The Dead Held Hands

The Temple of the Exploding Head Saga

A League of Elder Novel

arc (10)

The Dead Held Hands

The Temple of the Exploding Head Saga

A League of Elder Novel

Ren Garcia

Loconeal Publishing
Amherst

The Dead Held Hands

Copyright © 2011 by Ren Garcia
Cover Art by © 2011 by Carol Phillips
Interior Image Art by © 2011 by Carol Phillips
Interior Image Art by © 2011 by Fantasio
Interior Image Art by © 2011 by Eve Ventrue
Edited by Barbara Taft Verducci

Loconeal books may be ordered through booksellers or by contacting:
www.loconeal.com
216-772-8380

Loconeal Publishing can bring authors to your live event. Contact Loconeal Publishing at 216-772-8380.

Published by Loconeal Publishing, LLC
Printed in the United States of America

First Loconeal Publishing edition: April 2011

Visit our website: www.loconeal.com

ISBN 978-0-9825653-1-5 (Paperback)

Table of Contents

Prologue

Part One

Kay and Sam

Part Two

The Invisible World

Map Of Kana

Barrow

Kana

Sea of Kana

Sea of Esther

Sea of Elder

Sea of Ataba

Straits of Elder

Esther

Hala

Cabert

Zenon

Renoath

Fith Land

Hiei
Hiei
Pattern
Pais
Rustam
Green Sabre
Vincent
Bodicia
Zairy
Valenhelm
Tejmus
Shirster Point
Bloodstein
Midas
Hannover
Minz
Kandarr
Bell
Griff
Clovisc
Cham
Larkin
Colmma
Hazards of the Old Ones
Maqravine
River Sook
Walburn
Kenar River
Provost
Arden
Pridmar
Stamon
Acalan
Ataba
Tartan
Bern
Thirkill
Kelt
Bay
Feren
Horace
Champion
Caprina
Halil
Caroline
Bern
Falz
Sorrenson
Pela
Jacarta
Howell
Picock
Wiln
Want
St. Paris
Rolov
Twilight
Deep
Sammarcand
Mercia
Woodyard
Blue Pierce
The Great Blue Pierce River
Brynthia
Mystery
Kittle
Bere
Avernesios
Mellro
Kantaro
Lake Monama
Tyzo
St. Edmund's
Bartow
Deer
Calvert
Berz
Conwel
Dee
Camboa
Waddle
Withell Well River
Herman
Tyrol
Tardin
Effington
Hailathe
Green Sabre
Mt. Holly
Holly
Burgos
Durst
Blanchefort
The Gaston Way
Westron
Dare
Tuk
Sasa
Cotten
Rhoda

Castle Blanchefort

Towers

1. Harkness
2. Zom
3. Crandia
4. Elveria
5. Xyotol
6. Joab
7. Twellbor
8. Traveller
9. Zoe
10. Bell
11. Harper
12. Drella
13. Miller
14. Westron
15. Shereuger
16. Fum
17. Celebrandt
18. Bloodstein
19. Makara
20. Hooman
21. Prthnar
22. Josephina
23. Pendar
24. Solon
25. Cooper
26. Trembly
27. Maseron
28. Joliet

Blanchefort

The Telmus Grove

Inner Pleasure of the Telmus Grove

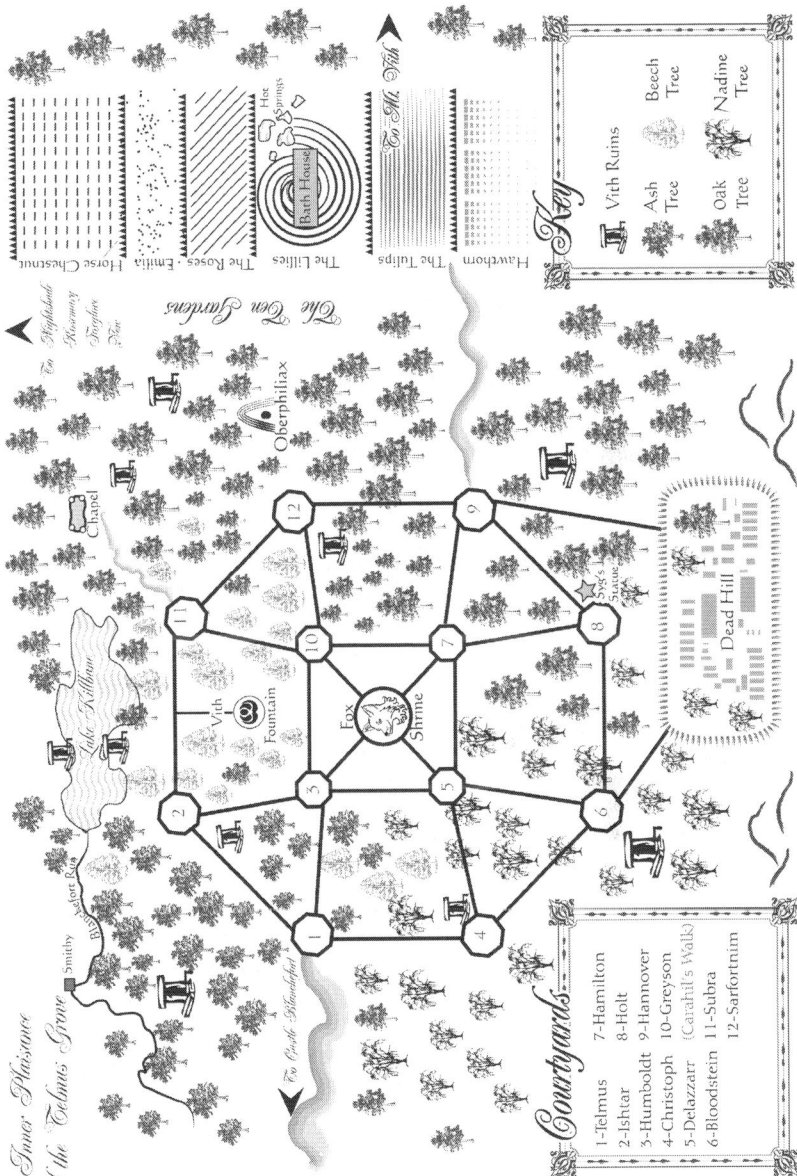

The Zen Gardens

To Mt. Zu

Key

🏛 Vich Ruins

🌳 Ash Tree

🌳 Beech Tree

🌳 Oak Tree

🌳 Nadine Tree

Horse Chestnut · Emilia · The Roses · The Lilies · The Tulips · Hawthorn

To Highlands · Rosemary · Foxglove · Fox

Hot Springs

Bath House

Chapel

Oberphiliax

Lake Killbow

To Mt. Zu

Vich Fountain

Fox Shrine

Dog's Statue

Dead Hill

Smithy

Robert Road

To Castle Bloodsbad

Courtyards

1-Telmus
2-Ishtar
3-Humboldt
4-Christoph
5-Delazzarr
6-Bloodstein
7-Hamilton
8-Holt
9-Hannover
10-Greyson (Carahil's Walk)
11-Subra
12-Sarfortnim

LIST OF ILLUSTRATIONS

The Dead Held Hands

The Temple of the Exploding Head Saga

A League of Elder Novel

*The Vith have a saying that the Dead hold hands and
lend the living their power.*

With the Dead, the Living are Invincible,

Without the Dead, the Living can do nothing.

PROLOGUE

I—The Temple

The latest round of Faithful filed into the huge temple complex. The temple was vast and stony, washed in dark shadows and unseen reaches. It was deep underground and, like a cave, was bereft of sunlight. Pillars, covered with lurid painted glyphs and symbols, lined the distant walls, and pagan idols lurked in the shadows like predatory beasts. Brass braziers on thin, stilt-like legs created fitful pockets of jumpy orange light. The light from the braziers did little except throw the huge space into a mass of flickering mystery.

The whole place seethed with energy, enough to light a thousand cities, but the temple needed more. It had to have more energy, much more, and the Faithful were there to give it just that.

Rugs of various types and materials were thrown out on the gritty stone floor, looking like a patchwork of cancerous skin. Incense burners in the shape of squat, angry gods filled the dank air with a heavy smell.

The Faithful made their way into the interior and took their places. They were naked. Their golden bodies of various shapes and configurations were washed and oiled—they glistened in the feeble brazier light.

They quivered in anticipation. If they lived through what was to come, they could expect to indulge in each other's flesh after it was over.

If they lived— and that was very much in question.

Far away, at the front of the complex, a naked priestess, her body dripping with oil and wearing a feathered headdress, climbed up onto a dirty stone platform. The steps leading up to the platform were dented in the center, from the slow wear of passing feet up and down through the ages. The Priestess was one of 10,000 who served the temple. She would stand there on the platform and lead the Faithful until she collapsed from exhaustion, and then the next one would take her place.

She lightly tapped a small tambourine-like instrument. Though small and lightly played with slim, oiled fingers, its tinkling sounds filled the vast temple from one end to the other. From the unseen sides of the temple to the right and left, throaty drums beat in answer.

Behind the priestess, ten nude figures were chained to several posts. Either drugged or tormented into a trance, they hung in their chains and vibrated with the drumbeats, insensate and mumbling in their obscure language. Several reeking creatures with no skin tended to the chained figures; they washed their pale flesh and tenderly stroked their long masses of black hair.

The chained people didn't have long to live.

The Faithful, spaced out on their motley rugs, fell to their knees (if they had knees, for some did not—some had no knees at all, and others had many more than just two) and abased themselves.

The ceremony continued, and would last for as long as this batch of Faithful held out. It was exhausting and would possibly be fatal for some in attendance, but they lived for this. There was no other place they wanted to be. To die here, to have their flesh consumed here in the dark, would be a blessing.

The brutal rituals taking place in the temple had been going on, without stop, for ages. The 10,000 feathered priestesses presided over the temple, each stepping alone onto the platform, each playing the tambourine, one after the next, daughters and granddaughters of priestesses before them. Likewise, the Faithful, in shifts, took their turn exploring the wonders and facing the consequences of the temple—such was the price it exacted. It was a like roaring fire that needed constant tending; otherwise, it would go out. The priestesses made sure that didn't happen.

That would ruin everything.

This temple was the anchorage. This was their portal and place of power supreme granting them mastery over time and distance, and they, in their depravity, gave it life, gave it power. Their age-old rule depended on the temple. They fed upon the riches the temple granted them, and, in turn, the temple fed upon them –a closed circle.

In an alien language, they began afresh.

"Bathloxi, hear our prayer ..." the priestess sang.
"Enemies of old, feel despair ..." the Faithful replied.
"Bathloxi, dance of light ..." the priestess sang.
"God of gods, invincible knight ..." the Faithful, entranced, mumbled.
"Bathloxi, our faith is sold ...
"Give to us what was foretold ..."

And on and on, over and over, through the hours, through the buried night, they concentrated. The temple needed strong emotion to function, and that's exactly what the Faithful were going to give it.

The Faithful focused on all sorts of strange feelings—though what they were truly feeling was known only to them. They felt something similar to hatred. It could be said they lusted. They might have envied, and probably they despised. Whatever they were feeling, it was passionate, and all of that heated energy condensed into a visible spark that danced off their prostrate backs and went to the nearest pillar like a leash of blue flame.

Eventually, a cloud of condensed energy filled the heights of the temple like an angry fog and became dense enough for the temple to feed upon it. Some of the Faithful strangled in the cloud, choked on its vapors and died where they were. The temple soaked the cloud up and converted it into raw, bestial power. Gouts of lightning from this newly collected energy arced every so often, charging the humid air with static. Sometimes, the lightning came down in belching strokes and hit select pockets of the Faithful, killing them by the score. If that happened, then so be it; again, the temple exacted its price.

If they managed to survive the noxious, energy-rich cloud and the random lightning hits, there was a further horror that vexed the Faithful. Every so often, some of the Faithful, clutching their heads (if they had a head, for some did not), suddenly stood in a panic. Spinning around in the fog, their bodies bulged, losing their shapes, and spread out in gold-flecked masses, enveloping those around.

And their heads (if applicable) exploded in a spray. The effort, the strange feelings they generated, and the greedy temple was too much for them.

The rest continued, having survived the cloud, the lighting and, so far, the exploding head chanting until their alien voices were ragged.

A few more fell apart in an endoplasmic gel and head spray.

Another lightning hit—more dead.

As the pagan night wore on, their prayers appeared to be answered. A strange creature appeared near the priestess. Four-legged, hoofed, antlered, it looked like a deer, though its sylvan eyes were flickering with bad intentions.

Slowly the deer began dancing to the drums and the tambourine. It reared up on its hind legs, and, when it did, its deer-like body transformed into a shaggy, man-like shape with horns.

A continual bolt of lightning came down and struck the deer in the antlers—apparently causing it no harm. It wore the lightning like a bright, spindly hat.

Bathloxi was a mixture of man, animal and pure energy. He'd come at last.

The priestess presented the ten chained figures as an offering. Having total mastery over her body, she gave herself many arms. They grew gracefully out of her body. With hardly an effort, she broke their chains and picked them up by the throat, holding all ten victims aloft as easily as new born babies. She presented them, dangling, to the god.

Bathloxi regarded them impassively; then, he sprang with passion. After a howling moment, some were consumed, others were electrocuted, and a few were burned.

The chained people with pale skin and thick black hair were dead. They were merely the latest victims of the temple.

"I am here; my body is bathed, my hunger is slaked. My conditions are met. I will do as you ask," Bathloxi said, blood drenched, energy crackling. *"My blood shall give this place of worship continued life ..."*

And energy flowed from the god to the Temple—the priestess and her Faithful successful once again in currying favor from Bathloxi, and that meant renewed energy for the temple—much, much more than they had been able to generate on their own.

Victorious, the surviving Faithful, as a reward for their efforts, fell upon each other and engaged in any number of travesties in the moaning dark. They copulated and fed upon their flesh. They tore each other's skin, gouged eyes, ripped hair and bathed in the flowing juices in an orgy of pain and ecstasy. To cause pain gave them ecstasy—the whole process sustaining itself. Eventually, they had no more bodies. They fell apart and flowed together as one prodding, jabbing mass creating a vast stagnant pool on the temple floor.

For ages the temple had stood there buried deep in the ground and exacted its tribute. For ages the priestesses, the Faithful, the sacrificial victims and their bloody god had fueled it.

Soon, very soon, their patience was to be rewarded. The subjugation of their enemy was at hand.

II—Lady Poe's Birthday

Lady Poe of Blanchefort's birthday was on February 14, apparently the date of an ancient holiday proclaiming love and togetherness; although, by the Kanan calendar, February had thirty-four days instead of the ancient count of twenty-eight.

Still, it was appropriate for Lady Poe was such a kind, loving person adored by all who knew her. As the month of February sat toward the very end of the cold winter season in the Vithlands of Kana, Poe and her family lived in their warmer southern residence, the Duke of Oyln's Grand Manor outside the city of Effington in the Estherlands. Her husband, Lord Peter, being in service to and good friends with the Duke of Oyln, was invited to live there with his family as he pleased. They had a whole wing to call their own.

To celebrate her birthday every year, the Duke and his Duchess, Lady Torrijayne, threw a large party with Poe as the guest of honor. Poe's brother and his wife and Lord Davage and Countess Sygillis of Blanchefort, helped in the planning and financing of the party and were always in attendance. Countess Sygillis and Duchess Torrijayne hated each other. Their long running feud went back to their sordid days as Black Hats and was a constant source of A-List news and gossip around the League. Socialites were always eagerly curious to see which of the two would make a fresh snide remark or fire a sarcastic quip about the other. There was even talk of heated private meetings and secluded hair-pulling fist-fights conducted between the two. However, for Lady Poe's birthday party, they mutually agreed to a truce and behaved themselves.

Lady Poe certainly loved grand parties and spared no expense, but, truth be told, it was the quiet, private celebration she enjoyed with her family that was her favorite birthday treat of all.

Her husband, Lord Peter of Blanchefort (formerly of Ruthven) usually had a surprise or two cooked up for her— a little something that he'd baked himself or possibly a clever trinket that he'd made, something quaint and hand-crafted. Lord Peter had skilled hands, and Lady Poe loved receiving hand-made gifts from her husband. Coming from a House Minor, Lord Peter was out-ranked by the House of Blanchefort and took its name by tradition upon their union. The often caustic social scene on Kana was a-buzz with the union, and a few Great Houses tried to block it through legal channels stating such a mismatched marriage in status violated League law. Others speculated that it would never last; however, Peter and Poe shared a loving relationship that held fast and grew through the years.

Their children also came up with something neat for their mother on her birthday.

Milos, their eldest son, sometimes wrote her a poem or a story which she listened to, eyes closed, hand in hand with Peter. Milos was so bright and creative that it was easy for him to come up with such things and captivate his mother.

The twins, Sarah and Phillip, had a harder time. They couldn't simply go out and buy mother something for Lady Poe of Blanchefort already had everything she wanted. They weren't quite as artistic as their older brother Milos, so they'd knock heads for weeks, trying to come up with something witty and charming to present to her. Fortunately for them, Sarah was the spitting image of her late grandmother, Countess Hermilane (Lady Poe's mother), and usually Sarah and Phillip acted out a scene from Hermilane's past, which many times involved some sort of sword fight or duel, as the late countess had been a known pugilistic hot-head in her day. Lady Poe watched their performance and clapped, giving the twins a big kiss on the cheek when they were finished. Also, if they really got desperate, all Sarah had to do to make her mother happy was put on a gown, which, being a proto-typical tomboy, was a tough chore for her.

Their fourth child Millie got a pass up to this point. She was still babbling in a high chair and couldn't actively participate, not for a few years yet.

There was a final child of sorts who always showed up on Poe's birthday, the one who brought with him the most surprises and jokes of all—Carahil.

Lady Poe, being a mighty Silver tech female, had made Carahil in a Vith fountain at Castle Blanchefort some twenty-five years prior. Her brother, Lord Davage, often told dinner-time stories of a saintly silver seal he'd befriended in the Xaphan city of Metatron, and Poe, listening, was inspired and re-created Carahil in Silver tech. She put a lot of effort into it, spending months of exhausting work until the fountain was overflowing with silver. When Carahil opened his eyes, he was wise and powerful in the form of a silver seal. As such, Carahil soon became a full member of the Celestial Arborium, and he soared over the cosmos defending balance and righting wrongs.

In short, Lady Poe of Blanchefort, using her Silver tech, had created a god and was its mother. Such was the extent of her power and the width of her character—to be content as an unassuming wife and mother rejoicing in the simple things, her vast power kept in check by her love for her husband and her children.

Carahil was so busy spanning the heavens far from home that he rarely saw his mother anymore, but, like a good son, he always remembered to visit Lady Poe on her birthday. He usually tried to sneak up on Poe and scare her—Carahil's love of pranks still knew no end. He'd jump out from behind a huge potted plant (Duchess Torrijayne loved plants and Grand Effington was a literal botanical garden in certain places), or he'd cut the lights and appear out of nowhere. Carahil loved making a grand entrance.

Everybody loved Carahil, and, once everybody recovered from their shock, they'd give him a huge hug. He reveled with his family for a time telling stories, playing with the children and basking in his mother's presence. After a bit the Duke and Duchess Torrijayne would come out and sit with Carahil as well, for they were his friends, too.

* * * * *

On this particular occasion, Carahil seemed a bit off-put. He wasn't quite his normal, happy self. He twitched his whiskers and asked if the children could give himself and his mother a few minutes in private. With a cry of displeasure they exited the area, the Duchess promising to give them all a treat from the kitchen.

Lord Peter began to take his leave along with the rest. "Please,

Lord Peter, stay," Carahil said. "You need to hear this, too."

Alone in the room, just the three of them, Lady Poe looked at Carahil, that happy faced, silver seal. She sensed danger. "Is there something wrong, Carahil?"

He twitched his whiskers. "Yes, Mother, there is."

Poe was shocked. Carahil usually didn't just come right out and say something. He enjoyed making people coax information out of him. His stark, concise answer alarmed her.

She gently placed her hands on the dome of his smooth silver head. "What is it?" she asked.

"I've come to you for advice, Mother, and for help. I need your help, and yours as well, Lord Peter."

"Anything, Carahil. Anything we can do," Lady Poe said.

Carahil reveled in her touch. Though he was a god with power supreme, he found comfort and solace in the soothing touch of his mother's hand as any child did.

Finally, he spoke.

"I need you to help me save the League, Mother."

And Carahil told them.

III—Born in a Jar

Her family didn't often come out of the fog; that was a sure way to bring the demons.

She had seen the Kanan sun many times, a lot more than her brothers and sisters ever had, though she was a girl not ten years old yet, the youngest of her large family by far. She was born in a jar, a blessed birth by any measure. Her ancient home on the black hill by the lake was thick in fog perpetually. Even the brightest noon was little more than a dull gray twilight at Castle Astralon. To see the sun meant to venture a distance from the lakeshore where the fog ended, but few ever wanted to do that. Again, fear of the demons ruled everything they did.

But that was they, her family and neighbors, not her. Fearless, she often traveled far enough from the fog near the lake to see the sun, to marvel at it, to feel its warmth. She'd done it lots of times and never once encountered a demon.

That's where *He* was, out there in the sun somewhere. The little boy she'd fallen in love with.

Great fecundity was a common feature of her people. All the tribes multiplied with abandon. She had twenty four brothers and forty-seven sisters. She was the youngest of the bunch by three months. She was born in a clutch of twelve, a rather standard amount in her family. The Searchers discovered her tiny, partially developed embryo mixed in with the others who were fully formed and ready to be born. "An Anuian is born to us! We are blessed!" they cheered as she was whisked away and placed into the brine filled jar. There she stayed for another three months, completing her development in the warm water and "knocking" when she was ready to come out.

As she grew, it became clear she was slightly different from the rest of her family. Though still only a girl, she was fuller, sturdier than others her age with larger eyes than usual, long eyelashes and "notched" lips. She was stronger and faster than the rest. She was an Anuian, a Greater Monama, and a rare treasure for Castle Astralon.

The Anuians, she was told, rebelled and fought the demons long ago and were hunted down and wiped out for their temerity, leaving the smaller, more docile Conox, or Lesser Monamas for the demons to torture. Though gone, occasionally, an Anuian was born amongst the Conox and placed in a jar, and was a jewel for their House. Already, the tribes offered their sons to her, to the girl born in a jar.

With all those brothers and sisters every generation, one should expect her family to be massive, getting exponentially larger with every generation until they filled a hundred Castle Astralons.

Such was not the case.

The demons kept them thinned out. Every year, and with greater frequency, she lost aunts, uncles, cousins, brothers and sisters to the demons. Sometimes they vanished in the night. Sometimes they'd be sitting right there, getting dressed, eating their breakfast or telling a story; then, in a flash, they were gone, their utensils clattering out of air to the table below. Vanishing into thin air wasn't an overly unusual thing; her people could disappear and travel great distances at will—it was a talent they all shared. But this was different. This was for good.

The demons had gotten them.

When the demons came, one never returned. Such was the sadness her people had endured for ages. Sudden death was something they lived with, both from the demons that tormented them, to the sundry wounds they chose to inflict upon themselves. There were the duels they fought, sometimes over petty arguments and misunderstandings. When her people fought, it wasn't a pretty thing to see. They were strong, and they had nails that could scratch iron.

And there were the Trials. One couldn't even enjoy the act of falling in love without the prospect of death lingering. One of her brothers had been killed while at Trial. He'd fallen in love with a girl from Nebulon on the other side of the lake, and the Trials for her love had killed him. One of her sisters had committed suicide after her love, a boy from the Zerb tribe, had been killed while at Trial for her. Unwilling to live without him, she soon followed him in death.

As far as the demons went, she'd lost thirty brothers and sisters to them, and she'd lost her parents as well in such a fashion—they went to bed one night and in the morning they were gone, never seen again. She was raised mostly by her grandmother, a large and bold woman, an Anuian, born in a jar just like she was. All she had left of her mother and father was the jar she'd been born in, which she kept on her window sill. Sometimes she grieved so much for her lost family that she forgot who she was and could do nothing but lie there, eyes blank, staring at ghosts. Her grandmother sang to her at such times with her magical voice to pull her back from her delirium.

Her name was Sammidoran. In her native Anuie tongue, *sammidoran* meant "The Far One," and she lived up to her name, for she was young and rather impulsive, doing things Astralon girls usually didn't do. That was the Anuian in her coming out defiant and strong.

She loved to run with the wild herds of gazelle and other grassland animals that grazed beyond the perimeter of her fog-bound home. With them she bounded through the grasslands, easily keeping up with the herd, running in the sun that she cherished so much. She ran all the way to the forest, and sometimes to the sea. If she removed her shoes, she could even change herself into the likeness of an animal or roam invisible if she wanted. The gods were in the earth, and they granted her people spiritual power over mind and body.

An odd paradox, she sometimes thought. Her people, even the common lesser ones, were mighty, gifted, swift and strong, yet they were powerless against the demons. The demons could not be met. The demons could not be crossed. The demons could not be fought.

So she was told...

Sammidoran had no friends to speak of. Some of the children of Castle Fphenook whom she knew were all taken by the demons. So were the Nebulons and the young Minzer children. The others who were left were afraid of her. The animals she ran with and the golden sun high above were her only sure companions. The demons could never take those from her.

* * * * *

She began having visions when she was five years old. All of her kind had visions, and hers were especially vivid. She could see the future, and she didn't want to. Many of her family saw their deaths in their visions, at the hands of the demons, and they crumpled up in sadness and waited for it to happen—waited for the end to come. She watched one of her brothers waste away in such a state. She went to her grandmother and pleaded "Why, why does this have to be?"

And her grandmother calmed her as only she could and said, "Nothing has to be. Nothing is indelibly etched. If you see bad future, or you see a darkness coming, then make it better. Keep your head clear and fight for what you want, as I have done. How do you think I've lasted so long?"

Her aunts and uncles didn't like that sort of talk. What sort of thing was that to tell a child? Filling her head with dreams and impossibilities. Their motto was simpler and much more stark: Live your life while you can and hope for the best, and, when the end comes, let your head swarm and take you to places where there is no pain and sadness, where the demons can't hurt you.

As if such a place could exist.

Though she was just a little girl, she took exception to her aunts' and uncles' advice. To give up and fade away? To be so frightened that the only place to hide was deep within oneself? What sort of life was that? On her runs far from home, she sometimes saw her gazelle being chased by predators. They didn't just give up, lay down and be eaten; they ran. They ran until they could run no more, often times eluding the predators that stalked them. Mostly, the predators went home hungry.

There was a lesson to be learned in that, she thought. Just because a monster was chasing close behind that meant to do harm didn't mean it was going to get you. She kept that thought in her heart.

Her visions began in the smoky pools of her dreams, and there was no denying them. She had visions of the people beyond the fog. The people with hair of differing colors. The people with the alluring eyes the color of sky, forest and earth.

She often heard her brothers and sisters talking about dreaming of Elders in their faraway cities, their *Arin-Dans* and *Cerri-Telas*, and how sad the dreams made them. She'd thought it was a lot of nonsense. Why would a mere dream make them so sad?

But now she was dreaming of Elders herself, and experiencing it was quite a bit different from merely hearing about it.

It was overwhelming.

She saw herself as a grown woman, standing on a hillside, tall and thin. She wore a black Bronta-covered gown with the usual Astralon bustle. Next to her was a man, with oddly colored hair (even for an Elder), a tailed coat, and a black, three-pointed hat. A long silver weapon hung at his side. Somehow, she got the feeling that the silver weapon was *her* weapon—that it belonged to her. In the future, he gave it to her on his knees, and she accepted it, writing her name into the shaft with her claw-like fingernails: SAMMIDORAN. It was cold where they were standing. Cold was bad. Cold hurt and made you go to sleep and never wake up. For some reason, the cold was not bothering her; she was resisting it. A special charm at her neck kept her warm. Where did she get such a thing she wondered?

She saw a great castle in the cold mountains. She saw her grandmother at the castle talking to the Elder lord and countess. She appeared to be friends with those people. Her folk rarely bothered much with the people beyond the fog, except for the occasional fortune-telling and prostitution that provided them with their meager income. Her grandmother, however, was an exception.

As night after night unfolded, she began seeing the man younger and younger each time. Most often she dreamed of the man with the weapon as a little boy, far away, living in that castle in the mountains. He was a boy with a perfect face and strangely-colored hair.

His eyes, look at his eyes, like the forest-colored pebbles on the lakeshore … They melted her. The things his eyes could see.

At first, she tried to distance herself from the image of the boy, to watch him impassively. She didn't want to become enraptured by her Elder vision, as her brothers and sisters before her had. But every night, there he was, emerging from the shadows, drawing her ever closer to him, lured in by wondrous things that he wanted to share with her. She was haunted by the little boy. Even as she opened her eyes in the first moments of morning, she could still hear his laughter.

A word began to enter her thoughts, one that she had previously thought silly and quaint: *Arin-Dan*. It meant "beloved" and "dreamed of." As with her brothers and sisters, this little boy was becoming her

Arin-Dan.

He was bright and cheerful. He had an inviting smile. And he was loving and kind, making her laugh, showing her interesting things in his castle and inviting her to sample delights from their kitchen. Her visions were so real that, in the morning, she often forgot the things she'd experienced were merely parts of a dream. It was heartbreaking sometimes to wake up and not have him there and to know that all the wonderful things she'd seen and tasted were not real.

She saw moments of sadness when he was hurting. His people were cruel to him. They thought him flawed and weak. She wanted to reach out and comfort him. If they didn't see the value in him, she did.

Don't weep, my Arin-Dan ...

There was another thing he introduced her to: desire. He was handsome, even as a little boy, and he had that Elder belly button that her people found so attractive. Trying to be coy, she ran from him through the corridors of her dreams, and he chased her. When she could stand it no longer, she allowed him to catch up, and together they fell into a feathery pile of bliss. Invariably, the dream ended, and she'd awake, her thin body alone and aching. "Come back here!" she'd say. "Finish what you started!"

Still, he wasn't perfect by any means. He was a bit spoiled and self-indulged. He was loathe to take action, to be as great as he could. He was a loafer; she hated that, and it infuriated her, but that stage wouldn't last. She saw him transform from a loaf to a great Vith lord, mighty and brave. All he needed was a push. She saw him taking her into his arms—she could feel his embrace. Once there, she felt safe and content. In his arms, nothing else mattered, not her family, not even the demons.

That was where she wanted to be, safe and sound, with him ...

She told her brothers and sisters about her visions, and they understood. They, too, had had dreams of their *Arin-Dans* and *Cerri-Telas*. They told her such dreams were dangerous and would bring the demons. She must be rid of them for her sake and for his. They advised her on what needed to be done. Pick a ceremonial White Emilia flower from the wild and go to the blackened Mourning Wall near the lake and plant it there. They told her that, once she completed the task, the vision will fade, and it'll hurt for a while, terribly, but then it'll be gone, and she'll be all right. She took their advice, went out and picked a single White Emilia flower and took it to the Mourning Wall, which was just a fragment of an old Anuian castle that the demons had destroyed centuries earlier. Around the base of the wall was a dense bed of White Emilia flowers, all planted there by her kin hoping to rid themselves of their visions. Holding her flower, she thought of the little boy somewhere out there beyond the fog. She thought of his laughter and his arms around her and what it would be like to not have that any more.

All those forsaken dreams growing there in a carpet of white.

The Anuian in her spoke. She didn't want the dream to end. She wanted it to be real. She wanted her *Arin-Dan*. Turning, she walked back home and planted the White Emilia in her jar, a reminder to her of what she almost let go.

Time passed. Her dreams continued and became more and more vivid. Her *Arin-Dan* was powerful—could do many things. She saw him turning invisible. Mouth open, heart fluttering, she watched him... *flying* ... through the sky in blasts of wind. And his lovely eyes ...

His Sight, splendid in time, can save both of your souls ...

All he needed was a little push, and he could be great.

But there was darkness too—horrible things lurking in the distance like an afternoon thunderstorm.

She saw the demons coming to her *Arin-Dan* and crawling into bed with him.

She saw the silver weapon with her name on it crossing with a demon's blade shaped like a phallus, the two weapons ringing as they clashed.

She saw him in a life or death struggle with a demon, covered in giant insects.

She saw him lying on the ground in a terrible place, the demons around him ... *eating him.*

No, no, no! Please! My life for his! My soul for his!

And, worst of all, she saw clawed hands around his throat, trying to wring the life out of him. The hands were chalk white, delicately formed with long fingers, and ended in a stout set of black, claw-like fingernails.

Those hands... could they be... her hands?

She forced the thoughts from her head where they simmered for a time, grew dark and came again.

And, strangest of all, she saw herself doing the unthinkable. She saw herself going against the demons, running from them, plotting their ruin, and it would begin with her walking into an Elder den full of mystery: THE MYSTERY DEN.

Sammidoran told her grandmother of her visions, and she listened.

"Who is this boy? What is his name?"

"I don't know. I want him. I love him. He's my *Arin-Dan*."

"*Arin-Dan*?" her grandmother replied, shocked. "Have you not gone to the Wall? Have you not been instructed to do that?"

"I did, and I chose not to plant my flower there. I didn't want it to end."

"Anuians!" she spat. "You understand you are condemning yourself to a bitter end? The demons will come for you and for your *Arin-Dan,* too."

"I won't let them. You taught me to fight. I won't let that happen."

Her grandmother admired her spirit, very courageous for such a young person. She saw the demons taking an interest in her, to take the love she felt for this Elder boy and twist it into a tragedy. The demons were always waiting to pounce upon their love and use it for their own ends. But, she also saw her granddaughter having great resolve and with this Elder boy at her side, what possibilities ...

She described the castle in the mountains, the cold, and her grandmother's frequent presence there. She described the weapon that hung at his side. A long sword-like weapon. But it wasn't a sword; it was a metal tube with a handle.

Sammidoran's grandmother smiled. "That is a CARG. That's what it is called," she said. "You are having visions of Castle Blanchefort far to the north. You are seeing the son of Lord Davage and Countess Sygillis of Blanchefort. He is not yet born, even now. He still rests in his mother's womb."

Sammidoran had been dreaming of a boy not yet a minute old.

She was intrigued. She began spending much of her time thinking about this unborn boy—this Lord Blanchefort. A boy who one day was to do great things. A boy who one day will hold her in his arms.

A boy who will be eaten by demons, or, worse, be torn to shreds ... by her own hands

No, I won't let them. I'll fight them. I'll figure out a way around this. I'll not let this happen!

She sat there in the fog, lost in a dream, addicted to it like a narcotic. She talked to him, though he wasn't there. She'd laugh; sometimes, she'd argue with him—he was so stubborn! Why did he have to be so stubborn?

She said his name, for she now knew it, too; it echoed to her from future's maelstrom: Kay. Lord Kabyl. Lord Kabyl of Blanchefort.

This unborn boy was her only friend, her confidant and her lover.

Living up to her name, she began using her power to "Blink" far to the north to Castle Blanchefort. There she prowled the castle and looked out the windows to the majestic scenery outside. She tried going outside to the wondrous Grove behind the castle to look around, but it was so cold. She could feel her skin freezing and her throat tightening. She could only withstand it for a few minutes before having to go back inside the castle.

In a dusty corner of the southern wing of the castle, she located the currently unused tower where the boy will one day live, and she walked around investigating it—haunting the place as an invisible little ghost. Although now a quiet and unused place, one day it will be brimming with life, for not only will Kay live in this wing, but so, too, his sisters and brothers and cousins, each getting their own colossal tower to grow up in.

Zorn tower—here was Kay's tower. That was its name.

Her Kay …

Rolling around in its darkened interior, she wrote her name on the walls in several select spots with her long, sharp fingernail. She explored the tower from top to bottom. It was a huge place, over one hundred, fifty stories high, bigger all by itself than the whole of Castle Astralon. She went to the dusty, disused places in the tower and sometimes visited the rooms and galleries where she would one day pass her time with Kay acting out scenes from the future to herself.

She became very excited when the Lord and Countess Blanchefort began getting the tower ready for the new arrival. Though his birth was still months away, she felt the wheels were in motion, that things were finally starting to happen. Seeing the

Countess, a beautiful, red-headed woman with her pregnant belly, she was desperate to reach out and touch it. It drove her mad. She sometimes considered presenting herself to Countess Blanchefort and demanding to touch her belly. That was Kay resting within, her *Arin-Dan*. He belonged to her. She felt entitled.

Patience, patience ...

Soon, her love will be born.

They had their staff clean the one-hundred, fifty story tower from top to bottom, and a team of skilled craftsmen were there building the furniture Kay would one day use.

She watched as they skillfully built Kay's bed. She was breathless as she watched them work.

Kay's bed. The things she and Kay will share there, do there. She sat in the corner and trembled.

She didn't want to wait. If only she could travel through time.

Kay's room and new nursery will be on the terraced levels, and Sammidoran helped get his room ready. Not an idler by any means, Sammidoran tried to help the staff out when she could. One day she picked up a sponge when the staff went down for lunch and began scrubbing the walls. She was shocked when Lord Blanchefort came in.

And he knelt down and smiled. "Well hello," he said as she stood there holding the sponge. He spoke in Elder, which her grandmother had taught her to speak. "Are you Lady Sammidoran? You must be. Your grandmother has told me all about you, and I've been eager to make your acquaintance," he said. He told her that, as she was the granddaughter of Countess Hortensia of Monama, she was always welcome there. He then grabbed another sponge and, together, the Lord and the pale little girl, finished scrubbing the walls.

* * * * *

She had a strange vision one night, and unlike the visions she had of Kay, she never had that particular vision again—but she remembered it. She never forgot a single detail.

The *Olonol* ... She dreamed of the *Olonol*.

It was a vision that could possibly change everything.

* * * * *

The day before Kay was born was when she saw her first demon in the flesh. She had run out to the sea with a basket full of stuffing and thread. There, out in the sun, she was putting the finishing touches on a little stuffed animal she had been working on. Her basket was open and all her materials were carefully arranged in front of her. It was a gazelle made of a colorful patchwork of red, blue, green and gold fabrics. It had green buttons for eyes—just like his eyes will be. Her grandmother had gotten her all the components for its making, and she'd spent weeks working on it. Like all of her people, she had strong, dexterous hands and, though she had never made a stuffed animal before, it looked quite accomplished; a master toy-maker couldn't have done better.

She was going to give it to Kay, as a gift from her to him. It was a modest gift. He was a Great Elder Lord with money and power and technological items that she could only wonder over. But, she had made this little gazelle all on her own and had poured every bit of care and love she had in its making. She hoped one day that it might mean something to him. She dreamed of talking to him about it one day: "Kay, I made that little gazelle for you before you were born. I made it just for you."

I hope you come to love it, Arin-Dan. Just like I love you...

She was restless and impatient. She wanted Kay. She wanted him born. She wanted him out in the world ... with her.

And then, she could feel eyes all over her. Watching, laughing.

Demons. There they were, staring at her from behind a tree: leering, bleeding, skinless.

"*Hi,ya, Sam,*" they hissed. "*What're you doing?*"

Frightened, she dropped everything and turned to run home.

Wait! The gazelle! She left it there. She turned to grab it and then run away as fast as she could.

A demon stood there holding the gazelle by the neck, squeezing it in her bloody fist. The demon was female, miserably thin, and dripping half-clotted blood. She was horribly bent at the torso.

She stank, as she heard demons always do.

"*You forget this?*" the demon said in a callow voice holding up the stuffed gazelle.

Sammidoran stood there powerful but helpless before the demon who could not be fought.

She'd worked so hard on that little gazelle.

That was for Kay. She hated the demon! She hated them all!

Moving like an uncoiling serpent, she tore off across the grassland leaving the demons behind in a hurry.

"HAHAHAHAHA! Run! Run, Sam!" they called to her. *"Run all you want ... we've got plans for you ... All in good time!"*

* * * * *

She sat by a favored tree later that afternoon and wept, her hands to her face. She'd always considered herself so bold and brave. She'd thought herself fearless. Yet, when standing face-to-face with the hated demons at last, she found herself powerless.

She had been afraid. She had been wracked with fear, and she lost Kay's toy gazelle. She felt herself a failure, and so she wept.

As she sat there and cried, she became aware of something creeping through the grass toward her.

The demons!

She stood and made to run away. Approaching the tree, low in the grass, was an odd sort of animal. It was small and shiny with a smooth-domed head and a set of long whiskers. It didn't have legs, but rather flippers, like the turtles that swam in the lake water. It seemed like it belonged in the water, or in the air, or anywhere else it wished to go. It was a beautiful little animal, and she didn't feel afraid any longer.

It held something in its mouth. It set whatever it was holding down and backed away. It looked at her expectantly with bright eyes and twitched its whiskers. She almost felt as if the shiny animal wished to talk to her. It seemed to be smiling.

The toy gazelle she had lost to the demons lay in the grass. There it was, unharmed, unblemished by the demon's hand, a patchwork of colorful cloth.

She was elated. She picked it up and looked around. She wished to bow and thank the little animal for delivering it to her. Surely he was a messenger of the gods sent to uplift her spirits. Perhaps he was a god himself. Now, she'd have a gift to give to Kay.

The animal was gone, as quickly as it had come. Cradling the gazelle, she ran home. She was bursting with joy.

As she ran, she thought she heard a kind voice say: "You worked so hard on that, Sam, seems a shame to lose it ..."

* * * * *

The next day, Sammidoran and her grandmother went north to Castle Blanchefort. She had been invited to be in attendance as the next Lord of Blanchefort was born. Many people were there—all Elders. She had never seen so many at once before. She stood there in her black gown next to her grandmother, as many came to peer into Lord Kabyl's crib. As they waited for their turn, she held the little gazelle to her.

It took some time, but, eventually, they arrived at the front of the line. Countess Hortensia picked Sammidoran up and allowed her to look down into his crib.

There he was, mere hours old, yet she'd known him for years. "Such kind fate," she said to her grandmother in her Anuie tongue as she stared at him, her heart racing.

Looking at this newly born baby, whom she had seen in her dreams, she made a promise to herself.

She would ignore and abjure what her aunts and uncles said about life, about fate. About giving up when things looked bad.

The things she'd seen: the goodness, the love, the laughs. His arms around her ...

And the darkness waiting for her that she tried to ignore. *"We've got plans for you ..."* the demon said. *A dark future is coming.*

She would follow her grandmother's advice. If the future looked bad, then do something about it ... change it. Fight for it. The things she had seen regarding this tiny baby who was now right in front of her, both the good and the bad, were worth it.

What will be created between them was worth it.

I'm going to be strong for you, Kay. I am going to watch over you. I am going to be there when you need me. I am going to keep the other girls away, for there is only me. Me!

She then took the stuffed gazelle she'd made and gave it to Kay as a gift. She propped it up against the side of his crib and was led away.

PART ONE

Kay and Sam

1—The Pale Ghost

*C*rash! Thump!

Lady Kilos of Blanchefort sat properly on the stone wall and watched with passing disinterest.

Her older brother was on the leafy ground, trying to stand. A tall woman in a Fleet coat stood over him.

"Ok, so all that pretty Vith fighting is nice for show, but, if you really want to win a fight, you do it street style, and you do it dirty, too. Right? And, don't ever hesitate to cheat. All that Vith honor I hear so much about—leave it for the dinner table," Lt. Kilos said, lending Kay a hand while pulling him out of the leaves.

They were out in the cold of the Telmus Grove surrounded by old, gnarled trees and fallen leaves. Kilo's silver Tweeter bird bounced around in the branches and fussed with the other birds.

She was showing Kay how to street fight, Onaris style.

Lord Kabyl of Blanchefort, or "Kay" as everybody called him, had had a crush on Lt. Kilos for as long as he could remember. She was an old friend of the family, his father's first officer and a trusted mentor to "Old Dav's" kids. There she was: tall, a lot taller than his rather tiny mother, wiry and lean in her ever-present Fleet uniform with a thick head of long brown hair that touched the small of her back. Kay had always thought she was so pretty.

"Let's go again," Kay said, raising his fists.

She laughed. "I think you've had enough for today, but you're doing well. Just get a little more meat on your bones, and you'll be tough as nails. Promise."

Kay reached down behind the wall and put his purple and black coat on. His younger sister, Lady Kilos, sat nearby in a minty blue gown watching them spar, her whitish blue hair done up in the Blanchefort style. She had been named in honor of Lt. Kilos, which got a little confusing sometimes with both of them running around. The Lady was growing up to be much more prissy and girlie than the brusque tomboyish Lt.

"Lt., I'd like to try," she said standing up. If she'd had sleeves to roll up, she would have.

"I like your spirit, Bottle, but you're too much of a lady to do things like fighting. Your cousin Sarah, on the other hand, oh boy, I think she's going to be in quite a few of them before she's done—the kid's a real blue-haired hothead." Lt. Kilos always called his sister "Bottle." Since they both had the same name, a nick-name was a must. Lady Kilos used to have a habit of throwing her bottle around, which Lt. Kilos thought was funny.

"I don't like Sarah," Lady Kilos said. "She's mean to me."

"She is not," Kay said.

"She does have a big mouth," Lt. Kilos agreed, "and that never gets you anywhere, but I think she means well."

Ki stared hard at Kay. "Come here, kid. Let me have a look at you."

Kay stepped in front of her, and she placed her strong hands on his shoulders. "You're getting so big. How old are you now, Kay?"

"I'm twelve."

"Twelve? Oh Creation, where's the time go? I still remember when you were bouncing off Syg's lap. I'm only a hundred and four, and you're making me feel like an old maid." She took a hard look at his eyes. "You've got the coolest eyes, Kay. What are they, sort of a jade color, creamy jade?"

"I guess. I don't know. All the bloody lords and ladies who come in to stare at me don't like them much."

"What is the deal with that? Every Tuesday, Dav and Syg have you downstairs standing there in the gallery, and all these stuffy blue folk come in and start pawing you like a mannequin at the stores holding a tray of free samples. What is that?"

"It's called 'The Review.' It's a Vith tradition. All the various Houses that think they might wish to ally themselves with the House, or arrange a marriage or do business with the House, come and have a look at the eldest children up until we turn fifteen. And we have to stand there and not move or say a word. I moved once to scratch my nose, and one of them wanted to cane me for moving, but Father wouldn't let them."

"Cane you? I wouldn't think so."

"I hate it," Kay said.

"I have to do it, too," Lady Kilos said.

"Yes, but they love you, don't they? They love your blue hair and your blue eyes and everything about you. Me? They say a green-eyed Vith lord is no Vith at all. They talk about me like I'm not even there. They say I'm too short, and they don't like my hair either. And I just have to stand there, lock still, like a bloody statue for hours sometimes and take it."

Lt. Kilos ruffled his hair. "I guess being a peasant like I am has its advantages sometimes. I couldn't put up with all that rigid society stuff. I'd have knocked somebody's damn teeth out by now."

Kilos squinted and looked at Kay's hair. It was purple, like a grape-flavored popsicle, long, wavy, tied-up in a tail.

"You know, I guess I'm used to seeing it this shade by now. I mean, you Blancheforts come in all sorts of cool colors, don't you? Your dad with his blue hair, Bottle over there with her whitish-blue, and Hathaline and your baby brother Maser—boy, those two have a carrot-top going, don't they?"

"I used to chase Kay around and try to put his hair in my mouth. I thought it would taste like grape," Lady Kilos said.

"Yuck!" Lt. Kilos replied. "I'll bet it doesn't taste like grape, does it, Bottle?"

"No."

"You don't have any kids, do you, Ki?" Kay asked.

"Me? No, sure don't. I've never had time for it. My husband brings it up every so often, but I'm not ready. I'm having too much fun hanging out with your mom and dad. I don't even have my womb turned on—Elder Women can do that, you know. If you leave it turned on, it gets messy."

"Really? You'd be a good mother, Lt.," Kay said.

"Think so?" She checked the time. "We'd best be getting back to the castle. It's getting late and your mom will have my head. Come on."

"You've been in fights with mother before, haven't you, Ki?" Kay asked.

"Fights? Yeah, yeah we used to fight all the time. That was before we became friends. She hits pretty hard for such a tiny squirt. She's a great lady, your mom. Great lady."

They got their stuff together, hats and coats, and headed back, crunching through the leaves and stepping up onto the cobbled path. It was a long walk back to Castle Blanchefort.

Lt. Kilos suddenly stopped and checked her coat pockets, slapping them frantically with her hands. "Damn! I think my flask fell out somewhere back there while we were sparring. It's missing. I've got it topped-off with some good stuff, and I don't want to lose it. Tweeter, find me my flask!"

Tweeter, glowing like a silver candle-flame, hopped off her shoulder and flapped back the way they came, ready for her to follow. "You two, wait here, ok? I'll be right back. I'm just going to get it."

She headed into the trees. "Don't move!" she called back one last time.

Kay and Lady Kilos stood still on the path as asked. She smiled. "I wouldn't listen to those stupid lords and ladies," she said. "I wish I had your eyes and hair, and I wish my face wasn't so puffy. You're so pretty, and I look like a marshmallow," she said, touching her swollen eyes with her hand. "I hate my face right now."

Kay made to respond when a noise came from the trees ahead of him.

"Kay!" he heard.

Kay gazed into the trees. "Who's there?"

He saw a tan, brown-haired face peek out from around a tree. "It's me, Kay. It's Kilos."

Kay stepped forward. "Lt.? Where'd you come from?" She had previously disappeared through the trees to the east but was now looking out at him from due west.

Kilos' voice was trembling. "Can you come here?" she said at a whisper. "Please?"

Leaving Lady Kilos behind, Kay stepped into the trees. There was Ki, leaning against a stump.

Ki?

Her clothes were different. She was wearing a crinkled black gown covered with intricate black-on-black designs, low cut, showing off arms and shoulders and a fair amount of her cleavage, pulled tight into an hour-glass shape. Odd—Lt. Kilos didn't have a girly figure;

she had more of an up-and-down tom-boy body like Sarah's, only taller. Kay, also, had never seen her wear anything other than her Fleet uniform, and seeing her in this black getup was a little disconcerting.

I've always dreamed of my Stepe-Vir, my "Beloved".

The final strange touch on her clothes was a chain wrapping around the skirt portion of her gown and dragging on the ground.

"What happened to your clothes?" Kay asked.

"My clothes? I lost them," she said, her whispered voice trembling.

"Lost them? What's with the chain?"

"Oh, it's a tradition. Don't pay it any mind."

She advanced on him, her large brown eyes wide and rather intense. Her lips and hands were shaking uncontrollably. Her hair was rather wooly and down to her ankles.

"And what happened to your hair?"

"My hair?"

"It's really long. Why are you shaking?"

"It's so cold. Aren't you cold? You fought well today, and I wanted to offer you a kiss as a reward. Would you like that?"

Kay's insides bloomed. A kiss from Lt. Kilos?

"Umm, sure."

She came forward and put her trembling hands on his shoulders. "You're so handsome, I've always thought so. Such colors."

Kay had thought she was going to give him a friendly peck on the cheek like mother often did, but, no, she lifted his chin and parted her lips to give him a kiss. As she came in, he noticed her fingernails were long, pointed, almost claw-like.

The kiss she gave him was like none he'd ever received before, slow and warm, moving and moist, and full of passion. He felt the tip of her tongue come wandering into his mouth.

"Kay!" came a voice. He surfaced from the kiss and craned his neck. Lt. Kilos was standing a distance away on the path next to his sister, hat on and blue coat parted, booted, holding her newly recovered flask.

There was a rustling and rattling of a chain, and the "Kilos" he'd been kissing was gone. He caught his breath. "I'm here, Lt.!" he said coming out of the trees.

The two Kilos' came running up. "I thought I asked you not to move!"

"I saw you bade me go into the trees," he replied.

"You what?"

"Yes. I heard you call my name, and then I saw you beckon from the trees. Right over there! It looked like you, only you were wearing a low-cut black gown, like for a funeral. You also had really long fingernails, kind of scary."

Kilos drew her gigantic Marine SK pistol from its holster. "Show me," she said.

Kay led them over to where the other "Kilos" had been standing. She leaned down and inspected the grass. "Right here," he said. "She gave me a kiss, tongue and all."

Ki looked up, open-mouthed. "What?"

"Yes. She wanted a kiss, or, I should say, 'you' wanted a kiss."

"Listen, I love you, kid, but you're a little young for me, right? And, by the way, when I want a kiss, I don't ask, I take, so it wasn't me."

"Did you give it to her, Kay?" Lady Kilos asked.

"Yeah."

Ki blushed a little and began inspecting the ground again. "Tweeter, was there someone standing here with Kay?"

He hopped a little and rustled his wings. "Hmmm," he says, "yes, I see a trail. Wait here." She stood and followed it back into the trees, SK at the ready. "And," she called back, "if you see me again, and I want another kiss, it's not me, ok?" She disappeared into the trees.

Kay and Lady Kilos stood there. "It might have been Sarah playing a joke on you," she said. "I think she's been developing the Gift of Cloak. Maybe it was Sarah."

"Sarah can't Cloak. Besides, she's not here. She's south for the winter with her mom and dad and Phillip; and, even if she were here, Sarah'd rather punch me than kiss me."

"It was just a thought." Another idea came into her head. "You know, Kay, it might have been the ghost!"

"What ghost?"

"I see a pale ghost all the time in the castle. It's a girl ghost, I think. She's always off hiding in a corner. I see her peeking out all the time when your back is turned."

"It felt too solid to be a ghost."

"Ghosts can feel solid. Father told me."

"What does this 'pale ghost' look like?"

"I think she's a kid, like us. A bit bigger than we are perhaps. She wears black, just like what you described, and her hair is black. She has a lot of hair, all the way down past her knees. Her skin is really pale, chalky white almost. That's why I call her the Pale Ghost, because she's pale, see? And she follows you around everywhere. I went to mother, and I said: 'Mother, how come Kay gets a ghost following him around, and I don't have one?'"

"And what did mother say?"

"She didn't say anything. Oh, and the Pale Ghost's fingernails are *really* long—I mean this big!" Ki lifted her hands and held them out several inches apart.

Kay considered the thought and shuddered. "That's creepy. What does she want?"

"I don't know. I've seen her coming out of your room, and once, when I was in the village with mother, I saw her standing on your balcony."

"Oh, Creation ..."

"I don't think she's a bad ghost. I don't think she means you any harm."

Lt. Kilos returned. "I found a fresh trail in the woods. It went back near to the clearing where we were sparring."

"You mean the ghost was watching us?"

"Ghost? Are we calling this kiss-seeking, gown-wearing manifestation a ghost? Well then, yes, the ghost was watching us. Come on, we're heading back."

* * * * *

When they returned to the castle, Lady Kilos followed Kay to his tower, Zorn Tower, one of the larger ones on the western face, southern wing. "Hey, you know what we can do, Kay?" she asked. "We can do an exorcism. Yeah. I have a book I inherited from Aunt Pardock that shows you how to do it. Let me go get it, and I'll meet you upstairs. Leave your door open." She stood straight up and concentrated. After a minute or so, she Wafted away. Ki's Gifts, at only eight years old, were manifesting quite well. Kay felt a little jealous as his Gifts weren't doing anything yet, and he was four years older.

He went inside and took the lift up. The floors, mostly empty, whizzed by as he climbed.

He got out and went into his bedroom. While not feeling scared, per se, he was feeling a bit anxious. Perfectly understandable seeing how a ghost just tried to put its tongue in his mouth.

He got his toy gazelle down from its shelf. It was his favorite toy; he'd had it forever. It always helped calm him on nights when he was certain there were monsters in the room with him. He swore it had a voice. He swore it sang to him sometimes.

As he waited for Ki, he sat to check his holo-mail. There were several new posts, mostly from Sarah.

His cousin Sarah, two years younger than he and the daughter of his aunt, Lady Poe of Blanchefort, had a love of the bizarre and the grotesque. She lived there in the castle in Xyotel Tower during the summer and went south with her parents in the winter. Everyday she trawled the Posts looking for lurid headlines and sordid articles, looking for stories of monsters and murder, never failing to find them in abundance. When she was there in the summer, she assailed Kay and her twin brother Phillip with all the sensational stories she'd found. When she was gone in the winter, she'd holo-post them to Kay's account every day. Sarah and Phillip, by all accounts, were Kay's best friends, their friendship growing with each passing year.

He'd get items from her like:

"DEMONS TERRORIZE CHRISTOPHER PARK!"

or:

"WRAITH OF GASTON' STRIKES."

He read the posts as Ki Wafted in with a crash of wind and noise. She was holding a huge book.

"Where did you get that?" he asked.

"I said I inherited it from Aunt Pardock. It belonged to our great grandmother!" Kilos put her hand to her mouth and whispered. "... And she was a Bloodstein Witch. Yeah."

"Oh," Kay said, impressed.

Ki flopped down cross-legged in the massive inverted funnel of her gown and opened the book, flipping through the creaky pages.

"Ah!" she cried. "Here it is. Ritual to perform an exorcism. It says the three points of a triangle are very important. It says the top of the triangle represents the present, the left side the past and the right side the future. It says that, if we can surround something of the Pale Ghost on three sides, then we can wish it away or do whatever we want. Oh wait! We don't have anything of it, do we?"

"I've got some of its slobber in my mouth."

"Good idea! Spit on the floor."

"Really?"

"It can't hurt."

Kay leaned forward and spat on the floor. Reading her book, Ki drew some symbols on the floor in chalk, front, left and then right. "There!" she said happily. That takes care of the Pale Ghost."

"Is that all?"

"Yep." She yawned. "I'm going to bed. Performing exorcisms makes me sleepy."

She Wafted away.

Kay looked at the little three-sided design Ki had made on the floor with his spit in the middle of it.

A Pale Ghost had come to him for a kiss. Why? Thinking back on it, he hadn't felt scared or put off; her clothes were a little strange and she had seemed a little intense, but that was all.

He looked around. "Hey, if you can hear me, thank you for the kiss. I wish you hadn't run away. Why do you hide? What's your name? Hello?"

No answer. Oh, wait—Ki's exorcism. Did it really work? Was the Pale Ghost no longer able to reach him in his room?

He debated it in his mind and then went to his bathroom and fetched a towel. He got down on his knees and rubbed out Ki's markings and his blob of spit.

He had decided to welcome the Pale Ghost and not shun her.

Kay sat up for a bit longer, wondering if she'd show. Not seeing anything, he went out onto his terrace. Across the way was Harkness Tower, where his sister Kilos, the exorcist-in-waiting, lived. The lights in her room were on. They went out a moment later; Ki must have just gone to bed.

Feeling sleepy himself, he undressed and crawled into bed. As he ventured into the warming realms of sleep, he heard a tiny voice.

That was the worst exorcism I've ever seen. It wouldn't have worked, but I'm proud of you for getting rid of it anyway. Don't be afraid of what's on the other side of the door. You might be surprised by what's there ...

2—The Last day of His Life

Kay had spent a lot of time finding the perfect spot where he would take his own life. He was now thirteen, and he couldn't handle it anymore.

The constant failure. The disappointment and blank stares as he stood there in the gallery, lock still.

The great lords and ladies chiding him in review.

Look at his eyes. Look at his hair.

It's his mother's fault.

His mother's fault!

Lord Davage chose poorly, and here's the result.

Ah no, his sister; now she's a classic Blanchefort and Vith. Too bad she's not a man.

Crying? He's crying!

His father coming up and whispering in telepathy. *<You ... need to be strong.>* Even his telepathic voice rang with anger.

Lord Davage's flawed, non-Vith son.

It wasn't just the Reviews that had him down. It was everything. Everything he tried, it seemed, he failed at.

Space:

His father was a great captain in the Stellar Fleet and commanded a star-faring vessel called the *New Faith* that he and mother were often away on. His father took him up in the ship several times, to help him get his "legs." He'd hoped Kay might one day follow him to the stars as father and son.

Each trip had been a disaster. Kay'd been badly sick the entire time. Once, they even had to turn back and send him home he was so sick.

The King CARG:

His father carried a CARG, the LosCapricos weapon of his House. His father's was a huge, coppery weapon called the King CARG that was monstrously heavy. Davage often talked loudly of how he planned to give it to Kay one day.

"It's very heavy. It's seventy-seven pounds, and I had to work up to lifting it when I was your age, Kay, so don't be put off if you find it too heavy to lift now," he said. "I have this—it's a mockup CARG called, the 'Runvanion'. It's the same size and nearly the same weight. When you can lift the Runvanion, you may have my King CARG. I shall leave it in the west wing library on a stand. Try it as you will."

And Kay tried it. It was like the Runvanion was nailed to the floor. He couldn't budge it. It was rather embarrassing. His cousin Phillip could lift it, and Sarah could, too, but he couldn't do a thing with it.

Kay's Skills:

He found a list one day, written by his father and Lady Poe, detailing his various strengths and failings. The list wasn't pretty:

Phy Strength:	Poor to Average
Appearance:	Exceptional (No childhood puffiness present)
Speed/Agility:	Fair
Dirge:	undetermined
Waft:	undetermined
Stare:	undetermined
Cloak:	undetermined
Piloting Skills:	Nil
Penmanship:	Exceptional
Linguistics:	Exceptional
General Aptitude:	Exceptional
Sight:	???????????

Kay's Piloting Skills:

Kay clearly had inherited his mother's skills as a pilot, and that was a terrible thing. His mother had wrecked a number of ripcars, leaving them battered and dented into shapelessness. His father Davage was an incredible pilot and was keen to teach Kay how to fly; however, Kay had zero instincts, feel or aptitude for flying. His cousin Phillip was a wonderful budding pilot; he and Davage would stand and watch as Phillip and his father, Lord Peter, cavorted across the sky over the castle. Even his seven year old baby sister, the red-headed Hathaline, could fly a level simulator better than he could. Much better. She showed real promise while Kay had none.

His Gifts:

"Kay," his father Davage often said. "We selected Zorn Tower just for you before you were born. It is, by far, the most haunted, phantom-riddled, chain-rattling place in the castle. We selected it for you as a test, for your Gift of Sight. The Gift of Sight is a proud Blanchefort tradition going back over a thousand years, and you, as our son and first-born, no doubt have a tremendous Sight. You will, most likely, have more than just one Gift, but the Sight is the most important. You shall see all sorts of things roaming about your tower, and, truth be told, not all will be pleasant. It's just part of the experience. Be bold and face your Gift with courage and a spirit of adventure. Feel free to share your experiences with your mother and me. We are always available to give ear and lend advice."

But, Kay never saw anything beyond the mundane. No Sight. He had strange dreams, always tinted in Amber. He had lots of those. He often dreamed of himself bearing a mark around his right eye, like mother had. But dreaming strange things apparently didn't have the same import as seeing them.

And he saw nothing.

He also heard plenty of things, such as His name whispered or shouted, strange titterings and the occasional rattling of chains. He heard laughing and chiding. He heard something speaking in a strange language.

Tena mortza, Arin-Dan.

Arin-Dan. He heard that word a lot but didn't know what it meant. It wasn't Vith; he didn't know what it was, perhaps some old ghost language or Haitathe. He'd research it later.

He also heard a friendly, jovial voice mixed into the rest, one that comforted him. It said things like: "*Hey kid, don't let them get you down*". He actually looked forward to hearing that voice. He thought the voice came from his gazelle.

But he saw nothing. Not even the Pale Ghost that Ki had mentioned, which was sort of a relief.

And then there was the humiliation with the Stertors. "The Stertors are coming to pay us a visit, Kay," his father said, calling him into his study. "It's a rather odd name, but the Stertors are a branch of the Sisterhood of Light, and they are our friends. They visit all the great Houses, and they shall observe you and proclaim what Gifts you have."

And the Stertors came wrapped up in their white robes and winged headdresses. They came in the summer when Sarah and Phillip and the rest were present in the castle, and all the children were tested and proclaimed, starting at the lowest rank, moving to highest. Between Lord Davage/Countess Sygillis, and Lady Poe/Lord Peter, there were quite a few children to sort through, the Stertor scribe noting them on an official parchment:

Millicent	Daughter of Lady Poe	Age: 6	Gifts: Sight, Stare
Phillip	Son of Lady Poe	Age: 11	Gifts: Sight
Sarah	Daughter of Lady Poe	Age 11	Gifts: Sight, Strength
Milos	Son of Lady Poe	Age: 12	Gifts: Sight, Dirge
Maser	Son of Lord Davage	Age: 3	Gifts: Sight, Strength
Hathaline	Daughter of Lord Davage	Age: 7	Gifts: Sight, Stare, Dirge
Kilos	Daughter of Lord Davage	Age: 9	Gifts: Stare, Dirge, Waft
Kabyl	Son of Lord Davage	Age: 13	Gifts: Cloak, Waft

The Stertors reviewed the list with Davage, Sygillis, Lady Poe and Lord Peter, her husband. Very impressive, they noted. A great diversity of Gifts, and most of the children had at least two. Look at

all the Sighters present. The House of Blanchefort was well-favored.
Davage looked at the list. "There must be a mistake. Lord Kabyl and Lady Kilos are not listed with Sight," he said.

"They do not have the Sight, my lord," the Stertor replied.

Kay remembered the expression of hopeless shock on his father's face.

No Sight. A Blanchefort heir with no Sight ... Thousands of years of tradition lost.

* * * * *

So, he'd planned his death, to rid the House of his imperfect green-eyed, purple-haired self. He put a lot of thought into it. He didn't want to leave his House in danger of extinction without an heir. His little brother Maser, three years old and red-headed like a ruby, would grow to become Lord of the House. Kay was replaceable. Not having Kay around would mean nothing, and his sister Ki would hold rule as House Regent until Maser grew old enough.

Ki would do a good job. She was a proper Vith. The House would be fine.

He picked a high balcony in westward-facing Pendar Tower, one of the smaller towers in the castle that Lt. Kilos often used as a guest tower. It was high up, and he would fall to the crags four thousand feet below. The crags had drainage access to the Bay of Bloodstein, so, after a little rain, all the blood and gore of his dead body would be neatly washed away; there would be no mess to clean up.

No fuss. Perhaps his little corpse would wash away, too.

Certainly mother and father and Sarah and Phillip and Ki, too, would feel a little sad, but they'd get over it. They were Vith and understood such things. And there were others to take his place. This House was secure and better off without him.

* * * * *

Today was to be the last day of his life. It was raining and the water would be up in the crags beneath Pendar Tower. Sarah and Phillip were away, gone south to spend the winter in Grand Oyln Manor with their parents. Ki was away on an outing to the south with father.

Pretty empty in the castle today. Perfect. Now, all he had to do was let the water accumulate, go up to the balcony and simply step off, and it would be like he never existed at all.

3—Sam

He stepped out onto the balcony in the wind and pelting rain. The stone was wet and slippery. Just over the rail was four thousand feet straight down to the flooded crags. He climbed up onto the railing, the strong wind ready to blow him off, and stood up straight.

This was it.

"Hey, kid," he heard a voice in his thoughts. *"Where's your note? You can't have a suicide without a note; why, that wouldn't be good form, would it? Why, they'd say, 'He threw himself off a balcony, and he didn't leave a note explaining his actions. Apparently, everything we thought about him was true.' Better come down and write your note."*

Kay climbed back down. What had he heard? Was that his conscience? In any event, the voice was right. What was he thinking? No note? That would be rude, so he looked around for paper and a writing implement. Not finding any, he exited the tower and went to his favorite reading room. There he sat down to compose his note.

He'd written a few lines when his mother appeared at the door, body-suited and barefoot as always when not in a gown. "Here you are, Kay; I've been looking all over for you." Standing at her side was his little sister Hathaline. Mother was carrying his little brother Maser—the heir to the House after he was gone. At seven years old, Hathaline was still barely larger than a toddler, her curled red hair a scarlet carpet spilling over her little girl's gown. Her thumb was in her mouth.

"It's been a while since we've done any exploring of the castle, and I thought I'd give you a task to perform on this rainy afternoon.

You must be lonely without your cousins."

She glanced at the note. "Your penmanship is coming along. Is that a note for your cousins or for a lucky lady out there somewhere?"

"No, mother, just a few musings."

"Ah. Well, come on, Kay. Let's go on an adventure."

Kay stood and followed his mother out of the room leaving the suicide note on the table.

His mother had many interests. She loved bowling in the secret Blanchefort alley, and she love crawling in the dark reaches of the castle. She'd personally mapped and re-discovered many hidden places under the castle, covered up by the newer sections and forgotten over time. Now that Kay and his cousins were getting older and more able to cope with the rigors of "castle-caving," she came to them more and more to share her passion. No doubt, bowling would soon follow.

"Have you ever heard of Countess Fercandia, Kay?" she asked as they walked down the corridor heading toward the eastern section of the castle, Kay's boots clicking on the tiles, his mother's bare feet making no sound.

"No, mother, I'm sorry I haven't."

"She's an old countess from long ago when the Vith still had to fight the Haitathe to survive. Countess Fercandia was a warrior who fought at her Lord's side, and she fought with a CARG, just like he did. Her CARG wasn't big and heavy like her lord's. It was smaller and lighter, something that she could use. It was still a CARG, just different. I wanted you to see it. I thought you might be inspired." Her face filled with motherly love and pride, and she touched his cheek. "And, maybe you wouldn't be so hard on yourself. Look at you, just a little boy, yet so burdened. I can sense it, Kay. I know you've been hurting."

"I'm fine, mother," he lied.

"You take things upon yourself that you shouldn't, Kay. Take your father's CARG for instance. Your father specifically told you that you wouldn't be able to lift the Runvanion right away; it's just too heavy. He told you you'd have to work up to it, but you didn't listen. You can't lift it now and, therefore, you consider yourself a failure now. Don't feel that way, Kay. All in good time. So, I wanted you to spend a little time with one of your ancestors who also used a CARG, just a different kind of CARG."

She pointed at a stone bench. "Look under the bench. You'll see a small grate. The grate trails off into a crawlspace, at the end of which you'll find the hidden chapel of Countess Fercandia. I want you to go there now and pay your respects. The going will be tight, and this is a four-out-of-five stone crawl, so it's a difficult one. But, if you stay small and take your time, you'll be fine."

Sygillis seated herself on the bench and bounced the tiny Maser on her knee. Little Hathaline stood to the side, still sucking her thumb. Kay took off his coat and laid it on the bench. "I don't like how this coat fits on you," she said. "I'm starting to take an interest in the doings at our factories, and I want to design you some clothes myself. I have all sorts of ideas and those people down there better start listening to me."

Kay thought about wearing his mother's clothes, but, of course, he wasn't going to be wearing anything much longer. He'd be dead soon. "Thank you, Mother. I look forward to it."

"Oh, wait," Sygillis said. She removed her pouch and held it out. "Take this. You'll need it."

Kay took the pouch and looked inside. There were two sweet pastries within to tide him over if he got hungry, a telecom should telepathy fail, and a never-dim neon flashlight.

A flashlight. He picked the flashlight up and looked at it in dismay.

What a disgrace he was.

Mother detected his distress. "It's just a flashlight, Kay. Use it if you can't see. It's all right."

He put the flashlight back into the punch and stuffed the whole thing into the grate.

"You know," Sygillis said as he wiggled headfirst into the hole. "Your sister, Kilos, the one whom all the lords and ladies can't get enough of, couldn't do this."

"Couldn't do what?" Kay asked, his baggy white shirt clinging to the grate in a frustrating manner.

"This. Crawling into tiny places. She's claustrophobic, Kay. She doesn't like small spaces."

"She doesn't?"

"No. You see, even a perfect Vith like your sister isn't perfect at everything. She fails and feels fear every now and again. Being afraid sometimes isn't a weakness. Take what makes you afraid and learn from it. That's what a great man or a great woman would do. Go on, the countess awaits."

He crawled into the tight dusty space. The way was tight going—mother certainly didn't give him overly-easy tasks, and, even he, with his tiny body, got stuck once or twice. The musty space was only twelve inches high at most. He lay there on his stomach, his head cranked to one side because he couldn't hold it out straight, and he crawled on his elbows in jerky stages, dragging his legs and boots along. He came to and S-bend and got stuck, his knees getting wedged. He was in a real fix. Suddenly, the cool open space of the long fall off the balcony he was soon to take seemed very free and inviting.

He tried to look around, but his head was stuck in a cranked position. Despite the confines, he remained perfectly calm and collected in the tight uterine fold. If his sister Kilos suffered from claustrophobia, then this straitjacket-like situation would probably stop her heart with fear.

<How're you doing, Kay?> his mother sent.

<I'm fine.>

<If you get stuck at the S-bend, you'll need to turn around and go in feet first. It's too small, and you'll get pretty stuck going headfirst. Going in feet first will allow you to bend your knees and twist with the contours. It's much easier that way. Trust me.>

<Thank you, Mother,> he sent. He pulled himself free and, balled up into the fetal position, wiggled around and plunged into the bend feet-first. Sure enough, he slid through like a bullet being stuffed through the barrel of a crooked gun.

Beyond the bend was what appeared to be a dead end. It was horribly dark, and he couldn't see much of anything. With chagrin he got the flashlight out and waved it around. Webs and old stone, a solid wall ahead of him. Where was the chapel? Had he taken a wrong turn?

He spied what looked like a crack in the stone face. It was small, very small—only about nine inches wide at its maximum. Peering in, he could see hints of a murky room beyond.

Must be the chapel.

Puzzling it out, the only way he could figure to enter the chapel without using the Waft—which he was still trying to master at thirteen—was to plunge in feet first again, a courageous thing to do not knowing what was waiting for him on the other side. The squeeze was harrowingly tight, even for a small boy like himself, and he had to control the urge to panic as the uterine stone caught and held on his clothes.

He paused and allowed the momentary hand of panic to go elsewhere. Fully composed, he stuffed himself through the hole into the waiting room on the other side.

<How are you doing, Kay?> his mother telepathied again.

<Fine, Mother, I just got through into the chapel.>

<Very good!! I'm so proud of you!! Do you know how hard that squeeze is to get through? Look how fearless you are—let the Vith lords choke on that! Take your time and look around, and don't forget to offer a blessing—you're in the presence of your ancestor.>

<I won't.>

He thought a moment and prevented a tear from coming. He would miss his mother.

Don't cry for me, Mother. I'm sorry I had to be a bother.

The room was bathed in a wash of lamp-black. He sat there trying to allow his flawed green eyes to adjust to the lightless surroundings. His hearing was rather acute, and he could hear minute little things going on around him, but he couldn't see a thing. He turned his neon flashlight on and waved it around.

The chapel beyond the squeeze was fairly small and dusty, mostly a faded blue color with complicated stained-glass windows dotting the walls which now looked out on packed earth and masonry; apparently, this chapel had once faced an outside wall and had been built over in the many years since its construction. That was a usual feature of Castle Blanchefort, the new covering up the old.

He looked around with the flashlight. A few ancient pews emerged in the dusty beam, as well as a life-sized marble statue of the Countess that was partially buried in the far wall. There she was. Pretty lady, he thought, admiring the serene-looking woman, a carved CARG resting in her left hand; her right hand open and inviting. The tiled floor was strewn with dried leaves—ancient and brittle. He picked one up and immersed it in the flashlight's beam; no, not leaves, they were roses! Dried roses littered the floor. He made his way to the statue to have a good look at her CARG. He was careful not to step on the roses as he made his way, he thought she might not like that. Those were her flowers, mummified or not, and he didn't want to hurt them.

The CARG in her hand was tapered and dainty, like a rapier. It was quite a bit smaller and lighter-looking than his father's accursed King CARG, which was like a lead club in comparison. He'd never thought of a CARG being dainty and light—it hadn't occurred to him.

There was Vith writing carved into the hilt of the countess's CARG, which Kay, from his lessons, could read.

Putting his "exceptional" linguistic skills to work, it said:

Killed one hundred Haitathe with Windamere

That must be her CARG's name. Windamere. And, it had killed a hundred Haitathe. He was impressed.

An image came to his mind of going to the castle smithy by the lake and forging a CARG similar to this one, something small and light that he could use without effort. He imagined the excitement, the heat and smoke. Perhaps his mother could add a bit of Silver tech to the forging, to make it stronger, make it glow. He imagined presenting it to his father.

He had a momentary dream in amber where he saw it in his hand, real and solid. It glowed with Silver tech power. There was something that he couldn't see clearly etched in the hilt: -AM-ID-RA-

The amber faded and he was back in the dark looking at the countess's CARG. All sorts of ideas entered his head. He could have a CARG just like this one. It could be real.

But no, it was too late for all that.

The balcony awaited him.

Recalling his mother's task, he approached the statue and bowed, head down, offering a simple prayer to her memory and thanks for this lesson, though it had come too late and he'd already made up his mind and was walking dead.

That's when the statue spoke to him.

<Hi!> it said in a cheerful female voice.

Kay looked up, startled. He thought, at first, it was his mother playing a trick on him, but no, mother was nowhere around. "Ummm, hello," he responded, holding the flashlight up to the statue's face in the gloom.

<What's your name?> the statue said, again in a pleasing, cheerful voice. The statue didn't move, its mouth didn't open and

close, but its voice was plain as day.

"Kabyl, my name is Kabyl. Countess Fercandia, is that you?"

<Kabyl's a very lovely name. And no ... I'm not a countess. Maybe someday I'll be one, but not now. My name is Sammidoran. That's kind of hard to say isn't it, so you can just call me Sam, or Sammi, or Dora. Or, if you feel brave, you can call me Sammidoran, whatever you like. May I call you Kay? Do you mind so much if I call you that? That's your nick-name, isn't it?>

"Sure ... I mean, no, I don't mind. Everybody calls me Kay."

<Oh, thank you, Kay, you're a nice fellow, I can tell that already.>

Kay waved his flashlight around, trying to find the source of the voice. It seemed to be coming directly from the statue.

<Why are you using a flashlight, Kay?> Sam asked.

"Because it's dark, and I can't see."

<Oh, you must be pulling my leg. You don't need a flashlight—use your Sight.>

Kay stood there before the statue, feeling a fresh wave of embarrassment. "I ... don't have the Sight," he said quietly.

<Sure you do!> Sam's voice shot back. Her voice was heavily accented with a trilling burr, and it sounded vaguely familiar, though Kay couldn't place it. It wasn't like a Remnath accent, or Esther, or Zenon either. It was most similar to Hala, like what his aunt, Countess Pardock, spoke, though Sam's voice was more musical and friendly in tone.

"Sam," Kay asked. "Your voice—it has an interesting sound to it."

<It does?> Sam replied. <You'll have to pardon me, Kay. Your language isn't what I normally speak. My grandmother taught it to me. I worked extra hard to learn it. I ... I hope I'm doing all right.>

"I can understand you just fine," Kay said. "What language do you speak, if I may ask?"

<Which one? Well, let's just say maybe I'll teach it to you here and there. A little at a time.I'd love to speak to you in my own language. Do you pick up languages fast?>

"I'm told I do."

<Well, great! I'm sure you'll be a natural.>

Sam was about to say something else but then paused. <Kay, I don't mean to sound rude, but do I smell something good in your

pack? It smells like something to eat. It smells really good, and I'm so very hungry. I've not lunched yet today.>

Kay opened his pack and pulled out one of the pastries. "You mean this? It's a fresh pastry from the kitchen;the cooks make them every day. My mother loves them."

<I can see why; they smell just wonderful. Is it be possible ... I mean, could I possibly ask you to share one with me? I hate to ask because I really don't have anything to share with you in return.>

"That's ... that's all right. I'll give you one, and you needn't give me back. I've always been taught to share."

<Oh!> Sam exclaimed, <you're so very kind.>

"Where should I go to give you this?" he asked.

<Ummm, simply place it in the statue's hand. I'll be able to get it there.>

Kay, without really thinking about it, stepped forward and placed the pastry into the old statue's open hand. "There, I hope you enjoy it."

After a moment, as he watched, the pastry vanished. <Ohhh!!> Sam exclaimed. <That was soooooo good!! Thank you so very much! You're such a nice fellow, Kay!>

Kay looked into his pack. "I have another one, Sam. I offer it to you, if you want it."

<You ... you don't want it?>

<No, Sam, you can have it. I offer it to you.>

Sam was quiet for a moment. Then, <Yes, Kay, I would like it very much. Thank you.> Her voice sounded strained as if she were on the verge of tears. Kay placed the pastry in the statue's hand, and again it vanished.

He backed away and sat down in one of the old pews, the old yew wood groaning as he did. He trained his dusty flashlight beam on the statue. "Sam, where are you?"

Sam stayed silent for a moment. <Well ...we've only just met, and I don't want you to think ill of me. Let's just say that I'm pretty far away.>

"Far away?" he said, repeating . "How is it that I am speaking to you?"

<Ohhh, I can do lots of things, Kay. I was poking around and saw you.>

Sam again paused. <I think you're cute, Kay. I hope that doesn't

intimidate you.>

"No, it doesn't," he said feeling a little bashful. "Can you see me?"

<I can. I like your hair. I like the color. Please, what do you call it?>

"My hair? It's purple. It's not a usual sort of color."

<Purple,> Sam repeated. <It's so lovely.>

"The great lords and ladies who come to gawk at me certainly don't like it."

<Who cares what they think? I like it. Your parents like it.>

"No, they don't. It needs to be blue."

<Blue? Is that a color?>

"Yes."

<Like your sister's hair? Your dad's hair? Sort of like the sky?>

Kay laughed. "Yes."

<Well, I think purple is very pretty. It sets you apart and makes you who you are. I saw you the other day standing there like a statue while all the people made mean remarks. I wanted to reach out and cheer you up. I saw you were upset, and who wouldn't be? I'd be upset, too. Your dad really got mad.>

"He got mad at me because the people made me cry."

<No! No, he didn't. He was mad at the people, for the things they said about you and about your mother. He'd had enough. Do you know what your father said? He said to them: 'Leave my home and never return. Should I catch you on our holdings ever again, it shall mean war'. What does 'war' mean?>

Kay shrugged. "Fighting. Killing, with armies."

<Oh. I wouldn't want to 'war' with your father; he's a great warrior. If he's willing to 'war' with the other lords over you, he must love you a lot.>

"I guess so. I'm sort of a disappointment around here. I can't fly, and I can't pick up father's CARG, and going into space makes me sick. And, I can't see anything. I can't Sight."

<And you consider yourself a failure?>

Kay thought about his response. "Yes."

<But you can see, and you can fly. You can't fly machines the way your father does, but you can fly none-the-less. You can't see the way your father sees, but you can see such things. Maybe you're just not looking in the right way. Your eyes are green and your hair is ...

purple ... maybe your ability to see is different, too. Have you ever thought of that?>

No, he hadn't.

Sam continued. <I can't fly, and I can't see, and I've never been to space, but it would probably make me sick, too. I can't do all those things, but I can talk to you from far away through the mouth of a statue, and I can lift your father's CARG. Hey, Kay, maybe we can help each other.>

"How so?"

<I can lift your father's CARG. I can help you to lift it, too, or come up with a suitable solution around it. Perhaps once you've lifted it, you'll figure out how to properly see, too. You never know.>

"You'll help me lift father's CARG? I suppose you saw me trying and failing? Is that right?"

<Yes.>

"Are you the Pale Ghost, Sam?"

<Pardon? Am I the what?>

"There is a ghost that's been following me around. A pale ghost with really long fingernails. Is that you?"

Sam laughed. <I'm not a ghost, Kay. My heart beats. My skin is warm. At night, I go to bed. And, there's nothing unusual about my fingernails. In our culture, ghosts are evil. I'm not evil.>

"Well, I'm sorry. I didn't mean to call you a ghost. So, you want to help me lift the Runvanion?"

<Runvanion? What's that?>

"It's the mock-up of my father's CARG in the library—the one I can't lift. You'll help me?"

<Oh! Oh, yes, I'd love to help you.>

"Wait. The Runvanion is seventy-seven pounds. I can't budge it, and you sound like a girl."

<I am a girl. So?>

"A girl couldn't lift the Runvanion."

<I can lift it. I'm stronger than all my brothers and sisters. Shall I prove it to you?>

"Yes. Please, prove it."

<Then turn off your flashlight and close your eyes. No peeking. Promise?>

"I promise."

He turned off the flashlight and couldn't see a thing. A moment later, he felt a soft hand touch his shoulder. The hand moved down his arm until it got to his, where it gently raised it aloft. He felt the cold, smooth shaft of the Runvanion fall softly into his palm. Feeling with his fingers, he followed the shaft down to the hilt. There, he felt a soft hand gripping the handle. The hand was soft and small. "Is that you, Sam?" he asked.

He heard her voice in his ear. "Yes, Kay, that's my hand." He heard the pew groan a little as she leaned over. He couldn't see her leaning over, but he sensed it. She whispered into his ear, so close he could feel her breath.

"See, nothing to it."

"How are you able to do this?"

She took his hand and moved it slowly up the length of her arm. Her arm was soft and girl-like in feel. He felt the bend of her elbow go by and then the jack-in the-box of her upper arm. She flexed, and he felt a machine-like network of muscle rise-up through the softness like a submarine ship bursting out of a calm stretch of water. Then, without an effort, she lifted him up off the pew, cradling him to her breast—and all while still holding the Runvanion.

She whispered into his ear. "So, have I proved my point? Perhaps you'd like to wrestle as well."

"I-I'm sure there's no need for that. So, what do you want in return?"

"In return? I don't want anything in return. Wait! I take that back. There is something I want."

"What is it?"

"I've always liked reading the news posts in the morning, but they don't come where I live. We don't have the holonet here. Will you read them to me?"

"Is that all you want?"

"Yes, I would like that very much."

"All right then, I agree. I will read you the posts and you'll help me lift the Runvanion. Please put me down."

"You promise?" Sam asked.

"Yes, I promise."

She set him back on the pew. He felt the cool Runvanion gently touch the side of his face, guided by Sam's hand. "You aren't just saying what I want to hear, are you, Kay? A promise is very important to my people, just as it is to yours. You've made me a promise, and now you're obligated to keep it. I don't want you, once we're done here, to go upstairs and do anything silly. Right? That would break everyone's heart here; it would never be the same. And, it would hurt me, too, as you just made me a promise that you didn't keep. I'm eager to hear you read me the posts."

Kay shuffled uncomfortably. "I don't know what you mean. I'm not going to do anything silly."

There was the balcony and the long drop to the crags hanging in his thoughts.

"All right. When may I expect you to read you me?"

"Tomorrow."

Sam's voice brightened, and the Runvanion fell away. The pew groaned again as Sam stood up and was gone. <Tomorrow it is,> came her voice from the statue. <You promised.>

He turned the flashlight back on. He was alone in the old chapel as before. They talked a bit more, then Kay thought he'd better be getting back to his mother.

<Kay ... I've greatly enjoyed meeting you today.>

"And so have I. Err, can you see me anywhere I am in the castle?"

Sam laughed. <You mean, can I see you in the bathroom and in the shower? Yes, I could if I wanted, but I promise I won't do that. Here is where we'll meet. This will be our special place, *zemfa*?>

"What?"

<Oh, sorry. What's the word I want? Ummm, oh!> She repeated herself: <This will be our special meeting place, *okay*? I think that's the right word.>

"All right."

<Until tomorrow, Kay ...>

And Kay left the chapel and returned to his mother. He told her about what he had experienced, and quickly his mother went into the chapel to see for herself. When she emerged, she said she had heard nothing. She pummeled him with questions, then apparently satisfied that it was a standard, run-of-the-mill ghost and nothing more, she and Kay returned to the central castle and had lunch.

* * * * *

Kay went back up to his reading room. It was raining hard, and the water would be way up in the crags below Pendar Tower. He could just head to the balcony and step off; there was nothing stopping him.

Only a strange promise he'd just made to a voice in a chapel.

He decided to postpone the suicide. He'd first keep his promise, read the posts to the voice named Sam, and then, once the conditions of the promise were fulfilled, he'd kill himself. He figured the afterlife might be pretty tough on those who didn't keep their promises.

Yes, he'd kill himself later.

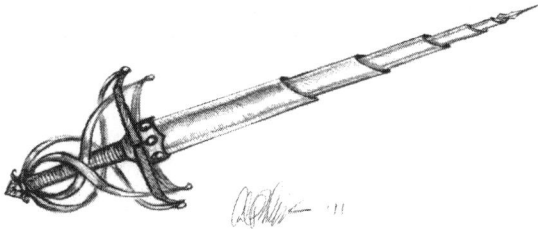

4—Forging his CARG

K ay didn't kill himself that day, or the next, or any day after that. In fact, he forgot all about it.

True to his promise, he returned to the hidden chapel and read Sam the posts with a tiny portable terminal. Nearly every day he was there. Sam wasn't a passive listener. She asked frequent questions and even liked to forcefully share her opinion on things, even if she didn't really know what she was talking about. Sometimes they argued about the posts.

Kay began to consider Sam a close friend, someone with whom he could share his deepest secrets.

And she loved to flirt. She loved to tell him how cute she thought he was, and every so often he'd feel a warm kiss on his cheek.

"Show yourself, Sam!" Kay often said, but Sam refused. She said she wasn't allowed.

True to her word, she helped him lift the Runvanion, mostly through encouragement, though she also taught him a few simple techniques for clearing his mind and focusing. He would sit on the floor in the chapel cross-legged, and, in the dark, he could sense Sam sitting next to him in a similar manner. Before the winter was out, he was able to lift the Runvanion off its stand, though the effort took everything he had, let alone trying to use it to fight with.

He could now lift it, and he should, by rights, inherit his father's King CARG, but, what good would that do? He couldn't fight with it; he couldn't even lift it up to level.

To that end, Sam had a much better idea. <You should forge

your own CARG. Is there any rule against that?>

"No, but my father was hoping to pass his CARG down to me so that I'd use it in battle as he has."

<Well, you're not your father—and he's not you. Did he never forge his own CARG?>

"No, he just uses my grandfather's. The King CARG was created by my grandfather."

<Just think how proud he'd be if you walked up to him one day and said, 'Look, father, I made this with my own two hands, and it'll serve me and the House well for years to come.' I think he'd be really impressed.>

Kay thought about it. It seemed to make sense. "You really think so?"

<I do.>

Kay was bursting with excitement and ideas. "All right. Let's do it! But, wait, I don't know the first thing about making a CARG."

<Well ... let's start with the basics. What is a CARG?>

"It's the traditional weapon of our House and designed to fight the Haitathe, the giants of old. It's a tubular shaft with a hilt, usually straight, and anywhere from three to eight feet long, the shaft being adjustable in length."

<Is it a club?>

"No, you use it like a sword, sort of. It cuts like a sword with the tube being micro faceted to cut. There are drums, I think, in the old smithy by the lake that machine in the correct grooves and facets that allow it to work." He approached the statue of Countess Fercandia and pointed at her CARG. "Something like hers. Something small and fairly light, though I don't like her hilt. My father's CARG has an X-shaped hilt, with each arm of the X being dedicated to a different season. I should have a similar X-shaped hilt for my CARG as a tribute to his."

<That's a great idea. I think he'd like that.>

"I'm going to get some books on the various kinds of metals to use, and I'm going to have to draft a design of some sort."

<Can I do that, Kay? I'm pretty good at drawing and inscribing things. I mean, it won't have any technical details, but I would like to contribute something if I could.>

"Sure, Sam, sure."

Kay left the chapel and got out as many books as he could find on the subject of bladesmithing, including several arcane Blanchefort texts on the subject of CARG-making, which was quite a bit different. He read all about drop-forging and casting and creating the machining for the various links that would compose the CARG's expandable shaft.

Look at all the math! Equations for calculating correct diameter and circumference. Equations for determining the center of balance, metal thickness, link weighting and on and on. It was rather overwhelming. His cousin Phillip was quite good with math, and Kay sent him several holos asking for help. Phillip responded and got him started. Phillip was curious what Kay was doing, and he replied:

"It's a surprise. See you in a few months."

Phillip must have told Sarah, as she sent Kay a basket-full of mail demanding to know what he was doing. She even requested that he stop whatever he was up to and wait for them to return in April; then, they could help him.

Sorry, Sarah. Thanks for the offer, but he wanted to do this alone.

The next morning, he awoke to find a packet of papers lying on his bed. It was a draft design for a CARG, hand drawn but laid out with incredible skill and detail. A professional draftsman couldn't have done better. There was a note attached to it.

What do you think?
—S

There it was—a beautiful facsimile of Countess Fercandia's CARG. The hilt was X-shaped, like his father's,with some exquisite designs Sam's had created to decorate each arm. Sam had done a wonderful job. She was a true artist.

It was Tuesday, and that meant it was time to go down with Lady Kilos and be Reviewed by the great lords and ladies. He normally dreaded those days, but today he stood like a statue without a care as his mind was elsewhere, turning on his CARG.

People came by, and he barely noticed or heard what they said. At some point during the afternoon a smallish man with a round belly and a plumed hat came up. He smiled and stood there for a while. He whispered in Kay's ear. "Hello, Kay, well met. I am Milos, Lord of Probert, a good friend of the family. I designed the ship your father flies around in. I knew your father when I was a just boy about your age. What a fine son Dav and Syg have. I have a son who's about your age as well. His name is Lon. I brought him today and hope you two might become friends, keep the tradition going."

After the Review had concluded, Davage and Sygillis led Kay into a ground floor reading room. Sitting within was a small, round boy wearing a long coat, knee-britches and buckle shoes. He'd pulled down a few books and was reading them, two at a time. The remains of a bowl of ice cream sat in front of him. They closed the door, and Kay and Lon were stuck in there.

There was a lot of silence as the two boys looked at each other.

Eventually, Kay, feeling rather uncomfortable, found a few books himself and decided to take advantage of the time to continue designing his CARG, the two boys sitting opposite at the table and saying nothing. He pulled Sam's drawing from his coat pocket and began trying to calculate the various lengths of the pieces using Phillip's equations as a guide.

He'd written out several pages of notes, when:

"Are you working on something?" There was Lon, sitting there on the other side of the table, trying to see what he was doing. He was clearly quite curious. A touch of chocolate stained his lips.

"Just a project."

"Oh." Lon stared at him. "Is your hair purple?"

"Yes. What of it?"

"Nothing. Just asking."

More silence. Lon's stomach rumbled.

"Can I see?"

"Why?"

"Just curious. My father's a great engineer. I'm going to be an engineer too, or maybe a scientist. My mother's a great scientist."

"It's a secret project."

Lon seemed impressed. "Oh, well, I'm great at keeping secrets. My mother's shared all sorts of secrets with me, and I've never told a soul. Not even the Sisters can Stare them out of me."

"Really?" Kay sized the tiny Lon up. "What If I came over there and beat them out of you? What then?"

"Oh, well, I wouldn't like that much, but you'd still not get anything of use out of me. I'm sure I'd say something, but you'd never know if I was secret-telling or not. I've memorized volumes of convincing-sounding fake secrets."

Kay laughed and showed Lon his drawings.

Lon looked them over. "Oh, you're designing a weapon?"

"I am."

"Very interesting. The most important thing is your center of balance." He came over to Kay's side and pointed at the design. "See, this length here is too long; your equation isn't quite correct, I think. It'll be top-heavy how you've got it. There are a few changes we can apply to this to right the balance. Here ..."

And soon Kay of Blanchefort and Lon of Probert were sitting side by side with their coats off pouring over the details. They started the day uncomfortable strangers and ended it great friends.

* * * * *

A month later, Kay was nearly ready. He stood in the old smithy where his ancestors used to make bullets and other such things. It had fallen into disuse after the Blancheforts switched from arms-making to fabric-making as a family trade. The last thing forged there many years ago was, oddly enough, the King CARG.

The kettle high overhead was bubbling with molten metal, kept hot by the ceramic furnace, spewing steam and heat. His father, seeing the plume of smoke coming from the smithy, had wanted to know what was going on. Thinking fast, Kay mentioned he was creating a cast statue of mother to present to her on her birthday. Davage was excited about the idea and was happy with Kay's initiative. To keep from making himself into a liar, Kay also was going to pour a statue of Sygillis. Once again, Sam, proving herself a wonderful artist, created the drawings of it. Davage came out every so often to see how he was progressing, and Kay showed him the drawings. He was pleased.

Standing before Kay was a vat of wet silica sand thirty feet wide and ten feet deep. Resting inside the wet sand was a form of his CARG, along with four pieces of what would become his mother's statue. The forms were made of springcyst—a polymer that would be evaporated by the molten metal. When the metal was poured in, it would destroy the springcyst and occupy the space in the sand, assuming the precise shape of the CARG and his mother's pieces.

Kay had made several mock-ups of the CARG and the statue pieces, starting with clay and finishing with a fired ceramic. He then gave the mock-ups to Lon, who, using his father's resources, had them scanned and recreated as the springcyst blanks.

Originally, Kay had planned on making a CARG the way his father's had, with billets of hammered metal creating each link, then machining them into a shaft. To that end, he'd acquired a raw consignment of carbon steel, titanium, vanadium, aluminum, molybdenum, tungsten, antimony, gold and lead. The steel was mostly for the statue pieces. All that changed when his mother Sygillis came down to see what he was doing. He decided to share with her his plans and showed her all he'd done, with the exception of the statue.

"This is wonderful, Kay. Truly. I'm so amazed by what you've done. The drawings, the metals. I'd like to contribute something, if I may."

And Sygillis filled a kettle full of glowing Silver tech straight from her hands. "Heat this for a month, keep it hot, add the other metals, and you'll be amazed by the results. You won't need to create links. Just pour it into a form. Trust me."

She kissed him and left.

After a month of keeping the Silver tech molten hot and adding the other metals, Kay poured the concoction into the sand, down the shaft and into the form of his CARG, the noise and smoke terrific as he did so. The form didn't fill up and burst out in a fan of sparks like he thought it would. Instead, he drained the kettle and then opened the gate admitting the waters of the Bloodstein Run into the vat. A clamor of steam escaped as the metal was quenched. He then reset the vat and repeated the process with the steel for his mother's statue.

When he dug it out after it had cooled, there it was, his CARG, perfectly formed. With the infusion of Silver tech, it did some amazing things that were readily apparent. It glowed, Just like Lt. Kilos' Tweeter bird, making a soft light.

It was lighter than anything, not even ten pounds, and it could change its size longer and shorted as needed. All he had to do was want it to change, and it did.

Running outside, he found a tree and swung, hoping to chop it in two. The CARG shook the tree and vibrated out of his hand. It took great skill to use the CARG in a cutting manner, skill he didn't possess.

* * * * *

"What's this?" Davage said as Kay entered his study.

Davage was sitting behind his desk. He was wearing his usual Fleet coat and frilly shirt, exactly what Lt. Kilos always wore. His blue hair appeared black in the quiet light of the study. Kay came in, got on one knee and held out his CARG. "I made this, Father."

He put down his pen and stood, taking the CARG from Kay's hands, turning it over, inspecting it. "Kay, you made this?"

"Yes, Father."

"All on your own, with no help?"

"Oh, I had lots of help. Phillip and Lon helped me work out the math, and I had help with the design, and mother contributed Silver tech in its making."

"Creation, what a thing. Look at it, so light. Balance perfect." Davage tried to bend the shaft. "Strong too. The general shape reminds me of Windamere, Countess Fercandia's CARG of long ago."

Kay nodded. "I used Windamere as a starting point. I can lift the Runvanvion now, Father, but it's so heavy, I don't think I'll ever be much use with it. I thought a smaller, lighter weapon would serve me better. I hope you're not disappointed."

"Disappointed?" Davage gasped. "Look at this, look what you've done here. What about your mother's statue that you told me about? Was that just a cover to prevent me from discovering what you were doing?"

"Yes, Father, although, I didn't want to disappoint or lie to you, and I created a statue of mother as well, cast in four pieces. It's not completed yet. It needs to be welded and finished."

Davage, gazing at the CARG, pushed his hat back and smiled, ear to ear. "God's Bodkins. See, this is what those lords and ladies miss in Review—that there's a heart in there, character and a soul to match. This is what it means to be a Vith, Kay, not your hair color or how tall you are or the shade of your eyes. It's how you overcome an obstacle, and it's keeping the promises you make—even those made in passing. I'm not dismissing your accomplishment with your CARG here, but I think keeping the statue part of your promise shows just

what sort of man you're going to become, and I'm very proud of you."
Davage looked at the CARG in his hands. "Look at this. Look at what
my son has done," he said over and over. "I'd like your mother's
statue completed and ready to present to her by her birthday. Do you
need help?"

"No, Father."

Davage gave the CARG back to Kay and unsaddled his King
CARG, a giant in comparison.

"Well now, Kay, you have your weapon, and a fine one it is.
Now it's time you learned how to use it. Are you ready to begin your
learning? There's much to train."

"I am, Father."

5—Five Questions

As time passed, Kay grew. He'd shot up over the years and added a nice coating of lean muscle. He carried his saddled CARG at his side, and, after four years of training, was quite good with it.

At seventeen, he was done with The Review. Now he could mingle in social circles and his purple hair and green eyes, once his bane, were now his greatest assets. Young ladies came up to him fascinated, and his mother often told him that his pile of correspondence should be getting quite big soon with interested young ladies. It never seemed to happen, though. His pile remained small and uninteresting.

He developed a core group of friends. His best friends were his twin cousins Sarah and Phillip, they being of fairly similar age and disposition, but every winter Sarah and Phillip left to go to Grand Oyln Manor in the south with their mother and father, and Kay was left on his own in the castle. He had his sisters and brother, and Lady Kilos wasn't bad to hang out with, though she enjoyed the social battlefield much more than what was to Kay's liking. Lady Hathaline tended to do her own thing and was a growing pilot, flying across the sky with father, showing great talent for it. Maser was still so young and chained to his mother's side. Lord Lon of Probert was also a good friend, but he was usually in Arden with his parents and was only around occasionally.

Kay still had a few mandatory duties to perform. The worst of these duties came when the "The Witch" was in attendance for a visit. "The Witch," as Sarah called her, was the Countess Hortensia of Monama, a close personal friend of his parents. She often came, apparently to tell their fortunes, as Monamas were adept at that. When she did come, Lord Davage and Countess Sygillis were always keen for Kay to visit with her in private, to get to know the Countess on a more personal level. On such occasions, Sarah relentlessly filled his ear. "The Witch is here," she'd say. "She's going to cast a spell, or throw you into a pot—look how big she is; her belly's full of little boys just like you. She might turn into a Berserkacide and eat you whole!"

With that in mind, Kay went to sit in attendance with her in the Firth House, a tearoom where guests were entertained. The Countess was a strange sight—a big, girthy woman, covered up with a blanket and sitting by a heater, chalk-white skin, black eyes. That marked her as a Monama, those coal-black eyes. But, instead of acting like a witch who wanted to eat him as Sarah had said, she seemed very friendly and kind and had a wry wit and easy manner. She told him stories and sang to him with her soothing Monama voice. Though Kay was hesitant at first because of the Countess's appearance, by the end of the session, this Monama had won him over. Her voice was strikingly similar in inflection to Sam's voice.

Monamas, if she was any indicator, weren't all that bad. But, the moment she left, Sarah, avid consumer of lurid Posts and cheap horror vids, filled his ear afresh.

Witch …

Berserkacide …

Eater of children …

And then the Countess Hortensia of Monama died, of long old age, and was buried by their lake in the far south. No more visits. No more singing in his ear.

Only Sarah's relentless voice remained.

* * * * *

In the winter, with Sarah and Phillip gone, Kay often crawled into the old chapel to speak to Sam. He usually brought her food, for which she was always very appreciative, deserts being her favorite. He also continued bringing a terminal into the chapel with him and read to her from the Posts. Kay considered Sam a close personal friend, his secret friend.

As the years went by, the obvious questions began to be posed with more and more frequency and force.

"Who are you, Sam?"

"Where are you, Sam?"

"What are you, Sam?"

Always, in a very polite tone, she skirted around the question. Always, she said she was afraid that, if she told him, he might not want to be her friend, or come and read to her anymore.

And she told him that she couldn't bear that.

So, Kay had to take Sam at her word, that she was a person from far away who could, obviously, do a number of very powerful things, spoke an odd language, and was too bashful to meet him in person, though Sam, safely hidden behind her mystical veils, was certainly not a bashful person at all. Kay liked to imagine that Sam was a Sister hidden away in one of their mysterious research centers. Sisters were told to be incredibly strong, and Sam was very strong, so she must be a Sister, perhaps yearning for something beyond the cloister.

Or, better yet, that she was one of those pretty, golden-haired Zenon-girls he'd seen at a recent ball, girls so pretty they'd make him blush and feel small.

Maybe Sam was a Zenon-girl who was also a Sister. Wouldn't that be neat?

* * * * *

Kay sat alone in Sam's chapel—he'd come to think of Countess Fercandia's chapel as Sam's chapel. It was chilly with winter in full force.

He had been talking and laughing with Sam all afternoon. They argued over a post that they disagreed on.

"Sam," Kay said on a more serious note. "What am I to you?"

Sam was silent a moment. <You're my friend, Kay ... you're my best friend.>

"And how long have we been friends?"

<Four years now.>

"Yes, four years, and I've never seen your face. I know almost nothing about you. It's not fair."

<I know, Kay. It's just ... I don't want to lose you ... as a friend. I'm afraid, if you saw me, that you won't want to be my friend anymore.>

"Why, are you a monster of some sort?"

Sam paused a moment. <No, I'm not a monster, silly.>

"Are you a Sister?"

Sam seemed astonished. <No, Kay, I'm not a Sister either.>

"Then I want to meet you in person."

<I have wanted you to look at me for some time now. You're my secret boyfriend.>

"You consider me your boyfriend?"

<I do. I've had a thing for you for some time now, Kay. And don't say you didn't know that—I can't possibly be any more obvious about it. Do you think of me as your girlfriend?>

"Well, no Sam. You're a voice in a chapel."

<You don't ... > Sam sounded a little hurt.

"I've never had a girlfriend. My parents have tried to set up meetings for me with various girls from around Kana, but they never seem to make it here."

<How sad,> Sam said with a tiny hint of elation in her voice. <They don't know what they're missing.>

"And, I don't get a whole lot of correspondence from girls, so, if you were my girlfriend, you'd probably just vanish on me and not write."

Sam laughed. <You're so cute, Kay. I'm not going anywhere. So, do I get to be your girlfriend?>

"I don't know. You're just a voice."

Kay felt something tap him on the shoulder. He turned to look, and nothing was there.

<I'm not a voice, Kay. I'm a full-fledged person.>

"Then let's meet. Let me see you."

<I'm not going to risk it, Kay.>

Kay crossed his arms, and they were silent for a bit. "I know, Sam," he said finally, "how about we play Five Questions? I'll ask you five questions, and I'll bet I can guess where you are within a hundred miles. Can we do that? And if I can guess where you are, then you have to agree to meet."

<Well, all right, Kay. Let's do that; it sounds like fun. I'm ready for your first question.>

Kay thought a moment. "Look out the nearest window; is it cloudy or sunny right now?"

Sam chuckled. <I really don't need to look. It's cloudy—foggy

actually. That's one question. You get four more.>

Foggy, eh? Kay smiled. His thoughts turned. Now he'll see how well he'd absorbed all of his sessions with his father. Five questions should be more than enough to home in on the unsuspecting Sam. "Okay, next question. Is it cold or warm where you are?"

<Warm.>

"Warm, all right. My third question: If you look out your window, in the direction of the sun, do you see any mountains or hills?" This was the key question.

<Hold on.> She was silent for a minute or two. <Nope, no mountains or hills.>

A flatland, huh? "Fourth question: Is there a sizable amount of water near where you are?"

<Yes.>

"Last question: Are you on the southern continent?"

<Yes.>

Kay smiled. "Sam, you're in the southern highlands, near or in the Zenon region."

He heard Sam giggle. <I'm impressed, Kay! You know your geography, but you're not quite close enough, so no deal.>

"I'm plenty close, Sam. Don't lie. You're in Zenon; that makes you a Zenon girl! I'll bet you're very good looking."

<Sorry, no deal, and, for the thousandth time, I'm not a Zenon girl. However, I have been told many times that I'm very attractive. I've had lots of potential boy suitors. I could have any of them I wanted, but I turned them away.>

"Why?"

<They're not you, Kay.>

Kay stood up and closed his terminal. "So, Sam, are we going to meet or not?"

<No, I'm sorry.>

"In that case, Sammidoran, I bid you good day."

<Kay, where are you going?>

"I'm leaving, and I shan't be back."

<Why?> Sam shrieked.

"I just told you why."

<Kay, don't go!>

As he slowly Wafted away—he was too large now to squeeze through the hole—he heard Sam cry out for him.

* * * * *

Several days later Kay received a strange letter in his pile of correspondence. It had been a rough few days, and several times he found himself heading to Sam's Chapel. He missed Sam. He missed her quite a bit, but, through sheer will, he put her out of his mind.

His name was written out on the envelope in a thin, twisting script written in black ink. It looked like something a skilled engraver might produce. There was no return mark or other indication where the letter came from.

He took the letter out—the paper was stark white against the flowing black lettering.

It said:

I've decided not to be mad at you anymore. If you insist that we meet, then let us meet. Just remember—I warned you.

Walk to the Grove tomorrow at noon, and I will be there.

Your girlfriend,

—S

P.S—I'm actually very excited. I've been eager to stand before you for some time.

6—Meet Sam

The next morning Kay got up and dressed in his best. He wore the purple and black coat that his mother had made for him, and his favorite boots. He made sure his boots were nicely shined. He saddled his silver CARG and popped on his black triangle hat. He had thought to wear his usual black fencer's gloves but thought better of it.

So attired, he strode out into the Grove, not really knowing where he was going. He wandered around for a bit and intentionally hid from Lady Kilos as she passed by yelling his name. She was holding a snowball and apparently wanted to dash it into his face. He'd get her later. For now, he wanted to be alone.

As the morning settled into afternoon, Kay became nervous. What if Sam was morbidly ugly or somehow deformed? Why else should she act in such a mysterious fashion?

She was from the south, near Zenon; she had to be. The Zenon girls were usually very pretty with tawny or auburn hair. In the past he had tried to zero in on her by the few words of her native tongue that she slipped out every so often. She was very careful about letting him hear too much of her language, and he made sure to write down as best he could the few words that got through. Clearly, Sam wanted to share it with him but was preventing herself. Sitting at a holo-terminal, he plugged the words in to see if he got any matches. Nothing ever came up—he was probably spelling them incorrectly. He recalled one word that she'd uttered on their very first meeting, *zemfa,* that apparently meant "okay." He hit the holo-net with gusto, trying every way he could think of to spell it:

zamfas
zambas
zembas
zimbas

Finally, a hit:

zemfa: (adj, adv, interj): 1:—All right; permissible, meeting standards.
Language: Anuie
Region: South Kana, Zenon Midlands
Addendum: Anuie. Regional language based on a family of similar tongues hailing from the south of Kana, west of Zenon, by the ...

Zenon!!

Kay read no further. Zenon! That's all he needed to know. Sam must be a Zenon girl. Great! Yes, yes, that was just fine.

Sam was a Zenon girl.

So, where was she?

As he waited, his mind began turning. How was Sam just going to "appear" in the Grove? For her arrival, certainly, there had to be a retinue of ships, coming from wherever. Certainly, the ships' occupants had to announce themselves, and, certainly, the staff would have a proper reception ready for them.

How had she done any of the things she was apparently able to do?

As Kay's thoughts turned, he barely heard a soft voice coming from behind him.

"Kay?"

He spun around. Standing in a thick copse of trees was a figure.

Kay smiled and took a step forward. "Sam, is that you?"

The figure nodded. "Yes, yes it's me, Kay."

"Why are you standing in that growth of trees? You could hurt yourself. You could twist your ankle. Come out here."

Tentatively, the figure emerged. She was hunched over a little, wearing a thick overcoat covered with a fur over top of it. She held the opening of the coat tightly shut.

She had a long wave of blonde hair that went down to her knees.

-

There was a flower nestled in the mass of her hair. She had sparkling blue eyes. She was trembling and seemed to be in some discomfort.

"Where did you come from?"

"Like I told you before, I can do a lot of things, Kay. You should know that by now."

"Did you Waft in here?"

"Sort of."

"Are you all right? Why are you trembling?"

"Cold—freezing actually, and I'm a little nervous, too. I've waited a long time for this meeting."

Kay held out his hand. "Cold? Oh, this is nothing, you big baby. You should be here when it's really cold. Well, it's probably a lot colder than you're used to in Zenon. Come, let's get inside."

Sam took Kay's hand. He noted her hand was elegant and slim. They made their way to the castle. Sam was moving slowly, bent over.

"Are you injured, Sam? Did you hurt your ankle?"

She spoke in a stutter, her breath coming out in a cloud. "I am so cold. This was a mistake, Kay. I should go home and come back when it's a little warmer, or we should have met inside. I didn't think it would be this cold."

She put her hand on his cheek and approached to give him a kiss.

The hand was chalk white, ghastly of pallor, like that of a corpse, and her finger-nails were like black daggers

Sam fell over struggling for breath. Kay rushed to her side. "Sam, let me help you! The castle's just this way!"

When she looked up, the blonde hair and blue eyes were gone. In their place was a shock of black hair dark as midnight. It wasn't simply very dark brown hair as most black-haired people had. It was coal black, matte black.

Her face— it was chalk white without a hint of color except for her lips, which were black.

And her eyes—huge, black, like two great holes in her head.

Monama! Creation! She was a Monama!!

Sarah's voice filled his head.

Freaks! Witches! Berserkacides going on murderous rampages. She's probably here to kill you—to eat you!

All this time … a Monama.

He jumped away, and she feebly reached out for him. Her coat and fur fell away. Underneath was a rail thin body wrapped up in a black gown with black on black designs stitched in the fabric, and there was a chain on her skirt.

"Creation! You're the Pale Ghost! You lied to me!"

"Kay ... I didn't lie, I ..."

Kay lurched back instinctively and unsaddled his CARG.

"Witch!" he cried. "Slavering beast!"

Sam pleaded with him, her black eyes large and strange. "Kay," she said, her voice strangled with emotion. "Kay, please ..."

Kay leveled his CARG at her throat, the same one she had helped him create four years ago. Her black lips pulled back in anguish. "So that's why all the secrecy; that's why all the hiding and lying! Have you been laughing at me all this time? Be gone ... be gone from here and trouble me no more!"

Sam's face crumpled up in sadness. A tear fell from her black eye—a plain old tear. She crawled away, summoning whatever strength she had left and was gone in a blink.

Only her coat and fur lying on the frozen cobbles bore proof that she had ever been there.

*   *   *   *   *

Several days later, the whole family was taking a speed barge to Saga, a large city on the windy western island of Barrow. It was a long way to go, but, once out in open water, the barge could move fast. Countess Sygillis had transacted a large sale of new fabrics to the House of Cotten, which was located in the south of Saga and was headed there to complete the sale in person. The whole family came to see the sights. As usual, Lord Davage piloted the vessel, which could fly and submerge if need be. Countess Sygillis, her dark red hair flying in the breeze, sat at his side. Kay and Lady Kilos sat behind them, and, in the back seat, all bundled up was Lady Hathaline and Lord Maser, locked in his little seat.

One of the children was in trouble. Hath was salty and had been punished by her mother—she had wanted to stand in the front with her father, as always, and help pilot the ship, and she raised a fuss when she hadn't been allowed to do so.

Finally, Lord Davage gave in. "Come on up here, Hath, and help me steer this leviathan," he said to her as the barge came around Mt.

Holly Cape and began to pick up speed. All smiles, Lady Hathaline went to the front. Everybody looked around admiring the scenery, except for Kay, who sat in his seat and sulked, the point of his triangle hat aimed at the floor, and Maser, who babbled and drooled.

Sam, a Monama witch, all this time. All the stories Sarah told—of the strange, lonely people hiding by the banks of their black lake, casting spells, seeing the future.

Freaks. Monsters that sometimes went mad with rage. Berserkacides.

He hated her.

He missed her. He couldn't even go into the eastern wing of the castle where their chapel was. It hurt too much.

Their chapel—what a sad joke.

Sygillis looked back, making sure that Maser wasn't trying to wiggle out of his seat, and she saw Kay.

"Kay, why the long face? You've not been yourself the past few days. Is everything all right?" Sygillis tapped him on the hat.

"He's never all right, Mother," Kilos said out of the corner of her mouth, trying to get a response out of him, her whitish-blue hair flying in the breeze.

Davage looked back when he could; Hath was holding the barge's controls in her eleven year old hands. "Well, Kay, out with it. You're depressing me. Perhaps we can help."

Kay shrugged, ready to sit there and sulk, and then changed his mind. "Mother, I've acted out of turn."

"And how so?"

"I have maintained a close communication with a voice for the last four years. I should have made that known to you."

"A voice?" Lady Kilos said. "Are you a nutter, Kay? Do you require a bib to drool on?"

Sygillis smiled. "I see. Please go on."

"I should not have allowed it. I should have gathered more information."

"Why, Kay?"

"Because the voice turned out to be that of a Monama witch."

"A witch?"

Davage let off the throttle a bit.

"Yes. She appeared to me a few days ago, and she was a Monama. I thought she was a Zenon girl, but she was a Monama."

"What would a Zenon girl possibly want with you?" Kilos asked, chiding. "How dumb can you ..."

"Ki," Sygillis said. "That's enough. Please leave your brother alone."

Kilos sat back and turned her attention to the passing seascape.

Sygillis turned back to Kay. "Go on, Kay. So, she revealed herself as a Monama, and then what did you do?"

"I unsaddled my CARG and told her to leave at once. I told her I never wished to speak to her again."

The barge slowed. Davage turned. "Kay," he said. "In seventeen years, you have been our pride and joy. You have always been such a wonderful, mature boy—we have been fortunate to have a son like you. All of our children are special, but you, Kay, are truly unique. I must say, however, I have never been so disappointed in you."

The words stung Kay. "Disappointed?"

"We have tried to teach you better, have we not?" Davage said.

"But a Monama ... Sarah has said—"

"Your cousin Sarah needs to grow up a bit, and, apparently, so do you."

His mother came back and sat down next to him. "Kay, how wet do you think your father and I are in our own home? A secret communication with a 'voice' from nowhere? Kay, we granted Lady Sammidoran permission to contact you in her special way four years ago. Countess Hortensia of Monama was our good friend, and Lady Sammidoran, her youngest granddaughter, was there the day you were born. She was just a girl about Hath's age at the time. I remember her grandmother lifting her up so that she could peer down into your crib, the wonder on her face. Her gift to you that day was that little gazelle."

"She gave me my gazelle?"

"Yes. She made it herself, just for you. She was so lonely—she didn't have a friend in the world, Kay, and for the very reasons you just mentioned. She was so excited when we gave her permission to speak to you—to try and strike up a friendship. We had hoped that you would be you, Kay, that you might choose to be her friend."

"Her eyes, her claws ..."

"That's why we were always so keen on you spending time with Countess Hortensia before she passed away—to show you that Monamas are good, kind people. Elders, rest her soul. But, you always seemed to harbor the same feelings most others do about Monamas, so Lady Sammidoran hid herself, waiting for the day that you might accept her for what she is. Yes, they are a little different. Yes, many, like your cousin, are afraid of them. Yes, many hate them as well, and that is their loss. Just remember, different doesn't mean bad, Kay. You, of all people, should know that well."

"Their rages, their madness."

"Propaganda," Davage said with bile. "There's no such thing as a Berserkacide."

"And, do you know what she told me, Kay?" Sygillis said. "I hate to pile on right now, but she said she thought that she was beginning to fall in love with you. I must admit, I thought that was a bit premature. I mean, you're only seventeen after all and yet to explore all of your possibilities, but I was flattered for you. As a mother, it's flattering for me to know that my son has affected someone in such a profound way. She was your friend for four years, Kay. Discard her if you wish, but please consider just who it is that you'll be hurting in the end."

Sygillis kissed him on the cheek and resumed her seat.

"Good going, Kay," Lady Kilos said, and Sygillis didn't bother to correct her.

Kay said nothing for the rest of the day.

* * * * *

Kay appeared in the chapel. It was dark and quiet. He looked around a moment and then sat down in a pew.

"Sam!" he called out into the hollow air. "Sam, I know you can hear me."

Silence. The statue of Fercandia stared at him, reproaching.

He'd struggled the last few days with his conscious. What he did to Sam was wrong, and he knew it.

The look on her face, the anguish. His CARG at her throat.

She gave him his gazelle—made it herself. The toy he cherished. He'd had it since before he could remember.

Sam, the Pale Ghost, watching him from afar since he was a boy. Why?

So the days rolled by, and he stayed away from the chapel. He remembered her standing in the Grove, freezing, her blonde-haired disguise falling away.

The lies. Perhaps that's what had made him so angry. Why didn't she just tell him—tell him that she was a Monama? Would his reaction have been any different?

He went back to the holo-net and looked up the word *zemfa* again. It came up:

zemfa: (adj, adv, interj): 1:—All right; permissible, meeting standards.
Language: Anuie
Region: South Kana, Zenon Midlands
Addendum: Anuie. Regional language based on a family of similar tongues hailing from the south of Kana, west of Zenon, by the Monama tribes of Astralon, Zerb and Nebulon. Known as "Monama Noble" it is ...

Monama. All he had to do was look, and there it was. Ki was right—he was dumb.

So, how was he going to do it? How was he going to say he was sorry?

Completely devoid of a plan, he grabbed her coat and fur and headed into the chapel.

"Sam, I'm sorry," he said in the echoing dark. "You were right. I'm an idiot. Come on Sam, I want to say I'm sorry."

Nothing.

"Sam, in the last few days I've been told, in no uncertain terms, that I have wronged you, and I acknowledge that. Maybe you should have just told me that you are a Monama. That would have given me a moment to ... be ready." He winced. "Oh, that didn't come out right. That didn't sound good—I'm sorry."

Nothing.

Kay held up Sam's fur. "You... you forgot your fur, and your coat, and I want to give them back. And, in any event... I miss you, Sam. How can I tell you such a thing without sounding like a total fool? I'll just lay it out. The day we started talking, I was going to kill myself. The only reason I'm alive is because of the promise I made to you. I can't even look at the posts without thinking of you. I can't enjoy anything without you. Are you happy? Here, how about if I say it like this: *Enier ane mirada*. That's Anuie, right? That's what you speak, I looked it up. That's Anuie for 'Will you forgive me?'."

Silence.

"At least get the last word in; tell me how stupid I am."

"You're stupid ..." he heard a quiet voice say from behind.

Kay turned, and sitting a few pews back was Sam, once again in black, all hair. Black eyes. Her clawed hands placed neatly in her lap. This time, no hiding, no covering her face. There she was ghastly white and matte black, hair all over the place. She looked like a ghost. Her mouth was small and sad. Her downcast eyes were huge, her eyelashes long and feathery.

Even ready for her appearance, Kay found himself choking back a hint of revulsion.

Why? She wasn't ugly; rather, she was quite pretty. She was beautiful in fact now that he looked at her—perfect. Just those huge eyes, those black holes in her head.

"You called me a witch," she said softly. "I've heard it before, I've heard it lots of times. But coming from you ... it really hurt."

"I'm sorry, Sam. I didn't mean it."

"Yes, you did."

"You're right, I did at the time, I didn't know what to think. But I've learned the error of my statement, and I have missed you. I didn't fully understand what you meant to me until you were gone. I'm asking you to forgive me."

Sam sighed. "Before she died, I went to my grandmother after her visits to your castle and asked her if she thought you were ready to see me ... I mean really see me. Always, she would say 'Almost, almost.' And I waited for the day when I could come to you as I am, unafraid, and you would take my hand. I was so eager for it." She paused and sat silent for a moment. "I guess 'Almost' was as close as I ever came. I'm going to leave now, Kay, and I'll not be back. I'm sorry I'm not what you were hoping for. I'm sorry I'm not some golden-haired beauty. I'm sorry I'm not a Zenon girl that you talk about all the time. I'm sorry I disappointed you—I think that's what hurts the most. I just wanted to say goodbye." She looked utterly miserable.

"Were you the Pale Ghost that used to follow me around and hide my things?"

"Yes."

"Why did you do that?"

"I've done lots of things, Kay, and all for you." She turned to leave. She moved in a haggard fashion. "Goodbye."

"Do you want to say goodbye to me, Sam?"

She didn't answer.

Kay stood and unsaddled his CARG. "Sam wait … before you go, the last time we met, I pointed this at you, I leveled it at your throat. I keep seeing the look on your face in my head, over and over. Please, take my CARG. You helped me create it, and I'm giving it to you as a token of my shame. I want you to have it."

Sam stood there and looked at the gleaming CARG.

"I made this with my own hands, Sam, just like you made my gazelle with yours. I've cherished that little toy that you made for me. It kept me safe when I was a little boy. Take my CARG, and let it keep you safe, too."

Sam reached out and took the CARG, holding it with both hands, her fingernails interlacing.

"Don't go, Sam… I'm begging you. I'm asking you to forgive me. I've learned my lesson. Let me prove it to you. I don't want this to be goodbye. *Enier ane mirada!*"

"You're not saying that right. It's *Enies ane mirada.*"

Kay stepped around the pews and approached her. "What do you say, Sam? If I am as important to you as you've always said, then don't punish yourself. Forgive me and let us move on."

She looked at the CARG. "Do you know how long I've waited to hear you say a few words in my language? I've wanted to share it with you for so long. Was it hard for you to learn?"

"I just practiced until I thought it right. I'm sorry I mispronounced *enies*. It means that what follows will be a question, right? I had trouble understanding that at first."

Sam smiled a little. "That's right. That's what it means. How do you ask a question without it? That was hard for me." She looked at his CARG. "I accept your gift."

With her black fingernail she scratched her name into the shaft of the CARG near the hilt, curled tendrils of silver twisting away as she worked. When she was done, she held it out. "*Ane forstas hithroe CARG ag-ane,*" she said. "Do you know what that means?"

Kay struggled. "It means you want … something. I—"

"It means I wish you to keep my CARG for me, Kay, and maybe you'll use it to defend me someday, to keep me safe."

"I'd like that, Sam. If you can deal with my purple hair, I can deal with anything you have to offer."

Sam laughed. "I love your hair, I think it's neat. And, keep the coat; I was wanting to give it to you as a memento."

Kay took her by the hand. "I'll always treasure it, Sam." He kissed her hand, long and soft, except for the black talon-like nails that were apparently hard enough to etch his CARG.

Sam took a deep breath and threw her long arms around him. "Oh, Kay—Kay ... I've missed you, too. I've missed you terribly! The past few days have been like a nightmare. I haven't been able to eat or sleep—I've felt so empty without you. If I had left just now, I don't know what I might have done. You have been my only friend, but you were all I needed." Tears dripped down her pale face. "And I'm sorry, too, that I presented myself as something I'm not, and the gods punished me. Does this mean that you don't care that I'm a *yendod* Monama?"

"A what?"

"A 'scary' Monama."

"If you'll have me, Sam," Kay said, wiping the tears away with a soft cloth.

She squeezed him tightly, their bodies fitting together nicely. "I've more surprises that you might, one day, discover. Are you willing to explore them with me? Are you going to freak on me again?"

"I won't, Sam." He kissed her on the cheek. "Have you lunched?"

"No, and I'm starving."

They Wafted out of the chapel—Kay's Waft still slow and blustery. Sam "Blinked" without noise or wind and waited for him to finish his Waft. Kay offered Sam his arm, which she took. "Well, come on. Let's get some lunch and say hello to my parents. They'll be happy to see you."

7—A Silver Hummingbird

Kay and Sam transformed each other over the winter. They saw each other every day, Sam appearing in the Grove in the morning. She still had no tolerance for the cold of the north, but, if she bundled up, she could withstand it for short periods of time. She wore a thick, fur-lined coat with furry mittens and ear muffs, all black of course. They would go into the castle and have breakfast, then make their way to some quiet place, usually a library or comfortable study in Kay's Zorn tower and read or look at the posts together via the Holo-net. Sam was fascinated by the Holo-net. She said she didn't have it at her home, and they spent hours toying around with it. She almost became as bad as his cousin Sarah, who was a true Holo-net/Airenet junkie.

Though elegant and somewhat frail-looking in her black gown, Sam was a lot more rough and tumble than she first let on. She loved to run and climb. She was much faster than Kay, even in a thick coat, gown and heeled shoes to boot. She could run like a deer and had the endurance of a championship athlete. She was a heck of a tree-climber and could scale the largest of trees in the Grove in a matter of moments, a feat that would have Sarah, a champion tree-climber, drooling. Sam used her nails; as he thought, they were every bit as formidable as they looked. Once she got to the top, she could jump all the way back down and not hurt herself, her hair trailing behind her plummeting body like a black comet as she fell.

Sam flooded Kay with Anuie, her native language, often switching back and forth in mid-sentence. Sometimes she refused to speak anything else, forcing Kay to listen and try to mimic her speech. Speaking in her language was rather important for her. Soon he was babbling away in a rudimentary fashion. Sam was delighted.

* * * * *

One morning, after they'd argued about an article in the posts, she shocked Kay by challenging him to a wrestling match to settle the matter. Kay tried to get out of it by stating that he didn't want to damage her gown. Sam, however, was determined and she made Kay take her to the laundry room, where she found one of his mother's Hospitaler body suits, cleaned and pressed. They then made their way back to the reading room and moved the furniture aside, giving them plenty of room to wrestle. Sam pulled her shoes off and changed into the suit behind a screen.

Then they went at it. Monamas, as a rule, were incredibly strong, and Sam had proved that. They were once prized on Hoban as arena fighters, and Sam, though quite thin and gangly, was, indeed, as strong as a bull. As they rolled around on the floor, a very real concern Kay had was with Sam's nails—he had thoughts of getting his throat accidentally cut, but Sam appeared adept at using her hands and not cutting him. They were both quite shy at first, confining themselves to headlocks and arm bars, but soon they relaxed and wrestled as hard as they could. Throwing each other around the room, grunting and straining, pretzeled-up in impossible holds, they wrestled for a good hour. Sam wasn't the first girl Kay had wrestled—he and Sarah often locked up in the Grove, but Sarah, unless she cheated and used her Gift of Strength, wasn't nearly as solid and tough as Sam was.

Finally, exhausted, they stopped, lay there for a moment and laughed. Then, they went down for some refreshments.

Wrestling Sam became a regular thing, and they did it almost every day.

Kissing Sam soon followed, their matches quickly fading into make out sessions. Sam was quite hot and slithery as they kissed, her long body all over him. She was unabashedly passionate. She seemed all hands, like she had more than just two, and often times they went places Kay felt they ought not to go. She also seemed to have quite a fascination with his bellybutton—she constantly touched it and caressed it with her fingernails. Sometimes she stared at it, and even licked it once, making him lurch with surprise.

* * * * *

"It's like my whole body just stops working," Sam said, lying next to Kay. "My heart, all of a sudden, slows way down, and I can't breathe. The cold air going into my lungs is like swallowing a razor blade. And I can't see. Even if I bundle up with my coat and furs, it doesn't help much. I feel it coming in through my feet. How do you stand it?"

"The cold? I don't feel it. None of us do. It can be below zero, and I can walk around outside in my shirt-sleeves and not be troubled in the least. They say the Vith are immune to the cold. The reason my cousins go south to Esther every winter is because my uncle, Lord Peter, hates the cold and he can't take it. He's an Esther, and I suppose they're not immune to cold."

Sam rolled on top of him. "What does snow feel like Kay? I can't touch snow without going into shock."

"Well, it depends. It can feel powdery, like sugar, or kind of crunchy, like wet sand. Here, I'll be right back." Kay left the reading room. Several minutes later he returned with a bowl of snow from outside. Sam sat up and looked at it with wonder. Just sitting next to the cold bowl gave her goose bumps.

"Watch," he said. He plunged his hand into the bowl and kept it there.

Several minutes elapsed. "You don't feel that, Kay?" Sam asked.

"No." He pulled his hand out and showed it to Sam.

"Oh, I can feel it radiating off your hand."

"Do you think you can condition yourself to it, little by little?"

Sam stared at the bowl of snow. She rubbed her hands together and then dipped her pinky into the bowl.

She gasped, open mouthed, throwing her head back. Kay pulled her hand out. Immediately, her whole hand turned blue, with her veins popping out in a spidery configuration. It took several minutes before Sam fully recovered, Kay holding her as if she had just been through a terrible ordeal.

* * * * *

He taught me many things, showed me ...

Gazing out of a terrace halfway up Kay's tower, Sam could see the village down below by the sea and wanted to go there and explore. She was bundled up in her coat and muffler as usual. They spoke in Anuie, Kay having developed a fair understanding of the language and a short vocabulary to go with it.

"*What is that road there to the south?*" Sam asked, leaning over the rail and pointing down from the terrace.

"*Bloodstein Road.*"

"*And those smaller buildings south of it?*"

Kay looked. "Cyantown. *That's where most of the villagers live. Quiet place.*"

"*And that pretty domed structure over there?*"

"*That's St Vith. It's a cathedral. We go there for service from time to time.*"

She panned her gaze farther north. "*What are those buildings there by the bay?*"

"That's Sarfortnim College. See that horseshoe-shaped structure down there? That's where they play brandtball."

"What is brandtball?"

"It's a game, Sam, played with three teams. Wish I could take you down there to see a match. I think you might enjoy it."

Sam shielded her eyes and stared at the arena. *"I want to go there and see, Kay. You'll teach me?"*

"It's too cold for you. You can take it for fifteen minutes at most, and brandtball games last several hours. You'll freeze to death before the first set is out."

"Isn't there anyplace indoors we can watch from?"

"Nope." Kay thought a moment and switched back to standard Elder. "It's too dangerous. And, I don't want all those people gawking at you bundled up like a coal-black polar bear."

"I know, Kay. I'll disguise myself … I'll make myself look like a Zenon girl that you were so eager for. It'll be hard because of the cold, and I won't be able to wear shoes while I'm doing it, but I'll do it for you. I can be anything you want me to be."

"But, Sam, let's think about that for a second, assuming you could survive out in the cold for an extended time. If we go to the village to watch a match, and you're Cloaked to look like a Zenon girl with no shoes on, people will, no doubt, have all sorts of questions. They'll want to know who was with me at the match. I am the next Lord of Blanchefort, and they're going to be curious."

"Well, let's make up a story."

"That's the worst thing we could do. Say we do that. People will still look into the matter and will soon discover that we were lying; then, it'll blow up into a full-fledged scandal. You watch."

Sam went on a short rant, trucking away in Anuie, but going so fast and using such complex words that Kay couldn't follow her.

"I don't understand," he said.

"Why are people so nosy?" she said. "We mind our own business in the Monama-lands"

"That's just the way it is in League Society—gossip's a big thing. It's one of the drawbacks of coming from a big Blue family. Besides, if I let you Cloak yourself to look a different way, that might mean that I tacitly wished you to be something you're not. I like you just the way you are. Look, you're the one who insists on secrecy, not me."

"Our relationship cannot generally be known," she said.

"Why not?

"Because it can't, Kay. Trust me."

Sam was sad. She leaned on the railing and stared at the village. Then she got cold and went inside.

* * * * *

Kay wracked his brains in the following weeks. Every two weeks, and on Tuesdays, Sam had to attend some sort of family function that she kept rather quiet about and stayed away. During that time, he walked the Grove alone moving off the paths and going knee -deep into the snow. He didn't feel the biting cold at all just the delicate lattice-work of the snow, a lovely feeling all in all. Vith must be impervious to cold, as was sometimes said. He recalled his lessons as a boy given by Lady Poe out in the Grove, no coat needed. He used to like throwing snowballs at Sarah while Lady Poe's back was turned, but her familiar Silver tech "Bark" always ratted him out.

Hmmm, Lady Poe ...

His aunt was known for her skill with creating Silver tech animals that could do all sorts of miraculous things. There was Bark and Shadow the cat, and her little bird Tweeter was a marvel, as was Fins the fish who could heal most any injury in a matter of moments. And Lady Poe had more, many more. Perhaps she could help. He had to remember, though, that Lady Poe knew nothing of his relationship with Sam, and she couldn't know. It was a secret Sam insisted upon. He'd have to pick his words carefully.

He went inside and Commed her up, reaching her at her winter home in Esther. As usual, Lady Poe was an affable, smiling lady with her short blonde hair and gigantic Shadowmark, much larger than his mother's. She was sitting in a lovely, terraced garden, a sweating summer drink sitting on the table top next to her.

"Kay," she said. "How goes it? My, I'm certain you've grown over the winter. Look at you!"

"I'm fine, Aunt Poe. How's the south?"

"Warm as always. I'm afraid the duchess isn't too happy with your mother right now, Kay. Something about an attack of cloth-eating StT's at a recent ball that forced her to retire before her gown fell off her body in tatters. I know nothing. I try not to get involved with those things, you see." She leaned toward the screen. "I think the duchess is preparing a revenge of some sort. Don't ask me what it is. I know nothing."

His mother and the duchess, always at each other's throats. He had to laugh a little. "And, Sarah and Phillip?"

"They are eager to return and see you. Sarah prepared a small bedroom that she calls 'Kay's Bedroom' that she's set aside should you ever chose to visit. The duke and duchess would love to see you."

"I will, Aunt Poe, I promise."

"Now, Kay, while I love speaking with you, you know the proper method of a Great Lord such as yourself in communicating with his peers is via long-hand letter. We are Vith, Kay, and that's how we do it."

"I know, Aunt Poe; however, a situation has occurred that requires prompt action, and I was wondering if I might ask a novel favor of you?"

Poe appeared concerned. "Certainly, Kay, anything I can do."

"Doubtless you know my friend, Lord Lon of Probert."

Lady Poe thought a moment and lit up. "Oh, yes, the son of Lord Milos and Lady Branna! What a delightful young fellow, very intelligent if I recall."

"Yes, that's him. He confessed to me in private that the climate here in Blanchefort is much too frigid for his south-Vithland tastes and finds he can barely stand it."

"Oh," Poe replied. "Many of my friends have mentioned the same thing, though I think the climate is just right." She lowered her voice and leaned into the screen again. "I think your Uncle Peter also has issues with it from time to time."

"I was hoping that you might be able to assist Lord Lon and make his visits a bit more comfortable. I was hoping you might be able to create some sort of Silver tech device that will keep him warm and toasty."

Poe thought about it. "A Silver tech device that will create heat? Well, I ..."

"Is that possible, Aunt Poe?"

Her large Vith blue eyes floated about her head, and she was lost in thought. "Well, certainly anything is possible. Hmmm, I hadn't considered ..." She took a sip from her glass. "Allow me a day or two to prepare something. I think we'll be able to assist Lord Lon nicely.

Shall I send my Silver tech device directly to Lon at his home in Arden? It is still Arden, correct?"

"Yes, it is, but you needn't send it there. Please send it to me here in Blanchefort, and thank you very much in advance, Aunt Poe, for your kind help."

In the background Kay could hear Sarah and Phillip running around.

"You're very welcome, Kay. Yes, I think we'll be able to help Lord Lon stay warm. Please give your parents my best."

"I will, and well met, Aunt Poe."

Sarah's blue-haired head popped up in the background. "Is that Kay? Wait!"

"Yes, it is, but if you wish to communicate with your cousin, young lady, you must write him a letter."

"Mother!" Sarah shrieked. "Wait! Kay, did you get my ... "

Lady Poe smiled and screened down, cutting Sarah off in mid-rant.

Kay was hopeful. Lady Poe could always be counted on to go out of her way for a person.

* * * * *

A few days later Kay received a post from the south. Sam had returned to the castle, and they quickly went up to their favorite haunt high up in his tower to open it.

"What is it, Kay?" Sam asked, looking at the drab brown box.

"It's something I've been expecting from my aunt. It's for you."

"*Prenta aine?*" she exclaimed, meaning, "for me?"

He looked around for a paper knife, and Sam took action cleanly cutting open the package with her fingernail. She was eager to get it open.

"*Bende,*" Kay said in Anuie, meaning "thanks".

"*Cerste,*" Sam replied, loving to speak in her language. She kissed him on the cheek.

Kay and Sam opened the box and peered inside.

Wrapped up in green tissue paper was a small silver medallion of a happy-faced hummingbird on a long silver chain. Kay took it out and examined it; clearly, its happy face gave it away as a Lady Poe creation. On the back side was Lady Poe's coat-of-arms, an assurance that the item would work as intended.

There was a note inside:

Kay

This is Snugs. I have a little workshop here at Grand Oyln Manor, and I whipped him up in an afternoon or two. An excellent idea, Kay. I'd not thought of it myself. Now, I can give one to your uncle and a few to some of my friends who are rather shy about visiting Blanchefort due to the climate. Now they have no excuse.

Snugs comes in two forms. My favorite, is a full-formed hummingbird which can warm up a whole room. The second is a medallion., which your uncle suggested. The medallion is not as potent as the full-formed one and must be worn to feel its effects. If you wish to have the full-formed Snugs, please let me know.

Give all my love to your sisters and your little brother, and to your parents, and we'll see you in a few months. Sarah and Phillip are dying to see you again—they miss you so.

Love

Aunt Poe

P.S—Sarah wanted me to tell you she helped out making the medallion and gave it its name.

Sam looked at the medallion in wonder. "This will keep me warm?"

"So she says. My aunt can do anything with her Silver tech."

Sam got up and bounced up and down. "Let's go see!"

They went down and out into the Grove, Kay carrying Sam's coat, mittens and hat just in case they were needed. Instantly, Sam recoiled a little bit as they stepped out into the outdoor air, her skin turning to rapid gooseflesh. She closed her eyes and held her breath. The lattice-work of her veins came to the surface.

Kay clasped the medallion around Sam's neck. A moment or two elapsed as the medallion swung on its chain. As the temperature dropped, the little hummingbird's wings began to flap in fluid movement; up, down, up down, flush across the face of the medallion.

Sam straightened up and looked around.

"How do you feel, Sam?" he asked.

Still holding her breath, she nodded. Her veins vanished, and her gooseflesh flattened out.

"Sam, breathe normally."

Carefully Sam breathed out in a cloud. She looked around. "This is amazing, Kay. I don't feel a thing." As she stood there, her body literally began to steam slightly in the cold air.

"You're steaming, Sam."

"Am I?"

"You don't feel cold?"

"No, I feel fine! I feel fine!" She took a deep breath and blew a cloud of steam. "I'm a dragon!" she cried. Off came her shoes, and she padded into the snow, whirling around, dancing in it.

Kay dropped his stuff and pawed up a large snowball. Before Sam could react, he pegged her with it in the face. Previously, any contact with snow was enough to put Sam into palpitations. She reached into the snow and scooped up a massive handful, throwing and missing. Kay ran and Sam tackled him, rolling through the snow, laughing.

As always, Lady Poe had created a marvelous Silver tech device that worked flawlessly. With this wondrous charm, Sam was free. The Grove was no longer a dangerous place where Sam could fall into distress at any moment. Now she could run outside in her gown as far as she wanted. Now she could touch the snow and marvel at its structure. She wore the medallion all the time, for she had always found the interior of the castle a bit chilly as well. One day, once they were duly announced, she wanted to approach Lady Poe and properly thank her for this remarkable gift.

"This won't be mine until I've thanked her," she said. "I must thank her as is proper."

8—Lady Kilos

With the problem of the cold defeated came another persistent and possibly more daunting issue. While Snugs did a great job of keeping Sam warm, it had an unexpected side-effect. Snugs totally fouled her ability to disguise herself and change shape. In fact, Sam couldn't do any of her remarkable abilities with it on.

So the fight to go to the village was on again in earnest.

"Sam, there aren't a whole lot of Monamas walking around in Blanchefort village. You're the one who says we have to keep our relationship a secret, not me, and you will stick out down there like nobody's business. Rest assured people are going to talk. Even your grandmother who was here fairly regularly for over 200 years never went to the village. Father tells me that, at their wedding, she nearly collapsed from the cold."

"So, how are we going to do this, Kay? *Ane-te-samma-ventinos!*"

"I know you want to go down there, Sam, but, things will be bad. Trust me. We have to think this out first!"

Kay and Sam wracked their brains. Sam had all sorts of ideas, most of which dealt with using Gifts and other outworldly powers. At one point, she got angry and insisted that he Cloak her himself.

"Cloak me, Kay. You can do it! Cloak me!"

"I can't Cloak you, Sam," he said. "I can't Cloak myself yet."

Sam had a bad moment—she lost her temper. She stood up. "Kay, I am so tired of your lousy Gifts! I can see the future, right? I see you doing such amazing things *but always in the future!* I'm tired of you being great in the future! I want you to be great *now*!!"

She picked him up by the collar. "You could Cloak me to look like whatever you wanted to without half trying if you only applied yourself. Do you know how frustrating that is? You know, Kay, I wonder if I were to throw you off this terrace, would you be able to Waft yourself to safety?"

"Waft? It takes me forever to Waft!"

"Sink or swim, Kay. I'm really thinking about doing it. I certainly hope you choose to swim, but I don't know. Sometimes you are maddeningly content being a do-nothing, and that makes me crazy!!"

"Sam, put me down!"

A voice came from the doorway. "Am I interrupting something? You left your door open."

Sam and Kay both looked, mouths open. Standing there in the threshold to the reading room was Lady Kilos, blue hair up, dressed in a minty gown. She was carrying a few parcels from the village. Sam dropped Kay and made to Blink away. It failed. She ripped Snugs off her neck and recoiled from the cold as if punched in the gut.

"There's really no need to be alarmed, I've known about you two for a long time. Please."

Kay came to Sam's side and put the medallion back on her neck. Sam exhaled harshly as her body warmed.

"Is she all right?" Ki asked.

"She's fine. It's the cold; she can't take it."

"Oh," Ki said.

They spent an uncomfortable moment. "Ki, how did you ..."

"You two really don't hide things well, do you? And you make a remarkable amount of racket up here when you're rolling around on the floor as you tend to enjoy doing. I also managed to worm a few things out of mother the other day. Not much goes on around here without me knowing about it. I'm very happy Kay chose to come to his senses and make up with you, Lady Sammidoran."

Kay was dumbfounded. His sister Ki was a noted gossiper and social want-to-be. If she knows, how long will it be before the rest of the League knows?

She appeared to read his troubled thoughts to some extent. She smiled and seated herself, placing her packages on the table. Sam slowly seated herself and looked at them with longing.

"Oh, go ahead and look if you like. Just some sundries that caught my eye."

Sam looked into one of the bags with wonder. "You were just in the village?"

"Yes. It's small, but it's actually a lot of fun. Father's warbird and other Fleet shipping help attract merchants from all over. Rundle Way is lined with wonderful shops; some are even from Bazz."

"Rundle Way is a dilapidated row of old buildings Father was going to have torn down," Kay said.

"Seems you've not been there in a while. It's completely rebuilt and occupied and is screaming to be explored." Sam listened and was enthralled.

"I think you two are going about this matter wholly wrong-footed," Ki said. "You want to visit the village, but you don't want to create a stir—yes? And, if I heard you correctly, you've been trying to puzzle this out using Gifts and other various feats of mind and body to either hide, Cloak, or move about invisibly. Why not simply go the most pragmatic and obvious route?"

Kay and Sam looked at each other, the two of them not having any thought as to what that route might be.

Lady Kilos smiled. "Lady Sammidoran, come here, please."

Dubiously, Sam stood and approached, still holding one of Ki's bags. "Please, call me Sam."

"Thank you, Sam, I will. And you may call me Ki. My, such lovely eyelashes. May I ask, are those real?"

"Yes," Sam said with a bit of uncertainty.

"There are ladies I know who would collapse for eyelashes like those. Turn around, please, if you will." Sam complied. "Such lovely, thick hair. Why do you wear a chain on your skirt?

"It's a tradition."

"Ah. May I see your hands, please?"

Sam slowly raised her hands. Pale, delicate. Her black fingernails, sharp as knives, glinted in the light.

"Thank you. Yes, this puzzle is much simpler than the two of you have considered. I can help."

Kay was dubious. He liked his sister Lady Kilos well enough. Sarah couldn't stand her much, too prissy. Too girlie. Those two attributes were bad black strikes in Sarah's tom-boy book. "So, if I am to understand, Ki, you'll help us and keep our secret?"

"Why is it a secret? I'm just asking."

Sam jumped in. "I have insisted on the secrecy, Ki. It's our way in the Monamalands. If it were to become publically known that Kay and I are seeing each other,… well, Kay is not ready for what would then have to happen after that. Nor am I. It is for his sake that I require our relationship remain a secret. I cannot say anything more."

Ki thought about it for a moment. "Well, that's good enough for me then. You may count on my discretion. I haven't said anything yet, have I? I could have ratted you two out years ago, but, Kay's my brother, and I'm not going to spread rumors about my own kin, except, maybe, Sarah. You know, Sam, Kay is considered bad luck with the ladies around Kana. Oh, they like him well enough. They fawn over him, and they ask me all sorts of things, but few, it seems, have any luck striking up a connection. Do you know anything about that?"

Sam blushed a slight bit. "No. How would I know anything about that? Their misfortune is my gain. Perhaps the gods are involved."

Ki smiled. "Perhaps. Fine then. So, if I'm understanding properly, you two want to go to the village and explore, but you're concerned about the gossip that'll no doubt be created. That is a good thought, as Kay correctly anticipated people's understandable reaction. Actually, I'm a little surprised he thought ahead far enough to recognize the problem. The only girl they ever see Kay running around with is Lady Sarah, and you do not look much like Sarah. And, if I heard you correctly, then you cannot use Gifts or sorcery to change your appearance."

Sam held out her medallion. "This keeps me warm, but it disrupts my ability to change my shape."

"You can do that?"

"I can, but not with this medallion on. I trade warmth and safety for my skills."

"Turn around again, please, Sam."

Sam held her arms out and turned around, the bustle of her gown rustling and her chain rattling. Ki laughed. "Yes, I'm fairly certain I can help you. I'll make it so you needn't fear in the village."

Kay wasn't sure. "You're going to help us?"

"That's what I just said."

"What do you want in return?"

Ki rolled her eyes up and thought a moment. "In return, I'd like to come with you. I won't be a third wheel. We can go and have some fun in the village—there are actually a lot of interesting shops and cafes down there, like I said. Good food, and, when we're done and you two want to start rolling around again, I'll leave you alone. I just want to be friends. So, what do you say?"

Kay thought about it. "And our secret is safe with you? No tricks?"

"No tricks, Kay. I'm not Sarah, always looking to get out of a promise like she does. You can count on me. I just want to be part of the gang for a change."

"Sounds fair enough. What do you say, Sam?"

"Oh yes," she replied. "Thank you, Ki. *Bende.* Your offer is most reasonable, and I look forward to becoming good friends with you."

Ki leapt to her feet. "Well then, Sam, please come with me to my tower, and we'll get started. You stay here, Kay, or go do what you want. Give me a few hours; then, you can come up and see. We'll be in my boudoir, 93rd floor. Let's go, Sam."

They left, and Kay stewed alone for an hour or two wondering what was going on over there. He could see Ki's Harkness Tower a fair distance away butted up next to the grand main entrance to the castle. Her tower, structurally, was identical to his. He looked at it, burning with curiosity as to what was going on within. As he waited, a post came in from Sarah. More ghastly stuff as usual:

"BERSERKACIDE NEST DISCOVERED IN CLOVIS RUINS."

She also left a note asking how "Snugs" was working.

Fine, just fine, he replied to her. A few more months and she'd return with Phillip as always. She and Phillip shared Xyotel Tower just a ways down off the East Wing. The guy wire they had setup from their tower to his for the purposes of sliding back and forth in dramatic style was still there, taut in the wind.

Finally, he went down to the foyer and entered Ki's Tower, up the lift and out on the 93rd floor. The whole floor and the two above it were designated as Ki's gigantic closet, and it was a wonderland of the frilly and the feminine. He'd only been in it once or twice previously. Sarah considered the place a purgatory for the living—a house of horrors containing all the girly things she despised. The layout of the floors were set up sort-of museum style, with a winding central path snaking its way past a number of vast display areas and eventually going up a floor to begin again. Ki had it very well organized: first unmentionables, then gowns, then shoes, then accessories, then an area for make-up and so on. Along the way, Ki had little holo-terminals going, chattering and caged to items of interest for her, like the latest fashion milestones from Esther, Remnath, and Zenon. Other terminals played music, and others flashed postings from her friends so that she would have instant news. Something was always flying by from her friends. Ki also had a number of Perlamum boards set up in alcoves so that she could keep track of the more notable games taking place around the League as they happened.

Kay moved down the path winding through Ki's closet. A chorus of animated mannequins wearing Ki's gowns danced about, whirling as he passed by. Many wore a variety of fashionable hats from the far corners of Kana and Hoban. Ki loved Hoban fashion. How she managed to pick what she wanted to wear every morning was surely a major labor.

Others carried pots of creams and trays of fruit, and they wore a bewildering array of shoes from all over.

He went up a level and moved into Ki's makeup area. Going through a vast pallet of watercolors shaded in every imaginable hue, he located the heart of Ki's boudoir. It was a large open terrace looking down on the village, situated in such a way that there was plenty of natural light coming in.

There was quiet chatter and laughter coming from just ahead accented by a little light music. Surrounded by colors and earthen pots full of powders and oils and a host of animated mannequins were Sam and Ki.

"Hi, Kay, come on over!" Ki said, holding a make-up brush. "You two had a problem, and your problem is now solved!"

"What did you do?" Kay made his way out onto the terrace pushing past a few whirling mannequins. Sam was sitting in a vast chair. When she saw Kay, she quieted down.

She appeared a little nervous. "Hi, Kay," she said softly.

"You two seem to be getting on well," Kay said.

"We have. Sam's a wonderful lady. You have fine taste, Kay. Notice anything different?" Ki asked.

Sam sat meekly in the chair as Kay looked her over. Firstly, she was wearing a red dress instead of her black Monama gown, which was nearby on a waiting mannequin, chain and all. Another mannequin was holding her black Monama shoes on a platter. Sam was wearing a stylish pair of knee-high black boots. "I had my mannequins whip up a quick dress for Sam. Looks lovely, I think. The boots are Esther. Esthers, short of Hoban, make great boots." Ki leaned down and gently brushed Sam's face. "I love those eyelashes. Now, I've applied a good layer of make up to Sam's face. Coming here as often as she does, she has taken on the slightest bit of blush. She's still very pale, but not anything so much as to create a stir. I've painted her lips a smashing color of red to highlight the rose in her skin, and I've added a gentle bit of azure eye shadow to give her a bit of depth."

Sam looked a bit odd. No black gown, no black lips. She appeared rather festive. She had her hands in her lap hidden under a cloth.

"What do you think, Kay?" she asked. "Do you like it?"

"You look very good. Great in fact."

Kilos beamed, proud of her work. "So, you wish to hide? Hiding in plain sight is always best and most effective."

A few problems quickly entered Kay's mind. "What about her eyes, Ki?"

"I was wondering when you'd ask me that." Ki put her brush down on a vanity and summoned a mannequin holding a fancy cardboard box. She opened the lid and pulled out a copper and silver pair of goggles. Ki put the goggles on Sam's face, carefully placing the stems around her ears.

"What in the name of Creation are those?" Kay asked.

"Gretnas," Ki replied, "from Hoban. They're all the rage over there. Everybody's wearing them."

The goggles contained an intricate set of interlocking lenses and silver and copper disks that were geared to move together like the mechanism of an old-fashioned watch. Looking at the goggles, Kay couldn't see Sam's eyes, just the complex layers of gears all nested together and sparkling. "Can you see, Sam?" he asked.

Ki adjusted the lenses and Sam looked around. "I can! Actually, I can see better than I normally do! It's so bright here, and I must be a bit nearsighted and didn't know any better. *Cul-lenor!*"

"What does that mean?" Ki asked.

"It means "amazing" in Anuie," Kay replied.

"You speak Anuie, Kay?'

Sam beamed. "Kay has picked up the basics of my language very quickly. I am so proud of him."

"I'm impressed," Kilos said. "So, with these Gretnas on, nobody will be the wiser. Sam will look like any stately lady about the League, no doubt of a high circle with money to afford these goggles. And, with those on, people will probably be more interested in them than in her, per se."

Kay nodded. He remembered something. "What about her fingernails?"

Sam blushed.

"Show him, Sam," Ki said. "Go on, show him."

"Kay, I hope you're not angry with me," Sam said, squirming in her chair.

"Angry about what?"

"About this." Sam cast her towel aside. Her Monama fingernails, once impossibly long and sharp, were now trimmed down to a very manageable length and were painted red like her lips.

"I had to get a file from the smithy. Her nails are hard as iron," Ki remarked.

"Our nails are a mark of beauty—we treasure them. I hope you don't mind me without them, Kay. Is it all right?" Sam was a bit panicked.

"It's fine, Sam. They look good." Sam got up out of the chair and gave him a hug. The boots she was wearing made her even taller than normal.

Kilos admired her work and then began putting her things away. "So, here's our story. Sam is the daughter of a prominent League House here for a visit and seeing the sights."

"And when they ask what House she's from?" Kay asked. Sam was still holding onto him. The gears inside her goggles clicked a little.

"We say her House is in the middle of a large business transaction with father, and we can't disclose it until the matter is settled. Happens all the time. They will understand that sort of thing in the village, and the matter will be settled."

Sam gazed at Kay, still wearing the goggles. "Do you think it'll work, Kay?"

"I think so. Ki knows her stuff."

* * * * *

So, with goggles, red lips and nails, they finally went down to the village, Sam wearing nothing over her red dress but a light shawl. As they plunged into the maze of shops and eateries, the locals were every bit as nosy and full of questions as Kay had predicted. He simply said she was a guest from the south, which was true. As Lady Kilos was present, the locals took it at that, though a few pressed the question as to which House she was from. Kay said that he was not at liberty to say—due to a pending business transaction. As Ki had predicted, that appeased them.

The three enjoyed the afternoon. Sam liked the shops and waterfront pubs in the village, and she positively loved trying the food, stopping at every eatery to sample the fare. She especially liked the view of the castle from down there. Once or twice Sam pulled Kay into a quiet alley, pushed her goggles aside and kissed him with her hummingbird-heated lips.

9—The Future-Telling

As the winter wore on, Sam, Kay and Lady Kilos became good friends. They often went to the village, Sam in colorful dresses provided by Ki and wearing the Gretna goggles from Hoban to cover her eyes. As their friendship grew, Ki told Sam she could have the goggles, as they tended to make her dizzy when she wore them anyway, but Sam wouldn't hear of it. She insisted on paying for them in some way, but Sam didn't have much money.

"I know," Ki said. "You can look into the future for me and give me a reading. How about that?"

Sam was dubious. "The future isn't a place I like to see, Ki," she said.

"Oh, come on. It'll be fun."

It took some convincing, as Sam clearly didn't want to do it; however, after a bit of talking, Sam relented.

They dressed down in sturdy clothing and went out into the Grove. Sam said she needed to be as close to the earth as possible in order to see. Being under the earth was even better. Kay had planned to crash into the vast underworld of Castle Blanchefort; however, Lady Kilos was too claustrophobic to follow them. She didn't like small spaces.

The best place to go, then, would be out in the Grove near the Holt courtyard. There were a number of easy, roomy tunnels to move through in that area, so Kilos should be fine. As they trudged out to the Holt courtyard, Sam was wearing one of her permanently appropriated bodysuits and a pair of sandals along with her usual Snugs medallion, the little wings flapping steadily. Her body steamed a bit in the cold air, especially from her head. Kay and Kilos wore smithy-style clothing that they didn't mind getting dirty. The Holt courtyard was wreathed in giant oak and nadine trees in the shadow of Dead Hill, the old Blanchefort necropolis atop the mushroom-shaped hill to the south. The low-slung confusion of tombs and vaults were spread out across the top of Dead Hill like a layer of gray frosting on a cake.

They got to the courtyard, and Kay plunged off the trail. Moving through the trees, he located a heavy-looking metal hatch half-buried in snow. "Here it is!" He tried the hatch and it wouldn't turn; rusted shut, it seemed. "This happens every winter." He struggled with it.

"Sam," he said, and she knelt down and gripped the handle. She struggled a moment, then the handle broke loose with a clank.

"That was really rusted shut," she said spinning the hatch open.

"We don't use this tunnel much anymore. It's for kids."

Ki looked within the dark hole with some trepidation as Sam cleared away the rest of the snow.

"Are you sure this is safe, Kay? I just don't like small spaces."

He held his hand out. "It's fine, Ki. This tunnel is big and straight, and it isn't very long. These tunnels here are pretty easy. This tunnel goes under this oak tree and comes back out on the other side. Mother doesn't even rate this one with her stone system. It's a 0-stoner, as Sarah calls it."

Ki, carrying a light, took his hand and entered slowly, carefully feeling her way with every step. The tunnel within went down about ten feet in an easy slope and then leveled out. The tunnel was about four feet high and made of hard-packed earth. It ran into the bowers of the oak tree above. The tangled, old-growth roots created a large, dry vault where they could stand straight. "This used to be one of my, Sarah, and Phillip's favorite hideouts when we were younger. We trucked all sorts of stuff in here for our adventures. Some of it is probably still lying around if you look for it." Sam quickly found an empty can of red gasol—left there by Sarah no doubt as red gasol was her drink of choice. Kay found a good spot in the roots and seated Ki.

"You ok, sis?" he asked. She was sweating and looked to be on just the verge of panicking. After a minute or two, she swallowed and composed herself.

"See, it's not so bad under here, right?"

She nodded tentatively. Kay set the light down as Sam removed her sandals and began digging at the ground.

"Why are we under here again, please?" Ki asked as Sam dug.

"You wanted me to see the future for you. I have to be near the ground to see the future. The gods are in the earth, and I must revel in it."

Kay set up several heaters, directed them at Sam and turned them on, the vault quickly becoming very warm.

Sam sat down and took the loose dirt she'd dug up and began rubbing herself with it. "Can you help me, Kay?" she asked. He came over and rubbed dirt into her back. He rubbed a little on her cheeks and she gave him a kiss. "Ki, are you sure you wish this? Sometimes, knowing a thing ahead of time makes the thing much worse than it actually is. Worrying about the future can be terrible. I'll ask one last time. Are you certain you wish this?"

"Yes, Sam, I do."

"All right." She removed her medallion and handed it to Kay. She instantly clenched up a bit even though she was centered in the heater's beam.

"You ok, Sam?"

She took a moment and slowly recovered. "Yes, I'm fine. So cold in here. Now, the future will come upon me, and I will fall into a trance. You may ask me specific questions, and I will answer. I will probably speak in Anuie; Kay will translate. These visions can go out of control, I want you to know that. I might start saying things that don't make sense. Just talk to me, say my name, and I will recover. *Zemfa?*"

"Sure, Sam, sure," Ki replied.

Kay seated himself next to Ki. Sam sat there in the middle of the vault, cross-legged, covered in dirt, trembling slightly.

"Now what?" Ki asked.

"Now, we wait," Sam said. "The future is here with us. It won't be long now."

Sam sat there motionless for awhile. Lady Kilos forgot about her discomfort at being in the tunnel a bit. "Kay," she whispered into his ear. "I have to go to the bathroom."

"Shhh," Kay said.

Then Sam stirred. She said a few things in Anuie. "What did she say, Kay?"

"I think she said you're not going to the bathroom."

Ki laughed. "Sure I am. Really, I'm going to pee."

Sam said a few more things. "Ki, Sam wants you to ask her something."

"Oh, Creation—what do I ask?" She thought a moment. "Ok, Sam, when will I get rid of my damn Puffies?"

Sam replied in Anuie. "I think she said five years from now," Kay translated.

"*Five years?*" Ki was beside herself. "Is she sure? Are you translating that right?"

Sam responded. "Yes, and yes, she's sure."

"Feature! Five damn more years of this? Will I be beautiful once it's gone?"

Again in Anuie. "She says you will be considered to be very beautiful. She also says Lady Togstra will not be happy about your beauty."

"Oh, she's a bitch." Ki smiled and sat back down, forgetting about her need to visit the bathroom. "Well, that's something anyway. Will I be prettier than her? No wait—when is she going to be married?"

Sam said something. Kay was confused. "What? Sam, I didn't understand that."

"What did she say?"

"She said something about Lady Togstra of Miles being taken in 003245."

"Really?" Ki said. "That long before she gets married? She's got awhile to go then. Ok, ok, Sam—who's she going to marry? Who's the unlucky fellow?"

More Anuie. "She said Cogster of Whalen."

Ki laughed out loud. "Lord Cogster of Whalen? The fellow from Esther with the fungal problem? Perhaps when they get married on 003245, he'll have cleared up a bit. Oh, this is great. He's a Shocktyte Jo-Boy!"

"Ki, watch your language," Kay said.

Sam mumbled. "She says they will be married in 003222."

"You said they will be married in 003245," Ki returned.

"She said Lady Togstra will be taken in 003245. Not married—taken."

"What does that mean? Where's she going?"

More mumbling. Kay was confused. "What did she say?" Ki

asked.

"I think she said Lady Togstra will die in 003217."

"Die? Well, how can she be married in 003222, be taken twenty-three years later in 003245 and be killed in 003217? That's just three years from now. I must say, though, that prospect doesn't really bother me much. I really don't like Lady Togstra."

"I think she's starting to skip around a bit. She warned us that might happen."

"Sam, who am I going to marry?" Ki asked wringing her hands.

Sam began to speak, but Ki shot up and stopped her. "Oh—no! No! I changed my mind. I don't want to know. You were right!"

She stood and made to exit the tunnel. "I'm done, guys. Thanks, Sam, you've paid for the goggles in full. Seriously, I have got to pee."

Sam's arm shot out and grabbed her by the wrist, holding her fast.

"Oww!" Ki cried. "Sam, that hurts!"

"003256," Sam said.

"What?"

"003256 is when they take you, too."

"Who takes me?"

Sam grimaced. "Hathaline."

"Lady Hathaline takes me? Where does she take me?"

"Tank," Sam said in the common. "She takes you to the Tank, where they all go."

Sam seemed lost. She switched back and forth in time. She spoke in Anuie.

"Kay, what did she say?"

"She said you and Sarah get into a fight."

"A fight? Me and Sarah? Well, fighting is so unlady-like. But, I hope I win. Sarah's mean."

"She is not."

"Not to you, but to me she's nothing but nasty. I get a little tired of it sometimes."

Sam was deep in a funk. She spoke again in Anuie.

"What, Sam?" Kay said. "What was that?"

"What did she say?"

"I think she said something about bowling?"

"Bowling?"

Sam began a long drone in Anuie, Kay following along as best he could.

"We bowl in a hidden place. Very dark. Somebody is there. They are there."

"Who's there?"

"I don't know. She says people I know are there waiting for us." Kay shook Sam a little. "Sam, Sam wake up."

Sam didn't stir.

"Sam! Wake up!"

Her eyes snapped open. She was panicked. In terror, she babbled in Anuie.

"Sam, I can't understand. What are you saying? Sam!"

She tore out of the tunnel, holding her face in her hands. "Sam, where are you going? You need your medallion!"

Kay ran out after her with Ki trailing. Sam was moving like a streak to the northeast, deep into the dense oak trees of the Grove. Kay followed as fast as he could, but soon she was out of sight. Fortunately, she left an obvious trail of deep footprints in the snow, appearing to stumble several times. "Kay, wait!" Ki cried from well in the rear.

Sam's footprints meandered through the trees, moving past an ancient Vith amphitheater, and continued on. The Ten Gardens was just ahead through the oak trees.

In a small oak clearing, he saw Sam slumped on her knees. She was holding a handful of snow, cradling it to her, turning her hands blue. Kay plunged in and came to her side. Her skin was spider-webbed with veins. He fumbled with the medallion for a moment then got it safely around her neck, great clouds of steam quickly working their way out of her hair.

"Sam! Sam, what's wrong?"

"*Olonol!*" she said. "*Olonol!*"

"What's that word? I don't know that word!"

"It will stand here!" Sam cried, her voice a mixture of triumph and cold-induced shock. "The *Olonol* will one day stand here!"

10—Kay's Gifts

S o, what exactly is this?" Sam asked holding the parchment.
"It's the official pronouncement of my Gifts by the Stertors. The
Stertors go around and determine what Gifts you have, and, if you
start developing Gifts not on the official list, you can get in trouble
with the Sisters."

Sam put the parchment down. "We don't think much of the
Sisters in the Monamalands. They seem rather off-putting."

"So, it says here I have the Gift of Cloak and the Gift of Waft.
My profile, as listed by the Stertors, makes me look more like a
Remnath than a Vith."

"This paper is meaningless. You also have the Gift of Sight."

Kay and Sam were underneath the castle, in the labyrinthine
quiet spaces. They crawled a long way. The passes weren't heated and
were formerly too cold for Sam to enter, but with her medallion, she
could follow Kay, her gown shed in favor of a bodysuit. They'd
crawled a long way and had made their way into a dusty space just
high enough for them to sit up. Kay's flashlight made a laser beam of
yellow light contaminated with passing stars of dust.

"So, you say that you've had visions of me and that you've seen
me having the Sight?"

Sam snuggled up against him, steam coming off her body.
"Yes," she said. Her hand wandered into his bellybutton as it usually
did when she was feeling amorous, and that was happening more and
more.

Perhaps it was Vith ego speaking from somewhere deep inside
or possibly his personal pride, but he didn't feel it was right to go

much further with Sam other than innocent kissing because, at this
stage of his life, Sam was a much more formidable person than he
was.

She was incredibly strong.

She was impossibly fast.

Her senses, especially her nose and sense of smell, were highly
acute.

She could Blink away and send herself virtually anywhere on
Kana.

She could transmute her thoughts.

She could change her shape.

And, she could see the future.

Kay just didn't feel he measured up, and, therefore, never
allowed himself to share a bed with her, though that's what she
expected of him with growing force. She had a favorite saying in
Anuie that she said when she was feeling particularly frustrated: *Te
mare Vith consomo!*, which meant: *The Vith are so damn demure!*

"So, what did you see specifically?" Kay asked. "What did you
see me doing?"

Sam's hand went into his shirt and farther down. "I saw you
seeing things far into the future and the past."

"Perhaps you misinterpreted what you were seeing."

"I did not."

"I mean, you said some very strange things during the Future-
Telling."

"Did I?"

"You said my sister was going to be 'taken' in 003256. You said
my little sister Hathaline takes her somewhere. Where does she take
her? Why? And you mentioned something about *Olonol*. I don't know
that word, and you won't tell me what it is. What is it?"

Sam, stopped, considered her response, and then abruptly
changed the subject. "That chain that I wear on my gown, do you
know why I wear it?"

"You've never said."

"It's for you, Kay. To protect yourself ..."

"From what?"

"From me. Monama women tend to get a little overly excited
when the time comes. I want that time to be now."

She crawled on top of him.

"I don't have the chain here."

"I won't hurt you ... much. I've waited for this for years."

Sam was all over him, and Kay couldn't move. She was like an impossibly strong octopus.

Kay felt waves of pleasure come over him. He was on the verge of giving in when a final bit of Vith pride spoke and prevented him from losing himself. "Sam, wait!"

She coiled up a little bit, her black eyes intense.

"Let's have a contest first."

"What sort of contest?"

"I'll find a place to hide, and you come and find me."

She snorted. "We've played this game before. You can't hide from me. Hide anywhere you want, and I can find you like that!" She snapped her fingers. "And ..." she took a deep whiff, "I can smell you, Kay." She licked her lips.

"I think this time you'll be a bit more challenged."

She got off and huddled up on the dusty ground. "All right. Go hide, Kay. Hide anywhere in the castle you want. You have an hour. Oh, and Kay?"

"Yes?"

She seized a piece of old mortar and shattered it in her hand. "You best get that chain and don't be afraid to use it when I find you. My gown is in the reading room. Oh, while you're there, take a close look at my gown—take a very close look. Those little designs on the fabric of my gown— they're called 'Bronta'. We put Bronta on our clothes, on our architecture and pottery. Everything. Take a look, and that should spell it out for you. Better get moving. Your time starts now."

Kay moved down the crawlway. He looked back once. Sam was huddled up like a wolf ready to spring. "See you soon, Kay," she whispered, waving.

Kay continued down the crawl and emerged in the east wing. He quickly went into their favorite reading room. There was her gown, neatly folded on the arm of the chair, and her shoes. He pulled the chain off her skirt. It wasn't a light chain by any stretch. It was fairly dense and could do some damage. He took it and readied to leave the room.

He recalled what she said and took a look at her gown. Stitched onto the black fabric were bands of intricate black swoops and whorls, very detailed and finely crafted. Other than being pretty designs, he couldn't make much out of them.

He left the reading room and checked his time piece. He had about forty minutes left. As he moved down the corridor, he felt that giddy, tingly feeling of being pursued, like when he hid from Sarah when they used to play hide and seek. Certainly, the consequences of being caught were not unpleasant. The chain rattled in his hand.

Kay wasn't really in a hurry. He knew exactly where he wanted to hide, and it wasn't all that far from where he started. He walked into the west wing and entered Cathomere's Cathedral—an old chapel dedicated to Lord Cathomere of long ago. It was one of the larger chapels in the castle; it was even presided over by a rector from the village. Kay entered, offered a blessing and then sat down in one of the pews, setting the chain aside. He enjoyed the vast quiet of the place, the smell of age-old incense and the lofty splendor of the stained glass windows. At the far end of the cathedral, standing in a dark corner, a bronze statue of Lord Cathomere stood proud, a slight smile hammered into his metallic face.

He checked his time piece. He had a while to go. He got comfortable and put his hat down over his eyes.

His thoughts raced. Sam was out there pursuing him, chasing him like a game animal.

... Like a game animal.

He slept and had amber dreams, like he sometimes did. His thoughts wandered. He saw Sam's gown in an amber hue. There were the designs on her gown, the Bronta designs Sam had mentioned. He saw them greatly magnified. The designs were made up of minute male and female forms in the act of having contorted sex. Apparently, as Sam said, sex made up a large portion of Monama culture.

He saw other things

He saw himself lying in bed, and there was a woman in bed with him. Not Sam—it was a glistening woman with red, twisted hair. She wore a golden mask covering the top portion of her face. She seemed somehow disfigured.

He saw that same woman watching him eat in the Capricos Hall, and watching him at CARG practice with father, and looking out at him from the boat house. He saw her whispering in Sam's ear.

There she was, inside some sort of glass coffin full of noisome brown fluid. She was beating on the glass, begging to get out.

He saw Sam wearing a thorny necklace of crystal spikes.
He saw himself in his bedroom sitting on the floor. A small, silvery creature sat next to him. Outside was Sam, beating on the door trying to get in, splintering the wood. Through his terrace, he saw a strange light coming from the west, low on the horizon. And there were bugs, swarms of them. Giant bugs from a dream. Buzzing wings.

Forty minutes came. His time piece chimed, and he woke up, the amber fading.

Kay looked around. He was sitting alone in the cathedral, the old smells and empty space filling him up.

Checked his timepiece.

One after.

Normally, Sam should have caught him by now, for she was that fast zeroing in on him. But no, he was still alone in the cathedral.

He wondered what he'd just seen, those visions in amber. What did they mean? He tried to reflect on them, but the visions quickly faded from his memory like a dream that was soon forgotten upon waking.

He heard a commotion out in the hallway. Through the crack of the open door leading out into the corridor, he saw Sam go streaking past, moving like a black and white panther.

The cathedral really works. Sam passed right by and couldn't detect him. There was no way she could find him in here unless she actually poked her head in and looked.

This cathedral was a sort of safe area, a quiet place. Many castles of the north had them, Castle Blanchefort being no exception. Here, within the serene confines of the cathedral, one could sit with one's thoughts and be assured of privacy. No eyes from afar could see, and no ears listening in could hear. No clairvoyance or clairaudience. No nothing. Here, one could be alone with one's thoughts. Even his father said he couldn't Sight into the cathedral. Kay had no idea how it worked; it just did.

More time passed—the rector even tried to evict Kay, but he could not as Kay's rank outstripped his.

More time passed. At some point he again heard Sam go clattering down the hallway. "Kay?" she yelled, a hint of concern in her voice, "Kay?"

He allowed her to run past. Apparently, she wasn't close enough to sniff him out.

He stayed in the cathedral determined to wait it out a few more minutes. He tried to ponder the meaning of his dream in amber, but so much of it had faded in his mind.

He remembered something about a golden mask and buzzing wings. Didn't make any sense.

"KAY!" came an enraged voice from the door.

Standing there was Lady Kilos and a positively livid Sam. She leapt over the pews, launching herself into the air, landing in front of him.

She seized him by the shirt and lifted him like a doll. "Kay! What are you doing? Do you know how concerned I was?"

"Sorry, Sam. I thought the object of the game was to keep you from finding me."

She cursed in Anuie.

"If Kay was hiding from you in here, Sam, then he was cheating. In this cathedral, you cannot be spied upon or located via technological or mystical means.

She was astounded, and her fury faded. She gently set Kay down. "You mean you can come in here and nobody watching you or listening to you can follow?"

"Nope—you couldn't find me, could you?"

She looked around at the place with wonder. She saw the bronze statue in the shadows and was startled. "Who's that?" she asked pointing.

"It's just a statue of Lord Cathomere, my great, great, great, great grandfather, I think, give or take a 'great' or two."

"Yeah," Ki said in agreement.

Mouth open in awe, her mind seemed to fill up with possibilities. "I had no idea. I had no idea. No visions, nothing. I didn't see this place."

The three of them sat in there for the rest of the afternoon until the rector demanded they leave.

11—The Pool

The next day, Sam, full of energy, wanted to take a walk. Kilos was away visiting friends in Remnath, and Kay's parents were off in their starship, the *New Faith*. They were, for the most part, alone. They waded into the deepest part of the Grove, not another soul around.

When they were assured of privacy, they fell into each other's arms, the cloud-covered summit of Mt. Vith visible in the distance.

Losing control of herself, Sam became like a wild animal, eyes wide, growling slightly. She slammed Kay into a tree and held him there with one arm. "I've been waiting for this for years, Kay," she said breathlessly in an odd voice, ripping his coat off. "You don't know... how hard it's been to... contain myself, to be so polite and proper when I've wanted to tear you apart!" Her voice was flecked with passion. "Kay... Kay! It's time that I showed you how I want you! It's time you discover what Monama women do to their men!"

She pulled the chain off her skirt. "You're going to need this." She threw the chain over her shoulder. Kay made to get past her and grab it, and she tackled him.

Kay struggled with the ravenous Sam. His clothes in tatters, her claws drawing blood, she picked him up and threw him down to the leafy ground, throwing herself on top of him. He was in the fight of his life. She loosened her gown by the straps and wiggled out of it.

Kay reached out and got hold of the chain. He wrapped it around her neck and wrenched her light body off him. She landed in the leaves and patches of snow and freed herself from the chain.

They circled. Sam tensed up and moved on all fours like an

animal. "Go ahead, Kay ... use the chain. Hit me with it," she growled, her voice unrecognizable.

She sprang, and he lashed her across the back with the chain raising an angry welt. She roared with passion, and he lashed her again and again. He got the chain around her neck once more and tied her to a Vith stone.

Sam tied up, the both of them bloody, he fell into her embrace, and they made love for the first time, drifting in and out of delirium for what seemed like hours, the afternoon turning to early evening unnoticed.

Another dream in amber as Kay, exhausted and slightly wounded, lay in Sam's arms.

Gonna' have some fun ...

He saw a woman leaning down over him, her face covered with a golden mask.

Gonna' make me jealous ...

He saw her standing there twirling Sam's medallion around on her finger. She hauled back and threw it somewhere into the trees.

Have fun ...

Just another dream in amber.

Sam screamed, and Kay awoke. Chained to the stone, Sam clenched up and stopped breathing. Her naked body was racked with convulsions. Kay gawked at her in a panic as her convulsing body broke the chain.

"Sam! Sam, what's wrong?"

She didn't answer. Her veins rose to the surface in a blue web.

Snugs! Her medallion was missing from around her neck.

Where was it?

Frantically, he looked around but didn't see it. "It could be anywhere around here."

Have fun... He remembered his dream, Sam's medallion spinning on the woman's finger.

Was that just a dream or ...?

She threw it off into the trees somewhere. Where was it?

Without Snugs, Sam didn't have long. Not knowing what else to do, Kay picked up her convulsing, nude body and ran with her to the nearby Ten Gardens, lost somewhere in the depths of the Grove.

In the center of the Lily Garden was a good-sized bath house featuring a large heated pool, partially under the bath house's stone roof, partially open to the elements. Countess Sygillis had put it in years ago; it was one of her favorite places. The children also used it quite often—Sarah often bemoaning the fact that Grand Oyln Manor didn't have a similar pool. During the winter it was a big hit. Lady Kilos used it just about every day to soak in the steaming water.

Now that pool was Sam's only chance.

In his fear and agitation, his thoughts spun, his heart pounded.

Panic! Things began to turn amber around him.

As he ran with Sam, he had a vague thought wondering what might happen should somebody—like Ki or his parents—be using the pool. But, no, they were all gone. What if Lady Hathaline was using it? Or one of the staff was there on his or her time off? Seeing the naked Kay, torn and bloodied as he was, come running in holding the equally naked and bloody Sam would, no doubt, create a huge stir, and he and Sam's secret would be lost.

He couldn't worry about that—Sam was about to die!

He saw the bath house approaching as he ran, and, for a brief second, he thought he could see through the stone walls and into the lavish interior.

"Creation!" There were two people in the bath house! A man and a woman. He didn't recognize them. They must be some of the staff. Whoever they were, they were about to get a juicy bit of gossip to spread around. What if they had a holomon or some other type of photographic equipment? He saw them casually watch as he approached. "You there in the bathhouse!" he yelled. "I order you to look away! Look away or face my punishment!" Kay usually tried not to order the staff around much; that's what his sister Lady Kilos and Sarah were for, and he never threatened them with punishment, but, this case was dire.

He looked down at Sam.

He was shocked. For a moment, he thought he saw some sort of strange, fibrous collar around her neck—one he'd never seen before. Interlaced in the folds of the collar were a host of small, diamond-shaped crystals etched with odd writing. The crystals were pointed and sharp looking, and the collar they were mounted in seemed somehow stuck to Sam's flesh like it was fused to her skin, or possibly stitched in place.

He blinked to get a better look, and the image in amber was gone, just Sam's perfect neck as usual. He must have been seeing things. He must!

He leapt over the low stone gate and neared the pool, running through the vast garden of lilies. There were a number of hot springs near the surface in this area of the Grove, and the ground felt warm under his feet.

There was the open end of the pool ahead, just a few more feet! Out of breath, Kay slid to the poolside and placed her into the steaming water. Her rigid body wanted to float at the surface like a log. He jumped in with a splash and held her body down. Her head with its mane of black hair refused to submerge, floating like a buoy.

She seemed dead, her face locked in a grimace. "Sam, wake up! Sam!" He splashed the hot water on her face. Nothing.

"You there!" he called to the people he'd seen in the bath house. "I need you to get help at once! My friend is dying! Make haste!"

No answer. Frantic, he looked around. The interior of the bath house appeared to be empty. He was certain he'd seen two people within. "Hello!" he said again. "Come out and get help or, by Creation, I'll have the two of you in irons!"

No answer.

Sam began coughing, and he turned his attention back to her. The warm water of the pool was having an effect, and she was coming too. She thrashed a bit in confusion, and he continued to hold her body down. She began kicking and nearly pummeled Kay to death as he doggedly held her down.

After a few minutes more, Sam was breathing normally again, her mass of black hair spreading out like an oil slick around her in the steaming water. She was calm and relaxed.

Finally, she opened her eyes and seemed no worse for her adventure. Kay sighed with relief.

"Gods, Sam, are you all right?"

"I think so. What happened? I thought I was going to die of the cold. It was overwhelming." She looked down. "Oh, my medallion, it's gone. What happened?"

"I'm not sure really. I had an odd dream where someone took it from around your neck."

"Who would do that?"

"I don't know. It was just a dream. Perhaps it came unclasped. We're going to have to do something about that, and get a second and third one available as backups to prevent this sort of thing. I'll go back and find it, Sam. You stay put, ok? You'll be safe in the water. Also, I thought I saw somebody in here before we arrived. Call them if you need help while I'm gone."

Sam looked around and squinted. "I don't see anybody. Kay, don't go. Where are we?"

"That is a bath house in the Ten Gardens. It's a place my mother had built to take refuge from the daily grind. There are no terminals here, no Holo-nets or any other sort of technological contrivances."

"This water, it's so much like home. And look, I can sit here and enjoy the evening without my medallion." She kicked with her foot and made a splash.

Kay saw the welts on her back and felt the scratches on his begin to sting.

"Are you all right, Sam? Did I hurt you with that chain?"

"I'm fine. I should have given you more preparation. When we get really aroused, that's how we are. Does that prospect give you pause?"

"No." He felt his back sting.

Sam looked around and was overjoyed. "Here, I don't need the medallion. Here, I can be anything you want me to be, Kay. Just command me, and I'll be it for you."

"You're fine as is, Sam. Just relax and stay put. I'm going back to fetch your medallion."

She put her arms and legs around him. He tried to pull free, but couldn't budge. "Don't go, Kay. Don't go. I nearly died just now, and I don't want to be alone. You'll find it later. My medallion's not going anywhere. Look for it later."

"But it's getting dark."

"Then wait until morning."

She drew him in tighter.

Night was falling, and it began to snow, the open-air bath house lit up in soft blue light, the large snowflakes sizzling when they hit the water, pillars of steam rising up into the darkening sky.

"Kay, why have you never brought me here before?" Sam asked basking in the warmth. "This is enchanting, the hot steaming water, the snow. Look at it snow. Now that I can properly appreciate it, it's so pretty. We have nothing like this." She looked up to see the sky interlaced with bloated clouds lazily dropping snowflakes amid broken cracks revealing stars. "I love it. I could sit in this pool all day with you."

"I never really thought about it, I suppose. I'm still getting used to you being free to move about."

She began kissing his neck. "I'll expect you to bring me here often, Kay. We can make this our place, where I can be anything you want me to be."

"Why do you want to change your image?"

"That's what Monama women do for their men. I want to make you happy."

Kay pulled away a bit and looked at her—he was completely used to her white pallor and her eyes by now; she was a beautiful young woman with a soul to match. He noticed something.

"Sam, where's your bellybutton?"

"I don't have a bellybutton. No Monama does. That's why we like yours so much, I guess. We love bellybuttons. We think they're so neat. I got hold of a picture of you several years ago swimming at the beach on Onaris or somewhere with no shirt on. "*You have a great bellybutton, Kay,*" she said with passion. "Do you think less of me for not having one?"

"No, Sam, it's just a bellybutton."

She looked down at his and probed it with her fingers. "Is that mine … is that my bellybutton?"

A tiny little bit of logic somewhere in his mind took exception.

Wait a second! If you don't have a bellybutton, how are you … born? How were your sustained during your maturation in your mother's womb?

She snuggled in close, her finger in his bellybutton, and whispered into his ear. "And, there's one more thing …"

Oh, here it comes, he thought. "What is it, Sam?"

"We, also have something we call *Veda-mena*, the 'Glory Hands'. They are a pair of extra arms that our old ancestors used to have. Old Monamas, centuries ago, used to have four arms, but that trait is mostly gone. Modern Monamas only have two fully developed arms. The second pair is still there, but in a tiny, vestigial state."

She lifted her left arm. There, under her armpit, was a tiny bump. Kay examined it closely.

"Sometimes, if we get very old, the arms sprout and develop, but that only happens every so often. My grandmother's sprouted in the last few years of her life."

Kay continued to examine the bump. "Why did you lose your extra set of arms?"

"I'm not certain. We have old stories of a time long ago when we were four-armed and evil and worshipped a Horned God deep in the ground. And then the gods of jade and sapphire came from the sky and took the evil from us, as well as our second pair of arms. I'm glad they're gone."

She took him by the chin. "There is a word in my language that I've wanted to say to you for a long time. It's a word we don't utter lightly. I've said it to you before, but you weren't listening. When I made your little toy gazelle, I said it. When you were a little boy, I sang it to you. Now, I want to say it to your face, and I want you to understand. How many of my people long for this moment, and how few actually get to live it."

K a y settled into Sam's arms. She cradled him, savoring the warmth of the water.

"*Arin-Dan*," she said. "You are my *Arin-Dan*."

"What does it mean?"

"It means a lot of things. It means, most literally, 'beloved'. It also means 'dreamed of' and 'sacred'. It means that I love you, Kay;

that I've dreamed of you my whole life." She grew misty. "I don't know how Elder girls are with the language they use. I don't know if there's a word in your tongue that means as much to them as *Arin-Dan* means to us. *Arin-Dan*, I've always loved you, since I was a little girl haunting your room, afraid to present myself to you. The first day we spoke in the chapel, I was so happy that I cried myself to sleep that night. I told my grandmother that I finally spoke to my *Arin-Dan*. I've done some things that I'm not particularly proud of through the years. Everything I've done, I've done for you, for my *Arin-Dan*." The water steamed, and the snow fell.

"Why, Sam? Why me?"

"Because I saw you, and me, in future's night. It happens sometimes. Monamas often see Elders in their dreams, but mostly we just stay by our lake and hide in the fog, wishing we weren't so afraid. And then we go to the wall and plant our flower, and the dream fades leaving us with sadness and regret. We wear black to match the sadness in our souls. I didn't want to stay away, Kay. I didn't want to be afraid. I wanted the dream to become real, and I wanted to give you some of what you've given me."

"You said you and your people are afraid of something. What is it?"

Sam paused and considered her response. "Like I said, we were evil once, and we're still being punished for it."

She waited for a response from Kay. She had just bared her soul. Her heart was out in the open, to either be anointed in love or ripped out and burned.

"Sam," Kay said, "In Anuie, words often have a male and female version, right? Is there a female version of *Arin-Dan*?"

"*Cerri-Tela*. It's *Cerri-Tela*."

"And, if I were to say that to you, how would it make you feel?"

"Like nothing else in the world matters. All my troubles gone."

"Then, you are my *Cerri-Tela*, Sam, no bellybutton and all."

"Say it again.*"

"*Cerri-Tela.*"

She smiled and pulled him down, and they made love again and again.

12—IN LOCK

Now that they were lovers, Sam often visited Kay at night—something she'd never done before. Kay lay in his huge bed, and then there was Sam, appearing from nowhere, quickly donning her medallion. The interlude in the Grove and the bathhouse truly opened the floodgates, for Sam now loved to have sex—she was crazed for it, and she wasn't gentle either, often scratching and bruising him. Sometimes when she appeared, she had on a thin nightgown, or, when she was more ravenous, she appeared naked, quietly climbing into bed and attacking him.

Sometimes, Kay needed the chain.

Trips to the bath house became frequent, usually late at night so that they could have it to themselves. At Sam's insistence, Kay began picking forms into which Sam would transform. He was shy at first, picking simple things like blonde hair and swarthy skin, though eventually things took an exotic turn. Sam insisted he open up and share his soul with her, to let out all the things that were there deep down inside.

Shame, she said, had no place with his *Cerri-Tela*.

There was a cook in the kitchens with a 4-D tattoo who was rather ugly, but whom Kay found oddly seductive.

Sam became her for him, tattoo and all.

Admitting to his old childhood crush on Lt. Kilos, Sam became Kilos for him, a passionate, ravenous Kilos nude in his arms. Then he chose a Sister once, and, another time, she became a demon for him from the pit of his nightmares, winged, fanged and hoofed. Those encounters were truly memorable.

One time, just to see what it would be like, Sam became Sarah for him, but that was a bit too strange, though, just that one time gave him unheard of pleasure.

* * * * *

And they conducted themselves in such a way for nearly five years—a secret couple, married in all but name. The only people, other than Kay's parents, knowing about their relationship were his sisters and the staff. Lady Kilos was a friend and proved remarkably good at keeping secrets. Lady Hathaline did her own thing and didn't give a hoot, the House staff minded their own business, and Maser was still too young to really know what was going on.

Sam sometimes had terrible nightmares late in the night. She yelled and spoke Anuie too fast for him to understand. She pleaded and begged before some unseen tormentor. Then, she began to cry in her sleep, her whole body shaking. Kay always woke her, and she never recognized him at first. Then she'd embrace him and continue weeping until she cried herself back to sleep. In the early morning he always asked her what she dreamt of, and she wouldn't tell him. She refused to tell. She often said she couldn't remember what had upset her so, but Kay could tell she was lying.

Their relationship was still mostly a winter event. Come summertime, with his cousins, Sarah and Phillip, dominating Kay's time, Sam had to stay away, and, though she rarely complained, Kay knew that, with each passing year, she began to resent it more and more. Not having the Holo-net at her home in Castle Astralon, they communicated solely via correspondence in the summertime and with occasional conversations in Sam's chapel. Talking to Sam in the chapel was frankly an unpleasant experience as she was often surly, bemoaning the fact that she had to stay away. The letters she wrote him in the summer weren't much better, hinting at her growing impatience.

It was her choice—she insisted on secrecy, so she had to live with it.

* * * * *

He received a strange correspondence during the summer when

he was twenty. Kay's correspondence pile generally shrank in the summer, drying up to only the most droll and uninteresting of letters to which he had no choice but to respond. He got letters from Sarah and Phillip and correspondence from his "aunt," the Duchess of Oyln, a forbidden person around the castle, his mother hating her with a passion. However, he got few letters from prospective ladies.

That was rather opposite of how it should be. In the winter with Sam around, his pile of letters generally grew, including even a few letters from various ladies from around Kana, though he had little time to answer them properly; Sam made sure of that.

The letter received was hand delivered to Kay by courier. It had no return label. The letter had a small notice stamped where the return address normally went. It said: HELD IN LOCK with the current date, meaning that the letter had been mailed at some unknown time in the past but was held at the sender's request at the Vithland Delivery Center until just the day before. People sometimes mailed letters IN LOCK to ensure that a letter was delivered at a certain desired time and date. People most often sent "Dear John" letters IN LOCK to ensure that they were far away, possibly on another planet, when the letter was finally delivered.

Inside the envelope was a folded, two page note and a single dried flower, rather like a small daisy with fewer petals. The note was written in red paint and was hopelessly smeared—apparently the letter had been IN LOCK for quite some time and had gotten either wet or had been stored in a humid location. The flower was white with a black "button" in the center. He didn't know what sort of flower it might be, or what meaning it had. He sent the flower to his "aunt", Duchess Torrijayne of Oyln, who was a noted expert on Kanan flowers and knew their lore. Several days later he got the flower back from the Duchess, along with a short note.

It's called, in the common vernacular, White Emilia, a hearty flower hailing from the south of Kana—a relative of the common daisy. Likes lots of shade. Its nectar is rich in sugar, but can be poisonous to many species of insect if the flower isn't fully matured.

You need to come down here and visit more often.
Signed—Dimples

The Duchess always used the code name "Dimples" when she corresponded with Kay—just in case his mother got hold of the letter.

Sam swore she had nothing to do with either the letter or the flower. Kay liked a good mystery as well as anybody and hoped that Sam would one day fess up to sending the note and flower, and reveal what was on her mind. He showed it to his father, hoping he, with his Sight, could make something out of it, but, no, the note had been written in brush-strokes and had no pen scoring marks on the paper that might be followed. The only way to read this note was to go back in time and read it before it had bled into illegibility. He stuck the note in the top drawer of his dresser and let the matter drop.

13—The Falling in Love Ball

Y ou wanna' step outside?" Sarah of Blanchefort said, throwing down her napkin and standing up, knocking her chair over.

Kay sat there at the table and shook his head.

Oh, this was a bad idea.

* * * * *

"So, what is this event that's coming up?" Sam asked as she watched the workmen haul in float-loads of supplies from the village.

"It's a ball. Every so often my mother and my aunt, Lady Poe, talk my father into hosting a lavish ball. My father hates big society functions, but he can't say no to my mother, and she just loves them."

"A party? When will it take place?"

"Next week, on the full moons. Mother and my aunt always pick a theme for their balls, and 'Falling in Love' is the theme of this one."

Sam watched dreamily. "I'm in love. May I come?"

"Certainly you can come if you want, Sam. Of course, nobody knows we're seeing each other, so we couldn't present as a couple."

"We could pretend we don't know each other. My grandmother was your father's seeress, so my having an invitation won't be so unusual. It'll be fun to pretend we don't know each other."

Kay thought about it. "All right, but there's a few things you'll need to be aware of."

Sam was leaning over the rail of his terrace watching the staff haul the supplies in, her medallion dangling.

"Are you listening?"

"I'm sorry, Kay. What is it?"

"As we're both under thirty, we'll be consigned to the children's area. Under thirty is always considered a child in League Society. Also, you're going to notice most of the children in the hall with us shall look a little strange."

"Strange?"

"Puffy faces, like Lady Kilos's. It's just something we Elders have to go through. We live well past our two-hundreds and generally live disease and age-free; however, the trade-off is a rather mal-formed childhood. Some have it worse than others. I always keep it to myself, but I think Ki looks rather like an unbaked biscuit right now."

"That's mean. Your face isn't puffy."

"I never had it. I don't know why. So, with that in mind, it's a tradition to keep the children separated in their own little area at special functions such as a ball. We'll be seated in the Capricos Hall with the others."

"That's fine."

"Now, there are going to be several people seated with us at our table. One will be my friend, Lord Lon of Probert."

"Who's he?"

"Oh, he's a delightful young fellow from Arden. He helped me work out the technical details of my CARG a few years back. I think you'll like him just fine. Also, there'll be my cousin Phillip. He's coming up from the south specifically for this event."

"Phillip? The brown-haired boy who leaves for the south every winter with your aunt?"

"The same."

"I've always wanted to meet your cousins. What is he like?"

"He's a good fellow. He's quiet and rather cerebral, like his father, Lord Peter. He's a natural pilot and can fly the *Goshawk* ship like anything. He and my sister Hathaline are both great pilots—they must have inherited all the piloting skill that I didn't."

"Do you think Phillip will like me?"

"Certainly Phillip will like you; there's no doubt. The problem isn't Lon or Phillip—the problem is Sarah."

"Sarah? Who's Sarah?"

"She's Phillip's twin sister."

"Oh! The blue-haired one who dresses like a boy, the one that I have turned into for you?"

"That's her," Kay blushed. "I think she's ten minutes older than Phillip is." Kay struggled for words. "Sarah ... is ..."

"She's the one Ki doesn't like, right?"

"Yes, that's her. Sarah prides herself on being a loudmouth and something of a bully, too. She's quick to judge, quick to jump to conclusions, hotheaded, pugnacious and rather stubborn as well. I'm told by my father that Sarah is the spitting image of my grandmother, Countess Hermilane of Hannover. My grandmother was known about society as a particularly nasty Black Widow, and Sarah is every bit as nasty. Ki just can't stand her."

Sam was perplexed. "I don't think I blame her. She doesn't sound like a very pleasant person, Kay."

"It's mostly a lot of bluster, and Ki can't get past it. Deep down, Sarah is a lot more like her matronly mother, Lady Poe, than she cares to let on. She's a devoted sister and a loyal friend and there's nothing she wouldn't do for you once you have her trust. The big problem with Sarah is that she does not like Monamas at all."

"Why not?"

"Sarah has a big imagination and she loves the lurid and the bizarre. She has a library taking up the entire 50th floor of Xyotel Tower where she keeps all the creepy stuff she's collected, and it's a lot. She has a fascination with Berserkacides most of all. I think she's actually frightened of them a little, and, when she sees a Monama, all she sees is a Berserkacide hiding within."

"I see," Sam said quietly.

"So, she probably isn't going to trust you much and might even go out of her way to be nasty. One thing to keep in mind with Sarah is that she values strength above all else. If she gets in your face, don't back down. Don't overdo it, but don't be meek either."

"Perhaps I should teach her a lesson in humility. Perhaps such a thing might do her some good."

"I'd appreciate it if you didn't, Sam. Sarah's a blowhard, and no doubt she'd have it coming to her, but as she's my friend and my cousin, just let it go and be bigger than she is. All right?"

"All right," she said. "I promise. Oh, one thing to be aware of. Will there be alcohol?"

"Doubtless. Some light stuff for toasting."

"I cannot drink alcohol. We don't handle it very well."

"That's fine. Just request some gasol from the servers. It won't be a problem."

Sam put her head down on the rail and watched the staff haul crate after crate of supplies into the castle.

* * * * *

Sarah of Blanchefort had been giving Sam the evil eye all evening. She was sitting across from Kay in a lemon-colored Blanchefort gown. Sarah detested gowns and was clearly uncomfortable in it. Her royal blue hair was also done up high, and she fussed with it constantly.

She had been talking with Kay about some of the new places she wanted to explore in the summer. " ... And there's this thing I heard about down south in the Gaston Way pass called the Wraith of Gaston. I want to do some investigating and catch this entity cold."

Her brother Phillip stirred. "The Gaston Way doesn't sound like any fun to me, Sarah," he said. "Just a lot of nothing out in the mountains."

She was on a roll. "Oh, yeah? The stories coming out of there say there's this freakin' monster that chases down passersby in the wild where there's no help. Then, it disables their transports, hauls them out and murders them."

Sam sat at her seat at the far end of the table and rustled uncomfortably. She'd been very quiet all evening, getting a constant angry eye from Sarah. "Your pardon," she quietly said. "I don't believe this creature has hurt anyone."

Sarah's gaze snapped to Sam. "Yeah? What do you know about it?"

"Well, I ..."

"I can't understand you!" Sarah yelled. "What's with your accent? Don't they teach you how to talk down there?"

Phillip, wearing a lovely green and black tailed coat, spoke up. "Sarah, you're being very rude." Phillip turned to Sam. "Apologies, Lady Monama."

"Don't apologize for me, Phillip! She needs to get the marbles out of her mouth, or, better yet, move to another table! She ought to be apologizing to me for damaging my calm!"

Lady Kilos was sitting next to Kay in a white gown. "I can understand her just fine, Sarah. Perhaps you've got cotton in your ears."

"Who's talking to you, *Tez*?" Sarah said in an ugly voice.

Sarah loved calling Ki "Tez," which was an Esther word for "cheap prostitute". The Duke of Oyln had taught it to her, and she loved using it, finding it a particularly demeaning name to call a person.

Kay, sitting opposite of Ki, had heard enough. He and Sam shared a few glances here and there. He could see Sarah's sour attitude was wearing on her. "Sarah," he said, "Your enthusiasm is appreciated, but you need to tone it down a little, right? And, don't call my sister Tez. You know I don't like that."

Sarah usually listened to Kay, and she quieted down for a time. Still, she kept a mistrusting eye on Sam. *"She could go Berserkacide on us at any moment, Kay,"* she whispered.

"Shhhh," he responded.

Lord Lon seemed to be having no trouble speaking to Sam. He sat next to her in his ill-fitting blue coat and buckle shoes, chattering away. "... and this pin here, my lady, I won at the annual Science and Space Jamboree the Sisters hold every year in Arden," he said pointing at a collection of pins stuck to his coat breast.

"Congratulations, my lord," she said.

The staff came by with a tray of watered down kid's wine for a toast. They set a goblet of the purple drink in front of Sam. *"Sen-tre,"* she said in Anuie, "may I have a glass of green gasol instead, please?" The staff member bowed and went to get it for her.

Sarah watched her with interest. "What's the matter, our wine not good enough for you?"

Kay was about to shush Sarah up again when Countess Sygillis came rushing into the hall. "Kay, there you are! Can you come with me, please? Lady Hamilton would like to see your coat and pattern I designed. She might wish to make a sizable purchase." Sygillis had designed Kay's clothes, Phillip's too. Kay stood and Syg adjusted his lapels and looked him over, hands on. "You look wonderful. You, too, Phillip. Come with me, please. It'll only take a moment."

Phillip stood and Syg took both of them by the arm and led them out of the hall.

Alone at the table, Sarah wasted no time. "Aren't you a little old for green gasol?" she asked Sam.

Sam sat properly as her glass arrived and was placed on the table. "We enjoy such things," she said.

"What? I can't understand you!"

"I said that we like gasol in the Monamalands."

The time for the toast came, and all stood and raised their glasses. Sam stood with her gasol.

"What's the matter?" Sarah said. "Can't take it, can you? What a little peasant you are."

"Lady Blanchefort, you are ..."

"Blah, blah, blah ..." Sarah said. "Can't understand a word you say. By the way, I thought I caught you making eyes at Kay. Do it again and I'll have you flogged out of the castle, understand?"

"Not while I out-rank you in this household!" Ki said, jumping in.

"We'll see what Kay has to say about that."

"You really are incredibly stupid, aren't you?" Ki shouted.

"Shut up, Tez, this is between me and her anyway. Butt out!" She turned back to Sam. "Now, pick up the wine and drink it. Pick it up!"

Lon spoke up. "Now, see here, Lady Blanchefort, you are behaving most inconsiderately."

"Lon, when she goes Berserkacide, you're going to be the first one she guts!" Sarah responded.

The word 'Berserkacide' seemed to bother Sam. She pushed her glass of gasol aside and tentatively picked up the glass of wine. She sniffed it.

"That's right," Sarah said. "Drink it."

"Sam, don't!" Ki said.

"Lady Monama," Lon said. "If you don't want it, don't drink it. Don't listen to Sarah."

"No, no Lon, I think she wants to prove she's not a Berserkacide. Go ahead, Monama, drink it down," Sarah said. "You watch. She's going to go 'nuts' on us."

There was a wave of clapping and a tinkling of crystal as the toast filtered through the hall.

Sam closed her eyes and drank a few swallows and clanged her goblet with Lon's.

"Drink it all, peasant, don't be rude!" Sarah said.

Sam emptied her glass and sat down. Sarah watched her eagerly, waiting to see some outworldly transformation take place.

"So, how many people have you killed, Monama?"

"I've had it with your mouth, Sarah!" Ki yelled.

"Yeah? Want to do something about it, Tez?"

"I could Stare you down into a pulp! How would you like that?" Ki responded.

Sarah was alarmed. "You wouldn't dare use your Gifts on me! We're family! Who's side are you on?"

"Not on yours, that's for sure, and try me."

As Ki and Sarah faced off, Sam shrunk in her chair and leaned over, threatening to fall face first to the table. Ki was alarmed. "Sam! —I mean, Lady Monama, are you all right?"

Sam didn't respond.

Ki stood and went to Sam. "Lord Lon, Can you help me with her? I think she's sick!"

As she reached Sam, her eyes snapped up and gave Sarah a withering stare. "So, you love the horrid and the bizarre, do you, Lady Sarah? Shall I tell you about this creature in the Gaston Way you so crave?"

Sarah sat there, fully convinced Sam was about to change into a Berserkacide.

Sam spoke, droning in an odd voice. "It knows the future and sees danger and possible complications from afar. It's afraid of what it sees."

"What's afraid?" Sarah asked.

"It waits for them in the lonely passes, where it knows there's no help. It uses NIGHTMARE magic and makes itself more than what it is. And, when they pass by in their transports, it comes upon them. They think they are safe in their transport. They are frightened when it catches them, running along the ground wreathed in smoke. It attacks their craft, fouling its works and forces them to flee the pass."

"And then it kills them," Sarah added.

"It frightens them and allows them to flee."

"How do you know this?"

Sam narrowed her eyes and ground her teeth. "I can see the future."

* * * * *

Kay and Phillip returned to the table and seated themselves. "Been behaving yourself, Sarah?" Kay asked.

He saw Ki and Lon standing next to Sam. He saw the empty glass and residue of wine.

"Sarah goaded Lady Monama into drinking some wine," Ki said.

Kay was alarmed. "Sarah!" he said, angry. "Monamas can't drink wine! I think we should fetch a Hospitaler! I think I saw Beth in the main ballroom!"

"No, watch!" Sarah said. "Watch. She's predicting the future and is going to change on us any moment, and we need to rush her when she does! Watch!"

Sam sat there wobbling a little.

Lon put a protective hand on her shoulder. "Lady Monama, may I help you to a washroom?"

Sam belched and pushed his hand away. "So, Lord Kabyl, our gracious host," she said, her words slightly slurred, "I've listened to your friend here discuss his accomplishments. What are your plans, sir, if I may be so bold?"

"My lady, we should find you medical assistance, just for in case the wine makes you sick."

"I don't need medical assistance. I'm fine. I'm fine, so my question, please. I'd like an answer." She stood up unsteadily.

"I've currently no plans, my lady. I'm only twenty-two, after all." His jade-colored eyes met her black.

"Are you going to join the Fleet, soar the stars with your mother and father?"

"No, my lady, I find that space travel does not agree with me, I'm sorry to say."

"I see, and you've given no further thought to the future?"

"No, my lady."

Sam smiled. She had big teeth, accentuated by her black lips. "Come now, you are twenty-two in age, but look at you—no trace of puffiness or swelling. You look a man already."

"Thank you, my lady."

Sam gazed at him. "Is he not handsome, Lord Lon?"

Lon was startled by the question. "Well, certainly, I suppose."

Sarah began to get tense and hiked up her gown. "What did I tell you before, Monama? Don't look at him, don't speak to him."

Sam turned back to Lord Kabyl. "And you're certain that you've no plans then, Lord Kabyl? No thoughts for the future?" she asked again, pressing the matter.

Lord Lon brightened and spoke up. "Lady Monama, I am planning to attend the Sister's Twilight 4 technical seminary this summer. I was one of only ten students to be selected."

She turned her head and looked at him for a moment. She gave him a wry smile and patted him on the cheek. "*Sen-tre.* Quite an honor." She loosed another belch then quickly turned back to Lord Kabyl. "I am still awaiting your answer, my lord."

"No, my lady, and I do not intend to have any for the time being."

Sarah rustled in her chair. "And what about you? You're soon to be of age officially. What are your plans, other than dying and freaking out?"

Phillip gave her a kick under the table, knocking her heeled shoe off.

Sam grabbed a piece of meat off the table, her claw-like fingernails glinting in the hall light as she picked it apart and ate it. "I am to be married, Lady Blanchefort. Yes, I am."

"That's wonderful, Lady Sammidoran," Lord Lon said. "Will you share with us right now who your future Lord might be?"

She sighed. "Oh, let's just say my future husband is sitting here at this very table."

Everybody looked around at each other. The temperature most certainly seemed to drop at the table.

Phillip, brave and empirical as ever, spoke up. "Lady Monama, I congratulate you and Lord Lon for your upcoming union. I must say, I had no idea."

"Me?" he squeaked.

Sammidoran appeared off put and turned to Phillip. "*Mundi-ner-a!*" she exclaimed. "And why, Lord Blanchefort, do you say that I am to be wed to Lord Lon, charming and brilliant though he may be?" she said dryly. She tented her greasy fingers and clacked her long black fingernails together as she awaited his answer.

Phillip paused a moment and responded. "Certainly we've just met, so it cannot be me, and as I know most of the doings of Lord Kabyl here, it cannot be he either. Therefore, it must be Lord Lon, as I am not as aware of his doings."

Lord Lon swallowed.

Sam gave Phillip a hard, squinting stare with her piercing black eyes. "Are you so certain that it cannot be you, Lord Blanchefort? Are you so certain that you have not been ... *kranti-gomi?*"

"What does that mean, my lady?" he asked.

"*Promised* to me?" she said in a sly voice. "Are you certain that hasn't happened?" She waved her fingers at him. Her black nails were long and rather cruel looking, dotted with hanging pieces of meat, and she made sure to let Phillip admire them.

Lady Kilos raised an eyebrow and smiled. *<I think Sam's really drunk,>* she sent to Kay.

<She needs a Hospitaler. I'm going to find Beth or Ennez.>

<No, he's drunk, too. I saw him passed out in the foyer.>

Phillip was clearly shocked. "Yes, Lady Monama, I am quite certain. My mother and father would never do such a thing, and, in any event, my mother cannot keep a secret and would have—"

"She'd have let something like that slip a long time ago," Sarah said interrupting, ready to defend her brother to the death. She fished around under the table for her shoe that Phillip had knocked off.

Sam laughed boldly. "In any event, Lord Blanchefort, rest assured, it is not you. You may breathe easy, sir," she said cheerfully.

Phillip, though he tried to hide it, was visibly relieved.

Lord Lon, after some thought, appeared agreeable to get to know

Sam a bit more. Apparently, after a bout of inner turmoil, he'd gotten used to the idea. "Lady Sammidoran," he said in a shy voice lost in the blueness of his large coat, "have you ever attended the annual science and technology exposition in Arden?"

She looked at him for a moment and smiled. "No, my lord, I have not."

"Oh, well, it's a wonderful event and I would love to show you the ..."

"Lord Kabyl," Sam said, teetering a little. "You are looking particularly handsome this evening. I approve of your attire. It pleases me. Your mother is a genius."

"Thank you, Lady Monama."

Lord Lon looked at his blue coat that matched Lady Sarah's hair. It was an off-the-rack House Probert creation, not nearly as stylish and well-fitted as Kay's. "Do ... do you like my coat, Lady Sammidoran? It's new."

She ignored him. "And what shall we name our first child, sir?" she asked Kay abruptly. "Will you invite me to sit closer to you, sir, as we shall soon be very close."

Everyone was silent.

"You're fine where you are," Sarah said after a moment. "Kay's not marrying you."

"Oh, and I didn't think you were his keeper, Lady Sarah."

Sarah began to get annoyed. "I'm not, but Kay is my cousin, and he's my best friend as well. He's not getting pushed into anything he doesn't want to do. You're not his type, Monama."

"Think so? You'd throw down the baton, Lady Sarah?"

"It would never get that far. I'll throw you down first."

Sam leaned forward, displaying her handsome bosom to Kay. She locked eyes with him. "And what do you say, Lord Kabyl? Would you not want me as a wife and countess?"

Kay swallowed hard, not quite sure where to go with this. Sam, when not drunk, demanded secrecy. He had to be careful. "My lady," he said. "You are a beautiful young woman and doubtless have many gifts with which to share. However, as I have said, I'm merely twenty-two years old and haven't considered courting as of yet."

"You didn't answer my question, sir."

Kay looked at the table. "I really don't know what to say, my lady."

Sam saw Lon's half-finished glass of wine, picked it up and drank it down. She staggered and fell laughing, her pointed Monama shoes flying into the air over the tabletop.

"Sam!" Kay cried.

Lon and Ki knelt down and helped her. "It's all right, my love," she said as they hauled her light body back up. "I expected your reaction, and I forgive you, but you might as well know that, one day, you shall love me like no other."

She made drunken eyes at him relentlessly.

Lord Lon looked a little deflated. Sarah fumed.

"Quit looking at him!" Sarah said. "Why don't you go and freak out like your countryman in Calvert did last month and go Berserkacide. That's all you Monamas do, isn't it?"

"Sarah!" Kay said. "Be quiet!"

Sarah stood up, wobbling slightly as she was still missing a shoe. "She's trying to bewitch you, Kay! Can't you see it? I'm trying to help you out here!"

Sam turned and glared at Sarah. "Oh ... if you only knew what I've done with Kay. Up and down, back and forth, sideways and forwards. You don't know your cousin as well as you think you do. You're really not all that bright are you?"

"Oh, yeah? Want to step outside and discover just how smart I am, Berserkacide, I mean Lady Monama?" Sarah yelled, kicking her chair aside.

"Sarah," Kay ordered, "sit down!"

"I've *been* you, Sarah, for K—"

"She needs a Hospitaler!" Kay said cutting her off.

Sarah was frothing mad. "You and your pack of grave-loving freaks are the bane and laughing stock of the League, and the only reason you've been invited to this ball is because Lord Davage had a fondness for your late grandmother. Otherwise, he'd have nothing to do with the lot of you!"

Sam's normally white complexion turned bloody red. "Bold words," she said at last. "Coming from the daughter of a pirate," she said referring to her father's former, and alleged, membership in the Black Goshawk gang.

Sarah screwed her eyes up and leaned forward. "Better a pirate than a stinking fortune-teller waiting to soak your claws in Elder blood."

Lord Lon struggled to hold Sam up. "Now see here, Lady Blanchefort, that was …"

"And," Sarah began, on a roll, "if you think you're good enough for Kay, you're as blood-simple and freaked-out as the rest of your family. You're a useless peasant not worth shining his shoes, and that's all you'll ever be!"

Sam went to say something, then put her hands to her face. She jerked free from Lon and Ki and staggered out of the room toward the noise and pomp of the ball, her black gown and bustle trailing like a shroud.

Kay stood, fuming. "I appreciate your looking out for me, Sarah, but that was exceedingly rude and uncalled for," he said. He saw her elusive missing shoe on the floor near his chair. He picked it up and tossed it to her. "You're lucky I don't floor you right now!"

"Me? Look, I'm sorry, but she's a freak," she said catching the yellow shoe in the mid-riff. "And, what did she mean when she said she's been me? That gives me the creeps."

"I don't know," Kay said.

"I don't think she's a freak," Lon said defiantly.

"Kay," Phillip said. "Where are you going?"

"Lady Monama is a guest of our home, a guest who has just been insulted by my idiotic cousin here. I am going to find her and offer my apologies."

14—The Library

A few weeks after the big "Falling in Love" ball with winter in full swing, Sam became fascinated with libraries. After watching a brandtball match at Sarfortnim College, she and Kay toured the campus and ended up in the college's main library. Sam was astounded by all the information that was kept in books. She noted that many of the books in the library were dedicated to engineering and machines of various types. She has always assumed that all archived information in Elder country was stored via holo-node.

"No, Sam, on other League worlds, holo-node is the favored medium to preserve information, but, here in the north of Kana, we still use books and vellum quite often. Not always, but it's a tradition we have."

When they returned to the castle, Sam went on a quest. She insisted Kay show her all of the various libraries scattered throughout the castle. It was a tough task, as there were over a hundred, all in all. Some were fairly small, like the reading rooms in his Tower, while others were quite astounding in size.

"What are you looking for?" he asked.

"A device. One that we have at our home by the lake and doesn't work. I was hoping to discover how to repair it."

Kay wasn't certain he bought her response, but he left it at that.

They combed the castle seeking out and going through every library and reading room they could find. Some of the libraries Sam discounted right away—Lady Poe's favorite library in her tower was stocked mostly with romance novels and horticultural books. The massive library near the kitchen contained nothing but cookbooks, and Countess Sygillis's personal library in her study were mostly self-help and sewing books.

Here and there, Sam found books that interested her—again mostly of a technical nature regarding exotic machines. Lord Davage's huge collection in his study provided a healthy cache of interesting reading that Sam devoured—she took over fifty books out of there, each she promised to return. Kay had tried to collect as much information as he could, but so far he had nothing. Whatever machine Sam was looking for eluded the both of them.

And she didn't confine herself to old books. Some nights Kay woke to find her sitting at his desk using the Holo-net. She appeared frustrated, as using the Holo-net could be a tricky, and was a maddeningly quirky method to access information that you wanted. Sarah was probably the best person he knew at using the Holo-net. Eventually, Sam became quite proficient, moving the floating holographic controls about with ease.

Sam was consumed with something, and it occupied her days and nights. At night, Kay often woke to find her sitting up in bed lost in thought, or sometimes she paced about, her mind absorbed in what apparently was a difficult puzzle. He spoke to her, and she didn't hear him at first. Then, she'd turn to him and smile, totally mum on whatever it was that was riveting her.

They eventually exhausted every library in the castle, Sam becoming rather sad that her odd search had been in vain.

"There's one more, library, Sam, though you have to promise never to tell."

"Of course, Kay. Where is it?"

Kay led her into the north wing to an innocent looking bench. There, under the bench was a nine-inch high hole hidden behind a vent. They squeezed through it twisting and turning for about a hundred feet until they got to the library, lost in stone—the passage never more than twelve inches high. It was a tough crawl, probably one of the hardest in the castle, Countess Sygillis giving it five full stones out of five. They struggled to get through. They inched along, their progress painfully slow, but they made it.

Once inside, Sam was fascinated by the tempting shelves full of the arcane. "Why is this place so hidden?"

"It's where we keep most of our more forbidden tomes and

documents. It's a Blanchefort secret, and it's protected from Wafting and other arcane methods to enter it. You also can't Sight the walls and see it through the stone, not even Father."

Looking around, the library was fairly small and eight-sided. Shelves full of documents, scrolls and old books lined the walls.

They went through the books, Sam carefully going through each, using her nails to turn the pages. Her nails were back to long and sharp; she had grown them back for the ball to keep with appearances. Lady Kilos was going to bust them back down tomorrow, which was always a difficult task.

And then she stopped. "*Jestro!*" she said in Anuie, an exclamation. She sat there looking at a full-page picture of several legendary machines from the antiquity of Kana. Kay looked over her shoulder, trying to determine which one had caught her eye.

The machines she was looking at were all old and fancy, nearly magical in the abilities they were purported to have. He was familiar with some of them. "Which one are you looking at, Sam?"

Absently, she pointed at the mirror-like machine in the center of the page.

"That's the Mallus Mirror," Kay said. "Supposedly it transverses the planes of dreams and reality. You have one of those at your home?"

"What," she said, preoccupied. "Oh, yes, yes. It's very nice." Kay had the distinct feeling she wasn't focusing on the Mallus Mirror, but rather another machine on the page.

"These machines actually exist?" she asked breathless, holding the book with shaking hands. "This isn't a fantasy book?"

"Yes, these machines are all said to be real. I've actually seen the Mallus Mirror on display at Fleet in Armenelos. If you have one at your home, it must be very valuable, even broken."

"What?" she said, preoccupied. "Oh, yes, yes."

She stared at the page, her expression lost in thought. She closed her eyes and smiled and, after a moment, a tear leaked down her face.

"Sam? You all right?" Kay asked her. He placed his hand on her back and her heart was racing, beating like only a Monama heart could.

Without answering, she began greedily reading the book, asking him questions about this and that. "May I borrow this, Kay? Please, I promise I'll return it undamaged."

"Of course, but, are you really interested in the Mallus Mirror, or something else on the page?"

Again Sam didn't answer. With book in hand, she quickly exited the library, Kay crawling after her as fast as he could. When he exited the crawlspace, she was there in the corridor with the book, removing Snugs from her neck. "I shall return shortly, Kay. I love you! I love you so much, *Arin-Dan!* This is wonderful!"

"What is, Sam? Sam?"

And she was gone.

* * * * *

She returned later in the day, breathless and preoccupied. She stared off into space and only half-heard when Kay tried to talk to her. That night after bed, Kay watched Sam fooling around with the Holo-net terminal, a vast number of holographic displays danced about her head. She masterfully manipulated the holographic controls. She seemed to come to a dead end, and, frustrated, she gave up in a huff, shut off the terminal, and crawled back into bed.

When she was asleep, he worked himself free of her arms and opened the terminal, curious as to what she was so interested in. The usual holographic gentleman in the black coat appeared with his staff of knowledge.

The last thing she had accessed was a visual history of the House of Want.

The House of Want? That was an odd thing to look up. Recalling his lessons with Lady Poe, the House of Want was an old Remnath House that actually left the League several centuries back. Why they left the League and where they went, nobody really knew. The forlorn ruins of their old castle still stood in the hills north of St. Paris. The House had been known for their incredible technological creations, especially their wondrous, arcane machines. It was sometimes said that their knowledge, especially that of their patriarch, Lord Revis, surpassed the Elders, and the Sisters were jealous and gave them no peace. It was said they left to get away from the Sisters.

Obviously, whatever machine Sam was interested in, it wasn't the Mallus Mirror as she said earlier; it was something created by the House of Want. A quick search brought up literally hundreds of machines created by them, all interesting and well-crafted. There were too many to choose from and he'd probably never be able to guess which one it was just by wrote or elimination.

He shut down the terminal and got back into bed, Sam quickly enveloping him. He'd have to sly it out of her.

* * * * *

Just as Sam couldn't get him to improve his Gifts, he couldn't get her to talk. During this odd period, Kay often asked her what she was looking for and, smiling, she'd simply say that she was working on a project for her household. Her story held no water, as what would her Monama Household need with arcane House of Want creations, machines that, in many ways, replicated mechanically what she and her people could do naturally? It was maddening.

Her demeanor during her nocturnal visits also changed. Instead of wanting to go to the bath house and make love, she, instead, asked him about machines and technical detail, but nothing so detailed that he could draw out of her what she was up to. She had all sorts of questions for Kay and was somewhat annoyed when he couldn't really provide her with a lot of good information. Kay wasn't into technical matters. His uncle, Lord Peter, was a great technical resource, as was Phillip, his cousin. Lord Lon of Probert—now, there was a technical whiz. A real chip off the old block was Lon, as his mother, Lady Branna of Probert, was one of the League's top scientists, and his father, Lord Milos of Probert, was the Fleet's lead engineer.

"Lord Lon, the cute little fellow in blue at the ball? Yes, I believe I recall him talking about fairs and the sciences."

"Yes. He's a good friend and smart as a whip."

Sam sat there ... her brain wheels apparently spinning. "Lord Lon ..." And she dropped the matter.

PART TWO

The Invisible World

1—The *Olonol*

I had a vision when I was a little girl. I had it just once, and never again, but I never forgot a single detail. Through the years, my vision stayed in the back of my thoughts, simmering and waiting to come out.

I had a vision of the *Olonol* ...

And it could change everything.

I dreamed of a strange workshop. All manner of swirling metal gadgets clicked and bobbed about. There were unique tools hanging on the walls, and shelves lined with ... *things*. I'd never seen such *things*. Elder machines.

In the center of the workshop, a man wearing Elder clothing was working on some type of twisting, silver sculpture. He had arms and legs that were long and skinny, and his *frondont*-shaped head sat on the end of a bent *vembla* neck. He wore a little Elder hat, giving him a rather pin-headed look. I thought he looked funny, though I'd been taught not to snicker or laugh, so I just stayed quiet.

The sculpture he was working on was beautiful—so pretty, so wonderful, something only an Elder could create. I complimented him on his work. I don't know if he understood.

He looked at me.

"So, you're here," he said. "They say I'm crazy. They say I'm full of it, but don't you believe a word. This machine, this one right here, is my greatest piece of work yet! This thing does what they say is impossible."

"What machine?" I wanted to know.

"This one right here!" he said rapping the sculpture with his tools. "Those headdressed zipheads from Valenhelm will say it doesn't work. They'll scavenge it out of here when I'm gone, look at it and scratch their noggins and, eventually, they'll write it off as a bit of failed genius and forget all about it. They'll put it on display and truck it around like a prize trophy. They'll lose it." He pointed toward a window. "See them out there?"

Outside in the afternoon sun, I could see a number of robed forms wearing stiff white headdresses dancing on a nearby hillside. They bobbed around with lots of arm waving and spinning, something a child would do. I laughed; I couldn't help it.

"See them dancing around out there like idiots. Those fools won't give me a minute's worth of peace. Anyway, don't you believe their guff! This machine works! It works every single time." He gave "The Machine" another loving rap with his tools. "All you have to do is know how to use it. That's all."

I squinted and studied it in detail. The Machine was a type of silver archway, standing about seven *verdits* tall, maybe three *verdits* wide, easily tall and wide enough for a large man to walk comfortably through. It was constructed in a sinewy, organic style. It looked like a living thing, like a partially dissected tree trunk in all its various layers. Such incredible complexity and workmanship. I wanted to look at it for a while. I wanted to touch it.

If I quieted my thoughts, I could hear The Machine talking to me. In the center of the arch was a large, dark purple stone of some sort. Its color reminded me of my *Arin-Dan's* hair.

The man looked at the whole thing lovingly. "We're leaving. Going to Emmira. Ever heard of it?"

"No, no, I'm sorry I haven't."

"Great place, Emmira. It's a shame I'll have to leave this baby behind. This machine, this one right here, can save your soul if you let it. Do you hear me?"

"Yes, sir, I hear you."

The man looked at me with a walleyed Elder gaze. "So, you want to know what it does? I'm dying for somebody—anybody—to properly appreciate it. For lack of anyone else, you'll do."

"Yes, I want to know." I wanted to know very much.

"Well, sit back and I'll tell you."

He then started his talking. "Now pay attention! I'm only going to go over this with you once."

And I did. I listened. I hung on every word he said.

Gods! Can it be true? Can this be real?

And I never had that vision again, but I never forgot a moment of it. I set it in stone in my memory. I often thought about it at night, replaying the dream in my thoughts trying to sift hidden meaning out of any small detail.

The Machine can Save Us

I never forgot the machine I'd seen and the wondrous thing it could do. The man told me what it did in exacting detail.

Could such a thing actually exist? The silver machine was the key, a miracle. It could, indeed, change everything.

The only thing the man didn't tell me was its name or where it could be found. It was the *Olonol,* a machine of riches, a machine of lore.

And now, here it is, drawn on the page of Kay's book exactly as I recalled it! Exact in every detail.

And, what I've been waiting for: a name to go along with it!

Oberphilliax, designed by Lord Revis, House of Want, who left the League in 000011AX.

Just like he said in my dream, he left the League, and he used the *Oberphilliax* to do it. This machine exists, and it works as well.

It does something even the gods cannot do.

And it'll work for me and my *Arin-Dan,* too. All I have to do is find it.

* * * * *

I like to think that, if this somehow works out, we shall use the machine on a carefree day sometime in the future and go to this man, this Lord Revis, House of Want, and stand before him as man and woman, and thank him as he is due.

Thank him for his genius and his machine that he left behind.

Olonol.

Oberphilliax. Right there on the page.

The Old Poltava

2—A Pewter Pistol

S am fell into a genuine funk as winter faded, going through bouts of sadness alternating with euphoria, and then delirium.

Kay asked her what was wrong, and she would say nothing. Nothing's wrong.

She became watchful, looking over her shoulder, always aware of what she said and did, carefully considering every word she spoke. Sometimes she jumped back, startled. Sometimes she fled from nothing as if pursued, and then she wept.

* * * * *

One day, they were out wandering in the Grove and came into a clearing. Sam found one of the ancient oak trees that was so old it had reached giant proportions. There were lots of those old giants scattered about. She saddled up to the tree and began happily carving their initials into the ancient bark with her fingernail. Kay looked over her shoulder to see what she was doing. She turned, smiling, wanting him to see what she'd drawn; then, her smile faded.

She turned, and, picking up the folds of her gown, ran from him, chain rattling, covering the ground as only she could.

"Sam!" Kay cried taking off after her.

He thought he might have been imagining it, but Kay thought he'd seen a ghostly hand reaching out for her just before she took off.

* * * * *

Given Sam's odd behavior, Kay began to think that she was sick or addled by some sort of malady. He wondered if the wine she'd had at the Falling in Love ball was having some lingering effects. When she wasn't around, mostly on Tuesdays when she had familial duties to attend, he began doing research on the House of Monama, but there wasn't much out there other than the usual postings and inquiries for fortune-tellers, prostitutes and seers. Their ability to see the future and their skills as prostitutes seemed all they contributed; they didn't appear to be part of the League at all other than these select occupations. The lack of solid information was maddening.

He tried inquiring with Samaritan Ennez of the Hospitalers regarding Monamas, and he wasn't much help. Apparently, they knew little about them as well.

Pacing about in his tower one afternoon when Sam was gone, he had a sudden brainstorm.

Sarah! Sarah had all sorts of information she'd collected on Monamas and Berserkacides, one of her favorite lurid topics. And, Sarah was quite meticulous in the documentation of her passions. Of course, being gone for the winter in Esther, Sarah's tower was locked up tightly, and the exterior was proofed against the Waft as were all the towers at Blanchefort Castle. Once inside a tower, one could Waft all they wanted, but one could not Waft from outside to inside. However, Kay didn't need to Waft in; he had the zip line running from his tower all the way to Sarah bedroom on the 42nd floor.

He got his dusty zip liner out of the closet (he really didn't use it much—it was Sarah who did most of the zipping with her zip liner) and fastened it to the line. He turned it on and engaged the servo motors, and soon he was dangling in mid air by the handles, thousands of feet above the distant rocks below. The zip liner was fast in covering the distance, and, after only a second or two, he was standing on Sarah's balcony. The bedroom within was much neater and girlier than one might expect from the rough and tumble tomboy she liked to present herself as. It was done up in teals and yellows (Sarah secretly favored yellow) and had white provincial furniture, again of a distinctly girlish flavor. Her closet doors were open and mostly empty—quite different from Ki's three-story closet. There were stuffed toys from her childhood arraigned here and there along with a wall full of pictures, many of her parents, Lady Poe and Lord Peter, many of his father and mother and many of the Duke and

Duchess Torrijayne. There were also photos of her older brother Milos and baby sister Millie, and a healthy amount of pictures of Phillip, Kay, and her. Clearly, Sarah liked keepsakes, and she obviously cherished her family, Phillip and Kay especially.

Kay exited her bedroom and entered the tower's main corridor. Kay knew that Sarah's favorite place to practice her love of the sensational was in the Mystery Library on the 50th floor, an equal distance from Phillip's bedroom on the 58th floor. Everything was locked, so Kay settled back to Waft up. It took forever, his Waft really quite terrible.

How angry Sam would be at such a display.

After a few minutes, he appeared on the 50th floor. The entrance to the library had a large slate over the door stating who was welcome to enter and who was not.

On the WELCOME side was:

SARAH
PHILLIP
KAY
MILOS
MOTHER/FATHER

On the FORBIDDEN side was:

LADY KILOS
BATHLOXI and, recently added,
LADY SAMMIDORAN OF MONAMA.

Kay chuckled and entered.

Sarah's Mystery Library was well-stocked with books of monsters, ghosts, urban legends and local lore, all carefully shelved, categorized, and perfectly taken care of. The large room was a paradise of comfortable, over-stuffed chairs, a table, several terminals and a cooler always stocked with drinks and snacks, (though it was empty now with Sarah away for the winter.) Sarah would make a wonderful librarian. Her collection was truly quite impressive. Unlike many girls who were difficult to buy a gift for, Sarah was easy. A well appreciated birthday gift idea for Sarah was always a new book of the lurid. Against the north wall was a detailed relief map of the winding Gaston Way, haunted, the lair of another of Sarah's favorite new monsters—the Wraith of Gaston. Recorded in holographic projections were Sarah's meticulous notes on locations of various sightings and places where she hoped the three of them would investigate. There were even names of people she wanted to interview regarding the haunting.

At the other end of the library in a cozy nook surrounded by shelved books, she kept much of her Monama/Berserkacide materials. Sitting on one of the shelves was a bleached, partially fossilized skull, supposedly of a Berserkacide, though Kay doubted it was real. It was Sarah's prize possession and was, according to her, a gift from Carahil, an elemental spirit created by her mother some years ago. She said she promised Carahil she'd keep it safe here in the Mystery Library. Looking around in the quiet, orderly splendor of the library, Kay saw little images of Carahil all over the place, as wall decorations, as book-stops on the shelves, and as little smiling plushies pushed against the wall. Seeing him was comforting, like he was here protecting the place.

Grabbing as much as he could carry off the shelves, he sat down at the table and began reading, though he dreaded what he might find.

Berserkacides seemed creatures right out of a horror vid or cheap, scary book, but yet, there they were. Berserkacides were Monama men, women, or children who had gone mad and become deformed. With four-arms, they shrieked with rage and killed any who crossed their path. They were said to appear in people's homes, in people's bedrooms, naked and glistening, black claws flashing. They were said to be unreasonable, unstoppable and could absorb massive amounts of damage before dying. There were three topics that Sam refused to talk about. These included her home by the shores of Lake Monama, some of the more detailed aspects of Monama life, and the Berserkacides, whose name she rarely uttered.

Clearly they were monsters for a stormy night and a vivid imagination. His father believed that they didn't exist at all and were products of either a hoax or hysteria.

Kay sometimes had a nightmare in which he would wake one morning and find that Sam had become a Berserkacide, her claws reaching for his throat.

It was a dream he was ashamed of and pushed away, but still, the how's and why's were endless. If real, how did one become a

Berserkacide? If real, why did one become a Berserkacide?

Sam was mum.

He found all sorts of collected information on Berserkacides in Sarah's books and documents, but scant little on standard, healthy Monamas—apparently that didn't interest her as much. As he sorted through the documents, he tried to bypass the ones regarding Berserkacides, but eventually his curiosity got the better of him:

BERSERKACIDE

...bestial rage...

...extremely violent and dangerous...

...four-armed, extremely powerful...

...rush of anger, followed by great cunning and cruelty...

...death of personality...

...permanent...

...no known cure, no known cause...

...Monamas mistrusted in many quarters due to Berserkacide events...

...Monamas often escorted out of many Remnath cities...

...Under Sisterhood surveillance ...

Death of personality. Death of soul... Death of his Sam.

Shuddering, he continued on.

Finally, he found something which seemed promising and didn't involve Berserkacides.

It read:

HEAD SWARM:

A semi-catatonic condition entered into by members of the House of Monama, highlighted by extreme apathy and delirium, lack of recognition and place, lack of muscular control, general weakness and listlessness. Head Swarm is entered into when a Monama believes that he or she is about to die and is...

He put the document down and sat there.

Head Swarm. About to die ...

Sam seemed to be exhibiting some of these symptoms, but not all of them. Even in her blackest and most sullen of moods, Sam recognized Kay and knew where she was.

He read on, but those words kept popping into his brain:

Head Swarm

...about to die.
Berserkacide...
...death of personality...
...no known cure. No known cause...
...Monamas mistrusted... Monamas detained and escorted away...

He saw one more thing that caught his interest, a short entry reading:

WHITE EMILIA

Herbaceous flowering plant of family Asteraceae, common in the Lake Monama region of Kana that thrives well in shade and low light. Often used symbolically in Monama mating rituals, especially the Nebulon, Astralon and Minzer tribes.

That was the white flower he'd received in the IN LOCK letter. Mating rituals? That was interesting. Sam hadn't mentioned anything about that. He found little else of use. He put everything back where he got it, knowing that the anal Sarah would no doubt discover it and make a fuss when she returned.

Berserkacide ...
Head Swarm ...
White Emilia ...

These names floated through his head for the rest of the afternoon.

* * * * *

Winter moved on.

Kay tried to ease Sam's flagging spirits by taking her to the village one day when she was in a particularly sad mood. Lady Kilos tagged along as well. Trips to the village usually made Sam happy, but not today. They strolled the vast maze of shops and emporiums—

Kilos always wanting to stop in the more expensive stores. Quietly, Sam looked around, and Kay offered to get her anything she wanted. Sometimes she wanted certain things, but today she wasn't interested enough to want anything. Lady Kilos certainly had no qualms about buying—she soon had an armload of bags and packages.

Sam, in her usual red dress and goggles, seemed determined to be dour.

Head Swarm ... lack of recognition.

"Sam, Sam ..." Kay kept saying, trying to see if she recognized him.

"What, Kay?" she slowly replied, and he'd be appeased for a while. He also recalled from his reading:

Head Swarm ... lack of reflex.

He tried poking her in the shoulder and back every so often to see how she'd react. She got annoyed after a bit and poked him back in the sternum, hard.

"Oww!" he cried.

Lady Kilos became quite hungry as the afternoon of shopping wore on. As they walked toward a nice café, they passed a small curio shop near the waterfront called THE MYSTERY DEN. The window of the shop was cluttered with a vaudevillian arrangement of cheap and poorly made trinkets, bathed in flake copper and sprayed-on pewter. It was your classic souvenir shop, clearly a place for tourists and new Fleet crew arrivals to buy inexpensive items to send home to their families.

Kay and Lady Kilos didn't look twice at the place.

Sam, though, took one look at the eclectic and rather seedy offerings crowded in the window and immediately became interested. She put her pale hands against the glass and peered in; the intricate and expensive goggles she wore stood out in stark contrast to the crap items on display. The heat from her medallion quickly began to steam the window.

Whatever funk she had been in seemed to be gone in a moment.

"Kay," she said, excitedly, "may we go in?"

"You're not serious, are you?" Kilos said in a prissy voice.

Sam didn't answer. She went to the door and flew inside, ringing the bell. Looking around to make sure that not too many people were watching, Kay and Kilos followed her in—they felt a bit sullied, like they were walking into a dirty courtesan's den.

Inside, surrounded by the seedy claptrap, moribund intaglio, and shelf-lined standard trinket fare, Sam seemed intoxicated. Mouth open, she browsed around the semi-lit shop, picking up a whole armful of tacky things best left un-selected.

When the shopkeeper saw Kay and Kilos, he was thrilled. "My lord! My lady!" he exclaimed throwing his hands up. "This is a great day! How may I humbly assist you?"

Kay was mortified. "My friend here from the south seems keen on purchasing a memento," he stammered.

"Ah, I have many to choose from. Please, may I point out a new shipment of wonderful commemorative garments that have only recently arrived?"

He pointed to a far wall, and, there, neatly folded, was a hideous assortment of workmen's clothing all stamped with BLANCHEFORT VILLAGE somewhere on the cloth. A few had poorly constructed holo pictures of Lord Davage's and Countess Sygillis' smiling faces. Kay wondered if his father was aware that these items—or this wretched store for that matter—existed.

"Ah ... yes, if my friend wishes, we might select some of those later," Kay said wanting to get out of the premises immediately.

Sam appeared to have made up her mind on something. She approached Kay. "May I have this, Kay? Will you buy it for me, please?"

Kay looked. Sam had discarded most of what she had been holding and was apparently settled on a positively grotesque pewter casting of a long barreled pistol mounted on a flimsy stand. It was clearly one of the most garish and unsightly desk ornaments ever conceived. The base of the stand had a plaque reading:

BLANCHEFORT PtVa: The Old "Poltava"

Apparently, this grim trinket was supposed to be a likeness of the famous Blanchefort PtVa pistol, once made right there in the village in the factories now churning out his mother's fabrics. His grandfather, Lord Sadric, had abolished the practice of producing firearms, and the weapon immediately fell into lore as a prized collector's item. This brutally ugly piece of pewter-cast gimcrack, long barreled and ungainly, looked nothing like the PtVa, but rather like a dueling pistol. The Poltava was a short-barreled, elegant gun.

Kay could easily imagine this same image—most likely having been stamped out in some sweaty shop in Calvert— being passed off as a Grenville 40, or a Dare 88 or an Inseroth D4. Depending on where you were when you bought it, the plaque changed accordingly.

"Sam," Kay asked, "you want ... this?"

"Yes, please, Kay, may I have it?"

"But Sam, it doesn't even look like a Poltava."

"Please, Kay, I really want it."

Thoughts of *Head Swarm* again entered his mind. Without another word, Kay, holding the mounted pistol as if it were soaked in urine, walked to the shopkeeper and put it on the counter, the mounted pistol wobbling slightly on its flimsy, soldered metal legs.

"Oh, that's a true beauty sir—the old Poltava; nothing like it will ever be made again," the excited shopkeeper said.

Kilos selected a shirt with a hideous holo-picture of Countess Sygillis stamped on the breast and tossed it onto the counter. "I'm going to blackmail mother with this later," she whispered happily.

Kay looked at the shirt and had to laugh a bit. There was a terrible picture of his mother on the breast, truly terrible. Her hair was not set correctly, her smile was goofy and unready to be taken, and her finger was precariously close to her nose; in fact, it was in her nose, truth be told. He wondered how and why such a thing had been mass-produced and put out for sale in the first place.

He looked at the tag: It had been made by the D of O Clothiers. D of O? The Duchess of Oyln. Dimples, his mother's constant nemesis, had struck again. Kay shook his head and smiled. Dimples was a relentless prankster. No harm done.

The shopkeeper told Kay the price for these two items, and he was appalled.

"Four haders?" These things combined weren't worth a quarter of a hader, but, with Sam and Kilos standing there smiling and watching, Kay paid him the money. The shopkeeper put the items into a bag, and then the three shoppers exited the store, Kay very thankful to do so.

The purchase made Sam's day. She cast aside her previous funk and walked happily at Kay's side. Once or twice she pulled him into an alcove and passionately kissed him, whispering of the chain and the things she was going to turn into for him later. They went to lunch and all through the meal, Sam kept peeking into the bag, as if some rare treasure rested inside. It was the happiest he'd seen her in a while, so, ugly or not, he was glad he bought it for her.

If that was strange, the next day Sam did something even stranger. They went deep into the Grove toward the back quarter past the Ten Gardens, a walk of several miles, Sam chattering happily as they walked. She was carrying the pewter pistol that he'd bought her the day before. They entered a huge oak clearing somewhere in the far depths of the Grove, and Sam stopped. "Will you give me a few moments, Kay?" Sam asked. She gave him a kiss and walked away. Kay looked around, trees everywhere. Mt. Vith rose majestically in the distance. That huge volcanic mountain, the "Old Man," looked marvelous from here.

Kay admired the mountain for a bit then looked around. Sam had wandered far from him. She stood about a hundred feet away, busy doing something with the ground. She was leaning over, her hands digging into the dirt. Humorously, her rear end and bustle stuck up in the air as she worked.

"Sam, what are you doing?" he asked, nearing her. She had dug a hole in the dirt and had partially buried the ugly pistol he'd bought her in the village. "Are you a dog burying a bone, Sam?"

"*Delada*," she said in Anuie, meaning "hush" as she patted the dirt down, stood up, and examined her work. She looked at it and tapped her chin with her finger. She spoke in Anuie, something she often did when she was preoccupied "*Hmmm, do you think this will be safe out here, Kay? Do you think anybody will accidentally kick it or uncover it?*"

He responded in Elder. "Well, you never know, but I doubt it. It's a big Grove, and nobody comes out here too often. If you really wanted to get rid of that ugly thing, I suggest a trash bin."

Sam clapped the dirt off her hands and put her arms around him. "*No, no—it's fine where it is.*"

"Why did you bury it—other than for obvious reasons?"

"*I put it here as a reminder.*"

"A reminder of what?"

"*A reminder that here it begins.*"

Kay laughed and spun her around. "Okay, Sam, thanks. I'll make a note of it."

They began walking out of the clearing, Sam looking back over her shoulder several times as they walked.

3—Hiei

The Sisterhood of Light, the oldest Vith sect in the League, maintained twenty five strongholds across Kana. They also had a few on Hoban, Onaris, Bazz and Planet Fall, Tubruk and Carina, but Kana was their true bastion. These strongholds were, of course, much more than just places of worship or faith—they were research centers and repositories of great knowledge and learning. These centers were solemn and guarded places seldom seen by any outside of the Sisterhood.

There was the great bastion at Pithnar: a lovely Vith ruin on the surface, but a vast complex below where the Sisters continued to experiment and test the Gifts, a task they had been performing for ages. Testing the Gifts was their founding mission. There was the monastery of Attilan where the Sisters tended to their young and trained them for decades. There was the tall tower of Twilight 4 on the southern shores of the lower continent in Remnath where the Sisters researched the odd assortment of weapons the Xaphans and other enemies tended to use against the League (the infamous Fanatics of Nalls were taken to Twilight 4 and never seen again— their secrets removed from them by methods unknown and unspoken of). Some League circles insisted the Sisters had vivisected the Fanatics to get at their secrets, while other, more charitable ones, claimed the Fanatics had cooperated with the Sisters and lived at Twilight 4 in well-cared for splendor.

Either dispassionate, probing monsters or benevolent hosts, the Sisters were easily moldable to match the needs and expectations of any who observed them.

Their places were strongholds, places of impenetrable security. The Sisters were, if anything, jealous of their sundry secrets; that much was perfectly clear. Though always presenting themselves as polite and shy, they quickly could become bitter and spiteful to any who might choose to cross them, especially to those who might wish to tap their secrets; those were enemies to be dealt with swiftly. The Sisters had, at various times in the past, captured and executed various foolish Lords who tested them too much. They'd also dissolved whole Houses in a process they called *Shuw-shun*—the old House of Mutt being a notorious example, their holdings dispersed, their patents burned and their progeny lost to the ages in a blast of fire and smoke.

It was an unspoken understanding that the Sisters were the true ruling power in the League.

* * * * *

The central repository at Hiei, north of Esther, was a quiet and dreary place. As typical for a Sisterhood stronghold, it was located in an out-of-the-way area rife with old stories of ghosts and monsters. The Sisters liked using superstition and local folklore as a first defense in the security of their places. The ground Hiei sat on was old Haitathe land—the giants of old. It was situated near the northern sea, not another village or settlement for hundreds of miles.

All things being equal, Hiei was probably one of the more accessible Sisterhood strongholds, if one could call it that. The Grand Abbess of Hiei, a progressive and somewhat radical abbess, openly allowed those not of the Sisterhood to visit the stronghold and make use of *some* of its resources. Some of its resources were available for research, while some were not permitted to be viewed, *ever*, that being the capricious and heavy-handed nature of the Sisters—take it or leave it.

Hiei was a tall castle-like structure built of black rock and weathered masonry. It was an old Haitathe fort, and, as such, it was over-sized and rather bleak of appearance. It was once safely perched a fair pace from the crashing waves of the Sea of Elder, but with time and erosion pulling back the coastline, the storm-driven waves often rode up its sheer black sides.

It was notable as being one of the larger book repositories in the League. Books, nothing else, were kept there at Hiei, and usually the books were of an old and unique bearing. Even in the technological and modern League, with its Holo-net and imprinted data, books were still an important method of collecting and preserving information.

Books were silent and covert and didn't corrupt or crash. Scanned databases could be hacked, could be uncovered by the Gifted and exploited, so information kept in books was usually sensitive, inflammatory or arcane in the extreme. The cache of books stored at Hiei contained information that the Sisterhood considered too sensitive to be allowed to be copied and placed in the Holo-net for general use. Still, the information kept there wasn't considered *overly*-dangerous or *overly*-critical to the well-being of the League, and, if the proper channels were met and one was well-favored, outsiders could come and perform research there. The ground level of the castle was set up as a massive library. Readers came, made their request, and, if granted, the book was brought to the reader where they could study it at their leisure. Books could never leave Hiei, and the Sisters, kind and smiling but tirelessly vigilant, always watched. They allowed no holos, photographs or scans of the material, but users could make hand-written notes, provided the Sisters look over and approve the content.

* * * * *

It was a typical day at Hiei. The readers, coming from all over, had conducted themselves properly and, after the tenth bell, were kindly asked to leave for the day.

The readers gave their books back, exited, and the grand, over-sized doors were closed and locked.

None, not even the Sisters, noticed the dark figure crouching in the heights of the library. The Sisters, blazing with thought and mentality, should have instantly detected it, but, for some reason, they did not.

They were oblivious to its smoldering presence.

After they were satisfied that the library was empty and secure, they retired to their chambers and warm beds in the towers above, leaving only two sentinels to guard the premises. The sentinels sat down at one of the reading tables and tucked into a simple meal of unidentifiable food.

The figure, moving with speed and silent grace, came down from the heights and hid for a moment in the shadows by the door. It could feel that, not only was the door locked, it was girded with the Sister's power—nothing, either by opening it or by Wafting, was getting through that door, in or out.

It considered this for a moment. Perhaps it had over-estimated its own abilities. Maybe it shall die here today.

* * * * *

One of the sentinels was startled as she ate.

She heard something.

Not getting up to investigate, not even putting her fork down, she reached out with her mind, inquisitively seeking whatever was there. Her mind was all she needed. With it she should instantly determine what it was that was hiding in the shadows. If it were a patron, that person was immediately to be interrogated, mentally and verbally, and a determination would be made as to why that person was still there. Perhaps the person was in the bathroom or something of that nature when the library closed. If that was the case, then no harm done. That patron would be escorted to a room with a bed and, under observation, be allowed to spend the night.

If, however, the person was sneaking around for other reasons, then that would be immediately determined and that person set to tribunal. And if the person was determined to be a clear threat with sinister motives, then she would kill the person just as easily right then and there.

What the sentinel sensed in the reaching tentacles of her mind confused her. It seemed that *something* was there by the door, but what it was, she couldn't tell—that was odd. She got the impression of desperation and longing laced with a hint of fear. And, above all else, there was determination, backed with steel.

But that was all. Nothing more could be gleaned. The sentinel should know not only what it was, but who it was as well—the person's hidden thoughts and feelings made available to her like an open scroll.

Stymied, the sentinel put down her fork, got up from the table, calmly walked over to the door and looked with her under-used eyes.

She found nothing there, just the huge door, the tiled floor and the steps leading in. Perhaps she was simply tired. Soon, her duty would be done for the day, and she could go to her modest room in the tower high above and sleep. She walked quietly back to the table and continued her meal.

* * * * *

But, something had been there. It smoothly crept from the door, across the open tiles to the narrow staircase heading down into the vast, book-filled vaults below. Moving like a patch of excited darkness, it skittered down the stairs.

Perhaps it had expected to meet some resistance along the way— a roaming Sister or two, and it was tensed and ready. It had not planned to fight and kill, but it could not be caught and detained—it would not. If fighting a Sister was required, then it will fight to incapacitate. If that was not possible, then it will fight to kill, and it was more than capable of doing just that.

Fortunately, the stone stairwell, emptying out into a pool of waiting darkness below, was not occupied.

The vaults of Hiei were vast in the extreme and forever plunged in a cave-like dark. The Sisters didn't use their eyes for much of anything, and artificial lights were not required. The thick darkness also helped to preserve the books stored there.

The intruder could also see in the dark, and the ocean of black before it meant nothing. Still, the sheer size of the place took it off guard for a moment. If it hadn't had a good starting place, it would never find what it was looking for.

It turned to the right, moving silently at speed along the floor. Even though the vault was pitch black, it could see patches of darker darkness, like shadows existing within shadows. It moved from one shadow patch to the next. It had a map clutched in its hands that it could clearly see. Following the map, it made its way into the interior one shadow at a time.

It was headed for a restricted section—a collection of books not seen by any eyes other than the Sisters for centuries. Just a little farther in, and it will be there.

Then, it happened. In a crossroad it encountered a Sister who was busy returning large books to their shelves—it came upon her suddenly, literally bumping into her and knocking a book from her hand. They stood there face to face for a moment—the Sister trying to coil it in mentality, confused, and the intruder, tensed and ready.

Then they engaged, the two of them suddenly locked at arms. The Sister tried to open her mouth and wail an aural and mental alarm. The Sisters were thought to be massively strong—where this supposed strength came from was not known. It was possibly an adaptation of the Gift of Strength turned on permanently. The attacker, though, was strong, too, and had the advantage of surprise for a Sister never expected to be forced to physically subdue an opponent.

They grappled for a moment; then, with a devastating blow, the attacker flattened the Sister to the ground, their battle having lasted little more than a second. Dragging the unconscious Sister out of the way, it continued. It must hurry. It could not be captured. Being captured meant pain, death or worse—prolonged torment.

Moving on, it finally found the section it was looking for: a row of shelves about twenty feet high stocked with a multitude of books. It set to work, its eyes quickly scanning. It bounded up the shelves, one after the other, desperately searching, knocking the unwanted books aside as it did.

A few minutes later, it found what it wanted—a large tome bound with a blue cover sitting on the uppermost shelf. It pulled the ancient book down and looked at it for a second, thick and old, pages yellowed, the blue leather cover smelling of age.

This had better be worth it, it thought. It double checked to make sure this was the correct book; then, it began making its way back to the stairs.

The Sisters were now aroused. They entered the vault in force. They were shrieking, a horrible drone that filled its ears and caused it fear. It even thought it saw the Sisters growing in size as they filtered in, becoming monstrous in their anger as they searched.

Calm, be calm. It waited for a clear moment, and then made a break for it.

It wound its way through the maze of corridors and then up the stairs, passing a slew of enraged Sisters as it went.

Again, they appeared to be having issues detecting it. Such an advantage will not last and wouldn't be protection for much longer. They turned to pursue, still clearly having no idea what it was they were up against. No matter, for soon they would have it—there was no way out of Hiei.

It moved at speed across the open floor of the library. Behind, it heard the shrieking mass of giant-sized Sisters pursuing. It could feel the pincers of TK trying to grab hold of it, but slipping off.

It reached the door, but it was TK'ed shut and proofed against Waft. The Sisters might have issues seeing it, but they could hold the door shut without hope of it being opened. And, eventually, they would have it cornered; then, it would die.

Seeing one chance, it scaled the wall to a tiny window about a hundred feet off the ground, barely larger than the width of the book it was carrying. Breaking out the glass, it stuffed the book through and then it shoved itself in, its body compressing down to allow itself to squeeze through.

And it was through to the dreary night outside.

When the Sisters threw open the door, it was gone, having vanished into the night, leaving no trace.

4—Strange Doings

As the winter wound down and Sarah and Phillip's annual return loomed larger and larger, Sam was mysteriously absent for a few days. Normally, at the end of winter, Sam was loathe to be away, so her absence was markedly strange. Kay waited for her in the Grove, and she'd not shown. He'd lie awake at night waiting for her to appear—no trace. He went to their chapel several times and tried to communicate. He never got Sam to answer, though, he did get something else on one occasion.

He heard a whisper that he strained to hear: *"Hi, ya', Kay. Where's your girlfriend? She's being bad."*

"Who is this?" Kay asked.

He heard a small laugh in response. *"Who do you think?"*

Unlike Sam's voice, which always appeared to come from the statute of Countess Fercandia, the whisper sounded like it came from behind him. He turned and thought he saw something moving in the dark near the corner. He drew his CARG shining in the dark.

Nothing was there, thankfully.

He heard nothing more in the chapel, but the whisper unsettled him. He avoided the chapel after that.

He began to wonder if he'd angered her somehow, or that she'd found someone else. She had been acting awfully strange.

Couldn't be. Not Sam.

* * * * *

He lay there in bed dead tired, though his mind was racing. His heart was pounding, close to hyper-ventilating.

Where was Sam?

Where was Sam?

Worry and dread. Uncertainty.

Things became odd around him, and he had no idea if he was awake or partially buried in an uncomfortable dream. The starlight coming into his room was very bright and kept him from sleeping. Lots of light was coming from the distant ruin of Castle Durst, too. He wanted it dark so that he could quiet his thoughts.

As he lay in bed, he became aware of somebody in the room with him. There was a figure in the corner near the window staring at him, giggling.

"Sam?"

In silhouette, the figure raised a flask to its mouth and tossed back a large drink. It raised a finger to its lips. "Shhhhh ..." It came forward. He saw a slender female form approach the bed, staggering a bit, as if drunk.

It didn't look like Sam. She must have transformed herself again. "Where've you been?" he asked, his voice hazy with sleep. She began singing a soft song, filling his head with it. His limbs grew heavy, and he couldn't move. He could only lay there.

She was wearing a costume or beaded dress. She was also wearing a backpack or some sort of lumpy device on her back that made her stoop a bit. She stripped off the dress and let it fall to the floor, though she left her backpack on. Still singing her song, she pulled the covers and got on top of him. She was lathered in some sort of warm oil. Her body was slick with it. She was also wearing a brassy or golden mask that covered the upper half of her face. This was the oddest thing into which she'd ever changed herself.

"Just want a taste ..." she whispered.

Before he knew what was happening, he was inside her, feeling the roiling heat of her body and rolls of her muscles tightening. Sitting up she rode up and down, her slick body glistening. She grunted in an unfamiliar voice. As she came to a peak, she fell forward putting her slick arms around him, kissing his neck.

Kay became aware of something—a wretched odor, an overpowering reek.

What was that? He tried to recoil but couldn't move. Her song filled his head. Wait, was it a song? Was it Anuie? It didn't seem to be

Anuie. It seemed to be some kind of scream perhaps.

Yes. It was a scream.

He felt her teeth probe the soft skin of his neck, then she latched onto a tiny piece and bit down, tearing it off.

She sat back up and stuck her tongue out, the little bit of skin she'd bitten off resting on the tip. Then she put her tongue back into her mouth and swallowed. "*Mmmm.*"

She got off him and picked her dress up, staggering away. "*I'll be watching you. You'll see me again soon,*" she whispered as she glided away and was gone in a greenish flash.

His neck was stinging and, after a few minutes, her song left his head, and he could move again. He got up and went into the bathroom to run some water on it. When he turned the lights on, he was horrified.

He was covered with sticky-looking blood.

But wait; he blinked, and a moment later, it was gone. He must have been seeing things. He checked himself, and there was nothing there. He checked his bed, and it was clean as normal. The whole landscape of his bedroom took on a very unreal sort of quality. He stumbled back to bed and collapsed.

He woke in the morning, his neck fine and unblemished. He wondered if he'd dreamed the whole thing.

* * * * *

On the third day of Sam's long absence, Kay was in his reading room checking his Holo-mail, and, not unexpectedly, he had a lot of the usual correspondence from Sarah and Phillip. Sarah, always with an eye for lurid and sensational postings, sent him a stack that had caught her attention.

One said:

BERSERKACIDE FIEND TERRORIZES LORD CHRISTOPHER PARK

Synthnet—MERCIA. Chaos reigned as a quiet day at the park turned into a bloody spectacle as a four-armed Berserkacide maniac ran free through Christopher Park in central Lyra. Singled out in the attack was Lord Torval of Clarence and his family as they attempted to enjoy a lovely afternoon in the park. The Berserkacide was killed at length by the local militia after a brief but intense skirmish. Fortunately, Lord Clarence and his family were not injured in the attack. The militia commander had no comment.

Another curious posting read:

PARAFLY INFESTATION SPREADING THROUGHOUT KANA

Synthnet—ARDEN. The Science Ministry has posted a general warning regarding a planet-wide infestation of a large, previously unidentified species of insect being called "Parafly" by Ministry entomologists, who believe the insect is a stowaway from another world. The Science Ministry wishes it to be noted that these insects, though large and swarming, do not appear to pose an immediate threat to the public at large. Paraflies, appear similar to an ordinary dragonfly, and may easily be identified by their large size (twice that of a standard dragonfly), and a furtive buzzing sound they create. The Science Ministry advises, should a swarm of Paraflies be encountered, that they be avoided and the local Ministry chapters be informed of their presence as soon as possible. At present, standard anti-insect agents appear to have little effect upon them.

Sarah and her posts. The girl loved the lurid.

Moving on, he'd finished a few letters when, suddenly, in a blast of air, there was Lady Kilos, his correspondence scattering. She'd Wafted in, her white gown settling at her feet. Her blue hair was perfect as ever. Her blast even knocked down some of the trinkets Kay had arranged on his bookshelves.

His favorite toy since he was a small kid, the little patchwork gazelle Sam had made for him, fell to the floor.

Lady Kilos picked the gazelle up, her puffy cheeks flush with excitement. "Kay," she said ready to burst, "Do you know what I just heard?"

"What, Ki?" he said a little perturbed, and slightly worried. Her news had to be regarding Sam, and it probably wasn't good. He stood and took the gazelle from Ki's grasp. He brushed it off and put it back up on the shelf.

"I heard that Sam—our Sam—was seen having lunch the other day with … another man!" She panted, having a hard time catching her breath.

"Who told you such a silly thing?" he asked trying to sound disinterested, but the heavy hand of worry was building up inside him, fast.

"I don't reveal my sources—not to you or anybody else. But, there's no doubt about it. Sam was caught red handed— lunching. What are we going to do?"

"It's lunch, Ki—it's not a crime."

"Yes, but lunch … with a guy—who's not you! I thought you two were supposed to be tight. We're buddies the three of us."

"We are tight, you know that." Kay returned to his letter-writing, trying to not appear interested.

"Well, Kay?" she said. "Don't you want to know who it was?"

Kay was burning to know. "Not really," he said, trying to be coy.

Lady Kilos glared at him. "Well then, I'll be off." Kilos, practicing her Wafting skills began to Waft from the room, her wind scattering his pile of letters about a second time.

"Wait a minute, Ki. I know you're dying to tell me, so out with it. Who was it?"

As the Waft coiled up around her, she yawned and vanished.

Only ten seconds to Waft—she was way better at it than he was. His took a whole minute. He was impressed, despite himself.

Damn her and her gossip! Now, he had to know. He tore out of his reading room and combed the castle looking for her. He finally caught up with her later on the main terrace. After following her around the castle, practically begging her to tell, she appeared suitably gratified. Gossip was a powerful weapon. They got lunch and sat down in the Capricos Hall to eat it.

"Ok," Kilos said, bursting to finally tell him. "Sam was caught red handed eating lunch in Arden."

Kay chewed his food and thought a bit. "Arden?"

"Yes, Kay, Arden. Who do you know in Arden?"

Kay thought but couldn't think of anybody. Lord Lon was from Arden, but there's no way. "Will you just tell me, Ki!"

"Lord Lon, you bag!" she said yelling. "She was lunching with Lord Lon. And, of course, Lon, all suave and sophisticated, managed to spill his whole drink on her at some point during the meal."

Kay felt a wash of relief pass over him. "Lon, Ki? Are you kidding me? Lord Lon of Probert? Creation, you had me worried there for a second."

"You're not mad?"

"No, I'm not mad. Lord Lon is my friend, and he's not exactly known for his Lady-Killing ways, is he? Sam's been obsessed with machines lately, ever since the Future-Telling, and even mentioned Lon by name. She was probably discussing some technical matters with him."

"Machines?" Kilos said with a bit of distaste. "What sort of machines?"

"I don't know, and she won't say. Says she has some machines around her home that she needs help with, but I don't buy it. Since I don't really have a lot of technical knowledge, she probably went to Lon with her questions. That's all, perfectly innocent."

Kilos looked a bit deflated. "Maybe, but my sources tell me that Lon looked rather smitten. He seems to like her." She finished up her lunch. "So, are you going to have it out with her? Is there going to be a big fight?"

"No, Ki, there isn't going to be a fight. I trust Sam, and Lord Lon is my friend."

"Lord Lon doesn't know you're seeing Sam... remember?"

Damn her!

5—Lost in the Fog

The ripcar fell through the heights in a mad half-roll. The pilot surely was either dead or suicidal. As the ground approached, the ripcar leveled out, spun once or twice and set down on the flatlands, gentle as you please.

Lady Hathaline adjusted the controls and the ripcar's motor revved a bit before settling into a more sedate, idle condition. After all that wind and commotion, Hath's red hair seemed hardly out of place.

Kay's hair, on the other hand, was a mess. He ran a hand through it to salvage a bit of order and popped his hat on. He jumped out.

Four days since Sam had disappeared. Kay couldn't handle it anymore. He needed answers.

"Thanks for the ride, sis," he said. "I appreciate it." He reached into the back and got his CARG, which he saddled into place at his hip.

Typically a quiet kid, Hath simply smiled back at him. Her blue ripcar coughed a little in the warm air. Her name "HATH" was spelled out in glittery letters across the hood.

Kay looked around at the lonely landscape. "I shouldn't be too long, but I'm told that it's best to do this alone. The city of Blue Pierce isn't far to the north. Why don't you get some lunch and then come back for me later." Kay checked his timepiece. "It's ten bells; can you come back for me at twelve bells? I should be done by then. That ok with you?"

Hath nodded and held out her hand.

"Oh," Kay said. He reached into his coat and pulled out a small moneybag. "Here, use what you need."

Hath took the money and pointed at Kay's timepiece. She asked a question.

"No, thank you, I don't want anything. Go on, have some fun, but don't forget about me, right? Twelve bells."

She then grabbed the controls and hauled the rumbling ripcar into the sky, tearing off to the north, its shiny blue panels looking like a bluebottle fly as it climbed skyward.

Wow, she could pilot a ship. Sixteen years old and look what she was doing.

With Hath now miles away, Kay looked around. He was standing alone on a warm flatland, grassy and somewhat forlorn. Far away to his left was the long green line of the Great Armenelos Forest, stretching back for thousands of miles. Every so often, a high-flying vessel came down into the forest, no doubt heading for the Zenon city of Armenelos, which was at the tangled heart of the forest.

To his right were the rolling, bubbly scallops of Remnath with its gentle hills.

Dead ahead was a towering wall of churning fog like a great bag of cotton perpetually draped over the landscape. The fog rose sharply from ground level, up into the heights where it flattened out like an anvil several thousand feet up. Occasional flashes of lightning back-lit the fog in strokes of cherry red. At the very center of this morass was Lake Monama, the largest lake on Kana, going southward for a thousand miles until it ran into the southern Sea of Elder.

Somewhere on the shores of the lake was Castle Astralon, Sam's home. He was going to plunge into the fog, find the castle and talk to Sam. He needed answers.

He started walking south, into the fog. It wasn't like any fog he'd ever seen before. It had a definite boundary between clear, warm air and dank impossible murk, and the billowing clouds within the boundary rotated in a slow counter-clockwise movement. He reached the edge, took a deep breath and entered.

Immediately, day changed to a shapeless darkness. He was instantly lost. What was he thinking? How far was it to the lakeshore? He knew Sam's home was foggy, but he hadn't expected this. What had Sam told him once, that bright light hurt her eyes? That she could see much better in muted light. Those black eyes of hers were, no doubt, able to see perfectly in this soup.

His lackadaisical attitude toward planning was clear. Sarah would have carefully scouted out such a mission and would have been fully prepared. Kay, on the other hand, simply hopped into Hath's ripcar and came on down.

He turned to go back the way he came; this trip was not a good idea.

More fog. More murk. After just a few steps, he was hopelessly lost. Kay unsaddled his CARG and shined it about. Its silvery light was pinned in by the fog, creating little more than a fitful halo around its shaft. He fought the urge to panic, to lose all sense of decorum and dignity and start screaming for help.

He had to relax. This was Sam's home. She was here somewhere. Revel in her goodness.

Yes, but Sam had told him outsiders weren't welcome. She had never let him come down to the lake, had never invited him. Though this was Sam's home, it was an utterly hostile place.

He paused and knelt to the ground to collect his thoughts. He couldn't be far from the edge. It had to be near.

Calm. Be calm.

Slowly getting hold of himself, he began to hear a faint but steady flow of voices moving along the ground. It was Monamas talking to each other in Anuie and in another tongue that he didn't know. Just like Sam could speak to him in the chapel, here they used their abilities in place of technology.

He listened intently, and a pair of voices became clearer and clearer though the chatter. It was definitely Anuie.

<You forgot to pack my lunch again, bitch!>

<Call me that again, and I'll slice you in two right here and now! I'm in no mood.>

<Come on, hurry up! I want to be in the Elder city by late day! We've no money to feed our children or ourselves, or have you forgotten?>

<I'm pulling as fast as I can! You need to get these wheels fixed. They stick.>

<We don't have the money to fix the wheels, dumbass! You know I should have sold you to the arena on Hoban years ago!>

<Yes, and the first person I would have fought and killed there would have been you, slor-mouth! Now make yourself useful and get out here and help me pull!>

<I don't pull the cart, remember? You pull the cart! That's what you do, you pull the cart! Now put your back into it before I pull my finger and unleash a fart!>

The voices began laughing. They seemed to be coming from somewhere just ahead. Kay stood and moved in that direction.

Something massive appeared in the fog as a great, darker patch, conical and rumbling along the ground. It was a transport of some kind, about three stories tall and sixty feet long, craggy and hissing with steam issuing from geared engines strapped at the top. As it approached, lights mounted to its side blinked. Squinting, Kay could make out faded, once gaudy writing on the side of the transport:

The Amazing Clatera & Wife—Fortune-teller Extraordinaire: Fates Thwarted, Mysteries De-Mystified and Pleasures Explored.

The transport had eight spindly wheels, each at least twelve feet in diameter, spinning on delicate axels. Harnessed at the front of the transport by a single heavy chain and dwarfed by the transport's mass was a barefoot Monama woman. She was leaning in the harness, bending over, apparently pulling the massive transport all by herself across the ground. She dug in and set herself with each step.

Kay watched the odd procession go by; then, he called, "Hello!" with his hand cupped against his mouth.

<What was that?>

<Who's out there?>

The woman stopped pulling and stepped out of the chain where it fell to the ground with a heavy clink. She went to the transport and drew out a massive, spiked club from a sheath, wielding it with one hand. She sniffed the air and instantly locked on to Kay.

<It's a bloody Elder!> she said.

<What's an Elder doing in here? Sniff again! Your nose is as wrong and used up as your twat!>

She took a deep breath. *<Smells like an Elder to me. Smells like a rich one, too. It's a male, he's recently bathed, and he's wearing scented oils of some sort. Huzzah! I smell silver on him!>*

<He's bathed? He's got Silver? He can't be a damn Calvert then; they rarely bathe, and they never have money. Maybe he's from Zenon or Remnath. Maybe we've lucked onto our first customer of the day! What in the name of the gods are you doing? Get yourself prettied up in case he wants to screw! I'm coming down!>

The woman sighed. *<I'm too tired to screw! I've been pulling this cart for hours!>*

<You pull the cart. You screw the customers, while I bring you the customers, got it?> She put her club back in its place and disappeared around the back of the transport.

"I say!" Kay called out. "Can you help me, please?"

"Are you lost?" came a sly voice heavy with an Anuie accent from behind. Kay turned.

Standing behind him was a Monama male wearing a black suit and waistcoat with baggy white sleeves. Like Sam, he was skinny with a bursting head of black hair; however, he was thinner than Sam, much shorter and daintier. His eyes were much smaller than Sam's, and he lacked the long feathery lashes that he'd come to associate with Monamas. He smiled. "We don't see many Elders here in the fog."

Kay held his glowing CARG up. "Well met, sir. Well met. I am Lord Kabyl of Blanchefort. I am on my way to Castle Astralon."

The Monama man gave a short snicker. "That a fact? On foot? You understand it's about ninety miles that way?" He pointed with his right hand, his fingernails long and black. "Did you hear that, Mitz? He said he's going to Castle Astralon."

The woman who had been pulling the transport appeared over Kay's right shoulder. She was now wearing a slinky black dress showing off a generous portion of her pale legs and a pair of towering pumps. She smelled of Monama perfume and sweat. Like the man, she seemed smaller and less-full than Sam, a lesser version of her. "I wouldn't expect a warm welcome if I were you. They don't like unannounced visitors," she said.

"No," the man agreed. "Astralons don't like anybody."

The two Monamas stood very close to him, invading his personal space. Kay felt ill at ease. "Would you care to introduce yourselves, please?"

"Certainly. I am the Amazing Clatera, and this is my assistant Mitzilaran. Would you care to have your fortune told? As you are lost in the fog ninety miles from your rather prickly destination, you could probably use a Future-Telling."

"Thank you, no. If I may, what tribe are you from?"

The man smiled. "Cardinal, actually. We like the Elders in Cardinal. You're lucky. If we'd been Minzers or Zerbs, we probably wouldn't have stopped."

"Mitz" walked around and began toying with the fabric of his shirt in the region of his bellybutton. "Perhaps you would be interested in something more ... exotic, good sir? I can be anything you want me to be."

Kay wanted away. He began a Waft. Slowly, the twisting column of air began swirling around him. "Thank you, no," he said.

Clatera laughed and put his hand on Kay's shoulder. His Waft sputtered and died. Kay knew a Monama's touch had the odd effect of disrupting his Gifts, just like Snugs disrupted Sam's ability to perform many of her skills. Whenever Sam touched him, his Gifts went chaotic and uncontrollable. She thought it was very funny.

Apparently this Clatera character knew that, too. "You wouldn't be trying to disappear on us, would you? Come now, we mean you no harm. We're simply two traveling merchants from Cardinal trying to get by."

"And you with all that silver," Mitz said. "Certainly there's some service we could offer to earn a few pieces of it."

Kay lifted his CARG and pushed Clatera's hand away. He tried to go on the offensive. "Why were you pulling that transport?"

They both looked back at the hulking shape in the fog. "Because Mitz needs the exercise," Clatera said.

Mitz's feet appeared to be hurting in her high-heeled shoes. She lifted her leg and rotated her foot. "Our steam engine broke. Been like that for awhile."

Kay looked at the massive transport and had a thought. "Well then, sure, I'll buy a service or two. Do you take Blanchefort haders?"

"Haders? I've never seen a hader before," Clatera said. "I'm used to seeing solaris and rubicons and sesterces. Can we exchange them for solaris in the towns?"

"Haders are Vith currency."

"Vith?" Clatera said with a bit of shock. "My, you're far from home, that quaint freezing cold place you come from."

"Yes, and I'll have you know haders enjoy a very favorable rate of exchange."

Clatera made a few fists and spoke to Mitz in rapid Anuie. <*The gods are smiling, Mitz. I'll speak his fortune, predict his death and then take his money. We were due a bit of good luck.*> He switched back to common Elder. "Then, shall we step inside where we can sit?"

Kay laughed. "I don't plan on dying, sir. And, I do not wish a Future-Telling. I simply have a few questions I wish answered that have nothing to do with the future."

Clatera was astonished. "You speak our language?"

Kay responded in Anuie, albeit with a bad accent. *"I do."*

He shook his mane of black hair. "An Elder in the fog who speaks Anuie. This is, in fact, a rare event. Who taught you our language?"

"My *Cerri-Tela*."

Again, Clatera was astonished. "Really? Your *Cerri-Tela* taught you? And who, pray, might that be?"

"A princess of Castle Astralon."

Mitz approached and gave him a good long sniff. "I do smell a Monama woman on him. They've been having a lot of sex. She's even transformed for him."

"Goodness, this Monama woman must just love you to death. I can only imagine what she's changed herself into for you. You're just full of surprises, Lord Kabyl of Blanchefort. So, shall we go inside where you may ask your questions."

They strode through the fog and approached the transport. It was big and heavy-looking. It hissed and sputtered with a regular beat. The fact that Mitz could pull it all by herself said something about

Monama strength. "Those are the small secondary motors running, for the lights and accessories. The large drive motor is dead as a knocker," Clatera said. A door opened, and Kay stepped inside.

The main area of the transport was hollowed out, granting a very open sort of feel. It looked like a little terraced cafe with tables arraigned on the open main floor centered around a babbling fountain. At the far end was a curtained stage. Above was a terrace lined with a number of doors. As they walked in, Mitz removed her shoes.

"Put those back on!" Clatera scolded her in Anuie. *"They make your legs look better."*

"I don't think he wants to screw; besides, my feet hurt. And remember, he can understand us."

Clatera gestured. "Seems we're a little low on customers today; just grab a seat. On good days in a bustling Zenon town, we have this place full. Those can be tough days for Mitz, what with pulling the cart, serving the drinks and screwing the customers—she's got much on her plate."

"Seems to me she's doing everything. What do you do, sir?"

"I get the customers, and I predict the future. That's the hard job. Sometimes we bring some of our children, and they put on little shows, dancing and changing their form."

Kay found a table near the fountain and sat. Clatera pulled a chair opposite him. "Would you like something to drink? Elder coffee perhaps?"

"That's fine, thanks," Kay replied. Mitz disappeared through a beaded archway.

Clatera rapped his long fingernails on the metal surface of the table. "So, what sort of questions do you have for me? It's your silver."

Kay cleared his throat. "My *Cerri-Tela* is a very secretive person. There are many things she keeps to herself. She cries in her sleep. She looks over her shoulder and minds what she says. Why?"

Clatera considered his answer. "First, let me ask you something. How did this happen? An Elder and a Monama? *Arin-Dan, Cerri-Tela.* How?"

"She says she's dreamed of me since she was a little girl. As she's several years older than I am, I assume she was seeing me before I was born."

"Possible. All Monamas dream of Elders at some point or

another. Did she tell you that? We find you very beautiful. Your interesting hair, your jewel-like eyes, it's all very appealing for us. I'm certain your lady is quite fascinated with your belly-button, isn't she?"

"She is."

"Do you find us attractive as well? We don't come in neat colors like you do."

"Obviously. I think she's beautiful."

"Transformed, or in her natural state?"

"I have never asked her to change her shape, though she herself is rather keen on it. I fancy her as she is. She's a little different from you and your wife."

"How so?"

Mitz returned through the beads with a tray containing several brass cups and a pot of steaming coffee.

She poured three cups and passed them out. She finally seated herself and took her cup.

"*Bende, Hosfra,*" Kay said, thanking her and adding a respectful lady's name.

"*Bende-bende,*" she replied in response, lifting her cup. As with Sam, speaking Anuie seemed to put her at ease a bit. She drank her coffee down.

Kay studied her as she drank.

"You were saying," Clatera said, "that we are different from your Monama woman. In what way?"

"She's bigger than you both are, a lot bigger. Her eyes are very different. They're much larger, longer lashes."

Clatera and Mitz looked at each other. "Does she have little dashes on her lips, sort of like little notches?" Clatera asked.

"She does."

"Hmmm, seems your woman is an Anuian Monama. Very rare these days. Rare indeed. Most of us, present company included, are Conox. We're not as big and strong and fast as the Anuians, but we're still a lot stronger and faster than you are."

"Clatera!" Mitz scolded. "You needn't be rude. Sir, the Anuians don't exist much anymore. They were killed off, hunted down ages ago and wiped out; though, occasionally, Anuians pop up in Conox bloodlines. Doesn't happen much, but still."

Kay considered Mitz's words. "Hunted down by whom?"

Clatera took a drink and changed the subject. "So, yes, as I was saying, dreaming of Elders is not uncommon amongst our people; however, nothing good usually comes out of it. It's best to keep it a dream and nothing more, and that's normally what we do. There is a ritual we have where we try to purge ourselves of our Elder dreams. I had my *Cerri-Tela*, and I planted my flower and never met her."

"Is Lady Mitzilaran not your *Cerri-Tela*?"

"Mitz is my wife, and I love her very much. She is not, however, my *Cerri-Tela*, and I am not her *Arin-Dan*."

"I don't understand."

Clatera's expression drifted into nostalgia for a moment, and then returned. "Of course you don't. Let me make it plain. Your lady, by doing what she's done, by not planting her flower and by coming out of the fog, is risking not only her life but yours as well."

"How so?"

"Those of us who leave the safety of our little place here tend to become Berserkacides."

Berserkacides. Ah, Kay thought, now we're getting somewhere. "How? Why? Is it a reaction? An infection of some sort that creates a Berserkacide?"

Clatera considered his answer. "You don't have enough silver for me to answer that. Suffice to say there are certain truths to the world, and you're better off not knowing what they are. Ignorance is bliss, right? Isn't that what they say?"

Mitz spoke up. "Anyone of us, at anytime, can become a Berserkacide. Your lady, in seeking you out, has almost guaranteed that she will become a Berserkacide at some point."

"You talk too much, Mitz," Clatera scolded.

"So, you're saying as we sit here that the two of you could suddenly become Berserkacides?" Kay asked. "What sort of malady is that? It doesn't sound real."

"Oh, it's real," Clatera said. "and there are no guarantees. The best way to keep from becoming one is to stick to ourselves and keep our mouths shut. Makes it hard to do business though. There are some centuries that pass where not a single Berserkacide is seen, and there are others, like this one, where they are quite frequent. More and more."

"You see a red light, you best run," Mitz said, shuddering a little.

"Shhht!" Clatera scolded.

"A red light? I don't understand."

Clatera finished his coffee. "Like I said, you don't have enough silver. Next question."

"This Berserkacide business seems very odd to me. It seems to behave with a sort of intelligence behind it from what I can gather, almost like a punishment of some kind."

"Next question. We're done talking about Berserkacides."

Kay wanted to press the matter, but Clatera clearly wasn't going to budge. He would try to reintroduce the topic again later. "All right. *Olonol*. What does that mean? I don't know that word, and she won't tell me."

"It means 'machine'."

"Machine? What sort of machine? Does it carry any sort of special significance?"

"None that I can think of. It means 'machine'; that's it. You're sitting in an *olonol* right now."

Kay wouldn't let it drop. "She was pointing at the ground after a Future-Telling yelling, *Olonol! Olonol!* What did she mean?"

"Who was?"

"My *Cerri-Tela!*"

"She was probably out of her head with the Future-Telling. It happens a lot."

"You have no stories, no lore regarding machines?"

"Only that we like them and usually can't afford the more interesting ones you Elders make. Listen, Future-Tellings can get a little muddled. She probably saw some sort of interesting machine standing there in the future and was all happy about it. You'll have to ask her."

"I have, and she won't answer."

"Well, there you go. Next question."

"Wait!" Kay said. "This *Olonol* is important. Can you, perhaps, tell my future and determine if you see a machine there at some point?"

Clatera thought about it a moment. He put his cup down, leaned forward and sniffed Kay. He sat back. "I'm going to be honest with you, Elder, because I think I like you ..."

"If you like me, then quit calling me 'Elder'. My name is Lord Kabyl, or just Kay if you wish."

"All right. A future reading on you, Kay, wouldn't be safe."

"Why not?"

Mitz spoke up before Clatera could stop her. "Because you have the demon all over you."

Kay sat there a moment. "What does that mean?"

Mitz made to say something, and Clatera cut her off. "Nothing. It's just an expression we use. The future isn't with you. I'd just be making it up. I do that. In business, that's what you have to do sometimes because, occasionally, I look into the future and see nothing. I don't want to rob you. You've earned a bit of honesty."

"But, what is this 'demon' bit? I don't understand."

Mitz looked down at the table, and Clatera cleared his throat. "As I said, just a figure of speech. Pay it no mind."

Kay didn't know if he believed Clatera, but would probably get nothing more out of him with further questioning. He decided to move on and try to backtrack to the topic later.

"All right," Kay said. "What is Head Swarm?"

Clatera laughed. "Full of novel questions, aren't you, Kay? When you said you had questions, I thought you'd want to know where to grab a Monama woman to really make her squeal. All right: a choice, that's what Head Swarm is. It's a choice."

"I'd read it was a sickness."

"If you knew something unpleasant was going to happen, and you could either endure it, or place yourself into a peaceful state where you would suffer no anguish and feel no pain, wouldn't you choose the latter?"

"Not if my duty demanded I stay and endure."

"Ah," Clatera said, skeptical. "See that, Mitz? You talk like a Vith after all, sir. Talk is cheap. Sitting here safe and sound is one thing, but, I promise, when the moment you've dreaded is upon you, you'll take the easy way out every time. That's Head Swarm."

Mitz had a question. "Your *Cerri-Tela*? Has she spoken of this? Of Head Swarm?"

"No. But I've seen her do odd things and act with a considerable melancholy. I thought she was falling into Head Swarm."

Mitz shook her head. "No, if she was in Head Swarm, she wouldn't be doing anything other than sitting and staring. You could plunge a knife into her belly, and she'd hardly flinch."

"How do you roust one who is in Head Swarm out of it?"

"You don't," Clatera said. "You let them go and be at peace. They are at a dreaded moment, and you'd best leave them to it."

"I won't let that happen to her."

"What can you possibly offer that Head Swarm cannot?" Clatera wanted to know.

"So that's the whole of it?" Kay said. "You just give up when things look bad, do you? Is that a Monama-thing? My *Cerri-Tela* is strong and fast. If something terrible has come upon her, why doesn't she stand and fight?"

"Some things cannot be fought," Mitz said. "Some truths cannot be avoided, and some evils cannot be defeated. The invisible world is all around you, and it is not kind."

Kay continued. "Sam often says that you, as a people, were evil once and that the gods are punishing you, even today."

Clatera laughed. "That's right. We were predators long ago, savage and proud. And the gods won't let us forget it."

They sat by the fountain in silence for a few minutes, both Clatera and Mitz appearing quite sad. Clatera was uninterested in talking any further. "I think we're finished here, Kay. Five silver pieces sounds fair to me."

Kay stared at his cup. "What is it that hovers over you? You said there are truths to the world that I'm not aware of, so what are they? I'm listening. What are you so afraid of?"

Clatera stood up. "I said we're done. The exit is that way." He pointed.

"I am here for my *Cerri-Tela*. I want to understand. Whatever it is, I want to face it with her."

"Ah," Clatera said. "You want to face 'It', whatever 'It' is, do you? You Vith. Of all tribes on Kana, you always have your monsters to fight, don't you? Your battles to win. Have you ever considered, Vith, that we are the monsters, that we are the enemy? I'm no Anuian like your woman, yet I could still kill you right now and it would be so easy. What could you do to stop me?"

Kay stood. "Were you to do that, you'd face my CARG."

"I'd be around it in a moment, and at your throat."

"Perhaps and perhaps not. In any event, at least I'd face my death like a man. I wouldn't stick my head in the sand and wait for the end to come like a scared rabbit." He reached into his coat and pulled out his remaining moneybag. "Here's your money, five haders and more. Much more." He set it down and made to walk away. "Thank you for not answering most of my questions."

"Wait!" Mitz said. "Please, don't go!"

"Let him go, Mitz. He needs to go and be away from here, and perhaps he'll forget all about this, and us. It's for the best."

"But, his *Cerri-Tela?*"

"She should not have come out of the fog. She is doomed, and so is he!"

"But, she did, and here he is." Mitz scooted around the table and stopped Kay. "Please, sir, come and sit."

She seated Kay and pulled up a chair next to him, holding his hand. She looked at his face, taking in his features. "Oh, you Elders are so beautiful. Such amazing colors." She reached out and touched his purple hair. "I can imagine what your *Cerri-Tela* feels when you hold her in your arms and look at her with those eyes. She came out of the fog, testing fate, for you. Tell me, when you say that word, *Cerri-Tela*, what emotions does it make you feel?"

"Love, devotion. Heartache, confusion, pain ... sadness."

She smiled. "You have chosen to give your heart to a Monama. And with that comes a great deal of peril, but you must know that by now."

"Why? What peril? Why does she cry? Why does she look over her shoulder? What is it that I don't know?"

Clatera responded. "You can't answer those questions, Mitz, and you know it. You'll condemn him to death and us into Berserkacides."

Mitz was defiant. "We're doomed anyway, whether we hide in the fog or not. They'll come for us sooner or later." She squeezed Kay's hand. "I remember the Elder boy I dreamed of when I was a girl. Somewhere in Zenon, I think, not too far away. I mean, I am devoted to my husband, but I sometimes wonder what might have happened had I come out."

"Mitz..."

"There are things he needs to know, Clatera! And he will know. I do this not just for him, but for her, too; for that Monama girl who came out of the fog." Mitz turned to Kay. "There are eyes on us, all the time. We call them Demons—I don't know what else to call them. And they take us and hurt us and make us do things we don't want to do. As my husband said, the gods are punishing us. When they come for us, we fall into Head Swarm to make our suffering less. You asked how to defeat Head Swarm. The only way to do it is to make the here and now, the real world with all its troubles, more attractive then the serene space of her own mind. If you are her *Arin-Dan,* then make her remember that, and she will return."

Mitz continued. "Now, tell me, she has insisted you keep your relationship a secret, am I correct?"

"Yes."

"And she's never told you why? Why the secrecy?"

"No. Again, just one of the many secrets she has."

Mitz leaned down and picked a white flower from a nearby plant stand. She held it up. It looked like a daisy with a black button in the center. Kay recognized it from the odd letter he received, only instead of being dried, this one was fresh and alive.

"This is *Zoznol-Gera.* You call it White Emilia. It's a symbolic flower to us, and we use them in our jars—just like the one your woman was no doubt born in. There might come a day when your Monama girl presents you with a necklace of White Emilia. If you take it, if you let her put it on your neck, you will be at Trial," Mitz said.

"What does that mean?"

Something stirred from above. A door in the upper terrace slammed. Clatera and Mitz looked at each other. They appeared terrified. "We've said too much, more than any Monama should," Clatera admitted.

Kay looked up at the terrace and saw nothing. "What? What is it?"

"I'm sorry! I'm sorry!" Mitz said "Show her! Show her the White Emilia, and she will have to tell you. I'm sorry!" She Blinked away.

Clatera backed away from the table and pointed. "The edge of the fog isn't far in that direction. Go. We've said too much. Go, keep your silver. Just go!" he said. He then Blinked away leaving Kay alone at the table.

Slowly, Kay stood and lifted his moneybag into the air. "Here, use this to repair your transport and to buy something nice for your wife. She deserves it." He set it back down on the table.

Kay made to exit the transport. "Thank you, once again, and be well. I'll not forget the pair of you." He marked his bearings and plunged into the fog. After a bit of stumbling, he emerged into the sunlight. Sometime later, Hath plunged down from the clouds in her rumbling ripcar and picked Kay up.

The ripcar screaming into the heavens, Hath asked him a

question.

"Not really," Kay said looking down at the flickering wall of fog. "I didn't learn much of anything."

* * * * *

Two nights later, as Kay lay in bed, his thoughts were a carousel of motion and activity. He thought of Sam, and machines, and secret Trials. He thought of Lord Lon of all people, his friend since childhood. Was the dumpy and unassuming Lon suddenly a rival for Sam's attention? A bitter bloom of jealousy and a general feeling of dread began to fill him up. With Sam not being around and his not being able to confront her and know the truth, he felt even worse.

Eventually, he drifted off to a shallow, unfulfilling sleep.

He woke up some time later and there, wrapped around him, was a sleeping Sam, nude as usual. He thought to wake and confront her.

Why do you keep looking over your shoulder?

What are the Trials?

What are you so afraid of?

Tell me, *Cerri-Tela*. Tell me.

And, he wanted to know about this "lunch" she'd been caught having with Lon and thoroughly interrogate her, but he decided to wait until morning.

She seemed so peaceful, and he was just glad that she was back.

6—And the Dead Held Hands

With the morning came the inevitable slew of questions. Sam, as usual, was evasive and didn't answer.

This time, Kay was not going to be denied. He fetched his dried White Emilia flower, approached Sam, and held it up. "Tell me about the Trials, Sam."

She looked at the flower and took it from him. She was devastated. Sam stood there holding the flower for a long time.

Finally: "The cathedral," she whispered into his ear as she removed Snugs and vanished.

Kay dressed and went down to Cathomere's Cathedral. Inside the twilight interior, Sam was sitting near the front. She had on her goggles and was admiring the statue. The rector was standing near her, asking that she remove her goggles.

"Good sir," Kay said. "Will you give us this space?"

"I've a sermon to prepare," he said.

"I really don't care. Please leave us. We shan't be long," Kay said with a tone of finality as the rector stomped away.

Kay seated himself next to Sam. She sat there small and rather deflated in her gown. She stared at the floor. "I so love this place," she quietly said. "I'm going to miss it."

"Are you going someplace, Sam?"

Sam took a deep breath. "You have shown me the White Emilia, I am therefore compelled to tell you of the Trials. When a Monama girl gives her heart publically, and her Love is known to all, she must put her Love to Trial. This is what the gods demand." Sam spoke so softly, Kay had difficulty hearing her.

"A test of some sort? A contest?"

Sam looked utterly defeated. "Yes, and I'm not referring to a mere foot face, or a wrestling match." She wept. Her voice was down to a whisper. "Just what sort of contest do you think I'm talking about, Kay? Don't make me say it, please."

The silence of the cathedral around them was profound. Kay shuffled. "Are you going to have to try and kill me Sam?"

She removed her goggles, her black eyes heavy with tears. "That's right," she said, her voice lost in the vastness around them. "That's right." Sam sat there, contemplative and bitter. "That's why I've wanted you advancing your Gifts, so that you'd be more ready. I thought ..."

"You thought I'd stand a better chance of surviving?"

"Yes, of course." She hesitated and was desperate. "I won't give you any trouble, Kay. I swear. Just tell me to go away, and I won't be a bother."

Kay put his arms around her and she pulled away. "Why would I do that, Sam?"

" Kay, do you have any doubt that, if I wished, I could kill you? Do you?"

"I'm strong, too. I'm fast."

She savored his face and took it into her hands. "Yes, yes you are, Kay, but, in all honesty, if I were to come at you, as in the Trials, you wouldn't last long. That's just the reality of it, and so I'm asking you to tell me to leave and never return. Be done with me."

Sam put her face into her hands and started sobbing. Kay put his arm around her, feeling her body convulsing with her crying.

There she was, her arms skinny and wiry, yet impossibly strong. There were her slender hands ended with a set of deadly claws.

An odd thing happened. Sam had just admitted that she, one day, might have to try and kill him, and given her incredible strength, her wind-like speed and her gut-rending claws, she was easily capable of doing so.

He should have been terrified. He should be fleeing from her side and calling out the castle guard, but Kay did none of those things.

Kay was the son of a Vith Household, but, up to this point in his short life, he had never felt much like a Vith lord. Vith were proud and strong. Vith were fearless and eager to meet any challenge. Kay, so far, had been an aloof, castle-bound vagabond who couldn't fly, couldn't manage League Society and couldn't Sight. He was a talentless, purple and green oddity.

But, being with Sam had taught him several things about himself, that he was much more capable than even he had given himself credit for. He had allowed himself to fall in love with a Monama girl, looking past all of their strangeness and social stigmas. He had embraced her ways and tried to understand them, even picking up the basics and a decent vocabulary of Sam's language, which wasn't easy by any means. He created his own CARG and built a statue of his mother. He did these things all on his own.

And now, here was Sam admitting that she would be compelled to attempt his murder. He didn't feel a hint of fear. He wasn't shocked either. He drew from an unexpected well-spring of courage he didn't know he had, just like his father before him facing his evil Black Hat mother alone for the first time and just like his little sister Hathaline fearlessly flying her ripcar.

Just like a Vith.

Sam stared at him, holding her goggles, the fear and despair clear in her large black eyes.

"There's a saying we have, Sam. They say the Vith feel no cold and feel no fear, either, because our ancestors sit in the gallery of the dead and hold hands, lending the living their power. It's through the living that the memory of the dead is passed on, and, so, they help us when we are worthy of help, and they take our fear from us. You have just told me you shall have to try and kill me someday. If you expected me to be frightened, I'm not frightened, Sam. If you thought I'd be shocked, I'm not really shocked either. I am Vith—I might not act like it most of the time, but I am. We have faced many perils through the ages, and we have endured. As my father did before me, somehow, someway, I will discover a way to survive. The Dead have held their hands for me, and I am not afraid."

Sam sat there, open-mouth shocked. She wiped her eyes and put her arms around him. "And, you still wish me at your side? How many Elder men have to worry about such things?"

"I'm not other Elder men. My family isn't destined to walk the same trodden path as everybody else. Look at my father; he had to stare into the eyes of death to court my mother. Also, my grandmother was a deadly duelist, and my great grandmother was a

Bloodstein witch. And there's more, many more going back into antiquity. Had I selected to court some tea-drinking lady from Zenon, I'd surely be letting a lot of dead ancestors down. Maybe, in such a case, they wouldn't have held hands for me. There is a challenge to be faced, and I will face it when the time is right."

Sam laughed a little. "Kay! Kay! I've underestimated you then. How could I? Shame on me. I should have told you long ago and anticipated that you'd take it in stride. You are such a remarkable young man. It's fortunate for me that I lost my heart to a Vith Lord."

"Couldn't you have just consulted the future to see what I would have said?"

"Things like this can go many ways, Kay—there are many futures. Besides, as we are sitting in here, I don't think I could see this conversation anyway—blacked out. This cathedral truly is a place of wonder."

"So, you've revealed one secret; what about the other ones? Am I ready to hear those as well? Have I not earned your trust?"

Sam darkened a little. "Kay, if I have other secrets, and I'm not saying I do—I keep them because there are things all around us that you don't understand. I don't understand them either; please, I'm not trying to be condescending. There are things that are beyond me, Kay, things that I'm afraid of—things that I have no control over and nether do you. You might feel no fear, but I do. I'm afraid of many things, and I don't want to burden you with my fears that are mostly silly anyway. My people have a lot of primitive beliefs, and none that have any place out here in the world."

They stood and made to exit the cathedral, Sam holding onto Kay as they walked. She clung to him.

"I don't know if I buy all that, Sam. There is something that not only you but other Monamas shrink from, something that makes you hold your tongue and look over your shoulder. I'd like you to tell me what it is."

"I will make this pact with you, Kay. I have often spoken of you as being great in the future, and I'm ashamed for saying that. You are great now, and I love you so. Study your Gifts—with heart and effort this time, for you now know what's at stake. Develop them, and, when I'm satisfied, I'll tell you all my silly beliefs. It won't be long, I promise. Can you live with that?"

"Do I have a choice?"

Sam didn't answer. As they exited the cathedral, she quickly reverted to darting eyes and glances over her shoulder.

And, after lunch, she was gone again, vanished to who knows where.

7—The Invisible World

L ord Davage of Blanchefort's study was in the northern wing of the castle near the large Palantine Courtyard. It was a spacious, multi-storied edifice adjacent to mother's study, which was of a similar size and configuration. As Lord Davage was usually away in his starcraft, the *New Faith*, the study was normally locked up.

"Well, Kay," Davage said, "this is a surprise. You've never taken an assertive interest in your Gifts before. I'm very pleased."

Davage sat behind his ancient desk, going over any number of forms and obligations of the House that backed up while he was away. Mother was sitting in her favorite chair next to the desk. She was wearing a vermillion gown of fine fabric. She held a steaming coffee cup.

"What's brought this on, Kay?" she asked.

"I believe it's time I took an interest in such things, Mother. I'm not a child anymore."

"Well, fine then. Well done!" Mother said.

Davage set his papers aside and smiled. He was in his usual Fleet uniform with its embroidered collar and black sash. His hair, aside from its blue color, was near identical to Kay's and was pulled into a tail. "Indeed. Well, let's to it, then. This is most convenient, as there is a ledger I need up on the third balcony." He pointed. High above the floor of the study was a third-story balcony lined with shelves and books. A large portrait of mother was also up there, framed and lit up. "Can you get it for me? I wish to observe your technique."

Davage and Sygillis watched with interest as Kay stood and

centered himself. After about a minute, he appeared on the balcony with a crash of wind. He looked around and pulled a ledger off one of the shelves. "Not this one?" he asked, showing it to Davage.

"That's the very one, in fact," Davage said. Kay straightened and again began the long, unwieldy process of Wafting, eventually appearing with the usual fuss of wind and scattering papers. He handed Davage the book.

"How was that?"

Davage and Sygillis looked at each other. "Well, Kay," he said. "Perhaps you ..."

"What your father is trying to say, Kay, is your form is appallingly bad," Mother said. "I don't mean to be harsh or critical, but that was the worst Waft I've ever seen. Even worse than that Shocktyte Duchess Torrijayne of Oyln. Your sister is much faster and much more accomplished at this stage."

Kay felt a little embarrassed. "What did I do wrong, Mother?"

Davage answered. "Well, 'wrong' isn't really the correct word, Kay. You did everything required to Waft; however, you took a number of pedestrian steps to accomplish the act. First, you stood and centered yourself which isn't required, you waited until the wind started blowing before you really put an effort into it, and then you half-Wafted at the end there, further delaying your appearance. All you need to work on is your form, and eliminate some of your odd habits."

Kay seated himself. "Could you show me, Father?"

"Certainly, Syg, let's have a race to the top and back and show Kay how it's done."

Mother took a sip from her coffee cup and set it aside. "Oh, you'll beat me, Dav, but fine. I'm ready." A moment later they blasted away and promptly appeared at the top. With another blast they reappeared where they were, with Davage appearing a moment before Sygillis. The whole thing didn't take more than a second.

"Did you see that, Kay?" Mother asked. "Did you see how fast your father is?"

"He didn't arrive more than a hair before you did, Mother."

"That 'hair' makes all the difference, Kay. That little bit can be the deciding factor between life and death, should things come to that."

"Did you see how we didn't make a big production of performing the Waft?" Davage asked. "With minimal preparation, we quickly Wafted to the top and back down. Less is certainly more in this case. That's the key. Don't think about it as much. Wind and noise, Kay, is a byproduct of the Waft, not a required component of it."

Mother picked her coffee cup back up. "You just have to practice, Kay. We know you have it in you to be a fine Wafter."

"Is there anything you can do you help me along in the process?"

Davage thought for a moment. "Well, I could punch you in the nose. Pain, it seems, helps the Waft along—why I don't know. Your grandfather used to put me and your Aunt Pardock to the cane as we practiced our Waft, and it did yield results. However, I am not going to resort to such draconian measures. Just practice hard, try from a seated position even though it's counter-intuitive, and, in time, you'll improve. Work with your sister and don't hesitate to ask her questions."

Kay seated himself and tried to absorb what he'd seen. "What about the Sight? The Stertors said I don't have the Sight."

Davage's ears pricked up. "I'm convinced the Stertors are incorrect."

"Does pain enhance one's use of the Sight as well?"

"No."

Kay blurted out a question he had. "Father, could there be invisible things all around us, even as we speak? I don't mean micro-organisms and such, but hidden sentient beings?"

"Hidden sentient beings? What brings this question?"

"Sam. I think Sam believes that something watches her all the time. She refuses to say, but that's what I have come to believe. Other Monamas that I've spoken to imply the same thing. They speak of Demons and being punished by the gods."

Davage and Sygillis looked at each other. "Countess Hortensia of Monama never mentioned anything about 'invisible creatures'," Sygillis said.

"No," Davage said. "But, there was always an air of sadness about her and a certain 'rehearsed' quality about the things she said. The Sight, Kay, is a bewildering thing. I see all sorts of things all the time, and this castle has its share of ghosts. So, to answer your question, yes, I do see things here in the castle all the time." Davage looked hopeful. "Are you seeing things, Kay?"

"No, Father."

"Kay, it's not probable that you don't have The Sight. Whatever the Stertors say or do not say, it's not relevant. It's passed down. I have it, your grandfather and great-grandfather had it; therefore, you should as well. Your cousins have it, and your sister and little brother have it."

"I know, and I've tried, and Sam insists I have it. But, I've never seen anything."

"Kay, close your eyes, please."

He sat back and closed his eyes, seeing the reddish interior of his closed eyelids.

"All right," came his father's voice. "I'm now holding up an object. I'd like you to tell me what it is, please, and no peeking. Just relax. Be at ease."

Kay took a deep breath and tried to get comfortable.

"The Sight, of all Gifts, is an outward Gift. Let it flow out of you. Be unbound. See what there is to see."

"No peeking, Kay," came his mother's cheerful voice.

"I'm not."

He tried his best and, as usual, saw nothing.

"Anything?" Davage asked.

"No, Father." Kay opened his eyes. Davage was standing behind his desk holding a small box. The disappointment on his face was clear.

"Father, I'm sorry."

He was silent for a moment. "No, no, Kay. It's all right. Truly."

The three of them were silent for a moment. "What's in the box, Father?" Kay asked, trying to change the subject.

"Oh, it's a small trinket I bought your mother on Bazz last time out."

Sygillis reached for it. "Well, Dav, may I have my present?"

"Oh, yes. Yes." He gave her the box, and she opened it, pulling out a lovely jade ring. "To match your eyes, Syg," he said.

"Dav ..." She put the ring on, and they kissed. Even after twenty years of marriage, Mother and Father still behaved as though they were newly in love.

Kay stood and felt utterly defeated. He kissed his mother on the cheek and made to leave, wanting to be away from the study.

"Kay," Davage said. "You are our son, and we love you very much. What you can and can't do is not relevant. Be the best man you can be, and that will make us happy."

    Kay nodded and left the study. He'd never felt like such a failure.

*   *   *   *   *

    He knew of a small bend in the Blanchefort Run creek flowing with black water where Lt. Kilos kept a stash of hard spirits in a flask. She said the cold water kept the spirits at just the right temperature for good drinking. He walked to the Ishtar courtyard in the Grove and stumbled off the path through the tangled growth to the fast-flowing creek. He walked up to the bank and fished around for the rope held in place with a peg.

    There it was. He fished it out and, sure enough, there was Ki's trusty flask. It felt full, too. He'd make sure to pay Lt. Kilos back later.

    He took the flask and went to Cathomere's Cathedral. The rector was gone, no doubt sitting in his small home in the Cyantown district of the village at that time of night. Kay walked into the vast open space, hearing his booted footfalls echo about. He found a cozy pew, sat down and tossed back a healthy swig from Ki's flask.

    He immediately spat it out. Wow—like drinking freezing cold acid! Spirits dripped down his chin and dribbled onto his clothes. It burned his face, too, and he wiped it off.

    Ha! Couldn't Sight, and couldn't drink either. He held his nose and forced down a coughing swig or two, gagging most of it back up. The spirits were way too strong for him. He had hoped to get roaring drunk and wallow in his self pity. He'd come into the cathedral for privacy—he wanted to be alone. He didn't even want to see Sam, should she appear.

    Fortunately, though he coughed most of the spirits back up, the little he managed to swallow was more than enough to accomplish his goal of getting drunk. Sarah liked, on occasion, to sneak booze out of the bars and drink it, but, instead of getting drunk, she usually just passed out, so it was rather a downer. Kay quickly got dizzy and felt the cavernous room around him spinning in a lazy manner. He closed his eyes and was exhausted, possibly doing a "Sarah" and quickly ready to pass out where he sat. His mind encapsulated itself into a troubled package and withdrew deep into the recesses of his own consciousness.

Though he was sitting in the pew, he felt himself moving in a sickening ball. He couldn't determine if he was standing or sitting, or flat on the ground. Actually, it made no difference. He thought he opened his eyes, but couldn't see. Everything was a sort of muddled amber color, as if he were on the bottom of a muddy lake looking up at the sun.

He thought he felt something nudge him.

There was a noise. Something spoke. *"Hey! Hey, you awake?"*

Kay felt his mouth moving. He made a noise.

"Wow, you are really drunk. Maybe you should try a nice fruity wine or watered-down ale next time. Might do you a little better. That hard stuff's pretty rad."

He wanted to know to whom he was speaking. *"Oh, you know me, buddy. Look, since you're here, I want to show you a few things. Ok? I hope you're not in a hurry or anything."*

Kay felt something soft but strong prop him up.

"Look over there. Just there, please."

Fighting the urge to get sick, Kay's vision came into a confused, amber sort of clarity. He saw a group of staff members assisting somebody from their bed and taking them out into the tower hall.

"Look a little closer," the voice said.

Kay squinted and choked back a wave of vomiting.

Wait. Those staff members? What ... were they? They were hunched and misshapen. Some looked to be nude; others were wearing armor of some sort. They glistened and seemed to be missing their skin. Things were attached to their bodies, horns or something. And, the person they'd assisted from the bedroom—no, they weren't assisting this person. They were dragging the struggling body out by the arms.

Who was that? It was a young lady with long, whitish blue hair. She would have been beautiful had she not been terrified, her face not locked into a scream. Some sort of greenish gate or doorway opened in front of them and they stepped through and were gone.

Somebody needed help! Kay tried to move. Must help! "My ... sister ..."

"Yes," came the voice. *"What you just saw was your sister being abducted by Demons in the year 003256. Does that year sound familiar? It should. Your girlfriend, during her Future-Telling, said*

your sister would be taken in 003256—and you just saw it happen."

"Must ... help ..."

"What you just saw hasn't happened yet. Ok? That scene of your poor sister getting abducted is something that can happen, might happen. It might happen to ladies all over the place. Or, it might not. It's something still in the crap-shoot known as the future. Ok? Depending on a few things, it might not have to happen at all. Do you understand?"

Kay didn't understand.

"Look, there are some bad things in the world, Kay. Sound familiar? There are things that have always been here, content through the millennia to just sit back and passively watch. But, anymore, they are no longer happy to just watch. I don't know why. I don't claim to understand their motives. But, one thing's clear—they are actively moving against you. They have been at the Xaphans for ages, and now they're coming for you, for the League. Your Monama girlfriend knows all about them, and she knows what the penalty is for opening her mouth."

Kay reacted. "Ber ... Ber ..."

"You mean Berserkacides? If that's what you're trying to say, you're right. Just like you and your people were engineered long ago to remain young and healthy throughout your lives, the Monamas were engineered, too. In fact, they've been engineered many times. Long ago, right here on Kana, they were a pretty horrific people and they worshipped a pretty horrific god in a temple in the ground. They called this place Tevlapradah. You know Anuie pretty well, right? But there's another language the Monamas speak called Systerel. It's a religious language they use. Tevlapradah in Systerel means 'Hell', and that's what this place was. The four-armed Monamas were the dark angels of a Horned God and did his bidding, and that's how it was for a long time. But, nothing's forever, and the Horned God lost his dark angels. I'm a little fuzzy on the details, and I'm still trying to work that out, but, somehow, the Monamas were transformed into what you see today, two-armed and much more civilized. They turned their backs on the Horned God and forgot about him. He wasn't too happy about that, and he found others to follow him—new dark angels. These 'newbies' are the Demons that haunt the Monamas to this very day. They took the Monamas and sort-of figured out how to turn them back into what they once were—Berserkacides, and they

inflict great suffering on them. They now are turning their sights on you."

The voice paused. *"Those skinless creatures you saw take your sister aren't the masterminds of this all. They are mere foot soldiers. See, the Monamas are at the bottom, just the blunt instruments, the rabid dogs to be unchained upon command. Then there's the skinless ones doing most of the dirty work. Running it all are the Golden People—people who have no shape, who can be whatever they want to be. Monamas can change their shapes in a small, topical sort of way, but not like this. The Golden People can be literally anything they want: tiny, huge, powerful, whatever. The Golden People are the new disciples of the Horned God. I really don't know what they're doing or why; their motives don't make a lot of sense to me, but, it seems clear they are planning the death of the League. An important initial phase of their plan appears to be to strike at the Vith, as the Vith will be most able to defend themselves against their preferred method of attack. I don't want to go into it, but it's horrible. Trust me. Now, I'm on your side, you know that, right? Just like I'm on your side, they've got the Horned God on theirs, so we're sort of working against each other, he and I. Therefore, I can only do so much. I'm going to need you to take action for me."*

Kay tried to talk, but the voice kept on. *"Shhh. Just listen. There's going to be an attack soon, against your House and many other Vith Houses all at once. I think their goal is to try and remove the fighting heart of the Vith and get them out of the way right off the bat. I've done something to your room, Kay, up in your tower. I'm not supposed to, but I did it anyway. They won't be able to get to you in your room, unless they climb in through the window, but it'll be awhile before they figure that out, and that should give you all the time you need. Here's what you're going to do. You'll head out to Castle Durst and go to the top. There, you'll encounter a device emitting light, like a searchlight. Your task will be to destroy that light at all costs. All right? Nothing else matters. Get rid of that damn light. That's the main thing."*

Kay felt himself being lifted away. *"I'm taking you back to your room to sleep it off. When you wake, you'll not remember any of this that I've told you, right? I have to take all of this from your memory, least the Horned God gets wise and take steps. But, when the time is right, you will remember, and you'll know what you have to do."*

He was surrounded by warm sheets and a soft pillow under his head. He thought he saw a small, silvery form leaning over him. *"There's probably going to come a time, Kay, when you feel like you're all alone. You're never alone. I'm never too far away. Just be yourself, all right?"*

Who are you?

The figure retreated. *"A friend. Oh, don't worry about Lt. Kilos' flask. I'll put it back in the creek for you. I'll even top it off, `cause I'm a nice guy and all. Oh! Look who's back."*

Kay felt someone crawl into bed with him. It was Sam. He felt her warm body all around him. Sam leaned over him and sniffed, smelling the spirits on his face. She got up and soon returned with a wet cloth from the bathroom. She dabbed his face, softly singing a Monama song. She sang in Anuie, of love and home. The sound of her voice slowly pulled Kay back from wherever he was.

As things became clear, the silvery form he'd been talking to seemed to drift out of the room and hang in the night sky like a silver star. *"Night, Kay. Rest easy, and kiss your lady for me."*

When Sam was done, she set her washcloth aside and curled up in his arms. The two of them slept.

8—The End of Winter

The next morning, as Kay and Sam ate breakfast in the Capricos Hall, they had a blow out fight, but not over Death Trials and secrets, or even Lon—it was over Sarah and Phillip.

"Kay, be it known that I am no longer content to lose you to your cousins in the summertime any more. I'm sorry, but our relationship has matured to the point that your future wife's needs outstrip those of your friends—and, yes, I am assuming that I am going to be your future wife. Therefore, it is *Me* first, *Them* second," she said, rather rank as she ate her food.

He had a wracking headache and was still reeling from a night full of odd dreams. "Well, Sam, it is you who insist that we maintain our secret relationship, though I am willing to present ourselves to the League and have told you so many times."

"You now know why I keep us a secret."

"And, as Sarah and Phillip live in this castle, I don't see how we are to conduct ourselves without them becoming wise to our activities."

"Avoid them."

"I can't avoid them. This is a big castle, but they'll seek me out. The three of us are normally inseparable in the summer. If I suddenly started avoiding them, they'd instantly know something was up." Kay glared at her. "Where have you been? Where do you keep going?"

"I've been busy. I had to attend to some business. I returned as soon as I could. I didn't want to be away, but I had to."

Sam stewed, clearly upset. "So, I cannot have you in the summer? At least we have the evenings."

"No Sam, we won't have the evenings either; you know that. Sarah and Phillip are known to barge in on me at all hours. Imagine the scene if you were there, all naked, and in they come."

Sam slammed her fork down. "Lord Blanchefort, it appears you are in quite a situation! I am almost to the point where you need to make a choice right here and now between them and me, and I will advise you that choosing them over me would be a bad, and possibly painful mistake for you!" She seized a large walnut from a nearby basket and shattered it in her pale fist.

Kay was unimpressed. "Really? I hear tell that you have been enjoying lunches in Arden with Lord Lon. What's that all about?"

"How did you find out about that?"

"Never mind. The point is that I know. Where have you been, and what were you discussing with Lon, if I might ask?"

"As I have said, I've been busy, and, regarding my lunch with Lord Lon, you may not ask, Kay. We were discussing a private matter, nothing that would interest you."

Kay was incensed. "Is that a fact? Sam, I want to know what you were talking about with Lon, and I want to know where you've been—now!"

"Or what?" she said rolling up her sleeves.

"Or, start eating this table, plates and all!"

And before another moment had passed, Kay and Sam were locked in a full-fledged fight/wrestling match. They were all over the place, throwing each other around, rocking the huge table in the hall. They hit the floor and started rolling around.

Soon, Kay had Sam by the head, and she had him by the waist, her legs squeezing the daylights out of him, her crossed shoes sticking up in the air.

As they struggled for position, Lord Davage and Countess Sygillis came into the hall with Lady Kilos walking behind. They'd come for breakfast.

Kilos looked at them on the floor and shook her head.

* * * * *

A few hours later, they were up in Kay's reading room. Kay had a scratched face and a few bruised ribs. Sam was doing all right. She was treating his scratch with a damp cloth.

"I'm sorry about this morning, Sam," he said.

"It's all right, Kay. If you can't get into the occasional brawl with the person you love, who can you?"

She put the cloth down and settled into his arms.

"I'm sorry I've been so strange and moody lately, Kay, and I'm sorry that I was absent over the last few days. There are things that I can't tell you. I want to—I'm dying to, but I can't. Just know that everything I do, I do for you—for us. You mean everything to me, *Arin-Dan*. And, most of all, I'm sorry about this morning. Not about our little tussle—which I thought was kind of fun—but about almost making you choose between me and your cousins. That was very selfish and unfair of me."

Kay kissed her. "Sam, I think it's time we told Sarah and Phillip about us. They're trustworthy—they won't give up our secret."

"They won't accept me. Sarah hates me, and I don't think I like her much, either."

"She'll just have to see reason. Phillip will be fine. For Sarah, just remember, she values strength. If she gets in your face, don't back down no matter what."

* * * * *

The sun set on winter. Tomorrow, Sarah and Phillip would return with their mother and father for yet another summer.

That evening Sam, true to her word, returned all of the books she had borrowed, and there were a bunch of them. They went to Lord Davage's study and put back the fifty or so books she'd borrowed. They went to the garden library in the west quarter and put back three books. In the big reading room in Countess Pardock's old tower, they put back ten books. Finally, they went to the hidden eight-sided library. They put back several books she had taken out.

"Did this book help you, in whatever you were looking for?" Kay asked.

"I hope so," she said vacantly as she fiddled with a huge blue book that didn't seem to fit properly on the shelf. She had to adjust several books and lay one on top of the others to make room.

Odd, Kay didn't recall any trouble fitting the books in before.

A large blue book?

"Hey," Sam said, "have I told you how much I love you lately?"

She didn't answer. "Sam?"

She lay there, unmoving, almost like she was dead.

* * * * *

The thing she had feared for years was nigh at hand. The thunderstorm she had tried to ignore was ready to darken the skies at long last. She couldn't hold it back—it was here.

The demons were coming. She wasn't ready.

She wasn't ready!

All the knowledge she had gathered, all her preparations— too late.

Her *Arin-Dan,* dying ...

The sadness that flowed through her was too much. It was just too much.

She saw her death, four armed, enraged. The demons watching and laughing, victorious as always. Her clawed hands at Kay's throat.

She wasn't ready.

She felt her mind detaching from her body, drifting away. All the fear she felt, all the dread began to fall to the wayside, replaced with a pall of sweet indifference. In this lukewarm state, it just didn't matter.

Head Swarm. She was falling into Head Swarm to protect herself from the unbearable torrent to come.

She casually noted that this was a big Head Swarm. Once in it, she probably couldn't be pulled out, ever. She would wither away over time and die.

As she drifted away, she heard a voice in the distance. She heard singing. It was a song she'd never heard, sung with love and care. It was a song that tempted her, prompted her to stay, to come down from the inviting paradise of Head Swarm and return to the fear and troubles of the real world and listen.

Who was singing? Where did it come from?

She fell back into her body and listened.

It was Kay. In the hidden library, he was holding her limp body and was singing an Elder tune. He sang it softly into her ear. She felt his arms around her and listened to the song. She fell into a contented state, a much more blissful one than even the fields of Head Swarm could offer.

Kay's touch and his loving voice kept her from Head Swarm,

gave her the strength to fight it off, and the courage to remain in the real world with a clear head, though the real world was soon to offer little but pain and sorrow.

How few Monamas had chosen pain over forgetfulness?

She couldn't have made that choice on her own—Kay helped her make it.

She'd forgotten how strong Kay would one day be. Up until this point, it had been Sam who was the strong one, and Kay, blissfully unaware, the weak one. She and Kay were about to enter a new phase of their lives, where she would be in need, and he would have to be strong, where he would have to face the demons that were about to fall on him all alone.

Was he up to what was coming? She had to have faith that he was.

"Don't let me go away, *Arin-Dan*," she finally said, her eyes opening.

"I won't, *Cerri-Tela*. I want you here, Sam, with me."

He held her for the rest of the night and sang in her ear.

Despite the storm that was about to rage, it was the most contented and safe she had ever felt.

* * * * *

The following afternoon was the usual cool, deep blue affair common in Blanchefort. Lord Davage and Kay were completing his afternoon CARG practice in the Holt courtyard in the Telmus Grove. The larger-than-life statue of Syg that Kay had made for her birthday stood in a pebbled nook overlooking the courtyard. Kay had sheathed it in copper, and the statue had developed a nice greenish patina over the years. Syg loved the statue, showed it to all her friends and spent a lot of time in the courtyard. "My son made this for me," she'd proudly say.

A close-knit family, everybody was nearby doing their own thing in the statue's shadow. Countess Sygillis and Lady Kilos were sitting on the low stone wall, arguing as usual. This time, their fight was centered on the cut of a new gown his mother was designing.

A fabric dummy floated in front of Sygillis draped with a new gown she was working on. Lady Hathaline sat nearby, quiet as usual. Lord Davage had promised to go flying with her as soon as he with finished with Kay's lesson. Maser was playing on a little mound of dirt under a huge tree with Lt. Kilos.

A member of the House staff arrived in the courtyard and approached Countess Sygillis. She halted her argument with Lady Kilos and turned to her.

"I am here, my countess, as you requested," the staff member said.

Sygillis held up a novelty shirt with a terrible holopicture of herself on the front—similar to the one Kilos had made Kay buy in the village.

"You are to prowl every shop in the village, and, if you discover any more of these shirts, you are to confiscate them at once on my orders, am I clear?"

"Yes, my countess. And if I happen to see anybody wearing the offending shirts, my countess?"

"You are to reimburse the person and seize the shirt off his or her protesting back if need be. If anyone gives you misery, you are to advise them to see me personally. Off you go."

The staff member ran off. Lady Kilos had a devilish grin on her face, as she had stockpiled quite a few of the shirts to use for any number of nefarious purposes. No doubt, they would come in handy.

Sygillis turned to Davage. "Dav, I'm at my wits end with her."

"To whom are you referring?" Davage asked, as if he didn't know.

"Her—the Duchess of Oyln. I am ready to challenge her to a fight to the death in the arena with the whole League watching; winner take all. The loser dies."

Lt. Kilos laughed. "Isn't she ready to drop another kid?"

"I don't care. I'll fight the both of them."

"Syg, you promised you'd quit fighting with Torri," Davage said.

Sygillis wadded up the shirt and threw it at Davage. "I'm not the one who keeps launching attacks of humiliation."

Davage was having a hard time keeping from laughing. "Well, Syg, after you 'bare-assed' the duchess at the Hubert ball, you had to expect some sort of revenge coming your way, yes? Instead of wanting to get the poor, and, might I say, rather pregnant duchess in the arena, why don't you try using your wits? Get even. If she's circulating shirts with an ugly picture of you on the breast, then why don't you circulate a shirt with an even uglier picture of her on it? Fair's fair, I suppose."

"Mother, I think I can get hold of some naked and grotesquely pregnant pictures of the duchess if you want them," Kilos said.

Sygillis appeared inspired, then shook her head and turned to Lady Kilos, resuming their previous argument.

"Lady Kilos," Sygillis spoke in a firm, impatient voice, "I am not creating clothing for a courtesan. The neckline shall plunge no further, and that is final!" She adjusted and pinned the fabric.

"Mother," Kilos replied tartly, "the fashions coming out of Armenelos are much more courageous regarding the display and wear of cleavage this year, and I insist our Blanchefort fashions meet the challenge. I am trying to do you a favor."

Lt. Kilos looked at the dummy. "You know, Bottle, I remember when they were calling your mom 'Madame Thimble' down at the factories for her butting in all the time with all her little swatches and patterns."

Kilos, frustrated, turned to Davage. "Father, will you please talk some sense into Mother?"

Davage put his CARG down and took them both by the chin. "Oh, you two clucking hens, always pecking away at each other."

Syg turned the dummy to face Dav. "What do you think, love? Do you like it?"

Davage looked at the gown. "I love it, darling. Very nice shape. Nice colors."

"Ki?" Syg asked, pointing it at Lt. Kilos.

"Umm, sure, Syg. It looks good. I'm no gown-wearer, so I really don't know."

"Father, the neckline is unacceptable," Kilos stated firmly. "You shall not catch me wearing that gown."

Syg turned to her. "You'll not be wearing such a thing until you are thirty years old, am I understood?"

"Why not? Kay's allowed to get into a twisting, rolling fight on the floor with his girlfriend, so why can't I wear an interesting gown."

"You shall be involved in a fight here in a moment sure enough, young lady."

Davage looked at it again. "Well, Syg, perhaps you could be a bit more daring, perhaps a tad lower."

Kay, watching, smiled and put his coat back on and saddled his

CARG, the lesson over.

"So, Dav, how's my son coming along here in his training," Sygillis asked tossing Kay's hair and giving him a kiss on the cheek.

"He's got a fine sword arm, and he uses that CARG like he's done it all his life. Though, you shouldn't hold it one-handed like a rapier. It's a CARG, Kay. Use both hands. I keep telling you that, and you keep ignoring my advice."

Kay leveled it, holding it like a fencer. "But Father, like this I can easily cross any incoming attack, while leaving my open hand free to brandish a pistol perhaps."

"A pistol?" Davage smiled, and in a blazingly fast move crossed Kay's CARG with his own. Kay's silver CARG flew out of his hand and spiraled off into the trees at the feet of the statue.

"You see, Kay, now you have both hands free. Just imagine if I were an enemy. You need both hands on your weapon."

Kay turned to his brother Maser. "Maser, can you go get my CARG, chief?"

Maser said something inaudible and scurried off into the trees, returning a moment later holding Kay's CARG.

Overhead, a familiar black ship streaked across the sky, heading for the farther reaches of the Grove.

Davage looked up. "Ah, looks like your aunt, uncle and cousins have returned." He checked his timepiece. "Right on time, too."

"Father," Kay asked, "may I be off? I'd like to greet them." He was excited.

Davage pushed his hat back and checked his timepiece again. "Certainly. If you see your aunt and uncle, tell them we'll be along shortly. It's good to have them back."

"Ki," Kay asked, saddling his CARG, "Want to come with me?"

"And get yelled at by Sarah? No thanks. Creation it's going to be a long summer."

"Suit yourself." Kay gave his mother a kiss on the cheek and tore off into the trees.

9—Sarah and Phillip of Blanchefort

K ay roughly met up with his cousins Sarah and Phillip, and after a brief laughing melee, they were all hugs and smiles.

Sarah and Phillip were a perfect blend of Blanchefort and Ruthven. They were both tall and thin, like a standard Blanchefort, and they had the thoughtful yet rugged look of the Ruthvens. Unlike her genial mother and father, Sarah, with her rolled, tailed blue hair was a real firecracker and the spitting image of her grandmother, Countess Hermilane, also a firecracker in her day. Sarah had inherited every bit of her grandmother's rather pugnacious temperament. Sarah never met a fight she didn't like: words, fists, sticks or whatever. It didn't matter; she was always ready. Phillip, her younger brother of ten minutes, was the recreation of their father, Lord Peter. He was handsome and auburn-headed and had fully inherited his father's hands and thoughtfulness as well. Rather like his older brother Milos, he was highly intelligent and studious, but, unlike his scholarly brother, he had a love of fun and adventure, and hanging out with Sarah and Kay gave him more than he could manage.

The two of them tended to wear Ruthven garb: white linen shirts, brown pants and tall boots with the long black duster their father used to wear during his pirating days as a member of the Duke of Oyln's Black Goshawk gang. Lady Poe had long given up trying to get Sarah to wear a Blanchefort gown—she wasn't having any of it. "Peter!" she would complain to her husband, "will you please ask your daughter to wear her beautiful gown?" But Sarah, stubborn unless it was a special occasion or Lady Poe's birthday, wouldn't budge. Lady Poe, in frustration, often said, "Young lady, it's a good thing for you that I am your mother, and not your aunt, Countess Pardock, for she would slap your bottom and stuff you into one without mercy!"

* * * * *

After they finished beating each other up in greeting, they immediately decided to go to Subra Courtyard, a secluded and somewhat remote courtyard in the Grove near Carahil's Walk where they often went. This was their place, their secret spot where there was nobody but the three of them. Here they came to practice with their CARGs and SAPPs; they'd lugged in several practice ones which they stacked in a trunk behind the wall. Phillip had brought in a telescope, a hammock, a portable terminal and a small cooler in which to put snacks— a veritable home away from home. They came here simply to relax and share their thoughts, at ease to say whatever came into their heads.

Sarah was walking around with Kay's silver CARG. "So, there was this lunatic threatening the village of Green Sabre, and the locals came to the Duke for help. He and Uncle Johnnie went to investigate, and you know what they found?"

Kay was flopped in the hammock, and Phillip sat nearby typing into the portable terminal. "What did they find, Sarah?" Kay asked indulging her. The three of them were already well into summer mode.

"They found a demon with no skin. The demon was the lunatic, and the Duke and Father and Uncle Johnnie pursued it through Green Sabre." Sarah spoke with relish; she loved this sort of thing.

"Then, they cornered it at the gravesite of Junius, a great Esther hero, where the demon summoned a host of Berserkacides to fight the Duke. They met the Berserkacides and killed the demon. Creation, I wish I'd been there."

Kay shook his head. "Well, maybe next time."

"Did you get my posts, Kay? I've got all sorts of new places to investigate along the Gaston Way near the old Tardy ruins. I got a few tips. We're going to have a busy summer."

"Sounds grand," Kay replied.

Phillip was still typing away on the terminal.

"Who are you talking to, Phillip?" Kay asked.

Sarah replied. "He's got himself a new girlfriend. She's a Paulie-girl from Conwell."

"Not true," Phillip said, still staring into the terminal. "She's too tame. I happen to like them a little wild."

Sarah approached Kay. "Have you been practicing with your Sight over the winter? You said you would."

"I have, Sarah, but it didn't do any good. I don't have it."

Sarah lit her Sight, her eyes glowing a soft blue to match her hair. "Now, Kay, all you have to do is relax and let it flow. See, look at me. See how it works?"

Kay lay there on the hammock. "I am relaxed, Sarah. No good. I got nothing."

She knocked him on the shoulder with his CARG. "Come on, Kay, give it a try. Just think how happy it'll make your dad." Though Sarah tried to hide it with a lot of bluster, she was just as matronly as her mother, Lady Poe, though if one mentioned it to her, she would get rather rank.

Kay took a deep breath. "Nothing."

"You're not even trying, are you, you bag?"

Phillip smiled and closed his terminal. "Don't let her put you off, Kay. You should see her. She's got eyes for that Lord Posey fellow from Bern. She's probably just missing him right now."

Sarah quieted her Sight and shot Phillip a deadly look. "I told you not to say anything about that, Phillip! Besides, I'll not marry a guy named Posey. I am not a Posey. Do I look like a Posey?? I'll marry into House Champion, or Colt or Midnight, something that sounds cool. Sarah of Colt—yes, I like that."

Sarah went to the cooler and got out something to drink. "So, Kay, how's your correspondence? You got anybody floating around out there? Lady Krista of Gamboa wanted me to ask. She's all keen on you. Says she's written to you."

"I don't recall getting any letters from Gamboa."

Phillip laughed. "Lady Krista of Gamboa is rather ugly, Kay, in case you're wondering."

"She is not."

Kay shrugged. "Well, I've been wanting to share something with you two for awhile now actually."

Sarah took a drink. "What is it?"

Kay got off the hammock and kicked at the ground. "What if told you that I've been seeing someone for about five years running?

Somebody whom I feel very serious about. What if I told you that?"

"Five years?" Sarah repeated finishing her drink. "You've been seeing someone for five years, and you've not said anything?"

"Yes."

"How'd you manage that?"

"Well, it's pretty easy in the winter since you're not here, and in the summer, we just take a step back and cool it. But, it's gotten to the point where we don't want to cool it anymore."

Phillip was curious. "Why've you hidden her from us, Kay? Are you feeling shy?"

"No."

Sarah was getting perturbed. "Well, who is it? Who's this lady? You shouldn't keep secrets from us—we're your pals."

Kay sighed. "Sam, come on out. I'd like to properly introduce you to my cousins."

After a moment, Sam came walking out of the trees. "Hello," she said softly, all smiles.

Sarah reacted violently. "Her? Kay, you've been seeing … *her?"*

"I have, Sarah. I wanted to tell you two before, but it didn't seem the right time."

"What about the scene at the ball? You looked like you were going to be sick when she started making advances toward you!"

"That was just an act."

Sarah was incensed. "You don't know how to act, Kay, and, of all people, why her? For Creation's sake, if you're that desperate, I'll marry you myself—anything but her!" Sarah cried. "She's a pre-berserk Berserkacide!"

"Sarah …"

Sam interrupted. "Lady Blanchefort, Kay told me that you might object."

"You bet I'll object! Kay's my best friend. He's like a brother to me, and it's my duty to knock him in the head when he puts two feet wrong!"

Sarah cuffed Kay in the back of his head, knocking his hat off. "What are you thinking?" She turned to Sam. "What have you done to my cousin? You've bewitched him!"

"You're right; I have bewitched him. And he has bewitched me. It took years. We started off as friends, and it grew from there. He's my *Arin-Dan*, Lady Sarah. *'My love'*. Monama women do not use that term lightly."

"Talk normal!" Sarah shouted.

"We were hoping that you would wish to be my friend."

Phillip spoke up. "You know, Lady Sammidoran, Lord Lon has not stopped talking about you since the ball."

Sam smiled. "Has he? He is adorable—truly. But, I am in love with your cousin. I've loved him my whole life, truth be told. I will be his countess some day."

Sarah turned red. "The flaming hell you will! Kay, if you're hot for a lady, I've got a bunch of friends that I could introduce you to, namely Lady Krista of Gamboa! Anything but this Monama, Berserkacide scum!"

"Sarah, that's enough!"

"Where's your four arms, *Sam*?" she asked. "Don't all you Berserkacides have four arms?"

Sam approached her. "I don't have four arms, Lady Sarah. Kay has told me you are a fiery person, and I can see that. Kay has also told me that you admire strength above all else. Tell you what, why don't we step away into the woods and have a private chat, just you and me? I think you've got a bit of honesty coming to you."

"You'll use your claws on me!"

Sam showed Sarah her nails—they had been trimmed down and painted red. "For my Kay, I have shortened my beloved fingernails to a more Vith-like length."

Sarah poked her in the chest. "If we go into the trees, we're not going to be talking much!"

Sam dropped a few inches as she removed her Monama shoes. "That's fine; any way you want. I do not intend to come between you and Kay, Sarah; nor will I allow you to come between Kay and me. I want us all to be friends. I don't wish to make *Arin-Dan* choose between us."

"You'll use some sort of Monama magic against me! You'll go Berserkacide on me!"

"I will not. Just you and me. Come on, what are we waiting for?"

"It'll take me a minute or two to power up so I can pound you."

"Take all the time you need."

Same held out her shoes. "Will you hold these for me, please?" she said to Kay. He took them, and Sarah huffed.

"Be careful," Kay said.

"Thanks!" both Sam and Sarah replied. Together they walked out of the courtyard into the trees.

Kay and Phillip stood there. Phillip looked gobsmacked. "Well, Kay, this is a surprise. You keep a secret well. I had no idea, and there's been no gossip, which is strange. In fact, I heard Lady Sammidoran recently lunched with Lord Lon in Arden. I was happy for him."

"Boy, word gets around. She did. She's working on some sort of project that Lon's helping her with."

"A project? What sort of project?"

"Don't know—she won't tell me."

Phillip was still trying to absorb all of this information. "And Lady Kilos. Is she aware of this?"

"She is."

"And she's not said anything? I'd think she, of all people, an avid gossiper…"

"She's actually quite stalwart at keeping secrets when she wants to. She's been a big help and has welcomed Sam."

Kay stood there holding Sam's shoes and looked to the trees. "I don't like this, Phillip. Sarah doesn't know what she's getting into. Sam's pretty strong."

"Sarah can handle herself. I suppose if anything gets her respect, this will."

Dimly, they could hear a struggle in the distance. Leaves rustled, dry tree limbs snapped. Clearly, Sam and Sarah were going at it.

"And what do you think, Phillip? What's your reaction to all of this?"

"I think Lord Lon's going to be pretty disappointed; that's my reaction. I don't mind Lady Sammidoran. I think she's very beautiful; I noticed her at the ball myself. Again, I'm mostly shocked that you kept quiet about it for so long."

"I wanted to tell you guys, but Sam has insisted on keeping it a secret—it's a Monama tradition, so let's leave it at that."

There was a cry and the sound of bodies falling on top of each other coming from the trees.

"I think I should go over there."

"No, no, Kay, let them finish. So, Kay, do you really have feelings for Lady Monama?"

"Yes, Phillip, I do. I love her."

"Well, that's good enough for me. As long as you're happy, that's all I care about. And don't listen to Sarah. Lady Krista of Gamboa looks like a man in a gown. I suppose I should start looking around, too. We're not kids anymore, are we?"

"Anybody interest you? That Paulie lady Sarah mentioned, perhaps?"

"No, she seems fairly keen to begin something with me, but I'm not really interested. I have come to the conclusion that I like a rather wild woman—like those urchins trawling the streets of Calvert. Sort of like Lt. Kilos, or Sarah—I like that kind of spirit. Most ladies of standing are too tame. The Duke introduced me to Lady Spree of Conwell last winter, and I found that she didn't interest me in the least. Too quiet and shy. I like an element of danger. I like to run and be chased. Ladies of standing don't chase after anybody. Maybe I should hunt down a Black Hat like your dad and the Duke did."

Phillip looked up at the sky. "I've had an image in my thoughts for some time, an image in green and brown of a lady—a fierce one. I suppose I compare all the ladies I meet to this image in my head, to this woman who doesn't exist."

"You dream of a lady, Phillip?" Kay asked.

He laughed. "I suppose so. This lady, though quite pretty, is crass and rough—a real handful. I have no idea what I'd do if I actually met up with someone like that."

Sam and Sarah emerged from the trees. They both looked a little mussed up. Sam had the skirt of her gown knotted and hiked up between her pale legs. She pulled the knot, and it came down like a stage curtain. Kay handed Sam her shoes back.

"Lady Sarah and I have been talking. I think we've come to an understanding," Sam said leaning against him as she put them back on.

Kay looked at Sarah. "Sarah, are you all right?"

"I'm fine," she said gruffly. Her tightly rolled up and pulled back blue hair was all over the place. Dry leaves hung limply on her duster.

Kay went to the cooler and pulled out two cold drinks, handing one to Sam and a red one to Sarah. Sarah took hers and held it against her right eye. She was sure to have a shiner by morning.

Sam took a drink and approached Kay. "Lady Sarah is very strong. She is a fine fighter. She can fight every bit as well as you can, Kay."

The compliment appeared to make her brighten a bit. "You've been fighting with Kay?"

"We fight all the time. We had a big one the other day, didn't we, Kay?"

Kay nodded. "So, what do you say, Sarah?" Kay asked. "Are we all friends? Can you deal with this? And you better say 'yes;' otherwise, it'll be you and I walking into the trees next."

She looked at the ground and toyed with her drink. "I still don't know if I trust her. I'm going to be watching you, *Sam*, and, if I seeing anything funny, I'm coming after you." She popped her can with a gassy rush.

"Funny?" Sam said. "You mean like this." Sam grabbed Kay and gave him a huge kiss."

Sarah stepped in between them. "Yes, like that. By Creation, no kissing when I'm around. That's the first rule! And no touching, and no talking either!"

Phillip laughed.

"No kissing, oh that's going to be a tough one," Sam said.

Phillip smiled and clapped Sam on the shoulder. "Well, Lady Sammidoran, welcome to our little troupe. I guess the first order of business is to see if we can select somebody for poor Lord Lon. He's going to be heartbroken when he finds out."

"Kay has told me that I can count on your discretion. Our relationship must be kept secret for now—even from Lord Lon. Will you promise?"

"I promise," Phillip said. "You needn't worry about me, or Sarah either. Right, Sarah?"

She grumbled something and looked at the ground again.

"Wonderful," Sam said, "but that doesn't mean we can't find a lucky lady for Lord Lon. Whom do you suggest, Phillip?"

10—What Sam Did

S ummer was a busy time at the castle, full of noise and fighting. Kay's cousins, Sarah and Phillip, absolutely dominated his time, giving him little peace, day or night. Sarah was well known for using the zip line from her tower, shooting across in her pajamas and barging right in through his 89th floor window whenever she had a thought for a crazy new scheme.

And Sarah had lots of crazy schemes, so she was zipping in all the time. Sarah was *slowly* accepting Sam into the group, though she still watched her with a dubious eye.

The only time Kay was separated from Sarah and Phillip was when he had an official duty to perform, as the next heir to the House. Sarah and Phillip, being ranked much farther down the order, got out of all those things, Sarah often snickering as Kay was led away to do whatever. "Try to stay awake," she'd whisper.

* * * * *

It was Tuesday. Sam, as usual on Tuesdays, had gone home attending to her own required duties to the south. She would be back in the morning. Kay, Sarah and Phillip had gone to the bath house for a nice soak.

Before long, Kay was summoned via telepathy by his mother.

<*Kay, you're needed in the castle. You have a visitor.*>

<*I do?*> Kay was shocked. He never had visitors. <*Who is it?? Is it Sam?*>

<*It is not, Sam; however, a young lady is here to see you.*>

<Me? But I'm here at the bath house with Sarah and Phillip. We were planning an outing later.>

<You can play with your cousins another time. Come along. She's waiting for you in the Firth House.>

Kay dressed and popped his hat on. "Got to go," he told Sarah and Phillip.

"Where are you off to?" Sarah demanded to know, bobbing in the water.

"Got a visitor."

"You? Who is it?"

"Don't know."

Kay exited the bathhouse, walking west through the lily garden, his CARG swinging at his side.

"Make it fast! We're heading to the Gaston Way later to do some more investigating!" she called. "Don't forget!"

Kay made his way back to the castle and went into the Palantine courtyard. It was a vast octagonal courtyard taking up most of the northern wing of the castle, heavily landscaped and planted with flowering trees and quiet pools. Underneath a statue at one end of the courtyard was the secret entrance to the Blanchefort bowling alley. Four medium-sized towers, Cooper, Tremblay, Maseron and Joliet, were accessible only from within the courtyard.

At the northern end of the courtyard was Firth House, a tea-room built of black stone by the old Vith centuries prior. Legend told it was the original founding of Blanchefort Castle, now surrounded and dwarfed by it. It had fallen into ruin during an attack by the old Bloodsteins centuries back and had festered as a pile of blackened masonry for some time. Lord Sadric of Blanchefort had it rebuilt and made into a lovely tearoom for the family's private use. The Blancheforts used it mostly as a secluded spot to meet new acquaintances. Countess Pardock had first met her future husband, Ferddie of Vincent, in the Firth House. So far, Kay's use of the Firth House to meet young ladies visiting from across the League had been quite limited. Lady Poe had often used it when meeting new gentlemen callers before meeting Lord Peter.

Kay emerged into the sunny Palantine and made his way through the winding paths to the Firth House; its distinctive low battlements reached up just higher than the surrounding trees like a pair of hands holding palms up toward the sky.

He wondered who it could be awaiting him. He'd only had one previous meeting in the Firth House. It was with a girl named Mertha of Trim, a rather homely person from Remnath whose bad complexion was matched only by her bad teeth.

"Mert the Terrible," Sarah called her. She had been a nice enough girl, and Kay made a friend, but nothing more.

Now, somebody else waited within.

Kay approached the black-stone structure. A new oaken door waited bearing the Blanchefort coat-of-arms, and he pulled it open. Inside was a fairly spacious room floored in rare woods from Hoban and upholstered with fine fabrics of teal and canary. The staff kept the place in immaculate condition. Lord Sadric was a well-remembered host, and a full-sized statue of him greeted all those entering, forever presiding over the goings on in the house. Someone sat in a chair at the opposite end.

Kay bowed. "Well met and good afternoon. I am Kabyl of Blanchefort, son of Lord Davage and Countess Sygillis."

The figure turned. "Hi, Kay, it's just me." The figure stood, and Lady Kilos emerged into the light.

"Ki—you're my mysterious lady caller?"

"I am."

"What is this?"

She approached. "Well, it's awful hard to get a moment alone with you, what with Sarah taking up every spare moment of the day."

"You and Sarah really need to have a heart to heart, Ki. She's not a bad person really, and she's got a lot more of her mother in her than she lets on."

"Aunt Poe is a great lady. Sarah, however, is a rotten, loud-mouthed Shocktyte."

"Ouch."

"I sort of miss the winter so I can spend a little time with my brother. Anyway, I wanted to talk to you, and the only way to get a moment is to make an appointment, I guess."

"Ok, here I am, Ki. What's on your mind?"

Ki looked around and spied the statue of Lord Sadric. "Not, here—too many old ghosts rolling around. Let's go up to the top. I'll see you there." With that, she coiled up a Waft and blasted out of the room, shaking the chandelier in the process.

Kay chose a more conventional method to get to the top. He

made his way up the stairs and emerged into the sunshine after a healthy climb. There was Ki standing on the battlements, admiring the view of the courtyard below and the rising bulk of the castle all around.

"I like it up here," she said. "Very pretty. I can't wait until I entertain young gentlemen. I think I'll make them climb the stairs to see me. I suppose I've got five years to wait before my face clears."

Kay removed his triangle hat and agreed.

"Took you long enough," she said. "Why didn't you Waft up?"

"I thought I'd walk."

Ki smiled. "You need to work on that, Kay. Sam would never approve."

"Yes, but Sam's not here."

Ki smiled and pulled a locket from the folds of her bodice. She opened it, and two silver ladybugs of superior size came fluttering out. They moved lightly through the air like little jewels.

Kay recognized what they were. "Whispers. Those are Whispers, right? Some of Aunt Poe's familiars."

"You're right," Ki said. "They come in handy. Now, nobody can hear us talking, and nobody can see us up here, just in case Sarah comes blundering in."

Apparently, Ki wanted assurance of privacy, and two Whispers would provide just that. Kay moved to the edge of the battlement and stood beside her. Beyond the battlement wall, the green floor of the Palatine was about a hundred feet down.

"So, what's on your mind, Ki?"

"I wanted to get some time alone with you to talk about Sam, actually."

"What about her?"

Ki hesitated and considered her words. "You know that I like Sam. I like her a lot. She's my friend, and I'm very glad that we've all become close. But, you're my brother and my first loyalty is to you, and I wanted to make sure you're aware of certain things. What I have to say might change your mind about Sam, or color your feelings for her a little. I hope not, but, I have to say my piece, for good or ill."

Kay was a little taken aback by Ki's tone. "All right, Ki, I'm listening. Sarah's nowhere to be seen. Let's have it."

She thought a moment, collecting her thoughts. Her white-blue hair shimmered in the sun. Her face was still very puffy from her

childhood, especially around the eyes, but, once it cleared up, Ki
would be a true beauty. It was easy to see. One of the Whispers
buzzed past her face. "You, Kay, are unlike all of the other young
lords in Vithland, and in Zenon, and in Remnath and Esther, too. Did
you know that?"

"You forgot Calvert."

"No I didn't. I don't count them. My point is—you should be
here in the Firth House meeting young ladies several times a week at
least. Your correspondence pile should be huge. When was the last
time you were here to meet a lady?"

"Last year, when Mertha of Trim came."

"Yeah, Big Mert, I remember that. Don't you find it odd that you
are a virtual wall flower at the age of twenty-two, when you should be
one of the most highly sought after prizes on Kana? Traditionally,
unattached gentlemen and ladies begin formally courting as soon as
they get past their Puffies." Ki touched her puffy face for a moment,
hating it. "As you've never seemed to have had it, Kay, you should
have been courting actively for the past two years, and I recall
mother stating she would not allow you to court until, at least, the age
of twenty. So, here it is, two years later, and you see virtually no
one."

"I'm not really looking, Ki. I've got Sam."

"Yes, you do, but that's a secret relationship, Kay. As you've not
announced yourselves to the League, you are officially available. As
the next Lord of Blanchefort, you should be on the top of anybody's
wish list."

Kay seated himself on the battlement, the hundred foot fall to the
cobbled path below precariously close. "Just give it to me, Ki. What
are you getting at?"

"I'm saying you are isolated in the League, Kay. Look at me, I'm
only eighteen and puffed up like a marshmallow; yet, I'm already
getting more correspondence from young gentlemen than I can
handle. I can't actively court them yet with my damn face and mother
monitoring the situation, but I'm already lining up my prospects for
the future. Phillip has lots of mail, Hath is starting to receive notices,
and even that Jo-Boy Sarah is getting some. And you, out-ranking us
all, have almost none. Doesn't that seem odd to you?"

Kay sighed and adjusted his hat. "Sure."

"I think Sam has done something over the years to keep you

isolated from those who might prove to be a competition for her. Kay, it's obvious that Sam has had her sights on you for a long time. I remember hearing a voice coming out of your room once when you were sleeping. "*Arin-Dan, Arin-Dan,*" it said. "Do you know what that means?"

Kay nodded.

"From my research, that word isn't something Monama women just toss around. It means she is serious about you, Kay, that, in her mind, you are hers. Having gotten to know Sam, I don't see her as the kind of person to sit back meekly and allow things like fate or chance to get in the way of what she wants—to get in the way of her *Arin-Dan.* I think she's taken matters into her own hands. I think she's actively eliminated her competition, either literally or mechanically."

One of the Whispers landed on the black stone surface of the battlement. Kay watched it move about with interest. "Be specific, please."

"All right. Do you know Lady Wilhelmina of Pole?"

"No."

"She's a friend of mine from Saga in Barrow. A real chatterbox—you think I like to talk; I'm nothing compared to her. She's soon to become the Duchess of Holly, I think, if all goes well. It's not a great Household to attach herself to, but it sounds good anyway. She's told me that she has written to you over ten times through the years and never gotten anything back. Now, I know you're not the most attentive letter-writer; however, you're not so rude as to ignore a lady's query ten times in a row."

"I don't remember ever getting a letter from her."

"No, I don't think you did. What about from Hadjinal of Effington or Lycona of Pert? Hadjinal told me she's written to you seventeen times and Lycona eight times. Lycona even told me she bought a magical doll from Bazz to cast a spell on you with it out of revenge for ignoring her. However, neither of those two hold a candle to Lady Roethaba of Mystery; she's the record-holder, I think. She has written you over thirty times, she says. She even gave me a letter to hand-carry to you."

"Again, that name doesn't ring a bell."

"No—though I set it on your pile personally last year. I guess it vanished, didn't it? So, I'm asking the question—what happened to all these correspondences? The Vithland Guild of Posts is not so bad to mishandle *all* of those letters."

"So, you're thinking that Sam intercepted them."

"Yes, I am. Sam can do some amazing things, and she can see the future. She probably knows exactly when some babe out there is penning you a note and goes and fetches it before you have a chance to read it. And, that's not all. Stealing letters is tame compared to what else I think Sam's done."

The stream below babbled and caught Kay's interest. "Now what? What else has Sam done?"

"Sarah loves talking and reading about the bizarre, correct? The unusual and gothic? She's so droll. I hear tell she is fascinated by the Wraith of Gaston."

"That's right. In fact, she wants to head out there again today to do some 'investigating' as she puts it near Tardy."

Ki laughed. "Oh, Sarah and the little things that drive her. Would you be so shocked if I told you that I'm quite certain that Sam *is* the Wraith of Gaston? That you've been kissing and wrestling with one of the biggest phantasms of Sarah's imagination?"

An interesting series of images flashed through his head. He laughed. "And, I suppose you have compelling proof?"

"I wouldn't have mentioned it if I hadn't" The sun moved past the edge of the towers surrounding the courtyard, and the two of them were suddenly in shade. "I didn't even think the Wraith of Gaston existed—I mean it's a rather silly story isn't it? A pale, spectral creature, wreathed in black, occasionally haunting the lonely mountain passes of the Gaston, vexing some passers while sparing others."

"I'm aware of the story."

"Wilhelmina of Pole—yes, she, once again. A few years back, mother transacted a rather large business agreement with her father, Lord Venture of Pole. Apparently, at some point in the transaction, you came up as a topic of discussion, as did Lord Venture's daughter Wilhelmina. That happens quite a bit, Kay, in case you were wondering, with businessmen and women mixing business and pleasure liberally. Mother and Lord Pole began comparing notes, discovered you and she were of similar ages, and she invited her here, to the Firth House, to meet you. She thought, perhaps, you might make a friend, possibly more."

"I wasn't aware of that."

Down below in the courtyard, Sarah and Phillip appeared through the south gate, dusters flattering, the both of them heading toward the Firth House. Sarah was loudly muttering something about being late to the Gaston.

Ki laughed and leaned over the side. "We're up here, you manky git!" she yelled, Sarah and Phillip hearing and seeing nothing past the Whisper's veil. They went into the Firth House clearly looking for Kay and then came back out a few moments later, Sarah in a froth. She headed toward the secret entrance to the Blanchefort bowling alley, opened the hatch and went down. Phillip stood on the path. He lit his Sight for a moment and looked around. He quickly saw them standing on the battlements. He waved, and Kay waved back.

"He's seen us. Don't worry about Phillip. He won't give us up to Sarah."

Ki also waved. "I like Phillip. I'd like a man like him to court me someday, calm, fairly cerebral; I can't believe he's Sarah's brother."

"You need to come off Sarah a little. She is a good friend and a good sister."

"She started this, not me."

"True, but perhaps if you swallowed your pride a little, you could end it, and we could all be friends."

Sarah came storming back out of the bowling alley entrance. She closed the hatch, and they both headed back toward the south gate, Sarah in a clear tizzy. Phillip glanced back at them once as they went.

"Looks like you're in for it later, Kay. Anyway, back to the topic at hand. Guess what happened to Wilhelmina as she made her way down the Gaston?" Ki continued. "I'll give you three guesses, but I'm hoping you only need one."

Kay watched Sarah and Phillip disappear back into the castle, marveling at the effectiveness of the Whispers. "She travelled here in her coach, dropping into the Gaston Way to avoid the restricted skyways of Pithnar and Atalan, and met the Wraith somewhere along the way. Is that right?"

"She certainly did. She described the ordeal in hearty detail. It made quite an impression on her. She said it came upon them in the wild and ran upon the ground, as fast as their coach could fly, and when they took to the air to escape it, it followed, running through the air after them. Wilhelmina got a good look at it; it was like a thunderstorm with a glowing person hidden within. Those black eyes on a pale face, she said, enough to chill her soul. She said it 'glowed' with an infernal light. She said she didn't remember it having a mouth, but it definitely had claws. She said it disabled their coach, doing a fair amount of damage in the process, until they had to veer out of the Gaston and return to Barrow quite convinced the Vithlands are haunted. That's when Wilhelmina started writing to you, as she was too chicken to return."

"You're assuming that Sam's capable of such an incredible feat."

"Kay, we both know Sam is capable of doing a lot. Look at how strong she is, how fast. Look how she can alter her appearance and how she can zero in on you just by using her nose. And what about when she speaks to you even when she's not here—no com, no holonet? How does she do that?"

"She told me how that works. She may transmute her voice across the earth."

"All the more proof to illustrate my point. Sam is very powerful. Also, do you remember the word she said during the future-telling?"

"She said: '*Olonol*'."

"I looked it up. It means: 'machine'. What machine? What was she talking about?"

"I don't know. I asked her, and she won't say. She's like that. Has all sorts of secrets she doesn't think I can handle."

A few staff members came out and began tending to the grounds. Kay and Ki sat silent, listening to the sounds of their tools as they clipped the bushes and raked the gravel, the sounds carrying. "I'm sorry I had to tell you this, Kay."

"I'm sorry too," he replied. "I'm sorry you think I'm so stupid, Ki."

Ki turned to him. "Kay, I …"

"Of course you're correct. About everything. Sam is quite powerful. She can do all sorts of things. She could break me in two if she wanted, or gut me in an instant. The only variable you didn't figure into your thoughts was me. Ki, I've known Sam has been doing something all these years to keep me from exposure to potential rivals. I simply never bothered to rationalize it out in such a forensic manner as you have—it had no meaning. As you mentioned, I know that Sam has been near to me my whole life. I have no idea what drew her to me, or what compelled her to leave her fog-bound home and come to the north in the killing cold. What Monama besides the paid seer does that? I have no idea what Sam sees when she looks at me. A great man? A powerful man? A fool? What is there to be seen? I really don't know, and I'm sure if I were to ask, she wouldn't answer. All I know is that if I have been fortunate to command such devotion from someone like Sam, and who am I to question it? I have been blessed. I have been enriched by the girl with the pale face and black eyes."

"You're not disturbed? The letter stealing? The Wraith?"

"I wouldn't expect anything less from her. And, if I were to shrink from such a thing, I wouldn't be a Vith, would I? As you said, she's not the sort of person to simply sit back and hope for the best. I actually admire that about her. And, I'm certain Sam is not the first lady in the League to take steps to sabotage a rival. Such things do happen, right, Ki?"

Ki smiled. "Yes, they do. I just can't think of anyone who went to such extremes. Usually ladies pay to have somebody else perform such things for them. There's a guild on Planet Fall specializing in just that."

"Sam doesn't do anything half-way, and she doesn't have the money or the means to contact a guild on Planet Fall. No, Sam would take matter into her own hands. Isn't that the Sam we both know and love?"

"I suppose so. So, Kay, how long have you known about this?"

"A long time. I'm not sure when I put it all together, but it makes sense. None of what you've just told me is at all surprising."

"And, you're just acting when you present yourself like a complete, dull-witted moron?"

"Well, let's not quite go that far, shall we, Ki, with the name calling?"

They laughed. Kay held out his hand. "Come on, Ki, let's get out of here."

Ki took his hand, and they exited the battlement, moving down the black stairs. She collected her two Whispers and put them back into her locket. "One last thing, Kay. You're certain you are at peace with this? I mean, to be spoken for your whole life? Have you no thoughts of what else might be out there?{

They exited the Firth House.

"Not really, no. I've no need to look anywhere else. I have all I need." They moved down the path and re-entered the castle.

"Hey, what are you doing?" came Sarah's loud voice. "Creation, we were about to list you as a missing person! Where've you been?"

"*Speaking of morons*," Ki said under her breath.

"Just having a talk with my sister, Sarah."

Sarah marched up. "What do you want to talk to her for? Your sister's making us late. The Gaston? Remember, we're heading out there? I don't want it to get dark on us!"

Ki spoke up. "Why do you want to go to the Gaston, Sarah?"

"No reason that would interest *you*," she replied in a rude voice. "Come on, Kay, let's go. Phillip's got the Ripcar ready and waiting!" Sarah grabbed Kay by the shoulder and pulled him down the corridor.

Kay looked back. "Hey, Ki?"

Ki stopped.

"Thanks for caring."

She smiled and waved as Kay was dragged away to go crouch in the weeds and cold rock planes of the Gaston to investigate the Wraith.

The spectral creature that loved her brother.

11—The ARLISS

They ate dinner in the Capricos Hall that evening. Everybody was there, along with a few guests. Dinners at Great Houses could be staunch, rigid affairs full of protocol and hidden rules, but not at Castle Blanchefort. Lord Davage, often starved as a child for failing to abide by the many rules Lord Sadric had put in place regarding meals, abolished every one of them. As a result, meals in the castle were informal, pleasant occasions full of good food and company. Lord Davage and Sygillis always sat side by side, laughing, talking, often times holding hands under the table. Lady Poe and Lord Peter followed suit. Countess Pardock of Vincent was often there for dinner, her husband dead and her children grown, but she was not there today. Milos and Millie often sat near their parents, Millie, being so young, still needed attention from Lady Poe at meal times, which she got in doting quantity. Milos wouldn't be around for much longer—he was soon to begin attending the old university in Arden. He already had his school pin, which he wore proudly on his lapel. Lady Kilos and Hathaline sat in random spots, as did Kay, Sarah and Phillip. Maser, that ridiculous kid, sat in a highchair near his mother Sygillis eating that soft kid's slop that Kay recalled hating.

Lt. Kilos and her Tweeter were also there sitting at the far end of the table. After his pool-side exploits with Sam transformed into Kilos's likeness, Kay wondered what the real Kilos was like during an intimate encounter. Sam portrayed her as a brutal, slightly sadistic lover, but, having gotten to know her over the years, Kay imagined her as a more passive, laid-back lover in bed. Who knows.

Sam was missing. Sam rarely missed dinner at Castle

Blanchefort as she loved eating Elder food.

Sarah was rank. "Sarah," Davage said, "how was the Gaston today?"

"Oh, it was fine, Uncle," she said, working on her plateful of roast beef. "We didn't see anything."

"Well, it's not surprising, Sarah. I've gone up and down the Gaston more times than I care to recall. I've never encountered a spectral creature there before."

"Are you certain, father?" Lady Kilos replied. "You never can be too sure when the Wraith might turn up."

Sarah tried to absorb the meaning of that and then dismissed it. "Lord Davage," Sarah said, "are you to be heading out soon?"

Davage wiped his lips. "Indeed, Sarah. Several days hence. Heading out for three weeks."

"Anything hot out there?" she asked.

"Actually, yes. We, along with several other ships, are headed to Hoban to lend support to an investigation of odd activity there. Just like the days of old, when the Xaphans were a constant threat, I'm rather looking forward to it."

Lt. Kilos took a drink from her tankard. "Kay, are you ever going to head out with your mom and dad … see the stars?"

"I don't like space travel, Lt. It makes me feel ill."

"Ohhh, you get used to it, kid. I used to get sick, too, in my early days. Want to know what cured it?"

"Um, yes, yes Lt., please. Tell me."

"Booze, kid. And lots of it."

Sygillis put her fork down and spoke up. "Ki, please don't encourage my son to take up drinking."

"Syg, lighten up, will you? Don't listen to your mom, Kay—a tankard of narva will cure anything."

"Ki," Sygillis said tartly, "it's been a long while since you and I stepped outside. If you would like a refresher, then please continue."

A footman entered the hall and spoke, "Lords and Ladies, may I present Lady Sammidoran of Monama and Astralon." Everybody at the table stood.

Sam glided into the hall in her usual black gown and bustle. She approached the table, looking a tad windblown. "Please forgive my tardy arrival. I was detained at home."

Kay pulled out a chair and properly seated her as another

footman handed Sam a menu of the evening's choices. Sam made her selections, and the footman retired to the kitchens to fetch them for her.

"I'm so hungry this evening," she said.

"We were just discussing the Wraith of Gaston, Sam," Lady Kilos said.

"Oh," Sam said, unfolding her napkin. "A lot of sensational nonsense."

"The Wraith is real all right," Sarah said. "Too many people have seen it to be a hoax. I've got all kinds of stuff on it."

The footman returned with Sam's selections. She picked up her fork. "And, what would you do should you ever come face to face with this creature?" Sam asked.

"I'd stand before it and demand it reveal its identity. I wouldn't be scared."

"Really?" Sam replied.

Lady Kilos jumped in. "What if, Sarah, you were actually sitting right next to the Wraith and didn't know it? What then?"

Sam looked around, noting all the weapons lining the walls. "Lord Davage—all of these weapons, they are the famous LosCapricos weapons of old, yes?"

"They are, Sam, every known type is displayed here. These are mostly mock-ups. They do not function."

Sam looked at the wall behind Davage. "That wand-shaped example behind you, my lord— what is that one?"

Davage turned to look. "This? This is the ARLISS of House Dare."

"It is very pretty."

"This mock up is made of ivory, but they are normally made of gold or silver."

Sam seemed a bit preoccupied. "Do you see that, Kay? The ARLISS. Do you think the ARLISS is pretty?"

Confused, Kay looked at it—it was just a plain ivory wand. "Sure, Sam, it's very pretty."

"What's it called again?"

"The ARLISS."

"ARLISS. Will you remember that for me, Kay, the ARLISS?"

"Sure, Sam."

* * * * *

A few days later, Kay, Sam and his cousins went down to the village to buy a birthday present for Duchess Torrijayne. Having no luck in finding inspiration for her gift, they ended up in a jewelry store on the Rundle Way, Phillip thinking a nice blue stone to match her eyes would be a nice touch.

As Sarah and Phillip looked around, Kay saw Sam, in her usual goggles, talking to the jeweler. She seemed to have him quite perplexed.

"No ma'am, I do not have one of those, and I don't know of any who might. If you need a purple stone, I have a fine quantity of amethysts and purple topaz."

"I do not want any of those. I must have a spinel, and it must be at least 300 carats in weight."

The jeweler shook his head. "You might try a store in a larger trade city, like Minz or Atalea. Certainly Armenelos would have such a thing. And, be ready for a hefty price."

Phillip and Sarah decided on a lovely sapphire ring for the Duchess. As they paid for it, Sam stood there next to Kay and looked rather sad.

* * * * *

Sarah had gotten a little nicer to Sam over the last few weeks. Strength impressed Sarah, and Sam had that in abundance. There was a soft mound in the Grove called Lennybus' Cone, and they loved to play King of the Mountain on it. Sarah, with her Gift of Strength, usually won such contests, Kay and Phillip not being able to dislodge her, but Sam could. Even at full strength, Sarah was no match for Sam, her wiry arms strong as a bear. Once Sam got to the top, she was there for good. Sarah grumbled about cheating but was still suitably impressed.

The bath house was another favorite haunt. In the evenings, they changed into swimwear and got in the huge heated pool. Lady Kilos often joined them, Sarah normally chasing her out, but Sam insisted she be allowed to stay and sit with them as Sam and Kilos were close friends.

One evening, Sarah was going on and on about a brandtball

match taking place in Rustam; apparently, she was a big fan. One of the annoying things about Sarah was her love of holonet, and she had to have it blaring at all times, or she wasn't happy. The bath house didn't have a holo-net terminal, and Sarah had forgotten her portable unit. She was making an awful racket about missing the game but didn't want to leave the soothing pool to go and get it herself.

Kay laughed and said he'd go and get it for her just to shut Sarah up.

"Don't be long," Sam whispered in his ear. "Want me to come with you, Kay?" she asked.

He kissed her pale skin. "No, Sam, it's fine. I'll be right back. I'm going for your terminal, Sarah," he said.

"Make it quick; I might miss the first set."

Kay pulled his boots on and donned a robe. He then made the long walk through the Ten gardens back to the castle to get Sarah's terminal. It was quite a slog. If he were a better Wafter, he'd do that to save himself a walk, but his Waft was awful. Sam didn't approve. *Work on your Gifts, Kay, for me,* she always said, and for good reason.

To save himself a bit of time, he walked through a large oak clearing populated by several ancient trees. The footing on either side of the clearing could be hazardous, but he knew the terrain so well he wasn't worried about it. He pressed on, walking at a good clip.

Ahead, a figure stood at one of the trees staring at its gigantic trunk. From a distance, he couldn't see clearly; the figure was tall and slim, female; it looked like his aunt, Lady Poe. He quickened his pace to say hello to her.

Slowly, the figure turned toward him.

"Kay?" he heard to his left. "Kay, is that you?"

Sitting some distance away in a wicker chair was his aunt, Lady Poe. Her head was lolled to one side, as if too heavy for her neck. Her eyes were rimmed with bags. She held a drink that had tipped over and spilled. She looked on the verge of death.

"Aunt Poe?" he said approaching her. "What's wrong? You look ill."

She managed a small smile, her eyes long slits. "I'm fine, Kay," she whispered. "Just tired. I need rest."

"What are you doing out here?"

"Getting a little air. Peter went to get me a blanket."

Kay was worried as she looked terrible. "Is there anything I can do for you, Aunt Poe?"

She slowly raised her hand and touched his cheek. "No, Kay, no. Did Snugs work for Lord Lon?"

"Oh, yes, Aunt Poe. It worked perfectly."

"Good. You and Sarah and Phillip, how close you are. That's important. Families need to be close. I love you like my own child."

She appeared to fall into a delirium. "Everything I do is for you and the children. Don't be afraid, Kay."

"Afraid of what, aunt?"

"The Tulees. Don't be afraid of them."

Kay was confused. He was about to ask her what a "Tulee" was when Lord Peter returned carrying a blanket. "Evening, Kay," he said.

"Evening, Uncle," Kay replied as Peter pulled the glass from Poe's limp fingers and began tucking the blanket in around her. He looked at Kay and appeared to note his concern.

"Don't worry about your aunt; she's fine. She's had a busy time of it lately. She just needs rest."

Kay knelt down, gave Lady Poe a kiss on the cheek, and took his leave. "Good night, Aunt Poe, Uncle Peter," he said.

"Good night, Kay," Peter replied.

Kay walked away and continued on toward the castle. It occurred to him just then—there was Aunt Poe sitting in the chair, so who was that he previously saw near the tree? He had been sure that was his Aunt Poe, too.

He walked back to the tree to investigate.

Nobody was there.

12—The Quest for Bowling

S arah had been dying for this for weeks. The four of them had been planning a bold adventure, and, now that the time had come, Sarah was beside herself.

* * * * *

Blanchefort Castle's nearest neighbor was Castle Durst, about seventy miles to the southwest-. It was a grand Vith structure like Blanchefort Castle, but much smaller and less well appointed. The Dursts were gone—no heirs, and the standing House name was officially extinct before the Sisters and the League Ex-Commons. With the passing of Countess Medaline of Grimm some ten years back, the castle stood empty. None of the remaining five Durst daughters, all married off and living elsewhere, chose to occupy the old ancestral castle.

Castle Durst was officially a ruin, one of the many floating around the Vithlands of Kana.

As per League custom, all of the Durst's possessions were to be appropriated and redistributed to any with legal claim to them. The Durst daughters, though direct descendants, had no legal claim to their own possessions, such was the very unfair but traditional male-oriented law of succession in the League.

However, Lord Blanchefort, having sworn to protect and maintain the Durst name until, with good fortune, the House could be legally reconstituted, secretly stole in and made off with the Durst's most valuable and treasured possessions. He hid them in a secure secret location until such time as he, or his progeny, could give them back to the future Dursts. When the hoard of claimants fell upon the castle, they only found an empty stone building and rotten food in the pantries.

Of the few possessions that Lord Blanchefort allowed to remain in open viewing were the blueprints to the castle, showing the many hidden areas and secret places that all Vith castles had in abundance. Sarah and Phillip had gotten hold of the map and poured over it, greatly interested in seeing them for themselves. On several afternoon expeditions, they had located the Durst holding room, several arcane libraries (now empty), a room that appeared to be a torture chamber, and a distillery where they fermented illegal spirits, the smell still thick in the air.

One thing that Sarah and Phillip were keen to find but couldn't was the Durst bowling alley. They knew it was there somewhere—all Vith Great Houses had hidden bowling alleys placed somewhere within the castle or on the grounds. The seven Durst daughters grew up with very good bowling averages. The deceased Lady Hathaline was said to have bowled a 300 game in the lost alley. However, try as they might, tearing the blueprints apart, they found no hidden alley. Sarah, bold as always, wrote to Lady Analine of Twill, the second of the last seven Durst daughters, and flat out asked her where the hidden alley was located. Analine wrote a terse response stating that was "none of her (expletive) business".

Sarah, however, took the rebuke as a victory. "That proves it's there some place, and we're just too dumb to figure it out!" Analine's response did nothing but whet Sarah's appetite.

* * * * *

One lazy evening they all sat in Kay's Tower, in a favored reading room on the 63rd floor. Sarah and Phillip were flopped out on couches, their dusters tossed aside and, as per usual with Sarah, the Airenet was turned on and some show bounced loudly in mid-air. Phillip typed into a terminal, as was his habit.

Kay and Sam sat on a couch by themselves near the terrace. Sam, shoes off and wearing one of the Countess's bodysuits, lay on him casually, her finger toying with his bellybutton that she found so fascinating. She loved quiet evenings. In a contented dream, she hummed a Monama tune.

They all sat in easy silence doing their own thing.

Sarah wasn't paying attention to the blaring Airenet. She was pouring over her copy of the Castle Durst blueprints, determined as ever to locate their alley. She was hoping to see something in the plans that had previously eluded her but wasn't having any success so far. Flopped on her stomach, her booted feet rocking carelessly back and forth, she tapped the paper with her fingers.

"We tried the west wing, already, right?" she asked.

"I believe so," Phillip responded absent-mindedly.

She poked the map. "I see a promising dead spot in the walls near western wing. I think, given the dimensions, a small bowling alley could be shoehorned in there."

She turned to Kay. "What do you think?"

"I think you should just leave it alone, Sarah. Would you want somebody poking around our castle looking for the Blanchefort alley?"

"No, but that's different. Castle Blanchefort's never going to be a ruin. I'll blow it up myself should it come to that."

There came a knock at the threshold. Lady Kilos stood there in a white gown holding a box of Perlamum pieces.

"Hi, everybody," she said in an uncharacteristically meek voice, "I was wondering if anyone was up for a game of Perlamum?"

Sarah took immediate exception. "Nobody wants to play Perlamum, *Tez*," she said in a rather ugly tone. "This is the fun room. The boring girls-wearing-gowns room is elsewhere. Push off!"

Kilos, holding her box, swallowed and made to leave.

Sam looked at Kay, silently demanding he speak up. "Hey, Ki, don't go. I'll play a game with you," he said.

She smiled and entered the room, seating herself across from Kay and opening her box. Sarah scowled—Sarah had never liked Lady Kilos much and wasn't shy about making her thoughts known.

"How can you wear those things?" she asked, noting Kilos's Blanchefort gown.

Kilos arranged the jade and turquoise Perlamum pieces on the fold-out board. "This? I love wearing my gowns. They feel quite comfortable to me. Your mother certainly wishes you'd wear a gown every so often, Sarah."

"Mother's going to have to soak it up on that one, isn't she?

Never catch me in one of those. How do you go to the bathroom I wonder?"

Before Kilos could answer, Sam spoke up. "No need to answer that, Ki. I think you look lovely in your gowns."

Kay and Kilos began playing, Sam sitting and watching. Eventually, Sarah forgot about Ki's presence and returned to staring at the Durst Castle map.

Sam sat up and stretched. *"Sar-te, inge fortencar?"* she said in her musical Monama language. She was now speaking more complex words, with Kay having mastered the more basic ones.

Kay thought a moment. "Wait, you asked if I …"

"Te, te, not *Ane,"* Sam corrected. "I was speaking to everybody."

"All right, you asked if we'd like something to eat, right?"

Sam was elated. "Close, Kay. Very good. I was asking if anybody would like something to drink: *fortencar,* not eat. To Eat is *dradzar* I was planning on getting something from the kitchen."

"No, thanks," Kay said puzzling at the board.

"Well, if you're going, Sam," Kilos said, "I'll take a Blue Gasol."

"That figures," Sarah replied in a loud voice. "Give me a Red Gasol, Sam, if you wouldn't mind," she said.

"I'll be right back," she said. She removed Snugs and Blinked away.

Kay and Kilos continued playing. Glancing over, Kilos became curious as to what Sarah was pouring over so intently. "What are you looking at?" she asked.

"None of your business," she replied.

Phillip stopped typing. "Sarah, give her a break, won't you. It's the plans to Castle Durst, Ki. We got them from Lord Davage."

"Oh," she said. She thought a moment. "Why are you looking at those?"

"Full of questions, aren't you?" Sarah responded.

Phillip made to respond. "We're …"

"Shhhhh!" Sarah said, cutting him off. "It's a damn secret! You want the whole League to know telling this motor mouth?"

Sam reappeared holding a try full of drinks and snacks. "She's looking for the Durst bowling alley, Ki," Sam said, apparently having heard the conversation. She set the tray down and picked up a green can. "Here, Kay, I brought you a Verdalar anyway."

"Thanks, Sam," he said vacantly, gazing at the board.

Sarah, taking her can, looked rather annoyed that her secret was out. "Great, Sam—you just blabbed to the blabber!"

"I'm not going to tell anybody," Ki said taking a drink. "What do you want with their bowling alley anyway? It's stripped. I saw the pins for it in the secret storage area down in the village. I went with Father as he supervised the process."

Sarah was jubilant. "Aha! You saw their pins? That proves it exists, and we just can't find it!"

"When you find it, what are you going to do?" Ki asked, taking Kay's jester. He sighed in misery.

"We're going to go there and bowl, Tez! What do you think we're going to do?"

Kay was annoyed, both from losing his jester and from Sarah's sour attitude. "Sarah, what have I told you about calling her that? She's my sister."

"Yeah?" Sarah replied. "What are you going to do about it?"

"I might have to kick your little butt right out the window."

Sarah sat up and pushed the blue prints aside. "Well, let's go then. I don't see anything between us but empty space." Phillip and Sam didn't pay them any mind. Kay and Sarah were constantly getting into little wrestling matches.

Kilos, unused to this sort of confrontation, was uncomfortable. "Well, there's no need to have an altercation on my behalf. It's fine, Kay."

They both stood up, and Sarah put her hair back. "They do this all the time, Ki," Sam commented, putting her feet up. "If I didn't know Sarah was Kay's cousin, I'd be pretty jealous as they're always rolling around with each other. *Parjen-thar will*: little 'snapping turtles'."

"Well, there's really no need to ..."

"Sure there is, Tez," Sarah said, rolling her sleeves up. "I'm going to mess your brother up a little right here, right now."

Kay and Sarah locked up. Quickly, Kay had her in a tight headlock, her blue hair squirting through the crease of his elbow.

Kilos sat there holding her Queen Perlamum piece, feeling a little put off, and glanced at the forgotten blueprints to Castle Durst. "Sarah you said you couldn't locate the Durst ancestral bowling alley, is that right?"

Sarah grunted something inaudible as she tried to free her head.

She flailed around, trying to grab hold of Kay's tailed hair. She wasn't allowed to use her Gift of Strength indoors, so she had to get by as is.

"Well, I see it right there on the blue prints plain as day."

Sarah reacted. "What? Wait a minute! Wait a minute! Let me go!" she said, her voice muffled. Kay released her, and she grabbed the blue prints. "Where do you see it?" she said, skeptically. "There is no possible way you see it so fast."

"Right there," Kilos returned, pointing.

"Where?" Sarah marched to the table and laid the blue prints out, scattering the Perlamum pieces.

"Hey!" Sam said. "You've ruined their game!"

"Who cares, Sam? Now then, Tez, where do you see the hidden alley?"

Kilos looked at the blue prints and pointed. "Right there." She pointed to the drawing of the large central tower, Rhoda Tower, easily the castle's tallest and largest feature.

Sarah looked at the drawing. "No, no, that's in the upper levels of the tower. The alley can't be hidden in there. It has to be below the ground level of the castle. You got me all worked up for nothing!"

"But why not? Our bowling alley is located underground, but that doesn't mean their's has to be as well, right? Also, I recall father mentioning the ground at Castle Durst is much more water-saturated than ours is; therefore, it seems to make sense that they would put their hidden alley in an elevated area. Rhoda Tower is quite large and should easily be able to accommodate such a thing."

Sarah studied the drawing intently. Phillip, becoming interested, came over and looked as well.

She tapped the paper with her finger. "Well, I see a fairly large blank area here between the sixty-forth and seventy-third floors. What do you think, Phillip? Kay?"

Phillip rubbed his chin. "I have been operating under the biased notion that the Durst alley is located below ground level, as that's where ours is, and the same at Oyln Manor."

"Will you shush-up on that!" Sarah yelled. "That's a secret!"

Phillip continued. "And the soil is, in fact, much wetter there than it is here. Lady Kilos could be correct. I'm rather embarrassed that I didn't think of that myself."

* * * * *

The next morning, they got the big old silver ripcar out of the park and began loading it. Kay and Phillip were there wearing their best coats and hats: Kay in his usual black and purple coat, custom-made by his mother, and his black Vith hat, and Phillip wearing a smaller Esther hat that he favored and a hunter green coat with tails. Both Phillip and Kay were wearing their CARG's, Kay's silver one and Phillip's verdant one that he rarely used. His SAPP hung about his neck as a scarf.

Sam blinked in, also wearing her nicest gown, a gothic black gown of taffeta and lace with a huge bustle with rather pointy Monama shoes. Lady Kilos was also there wearing a minty blue gown.

They were heading to Castle Durst to bowl in their secret bowling alley.

"It looks as if we should be heading out to a wonderful ball or an evening at a lavish restaurant, not going to a sinister castle ruin to play a simple game," Sam remarked.

Phillip laughed as he loaded his bowling equipment, his balls, gloves and shoes, into the back of the ripcar. "It's tradition, Sam. We're supposed to dress up when we bowl. That's how all the ancestors did it."

Kay threw his bag into the back. He noted the large dent toward the rear of the craft—mother had done that. "Of course, mother has a thing about bowling nude, which we seldom speak of. I'm bringing the yellow ball you favor, Sam. Do you want anymore?"

She took his arm. "No, no, the yellow is fine. Thank you."

Down the path, Sarah emerged from around the bend. Unlike the rest standing by the ripcar, she was wearing her usual duster and boots. Her hands were pretty full. She was carrying a bowling bag with her ball and shoes and travelling cover containing her usual lemon-colored gown. She was also carrying a cooler full of stuff.

"Why aren't you dressed, Sarah?" Phillip asked.

She approached, somewhat out of breath. "Because I'll change once we get there. I hate gowns."

"Then why wear one at all?" Sam asked.

"Because we're bowling, and a gown is the uniform you wear when you bowl."

Sarah piled her stuff into the ripcar and took inventory.

"Everybody got everything?" she asked.

"We're ready to go," Kay replied.

"What about pins? We'll need pins to play."

"Already loaded."

"And power? What about power?"

"I brought several portable power units, Sarah," Phillip said.

Apparently satisfied, Sarah climbed into the back.

With everybody present, they piled into the big silver ripcar, and Phillip lifted it into the air. He moved south around the formidable bulk of the castle, rising high.

"Look there, Sam," Sarah said pointing. "That notch in the mountains over there is the northern portal to the Gaston Way. Just a big, old pass through the mountains that goes all the way to Arden. It's flippin' haunted!"

Sam turned to look and adjusted her goggles. She saw the long line moving through the mountains, vanishing in the haze far to the south. "Really?" she said. "What sort of apparition haunts it again, please?"

"A creepy ghost that chases you in your ripcar! I've seen it myself!"

Sam appeared rather surprised. "Have you?"

Phillip looked back. "You have not, Sarah!" he said. "That was foxfire, and you know it!"

Sam, her incredible mass of black hair flowing in the breeze, laughed. "I wouldn't count on any further hauntings down that way, Sarah. I foresee no further troubles there." Sam removed her goggles and settled into Kay's shoulder, shutting her eyes.

Phillip cleared the castle and the coastal shelf and settled into the vast valley between two ridges heading south-west, following the natural contours and passing the great cone-shaped mountain of Mt. Durst. He picked up some altitude and came out of the valley bearing west.

Ahead, in the cold distance, was Castle Durst, sitting at the highest point between two mountain rivers. They passed over the walled outer compound, which was crumbling in places. The grounds within the wall were once carefully tended; now, the greenery had fallen back to nature and was overgrown and threatening to tangle. Ibex's had claimed a healthy portion of the south grounds through a breach in the walls, and the northern part was flooded a bit as the river was up. Elsewhere, wild, predatory animals were on the prowl. They passed fast-flowing Durst creek and were over the inner-compound. Here, Lord Davage's crews worked once a month to push back the tide of growing things, and it still appeared fairly-well tended.

The castle at the center of the grounds was quiet and forlorn. The white paint was starting to peel, revealing the old, gray rock beneath, and the whole place had a stark and singularly "vacant" feel to it. The window panes, once glittering in rare crystal and stained glass, had been removed, and the dozens of gaping holes left behind gave one the impression of a mouthful of rotten and missing teeth. Unlike the sprawling layout of Castle Blanchefort, Castle Durst was built around a central axel, like a great wheel, with smaller and larger spires rising up at regular points along the spokes of the wheel. The central feature of the castle was Rhoda Tower in the center. Though the castle was much smaller than Castle Blanchefort, Rhoda Tower was far and away larger than any single tower at Castle Blanchefort.

Phillip turned the ripcar and landed in the pebbled drive. He killed the engine, and they all got out. Sam put her goggles back on to protect her eyes from the afternoon glare. She craned her neck back and looked at the top. "How tall is this tower?"

Sarah, hauling her stuff, walked past her. "Two thousand, four hundred, fifty feet. I read it on the blue prints."

With everybody lugging their gear, they marched across the dragon-tooth moat and entered the open main doorway. Sam carried the impressively heavy box containing the bowling pins they would use for their game. The box's weight didn't appear to be troubling her in the least.

The emptiness of the place was astounding once inside. Once well known for its tapestries and lavish interior, all that greeted them now were bare walls and bits of garbage on the floor.

"So sad," Sam said, looking around. "The life and joy this place once must have seen, now all gone and stripped away. I don't like abandoned buildings, Kay. They make me uneasy."

"It's not abandoned now. Not with us here," Sarah said with a touch of optimism.

They worked their way to the base of Rhoda Tower. A massive spiral stairwell greeted them.

"The lifts are out," Sarah said in dismay. "Phillip, can you get this working? I'm not walking up sixty-four floors, no way."

He walked up to the panel and opened the cover. He attached the leads to a small portable power unit he'd brought just for this very purpose, and the lift came to life. "I figured you'd be a sissy about it, Sarah, so I brought this. I've got some more here with me for the bowling alley," he said.

"Good thinking," Sarah offered as the lift came down, and they piled in.

They went up sixty-three floors and got out into near total darkness. Sarah and Phillip lit their Sights and got out, the twin beams of their eyes panning about like flashlights; Phillip's was silver while Sarah's was an aqua blue. "Let me locate the junction panel. Just a moment," Phillip said, his silver beams shining bright and pooling on the walls.

Something brushed past Lady Kilos. "Sarah?" she said.

Two blue beams of light turned to her from down the hall, floating in the dark. "What?"

"Did you just brush past me and tug my gown?"

"No!" She turned away and resumed looking for the lights.

"Kay," Sam said still holding the heavy box of pins, "you should go out and help them."

"It's pitch black, Sam. I can't see."

"Use your Sight, Kay."

"I don't have the Sight, Sam. I wish you'd realize that."

As he stood there in the dark, he felt a sharp pinch in his lower back. It hurt quite a lot. "Ow! Sam, did you do that?"

"Do what, Kay?"

"Pinch me!"

She stood there holding the box with one hand. "Why would I pinch you, Kay? I can see fairly well in the dark. I'll help Sarah and Philip."

"Wait!!" He saw her pulling her goggles off and carefully put them into a pocket in her gown. In the pitch black he clearly saw her. "Sam, you …"

The lights came on with a click, revealing a musty antechamber of tight-fitting ochre stone blocks. "Got it!" Sarah cried in triumph.

Kay, Sam and Kilos exited the lift shaft. As below, the corridor was bare and windowless. Wire and metal hanging clips were pressed into the walls at various places indicating that vast murals and other hangings once decorated the corridor. Phillip was standing at an open panel at the end of the corridor trying to shore up the power connections he'd just made. Sarah was closely scanning the walls, looking for the entrance. "Well, don't just stand there, you people! Give me a hand finding the entrance to the place!"

"Don't bother with the east wall; concentrate on the west wall. That's where it has to be," Phillip added.

"I know that!" Sarah cried.

They put their things down and began a protracted search of the walls. "What are we looking for?" Kilos asked, feeling with her hands.

"Hidden panels, levers, buttons, wheels, anything that might open the door and reveal the damn bowling alley," Sarah said tugging on a slight imperfection in the stone.

They gave the stone walls the once over, feeling and testing but finding nothing. Sarah and Phillip gazed at the walls with their Sight, but they saw nothing through the stone but stone.

"I don't think it's here," Kay said taking a step back. "We're suspecting that the alley is hidden between the 64th and 72nd floors, so the entrance could be anywhere on those floors. It might even be elsewhere."

Sarah turned to him, her eyes lit up like cyan laser beams. "Better get climbing then. I want to keep searching here for a bit more, then we'll be up, right?"

Kay made his was down the corridor to the spiral staircase at the end. Sam clapped her hands together to clear the dust she'd picked up from the walls and followed him up.

"Hey, Sam, I think I got something here. Could you please help me?" Kilos asked, feeling about a suspect imperfection in the wall. Reluctantly she stopped and joined Ki at the wall.

He clambered up the stairs to the next level. The level above was plunged in darkness, and he couldn't see a thing. In the estuary between the light from the level below and the darkened corridor above, he squinted and tried to see, straining as hard as he could.

Nothing. He thought he'd been able to see Sam removing her goggles in the dark after feeling a pinch. He recalled his father talking about pain enhancing the Gift of Waft. Perhaps it would work with the Sight as well, though his father didn't think so. He took a pinch of skin on his forearm and squeezed, but all he did was hurt his arm and make it red.

Sure enough, despite what Sam said and thought, he couldn't see in the dark. He had no Sight and was therefore a great disappointment to his father and a setback to the House of Blanchefort. He felt a little coiling of shame building up in him somewhere, as he had previously in his father's study.

He drew his CARG. It always glowed a bit in darkness, an unintended side-effect of the introduction of his mother's Silver tech during its forging. The glowing wasn't directed into a beam, however, and the soft glow often did more harm than good as it completely fouled any night vision he might have had going.

"Phillip, I'm going to need light up here!" he yelled down.

Waving the CARG around, he found the wall. As below, it was bare stone and forgotten memories. The windowless interior here was more cave-like than castle. His mother often spoke of part of her soul having grown up here, in the good days when the Dursts were full of high hopes and the promise of ascendancy amongst the old Vith Houses. Surely a male heir would come. Surely the House would live on.

Kay moved his CARG along the stone face of the wall, hoping to see some sort of obvious lever or button that might reveal the entrance to the bowling alley. This was turning out to be more work than he'd been hoping for. Sarah and her little adventures. He pressed on into the dark, hoping to ...

What's that?

Something down the corridor caught his eye, and he stopped, turning his attention to the gummy darkness ahead. He was certain he'd seen something pickup the silvery light of his CARG and reflect it back, something flat and coin-like—like a pair of eyes. Kay felt a thrill run down his spine, and his loins tighten. He raised his CARG and held it steady.

"Who's there?" he said, his voice shaking slightly.

Listening intently, he thought he could hear something stirring in the dark.

" I know you ..." A voice!!

Down below, Phillip and Sarah got into a loud, cursing argument about something, and the din of their drifting voices drowned out all else.

Damn those two—he couldn't hear! Holding his CARG at the

ready, he stepped farther down the corridor, dreading to catch another glance at whatever it was. He got to the end and saw nothing.

Something was there, he knew it!

He felt a brush across his back. He whirled around.

"Kay!" Sam cried, startled. "It's just me. What's wrong?"

He put a protective arm around her. Sam's taffeta gown crinkled a little as he squeezed her. He raised his CARG and held it out. Sam's pale skin picked up the light and shown with a moon-like glow. "Creation, Sam, you startled me. I thought I saw something."

"Saw what?" she asked.

"I don't know, a pair of eyes possibly. I thought I heard something, too."

Sam looked around. "You must have been imagining it." She embraced him and offered a loving kiss. She put her hand over his heart. "Gods, Kay, your heart is pounding. It's all right, *Arin-Dan*. There's nobody here."

"Then what did I see?"

"Well, Kay, I don't know. It's dark and unfamiliar in here. Perhaps you imagined it? That's perfectly understandable." Sam embraced him in a protective fashion. He could smell the wormwood in her hair.

"Do you smell anything?"

"I can't smell much when I'm wearing Snugs."

"Take it off."

"I don't want to take it off. It's probably freezing in here. It was just your imagination, Kay. That's all."

There was a commotion coming up the stairs. Sights lit and bobbing, Phillip and Sarah appeared.

"Are you kissing?" Sarah cried in dismay, her two blue beams fixed on them in a pair of blue spotlights.

"What if we are?" Sam replied.

"It's time for bowling, not kissing!"

Phillip, his silvery Sight beams panning about, passed them and went to the junction panel. He opened it and attached a pair of cables. The lights came up a moment later.

Kay rubbed his eyes and looked around, seeing nothing but the water-stained stone walls. Sarah was already at the walls looking for the entrance. Lady Kilos was making her way up the stairs. Sam smiled and gave him another kiss, finally letting him go. They both went to the wall and joined the search.

"Oh, here! Here! What's this?" Kilos cried, spying a recessed lever in the wall.

They gathered around. At eye-level was a small metal lever sitting within a housing in the stone. It appeared to have once been behind a painting or hanging. Greedy and impatient, Sarah put her hands in and tried to move the lever.

"No, it's stuck. Damn! Phillip, open this! I'm not allowed to power up inside, remember? I promised mother." Phillip approached but couldn't get anywhere with it either.

"Sam?" Sarah said turning to her.

Sam took a look at the lever, reached in and pulled. BANG! The rusty lever broke loose and came forward. In the center of the corridor, a hidden doorway slid in and moved aside, revealing a cloudy darkness from within.

There it was—the Durst's hidden bowling alley. They all gazed at the open doorway.

"Wait!" Sarah shrieked. "Don't anybody go in; I need to get changed first!" She took her gown (still in its bag) and ran down the stairs with it.

They stood there looking at the dark space within waiting for Sarah to return. "I really don't wish to do this," Kilos said. "I feel as though we are treading upon the Durst's memory."

"We're honoring them by coming here to play and revel in their memory," Phillip replied. "I don't have an issue with it."

The doorway and whatever was beyond it beckoned. Nobody went in. "I wonder how many times Mother walked through this door to play?" Kilos said.

"Mother?" Kay asked.

"She always says a small part of her soul grew up here in this castle."

Sarah came back up the stairs. She was in her lemon gown, trying to cinch it up in the mid-section area. She was wearing her bowling shoes and holding her bag with her prized clear bowling ball within. "Ok, I'm back, let's go in." She pushed past everybody and got to the open doorway, standing there. "It's powerful dark. Phillip, can you bring up the lights?"

He shook his head. "Nope, not until we get inside. It must be in there someplace."

Sarah lit her Sight and plunged in, followed by Kay and Sam and Lady Kilos.

Kay and Sam stumbled through the dark, feeling their way. Sarah and Phillip's lit Sights panned about. "There's a ramp here leading down. Be careful," Phillip added.

Kilos groped about in the dark and took Kay's arm. "Kay?" she asked. "Can you see?"

"No, Ki, I can't."

"You can, too, Kay! *Jon-de Mi!* You make me so angry sometimes!" Sam yelled, sounding quite annoyed. In the dark she got into his face; he could feel her heat and smell her breath. "Come on, Kay, it's time for you to grow up! You promised me you would practice!"

"I don't have the damn Sight, Sam! How many times do I have to feel this humiliation?" Sam simmered in the dark, ready to lose her temper.

The lights came on.

The Durst bowling alley stretched out in flickering light as Phillip shored up the power connections. It was quite a bit smaller than the Blanchefort alley, having only one lane as opposed to the three that they had. It was sunken quite a bit, and there was a switch-back ramp trailing down to the alley floor. As in the corridor, the stone walls were bare. The whole place was plain and rather depressing, though, in its day, it was probably lavish with paintings and tapestries.

Sam seemed a little put off and went out into the corridor to get the heavy box full of pins.

Down below, Phillip was fiddling with the pin pit, trying to restore life to the pin setter, while Sarah stocked the small bar behind the scoring table with drinks and snacks she'd brought. Kay and Kilos made their way down as Sam reemerged through the door with the box.

"Hey, Kay, what's this?" she asked, her momentary morass forgotten.

She was looking at a stone pillar partially buried in the stone wall. On it, several generations of Dursts had scratched their names. There were many names ending with "line," the usual ending of a girl's name in the old Durst House, and many "thas" as well for the men. Sam was pointing at one name. "Look at this one, Kay!" she said.

The one she was pointing at read:

Hathaline loves Davage

Kay looked at it. Part of his mother's soul had written that inscription years ago.

"I would like to write our names, Kay," Sam said handing him the box. Kay staggered a bit under its weight as Sam began to scratch their names into the pillar with her fingernail.

"Hey, come on!" Sarah yelled, getting impatient. "No time for that, Sam!" Kay, still struggling with the box, headed down the ramp with a giddy Sam following, giving him little tickles as he worked his way down.

Sarah had placed her clear ball on the rails and was getting Phillip's green ball out of the bag. Kilos seated herself and put on her bowling shoes.

Phillip was having no luck in the pin pit. "The mechanism's gone!" he called out from down the lane. "Looks like somebody's going to have to stay down here and manually reset the pins."

"What did you say, Phillip?" Sarah yelled from the scoring table.

"Nothing, Sarah," Kay responded. "Look, I'll just get into the pit and reset them myself. I've never been overly big into bowling anyway."

"No, Kay, we'll take turns. It's not fair for you to do it all the time!" Sarah said.

"Sure, sure. I'll take the first shift."

Phillip stood and made his way up the lane and got his ball off the rails as Kay pulled himself into the tight confines of the pit. Sam followed him down.

"Kay, make room, and I'll join you back there," she called.

"No, Sam, you play and have fun. I'll be out soon. Promise."

She hesitated. "*Ange-zein ah stener-zwei, Arin-Dan?*" she asked him quietly.

"Of course I'm not angry with you, *Cerri-Tela*," he replied, understanding complex Anuie more and more. "Go on, Sam. Get your shoes on."

She leaned down and kissed him, then carefully made her way to the scoring table, not wanting to risk slipping in her Monama shoes on the waxed surface. Kay set the pins up and climbed up out of the way as Sarah wound up and took the first throw.

* * * * *

The game seemed like it went on forever, with ball after ball shooting down the Durst's old lane. Kay was nearly driven deaf as each throw made a commotion of noise in the pit, and he had to stuff his fingers in his ears so that his eardrums wouldn't split.

Midway through the first frame, Lady Kilos appeared to be in the lead, followed by Phillip, then a distant Sarah and Sam dragging the rear. Sam could throw the ball very hard, but she had no touch and could not pickup a spare to save her life. She had left a trail of open frames in her wake. Peeking up the lane through the pit, he saw Ki giving Sam pointers. It was odd seeing Sam, wraithlike in black holding a fruity-yellow bowling ball, her fingers stuck in the holes.

"Hey, Kay!" Sarah shouted. "Come out! We're going to have a bathroom break and get some refreshments before we continue. I brought drinks!"

"Come out, Kay," Sam said. *"Stantis meine arte kinder-loe!"*

"What's that mean?" Sarah asked.

"It means: I was hoping we could take a short walk before we begin playing again," Sam said.

"Well, don't be long!" Sarah said. "Creation, we've a game to finish!"

Kay, walking up the lane, had to laugh. That was clearly not what Sam had said. Sarah would freak if she knew what Sam had *really* said.

Sam was waiting for him. "Come on, slow poke," she said. He took her hand, and they explored the back half of the alley. In the rear was a door that opened up into a circular stair spiraling all the way up to the top of Rhoda Tower far away. There were small windows at regular intervals, so they had light to see. They went up about three floors, and then Sam put him up against the wall and rubbed into him.

"At last! We could make love right here and now, Kay. All that bowling has made me rather randy I'm afraid," she said into his ear, her voice changing into an earthy burr as it usually did when she was becoming aroused. "I find it oddly provocative with Sarah around, as she despises my touching you." She began feeling up his leg.

Despite himself and the close proximity of his sister and his cousins, Kay was fairly keen to try. He reached up through the volumes of crinkly black cloth of Sam's gown and found the hot apex of her crotch. Sam began to moan.

Sam had his shirt pulled out and was well on her way to unbuttoning his pants when Kay heard Sarah rooting around downstairs somewhere close. "Kay! Sam! Where are you? We're going to resume in a few minutes!"

Hearing Sarah's voice so close was a bit of a mood-killer for Kay. Sam, unmindful, began to wrap him up in her long arms. Soon there would be no reasoning with her, and she'd make enough noise that Sarah was sure to hear.

"No, Sam, we can't ..."

Sam licked his neck and began working him. "No, no, no, Kay. I want to make love."

"Shhhh, shhh!"

"I want to make love!"

She was steamy and unreasonable. "All right, but not here. Let's go up to the top. The prospect of Sarah catching us is not a pleasant one for me."

Panting, Sam let him go. She removed her Snugs and Blinked away. Damn, her Blink was fast. Kay tried to relax and calm his breathing. He settled and began to perform a Waft, trying to implement what he'd learned in Father's study. As usual, it took a great deal of patience and inner calm to begin the process. Slowly, he felt the twisting column of wind form around him, and he became light and airy. He felt himself moving in the direction he wanted to go, passing through the dozens of stone levels to the distant top where Sam was waiting. Things were indistinct around him. In a twilight, he saw the great, windowed lounge of the upper most room of Rhoda Tower appear, and he allowed the Waft to swirl to a stop.

Kay looked around. The room, once a grand gathering area featuring commanding views all around, was empty and surrounded by open terraces and galleries. To the east, Kay could see the distant confusion of spires from Castle Blanchefort like a reddish pincushion low on the horizon. Farther east he could see the domain of Bloodstein, his distant relatives, clinging to the leeward side of the mountains. Northeast was the ancient hamlet of Shirster Point locked in ice by the sea, and, to the west, was the Vith city of Mt. Holly.

Castle Durst certainly commanded a central viewing of most of the Vith's great holdings.

The notion struck Kay as odd for a moment. Castle Durst, from its central and rather elevated position, commands most of Vithland. Should somebody wish to launch an attack of some sort, it would be ideal to do it from this place. Kay was alarmed for a moment, almost panicked.

But of course, that was silly. Who would want to do such a thing, as Castle Durst was just a ruin.

He looked around. "Sam?" Where was she? He thought she might have gotten comfortable in one of the terraces; Sam liked to make love in odd places. He took his coat off and laid it down.

Ah, there she was. He saw a black form standing framed in the northern gallery, facing the balcony. She was holding some sort of red torch that lit her up in a garnet glow. "Sam, what are you doing over there? We don't have much time; Sarah will kill us."

He saw her head turn slightly. Over her shoulder, he saw the pale skin and black eyes.

"*I know you ...*"

The figure standing against the wall was not Sam. It was clearly a Monama with the pale skin and black eyes. It had the usual thin body type and massive head of black hair and was wearing a black waistcoat of some kind with baggy white sleeves. It was apparently male, with rather dainty features.

"Clatera?" Kay asked. "Clatera, is that you?"

Hearing his name seemed to wake him up a little. He stirred and turned to face Kay.

"What are you doing here?" Kay asked. "You'll freeze."

Clatera mumbled something. "I didn't hear you. Let me help, you're probably freezing to death."

He spoke again. "*I told you ... too many questions!*"

He sprang, covering a fair distance. Kay backed away, rubbing up against the wall. Clatera landed in a half crouch. He raised his arms, and he had four of them. Two were clad in his baggy sleeves while two more had burst out through the fabric of his shirt and were bare. Long, deadly claws glistened at his fingertips.

"*See what happens! See what they do to us! You did this to me!*" Clatera growled. He advanced on Kay, moving in a supple fashion like a panther.

Kay tried to back away, to give himself room. Up against the wall, he side-stepped to his left and bumped into something solid, yet fleshy. In an instant, four pale arms went around his chest. Claws dug into his flesh.

"Care for something exotic?" whispered a feminine voice in his ear. He pulled away and the arms parted, allowing him to fall forward. Looking back, there was Mitzilaran, four-armed, wearing her slinky black dress. She had a diabolic look on her face. *"I can be anything you want me to be."* She raised her arms and slowly advanced.

Kay was surrounded with Mitz in front of him, Clatera coming up from his rear. Despite his situation, Kay felt his heart break. He barely knew these two, but he considered them friends. Mitz had been so kind to him. She had understood how he felt. And now, here they were ...

Berserkacides. All of Sarah's lurid stories and postings hit him full. They had opened up to him a little, and now they were Berserkacides, as if they were being punished for speaking to him. He backed away and unsaddled his CARG preparing to wield it against his friends.

Berserkacide: Four-armed. Bestial Rage. Death of Personality.

Whoever Clatera and Mitzilaran of Cardinal had been was gone forever. Only the Berserkacides remained.

The gravity of the situation hit him full. This wasn't a rumble session in the Grove with Sarah and Phillip or a wrestling match with Sam; this was for keeps. "Phillip!" he yelled. "I need help! Sam!"

Where was Sam?

Mitz came at him, moving with incredible speed and grace. Kay held his trembling CARG out, one-handed as usual. Behind him,Clatera side-stepped to his right.

Mitz brandished her four hands barbed with glistening claws, allowing him to appreciate them.

From listening to Sarah over the years, he'd assumed Berserkacides were these raging beasts slavering to taste warm meat. However, Clatera and Mitz weren't making much noise at all, and that was even worse. Mitz darted about, staying at the end of his CARG, testing his defenses and gathering information on Kay. How fast was he? How skilled? Where was a weakness and how best to strike? Mitz seemed very deliberate and cunning. Clatera, stayed in his rear, readying to strike.

"Sam!" Kay cried. "Phillip!"

Mitz smiled a little and took a solid swipe at Kay's CARG,

hoping to either bisect the weapon with her claws or knock it from his grasp. Kay felt the CARG tremor, but he held fast. He tried a quick thrust, but she nimbly moved aside.

From behind, Clatera advanced. Kay whirled around in a wild swing, hoping to keep him at bay. Clatera leapt away, easily evading his wild swing.

They circled, and the two Berserkacides began a new tactic. They backed him up into the west gallery where he'd have no place to go except over the side in a long drop to the cold ground far below. Clatera feinted one way, and when Kay reacted, Mitz darted the other and got past Kay's defense, swiping him in the shoulder. She buried her claws into his shoulder where they bit deeply.

Pain.

Kay grimaced and saw stars. His wound was on fire. His eyes watered, and he felt instantly sick from the pain.

And he saw something through the amber haze of pain. In the gallery behind the Berserkacides, he saw some sort of strange, partially constructed device sitting in the center of the room, one that hadn't been there before, or at least he hadn't seen it.

His innards reacted to seeing the device. Something told him it meant no good, that if it was made whole or woken up, then terrible things would happen. The device could not be allowed to remain. He had to get rid of it.

It was imperative, but why he felt that way he didn't know.

He tried to get a better look at it, but Mitz was on him. She batted his CARG aside and got in close, her four clawed hands slashing his neck and head. Kay managed to keep his poise and forced her to draw back with quick strikes from his light weapon. She backed away and made to do a final lunge, either knocking Kay over the side or spilling his blood. It really didn't matter. To his right, Clatera coiled up for a side-strike.

Kay performed a sudden move that neither of them expected. Kay's CARG was a wonder. Imbued with Silver tech, it could do a number of useful things, including length expansion. He jammed the horn of the CARG into the floor and rapidly expanded its length. He rocketed forward, like a pole vaulter, over the flailing Mitz and landed in the center of the room, the two Berserkacides tearing after him.

He was standing right next to the device. Glancing at it, it seemed to be only partially constructed. Several obvious components were missing. As the two Berserkacides closed the distance, he hauled back and swung, cleaving the thing in two.

"*No!*" Mitz screamed. He watched it topple over for a moment and felt immensely relieved. Whatever happened now didn't matter. The thing was gone.

The two of them lost their sly calmness and roared in rage, thirsting for his blood.

Kay raised his CARG and readied to make his final stand.

"What are you two doing?" came an angry voice. "You better not be naked up here for Creation's sake!" Sarah shouted marching into the room.

"Sarah! Look out!" Kay cried. Mitz skittered to a stop and made to gut Sarah.

"What are you …" Sarah saw the Berserkacide beast coming at her. Instead of her usual bravado and love of fighting, Sarah's mouth dropped open, and, eyes wide, she froze in place.

She locked up solid as the slavering Mitz came at her. Kay had always suspected that Sarah's bluster when it came to Berserkacides covered up a genuine terror of them. Vith didn't feel fear, but Sarah was half Esther, and she was petrified. "Sarah, move!" he cried. She just stood there in her lemon-colored gown as death approached.

Seeing Sarah's bloody end mere moments away, Kay again turned to his CARG. As it could expand in length, it could also fire a blast of Silver tech. Kay could do a fair amount of damage with it. The trouble is that it did not always work, and there was no way to know if it would or it wouldn't.

Kay gripped the hilt and squeezed. Either this worked, or Sarah was dead.

The CARG grew hot, and then a molten blast of Silver tech came out, hitting Mitz squarely in the chest. Rolling with the blast, as if caught in the spray of a fire hose, flesh-shredding, Mitz rolled across the floor and was swept over the side of the gallery.

Clatera roared and altered his course and went at Sarah, also. "*First her, then you!*" He bounded in for the kill.

Another figure joined her as the reaching beast approached.

It was Lady Kilos. Though she only had a quick moment to take in and process what was happening, she acted fast. She got in front of Sarah. "*Stop!!*" she said in a fairly accomplished Dirge voice which reverberated around the gallery.

Clatera reacted as if hot oil had been poured over him. He fell to the floor, curled up and kicked and flailed, his claws sparking off the floor. He pawed at his head and pulled out fist-fulls of black, Monama hair. The power of the Dirge wore off, and he sprung again with incredible speed.

Ki put her arms around Sarah and, in a blast, Wafted away, leaving the Berserkacide only empty space.

Phillip entered the gallery, saw what was happening and drew his CARG and SAPP. He formed his SAPP into a black shield as Clatera squared off with him, trying to get around his shield.

Kay joined him, CARG at the ready. They worked well together, Phillip holding Clatera at bay while Kay threatened him with his CARG poised over top of the SAPP, like a horned, carapaced beast. Clatera tried to lunge to his right, and Phillip stopped him with his reaching CARG. Kay then attacked and impaled him through the ribs. He cried out and backed away.

They pressed the attack, relentlessly pushing toward the wall. Clatera tried to bound away and Phillip slashed, drawing blood. Kay came in and thrust, getting him deep in the thigh.

With a burst of strength, he pushed them away and staggered toward the gallery where he made to leap over the side and then down to the ground far below. Kay and Phillip charged in pursuit, but the Berserkacide Clatera was far too fast and would reach the side well ahead of them.

Something happened. They saw the beast's head, arms and torso go over the side and plummet away; however his waist and legs were still there. Then there was blood bursting from the legs in a torrent. Then, the sick mess toppled over.

"Kay!" he heard a voice. It was Sam. They ran to the gallery and looked over the side.

There was Sam, clinging there against the tower face with her claws like a rock climber. Her right hand was soaked in blood. She had killed Clatera with a swipe of her hand, bisecting him clean with her claws. Though she was fastened against the face of the tower with a two thousand foot drop below, she tried to hide her bloody hand from Kay. "The light, Kay, the red light. Is it gone?"

Kay looked around. Lying on the floor near the center of the gallery was a garnet pool of light. "I see it over there. Let me help you up!'"

Sam clung fast to the side of the tower and refused to move. "Dispose of that light, Kay. Destroy it!"

Phillip went to the light and poked at it with his CARG. It shattered, and the light went out. "It's out, Sam! It's out!"

He helped her up into the gallery and she could barely stand she trembled so. "I thought you were dead, Kay, and I couldn't help you. I was too frightened to help you!"

Kay pulled her straight and held her. "It's all right, Sam. I'm fine." Sam went limp with fright and shame. "Sam!" He propped her up and looked around. "Where are Ki and Sarah?"

Phillip lit his Sight and looked around. "I think I see them several floors down. They look ok."

They searched the area. Three floors down, they found Ki and Sarah, unharmed, though Sarah appeared out of her skull with fright. Ki stroked her hair and soothed her.

* * * * *

They returned the next day with Lord Davage, Countess Sygillis and the Magistrates of Blanchefort and Mt. Holly. A search of the area found nothing of note in the castle; however, on the grounds, Clatera and Mitz's transport was found, partially destroyed and hidden by brush. The remains of Mitz's body was gathered up and put in a box, as was Clatera's. Kay wanted to take their remains back to Lake Monama so that they could be buried with their people, but Sam said Berserkacides could not be buried on Monama lands. After some doing, he convinced his parents to allow him to bury them in a servants' graveyard deep in the Grove. He said these two were his friends, and he owed it to them. He felt it was his fault they were transformed into Berserkacides, that, if they hadn't encountered him in the fog, perhaps none of this would have happened. He swore, if he could someday make this right, he would. He would not forget them.

Of the strange device Kay said he saw and destroyed, not a trace of it could be found, no fragments, no nothing. Davage looked the area over several times with his Sight and confirmed nothing was there to be found. The Magistrates scanned the gallery with their best equipment: empty.

Perhaps Kay imagined it in the heat of the moment.

13—A Visit from the Sisters

A fter the incident at Castle Durst, Sarah became much friendlier toward Lady Kilos. She never actually thanked her for saving her life, but her gratitude was clear.

Unfortunately, her attitude toward Sam soured to almost the point of hostility. Sarah no longer differentiated between Monamas and Berserkacides and looked at Sam with a mistrusting eye, often leaving the room when she entered.

Sam never quite recovered after Castle Durst, as she allowed Kay to fight for his life alone, too terrified of the Berserkacides to help. She seemed diminished a bit, not quite the powerful figure she had presented herself as before. And Sam's absences increased. Always unexplained, never a reason for being gone offered.

* * * * *

Kay, Sarah and Phillip were surprised when they were called into Lord Davage's study one afternoon a week after Castle Durst. Sam, as usual, was not there, and that suited Sarah just fine.

Eagle-eyed Sarah had seen the procession come up through the village that morning. The floats, the flanking Marines.

She'd seen the Sisters coming to the castle.

The Sisterhood of Light had maintained a very close relationship with the House of Blanchefort over the years. When Kay's mother, Countess Sygillis, joined the House, the relationship became a bit rocky, as, she being an ex-Black Hat, created some measure of tension. However, after a tenuous first few encounters, the Sisters grew to trust and accept Sygillis and value her counsel.

The Sisters came often. It was said they, occasionally, needed advice, and Lord Davage was always good for that. It was also said that, when they had a question about the Xaphans, they asked Countess Sygillis, as she was once a Xaphan.

Others simply said they enjoyed Lord Davage's company and liked to be sociable when they could. In any event, their meetings were always private and not spoken of to any great extent.

Today, however, was different. Everyone present, in turn, was asked to come to Lord Davage's study and spend a few moments with the Sisters, staff included. It was an odd thing to be asked to see the Sisters. Everybody in the castle couldn't help but be nervous.

"I'll bet you it's about the Berserkacide thing in the castle," Sarah speculated. "I'll bet they think Sam's a Berserkacide and was in on it."

"She was not, Sarah," Kay replied, cross.

Kay, Sarah and Phillip sat outside the study, feeling a bit put off. Inside the study were the Sisters, and Creation knows what they really wanted. Lady Kilos and Lady Hathaline were there, also. Lady Kilos, usually a witty, somewhat sarcastic girl, sat silent in her lilac gown, obviously wanting to be elsewhere. She had her little terminal with her but wasn't typing anything into it. Lady Hathaline, ever the adventurer, didn't seem to care one way or the other. She asked a question.

"I don't know, Hath," Kilos replied.

The door to the Lord Davage's study opened, and Lady Poe and Lord Peter came out holding hands.

Lady Poe, looking drawn and rather tired, gave a friendly nod to everybody present, stopped and adjusted Sarah's collar, and fussed with her hair. "You should be wearing a gown for this, young lady," she said under her breath.

"Let her be," Peter said. "You look just fine, Sarah."

Sarah smiled at her father.

The door opened again, and Lord Davage called in Kay, Sarah and Phillip, Kilos and Lady Hathaline.

Slowly, as if they were going to their deaths, they stood and walked inside.

In the study was Countess Sygillis, sitting near Davage's desk in a bright teal gown. Sitting across from them were five Sisters, each wearing their usual white robes with blue cloaks. Their winged headdresses were large and pure white. A handsome, uniformed Marine stood by each one.

Davage returned to his desk and took a seat. "Come in, everybody, don't be shy," he said cheerfully.

One by one, they approached the desk, turned to the Sisters, and bowed. The Sisters acknowledged them with a short nod. There was a long, padded bench placed in front of the desk for them to sit, though, there wasn't enough room for everybody, so Kay and Phillip stood while Sarah, Kilos and Hathaline seated themselves.

There was silence for a minute or two.

Kay felt quite uncomfortable and wanted to look at the floor, but he knew proper etiquette demanded that one always look the Sisters in the eye, and he did, though it was hard. Phillip, standing next to him, was having less success, and his eyes often wandered to the floor.

After what seemed like an eternity, a Marine spoke. "Lord Blanchefort," he spoke for one of the Sisters, "you have truly grown into a fine young man. You do your House proud, as always. You and your kin are well favored, and we are honored to be counted amongst your friends."

Kay knew the proper response. "I am humbled to be in the exalted presence of the Sisterhood of Light and am also humbled that you find favor with me and my kin. I will, as the next Lord of Blanchefort, look forward to sustaining our age old friendship and open my arms to you, as you see fit."

The Sisters listened to his greeting and smiled.

Another Marine spoke. "You are, no doubt, curious as to the nature of our visit. We shan't keep you in suspense any longer. Several weeks ago, our sacred stronghold at Hiei was breeched, and an item was stolen."

Kay was shocked. "Stolen?"

"Yes. Fortunately, no Sisters were hurt or killed during the execution of the robbery. It is our wish to spend a moment with you to make you aware of this event, and to inquire if you have heard anything regarding the person or persons responsible. We are touring all of the Great Houses and asking for their help as well. Any information you have to share shall be most appreciated."

Kay could feel his insides churning a bit—the Sisters were Staring him up and down. If he had known anything about the robbery, their Stare would have dug it out immediately. The banter was, as they say, merely lip service.

Sarah was fidgeting hard, and Phillip looked sick—they were getting the Stare treatment, too. Lady Kilos bit her lip and sat as still as she could. Lady Hathaline seemed to be suffering the most. She rocked back and forth, holding her stomach. Davage and Sygillis watched. Syg, in torment, took Davage's hand and squeezed it.

Hathaline stood and slumped over, holding her face with her hands. Kay went to her side and held her up. "Sis," he said. "Just let it pass through. Ok, let it go."

Weeping, she held onto Kay and struggled to endure the Stare.

Sygillis stood. "Enough, you are hurting our daughter!"

A Marine responded. "There's a darkness with this one. Has she been to Esther?"

"No, she has not, Sister," Davage, replied. "She is sixteen years old, for Creation's sake, and I'll thank you to let her go."

The Sisters Stare continued. They dug deep, sifting for information and little Hathaline wasn't handling it well.

Whoever was stupid enough to steal something from the Sisters will be hunted forever. They were not forgiving about certain things, the Sisters. Nor were they forgetting. If he or Sarah or Phillip or anybody else had actually been the one who committed the robbery, they'd have been killed where they were.

They seemed to be taking a particular interest in Hathaline, peering deep into her soul. She made a gurgling sound.

"Sisters, enough!" Davage said in a commanding tone.

They let her go, and she staggered. Kay helped Hath back to her seat. "You ok, sis?" he asked, offering her a cloth.

She took it and nodded, wiping her face. Sygillis came to her side and held her.

After a moment, Kay resumed his spot next to Phillip and spoke. "Great Sisters, I am relieved to learn that none were harmed during the execution of this heinous act. Unfortunately, I have no information to share with you at this time. I will swear to keep a weather ear, and, should I hear anything of value, I will inform the Sisterhood at once."

The Sisters smiled. Apparently everybody had passed their Stare test. "Thank you, Lord Blanchefort. We would like to take this moment to remind you that our chapel at Kurtis in the Great

Armenelos Forest is always open to pilgrims and esteemed visitors, and we invite you and your fine kin to please come and share some of your time with us. It will be an honor to entertain you as our guests."

"Thank you, Great Sister," Kay said. "I will remember your invitation, and when my travels bring me close, I will certainly stop and share a moment with my esteemed friends, the Sisterhood of Light."

The Sisters smiled and nodded, and the meeting was over. Countess Sygillis looked at her son, and Davage stood and escorted them out of the study. Kay helped Lady Hathaline out; she was still reeling from the Stare.

"What the Feature was that all about?" Sarah said under her breath as they exited, shuffling her feet.

"I guess they want their book back,"

Hath cried in Kay's ear.

"I know, sis," he said. "I know."

14—Hocked Jewels

A few days after the Sister's visit to the castle, things were finally getting back to normal. At seven bells Kay was waiting in the Capricos Hall for Sarah and Phillip. Sam, too, should be by shortly, so she had promised, but, so far, he was alone. They had planned on taking a ripcar to the Clovis ruins and look for more signs of the Wraith of Gaston.

At seven bells, the morning table was set with heated trays of scrambled eggs and piled up mounds of bacon, hash, pancakes and waffles, fruit and an assortment of other delicious breakfast fares. Kay, expecting a vigorous afternoon in the lonely way of the Gaston, heaped his plate full of bacon and eggs. Nobody else had yet arrived at the table.

He didn't have a good feeling. No Sam. Either Sam showed up early, or she tended not to show up at all. She promised though.

Lady Kilos Wafted in with a blast, sending Kay's napkin flying.

"Ki, have you ever heard of simply walking from one place to the next?" he said.

"Well, you can't get good at something if you don't practice, can you? I intend to have fully mastered the Waft by the time I hit the Ball scene. I want to Waft in so hard I blow everybody's hats off."

Kay took a mouthful of eggs. "I suppose it's good that you've a goal in mind."

Kilos smiled and sat down next to him. She shuffled her feet and tapped her fingers on the tabletop.

"Are you not eating?" Kay asked, noting that she hadn't grabbed a plate.

"You know what, Kay?" she said in a sheepish voice, ignoring his question.

"What?"

"I have more gossip."

He rolled his eyes. "Oh, Creation, what now?"

Sarah and Phillip filtered into the room, Sarah yawning and Phillip putting his duster on. They sat down on the other side of Kay, and Sarah began filling her plate with eggs. For such a thin girl, Sarah had a big appetite.

"What's going on?" Sarah asked. "Where's your lady? We're hiking today, and she better not make us late. If she wants to hang out with us, she'd better be on time."

"Don't know, and chill out, Sarah," Kay responded. "We'll wait all day for Sam if we have to. She promised she'd be here."

"I have gossip," Kilos said, excited.

Phillip grabbed a plate and put two waffles on it. "You mean the news about Lady Sammidoran selling her jewelry in Armenelos? Am I correct?"

Kilos looked shocked. "How did you know about that, Phillip?"

"I, like you, have my sources."

Kay couldn't believe what he just heard. "Wait a minute!! You're saying Sam went to Armenelos and sold some of her jewelry? When did that happen?"

Before Phillip could answer, Kilos butted in. "Yesterday. And she didn't sell some of her jewelry; she sold it all. I heard she wanted to make a substantial set of purchases and, of course, she didn't have the ready cash, so she hocked her stuff—there's a market for that black Monama jewelry they wear. She even tried to disguise herself, but when she found out how expensive whatever it is she wanted to buy was, she dropped her disguise she was so flustered. I heard she also told a few people's fortunes to boot, as she was short on money."

Kay tried to ignore her. "Ki, why don't you get something to eat and leave me be?"

Lady Kilos wasn't having any of it. She was in full Gossip-mode. "So, Kay, what's Sam buying you? A gift of some sort?" Kilos saddled right up to him and started making a silly-sounding voice. *"Ohhhh, she loves you, doesn't she?"*

"Ki, I'm not aware of Sam buying me anything. Sam doesn't have much money. I've always told her to save her money. If she needs anything, she knows to come to me, and I'll give it to her."

"So," Sarah said chiming in. "Who's Sam buying the thing for, then, Kay?" she asked as she began tearing into her eggs. "It must not be for you. Must be for somebody else. See—Monamas—you can't trust them."

"I'm sure it's nothing to be concerned about. What's with you? Sam's your friend, and you're treating her like garbage."

Sarah looked at her plate and grumbled. "She's a good-for-nothing Berserkacide who was going to let you die. I'm not going to forgive her for that."

"She was scared, Sarah, just like you were. Give her a break, will you?"

"So where is she? Who's she buying the thing for? I don't trust her."

"You've got a suspicious mind, Sarah."

"You bet I do. It's a dangerous world out there, Kay, and the sooner you realize that, the better. So then, why the sneaking around? Why didn't she come to you if she wanted something?"

"Maybe she wants to surprise me with it."

Sarah, with a mouthful of eggs, continued: "Or, maybe," she said swallowing, "maybe she's buying something nice for somebody else, like I said before."

"Don't be stupid."

"Oh, don't be stupid, eh? Why don't you not be stupid for a second? Let's get one thing straight right here and now—Monamas do not hang out with Elders—they just don't. They stay in their creepy little area by their creepy little lake in the fog, and they don't come out. And when they do come out, they go 'Nuts' and kill people. They Berserkacide, just like in Green Sabre with the Duke and just like those two freakjobs in the castle!"

"Those 'freakjobs', Sarah, were my friends, and I got to watch them die! And, it's probably my fault they ended up like that, you see?" Kay said, becoming angry. "Take it back!"

Sarah sat there a moment. "Sorry, I take it back. But, it's the damn truth, Kay, and it proves my point. Monamas and Elders don't mix!"

Phillip finished his waffles. "Sarah, I think you're exaggerating a tad."

Sarah continued. "Ever given a thought that she's just hanging out with you for your cash? Ever thought of that, Kay?"

"No, Sarah, I haven't."

"Perhaps you should. Perhaps you should come to the realization that she's been playing you this whole time. She's probably got some impoverished Monama dude back there by the lake that she's feeding coin to—your coin. By Creation, Kay!! You're a Blanchefort; you're supposed to be playing people, not the other way around!"

Kilos looked conflicted. "Well, normally I'd agree with you, Sarah, but…"

Sarah cut her off. "Listen to your sister, Kay!"

"The sound of your voice is starting to wear on me, Sarah!" Kay said. He stood up and made to leave. He gave a questioning look to Phillip, who looked back and shrugged his shoulders. Kay then started to walk away.

"Where are you going? We're supposed to be heading out to the Gaston!" Sarah cried.

"I no longer feel like it."

"If you're going to your room to cry over your girlfriend, make sure you've got a healthy supply of tissues. When you're done bawling, come on back down and join us, and we'll forget this ever happened! Seeing a Monama—now I've heard it all!" Sarah, feeling victorious, began eating her breakfast in earnest.

* * * * *

That night, Kay wrestled with his thoughts. Kilos' voice. Sarah's voice.

Sam's voice …

They all mixed together. Could Sarah be correct—could Sam have been toying with him all this time? All that talk of *Arin-Dan*? Monamas are a reclusive lot—rarely mixing with outside Houses on a social level, and whenever they did, they oftentimes went berserk.

Look at poor Clatera and Mitz .

He decided to go to Cathomere's Cathedral and sit there in peace. If Sam did show up tonight, he didn't want her to know where he was. He thought, if she showed, that he might say some things that he'd regret later; such was his state of mind.

She had a lot of explaining to do, but now was not the time. Later, when he was more cleared-headed, when Sarah's voice was gone from his thoughts— that would be the time.

But not now. Sarah was allowing her obvious fear of Berserkacides to bleed over to a dislike of Sam, though she was hardly an unbiased source. Her head was full of tabloid Postings and lurid media junk proclaiming Monamas dangerous loners who could see the future, and were best left alone.

Loners who could go Berserkacide at any moment.

And that was horribly proved at Castle Durst.

He'd sat in there about an hour when he heard a soft voice coming from behind him.

"Kay? Kay, what are you doing in here, darling?"

It was Sam. She was peeking her head into the cathedral, wearing one of his robes. Her face looked drawn and tired. Snugs hung at her neck.

Kay looked at her, and, as he previously thought, he felt a great deal of bitterness build up inside him. "I wanted some privacy."

Sam walked in and sat next to him. "Why?"

"I didn't particularly feel like seeing you, Sam."

She looked hurt. "Kay, are you angry with me? Is it something I've done?"

Kay leaned back— he felt a cruel streak coming on. All his love for her seemed capsuled up in his brain, and an angry, hateful Kay took his place at the controls. "Why do you keep coming here, Sam?" he said.

"Because here is where I want to be. Because you're here, *Arin-Dan*, and I love you."

"Do you?"

"Kay, why are you acting like this?"

"Because I'm tired of … everything. I'm tired of the secrets and the hiding and the weeping, and the deals behind my back."

"What deals?"

He wanted to stop, but was helpless. He couldn't shut his mouth. "The deals—yes, Armenelos— I know all about it. You sold your jewelry to make a large set of purchases."

Sam, sitting there in his robe, looked desperate. "I … I was trying to keep that quiet, Kay. *Arin-Dan*, I didn't want you know about that. It's not what you think."

"Yes, just the latest in a long series of secrets that you don't want me to know about. I must say the intrigue is starting to tire me."

Sam looked utterly shattered. "So, what are you saying Kay?" she said in an unsteady voice.

Kay's mouth started moving on its own—his heart not able to stop it—a clawed hand pulled his internal strings. "I'm saying I don't know if there's a future for us. I'm saying I don't know if I want you here anymore."

How could he have just said that?

"Sarah thinks you've been playing me for a fool, and I think maybe she's right."

"Sarah?"

Sam reacted like she'd been struck. She stood up, holding her face in her hands and knocked over a small brazier which fell with a loud commotion. Every bit of Kay wanted to go to her and comfort her, but a tiny cruel piece held him back. He just sat there.

Sam doubled over and made a noise. She then ran out of the cathedral, her feet slapping on the stones and was gone.

Kay stayed in the cathedral that night, partially asleep in a shallow pool of nightmare water. Even though he was in a "safe" place, he was surrounded by phantasms: a happy Sam, a loving Sam, Sam crying, Sam angry, and an image of Sam that terrified him—she was crouching, four arms extended, ready to spring and tear his throat out. A Sam that wanted his blood.

Berserkacide.

His thoughts fell into the Shadowlands. He thought something small stood at the door of the cathedral. He heard a voice:

What did you just do, buddy?

The leering chorus jolted him from sleep. "Sam!" he yelled, but, of course, she was not there.

The cathedral appeared strange to him. Everything was in amber. For a moment he thought he could see Sam again, standing there doubled over in agony. Then she was gone. He saw the cathedral empty. He saw it fill with people there for service, then empty, then fill over and over again.

Then, he saw no cathedral. He was standing on a grassy plain overlooking the cliff to the sea far below. It is as if he was seeing back through the ages, to a primitive time before Castle Blanchefort was built.

He then saw something quite strange—he saw himself and Sam standing side by side on a distant hilltop. They faced away from him.

He blinked a few times, and it was gone. The amber haze cleared, and he was back in the cathedral, alone with his guilt.

As he sat there in the breezy airiness of the cathedral, he felt he'd come to a crossroads of some sort. He was either at the beginning of something new, or at the end of something old, but he couldn't tell which. He kept thinking of that distant hilltop, he and Sam standing there side by side, facing away.

Somehow, it comforted him.

15—"I Run for You ... "

The next day was like a waking nightmare. Kay stumbled through the day, honestly not knowing whether or not he was awake or asleep, alive or dead. Everything seemed strange and bile-tinged. Sam, and his caustic treatment of her, was always on the back of his thoughts tormenting him.

Maybe he'd gone insane. Maybe he had fallen over the edge after he'd been so cruel to Sam. It certainly felt like he was insane.

He walked around the castle seeing strange things. His mother appeared smaller than normal, hunched, and ready to spring. He'd look away, and for a tiny second, she'd be wearing her old Black Hat robes and mask. His father looked at him with a crafty, calculating eye.

He walked down a corridor, not really knowing where he was going.

He felt hands at his throat.

He turned, and there was his sister, standing there innocently.

"Did you just try and strangle me?" he asked.

"Yes," she said and bounded away, tittering in an unsettling manner.

He went to the kitchens to grab something to eat. He kept seeing the staff approaching with hidden knives and odd powders hoping to tap them into his food.

Sarah was running around in her yellow gown, screaming his name, paints and makeup smeared on her face like a harlequin.

Kay tried to avoid her, as she seemed rather sinister. He hid from her in the foreboding Hall of Portraits, lined with paintings of past

Blancheforts.

"KKKKKKKKKAAAAAAAAAAAAAAAYYYYYYY!!!!!"
Sarah screeched as she passed by.

Something spoke.

"Hey, Kay ... you remember that thing we were talking about the other day?"

Kay looked around, Surly he hadn't just heard a voice just now.

"You're not hearing things, Kay. It's me."

He saw nothing but the myriad portraits hanging from the wall.
"Who are you?"

"A friend. For the Love of Creation, Kay, you're going to have to trust me on this."

"What is happening?" he said.

"You are under attack, from Castle Durst. Remember me telling you this?"

"No, no. I destroyed the device in Castle Durst."

"They fixed it, Kay, and it's on! You have to give them an 'A' for effort on their part. They are using it on you even as we speak. Don't feel quite normal, do you? Everything seems a little off, doesn't it? It's their machine doing that to you, Kay. The light it creates drives you insane."

"Insane? Father, I'll get father and ..."

"Your father can't help you, Kay, nor can your mother or anybody else for that matter. They are under the light and are helpless before it. You have to get rid of it."

"What? How?"

"The light doesn't affect you like it does everybody else. You are able to shrug off its effects. I don't have time to explain why; just trust me."

"What? What should I do?"

"First, go to your room, Kay, and be careful; if it looks dangerous out there, it probably is. Don't stop for anything, no matter what you see, okay? Just get to your room; that's the main thing."

He exited the Hall of Portraits and made the long walk to his tower. He saw people along the way lying on the ground. He saw staff members on the floor here and there.

Was it nap time? It was so hard to think.

Up ahead, who's that? Phillip? Yes, it's Phillip, asleep too. That's not like Phillip. Kay went to his side to wake him up.

Blood all over Phillip. His throat was gone.

Looking back. Red everywhere. The staff were all dead.

"GET TO YOUR ROOM!!" rang through his head.

He continued on, stumbling through the castle toward his tower.

Everything was a muddle. Hard to think. Passing a mirror he saw his own reflection: it was odd, distorted. He saw a mark around his right eye, very similar to mother's Shadowmark.

Ahead was the base of Zorn Tower, his tower. There was a commotion going on down the corridor. There was a pile of yellow fabric on the floor with a patch of black over it.

Sarah in her gown, in pieces. Something in black was on top of her, tearing her body apart with relish.

It was terrible. Kay quickly stumbled into his tower and locked the door. He then took the lift up and up to his floor.

He closed the door and sat in a corner staring at the walls.

There were strange sounds coming from below, a steady droning of misery. He looked out his terrace and saw, far in the distance, a light coming from Castle Durst. It was golden and warming, rather comforting and pretty to look at.

There were knocks at his door, but he didn't answer.

Knocks at the door again. This time, somebody tried the latch, finding it locked. The person tried even harder, the old door shaking in its frame.

"Kay," he heard through the door. The voice was familiar yet distorted and wicked. *"Let me in, Kay; it's Sam. I want to kiss you."*

The door shook in its ancient frame. *"KAY!"* came a shriek from the other side as the door withstood a torrent of banging. He heard wood splintering and curling away as something sharp assailed it from the other side.

Eventually he got into bed, fully dressed, and pulled up the covers, listening to the door rattle on its hinge.

Suddenly the room was filled with silvery light, and his bedclothes were ripped away.

"Kay! What are you doing? No time for sleeping! It's time to go to work!"

"Who are you, and what do you want?"

Something wrenched him out of bed and set him into a kneeling position on the floor. *"Who am I? I'm your best friend, Kay; that's who I am! We've got a long night ahead of us, but, first, you've got a big mess to clean up!"*

"What?"

"I hate to do this to you, kid, but ..."

Kay felt a burst of agony bloom in his side. It felt like he was being bitten by a shark.

In a halo of pain, the room turned to amber, and things became muddled.

"My hands? Are those my hands?"

Though he might have been dreaming—it certainly felt like he was dreaming—he found he could see past the walls of his room through the depths of the Castle.

Carnage everywhere, death! Outside his door was a Berserkacide in the shape of Sam, his *Cerri-Tela*, clawing at his door, trying to get at him He felt himself get sick with heartbreak.

"Stay with me, Kay. I know it's hard, but you have to have faith."

Elsewhere, his father was lying on the floor—not moving. His mother was walking about in a strange stilted fashion, a blank look on her face with blood on her hands. His sister Kilos was holding her head spinning around in her room. Lady Poe and Lord Peter were laying on the floor of their bedroom huddled together, covered in giant bugs! Everybody else, Hathaline, Maser, Sarah, Phillip were still, like they were dead.

The swarm of insects covered Lady Poe and Lord Peter in a seething mass.

Kay tried to pull away, but was held down and in agony. *"Focus, Kay, focus. Be calm. I promise everything will be all right. Now, I need you to look out into the Telmus Grove, specifically, to an oak clearing where Sam once mentioned the name 'Olonol'. Do it now, Kay."*

"Everybody dead …"

"Kay!" the voice said with rising anger. *"Look to the Grove! Do it now!"*

As commanded, Kay saw out through the castle walls into the amber night, out into the Grove. He saw the stone walkways and ancient trees.

There it was. There was the clearing. Nobody there, lonely.

"Now," the voice said, *"this is going to be a little strange."*

The image of the darkened Grove changed. It began moving, as if in reverse. Night faded to twilight, which returned to dusk. Passing birds flew backwards, and a confusion of people appeared. They acted out a strange scene in reverse.

"All right, that's far enough. Now look."

Things seemed to slow down and stop and then resume a more normal running.

There was Sam, Blinking into the Grove. She looked around and then fell to her knees, slowly placing Snugs around her neck, not bothering to pull the chain through her hair. She wept bitterly. A knife fell out of her hand.

"Sam!" Kay cried.

"She's in a bad state, kid, ever since you said those things to her in the cathedral. You broke her little heart, and she also can't forgive herself for not helping you fight those Berserkacides at Castle Durst. She's at the end of her rope, and her head is not in a good place."

"I need to get to her. To talk to her!"

"What you're seeing has already happened, Kay, earlier today. You're seeing into the past, and pretty soon you're about to find out

what it is that Sam has been so afraid of through the years. Watch, just watch and don't be alarmed."

A cloudy green slit formed in the air behind Sam, and two people appeared through it as if from nowhere, a tall man in golden armor and a rail thin, bent woman wearing some sort of beaded dress. She had red hair that was styled into a towering bee-hive. Kay struggled but was held in place.

"Just watch!"

The man and woman approached Sam, standing at either side of her.

The woman spoke seemingly kind words in a rasping voice as the man looked on.

She told Sam that she had had a good life, that they had let her go on for a long time, relatively free. They told her they had allowed her dreams to come true, and she'd been so happy.

Wasn't that right?

The broken Sam agreed.

Now, she said, it was time to fulfill her mission, one that they had selected for her since she was a small girl. The woman told Sam that she was her favorite slave by far.

Sam reacted a little and searched for her knife. The man kicked it away.

Blink, Sam, Blink! No, she can't with Snugs on.

The woman gave her a tender hug and kiss, and then savagely wrenched her head back by the hair. She held something in her hand.

Light, red light, just like what Clatera had been holding at Castle Durst. The woman forced her to gaze into the light.

Sam struggled a moment, and then slowly stood up. A second pair of pale arms appeared through her black gown like two milky snakes.

"Berserkacide!" Kay wailed.

Then the woman gave Sam her command: Kill. Kill everyone in the castle, and leave *Arin-Dan* for last. Tear his throat out when you get to him.

Sam turned and ran as only she could toward the castle, her new arms held over her head.

Kay was about to begin screaming when the voice cut him off.

"I know what you're thinking, but don't! What you just witnessed is what happened earlier today, but, we aren't going to let that

happen, are we?"

"We can stop it? Prevent it?"

"We can. Take these."

Something small and slightly squishy fell into Kay's hand.

"Now, what you're going take a few steps forward, and you'll be out there in the Grove, in the past with Sam. Take what I've given you and scatter them around. Do not take your eyes off her! Do not blink, and do not look away! You won't have much time, so you better get her to leave and quick about it! Be warned—the past isn't like a scene from a film replayed over and over. You have one chance to step through and fix this; after that, this moment in time will be blacked out, and you'll never be able to see it again. Are you ready?"

Kay had no idea what to make of this. The voice allowed him to stand. "I'm ready," he said having no notion as to what was going to happen.

"Then go. I'll be waiting for you when you're done."

The scene reset itself. There was Sam entering the clearing, holding her knife ...

... and Kay was standing behind her.

She sniffed and whirled around. She looked at him with big eyes. She hunched over a little.

"What are you holding there, Sam?

She looked down and hid what was in her hand.

"Give me the knife, Sam."

She wiped a tear away and quietly held out the knife. Kay took it without looking. He kept his gaze fixed on Sam. "Please put your Snugs on."

She quietly put her medallion on and worked it through her hair. Sam looked at him oddly for a moment, and then burst into a smile. "You're seeing! You're using your Sight! I knew it! I knew you could do it!"

"What are you doing out here, Sam?"

She looked down. "I ... I've lost your love, and, after my performance in the castle, I don't deserve it." Her face cringed into sadness. "I was too frightened to help you, and I came here to end my life. I wanted to be near you when I did it. I thought perhaps you would bury me on Dead Hill and then, one day, you and I might rest near each other. I was hoping you would forgive me!"

"You don't need to be dead to be near me, Sam. There is

forgiveness that's needed here. Forgive my words. Forgive me, Sam."

Kay thought he heard something behind him. Gods—the things in his hand, he'd forgotten to scatter them! Quickly, he tossed them to the ground and several objects tumbled into the grass. A few objects remained in his hand.

There was movement and sounds, but Kay ignored them. He trained his gaze on Sam, not daring to look away.

Sam looked down again and held her stomach. "I didn't want you to see me like this."

Kay felt his eyes going blurry. Quick! Be quick!

"Sam, I said the things I said because I was hurt—because I thought you might be straying, or toying with my emotions."

"I would never. I ... "

"I know, but I let Sarah get the better of me. I repent everything I said. You know I didn't mean it."

"You ... love me still?"

"More than ever. I have seen the things that hover over you, and I know that they are soon to be here to change you into a Berserkacide."

Sam's mouth opened in terror, and she looked around.

"Have no fear, Sam. They cannot enter for the moment. You must get away from here for the time being and guard yourself. I want you to be strong. You have always taught me to be strong, now it's your turn."

Sam approached and put her arms around him. "I'll ... I'll have to run, Kay. They might be after me."

"I will stand at your side, Sam. Let's face them together. I'm not afraid."

"No, no I think I know what to do. I'm almost ready. My *Arin-Dan*, I have something planned that can save us—I know it will! That's what I've been doing, but I had to be careful because they're watching. They are *always* watching us. I just need a bit more time. No Monama ever runs from them, but, if I have your love, then I'll run for you. I'll do what I must until I'm ready."

"Then take my strength, *Cerri-Tela*. You have my love, and my adoration, and my CARG remains yours."

Sam breathed in and out, a new light in her eyes. She stood up straight. "Thank you for reminding me of what I already should have known, and for giving me new strength, *Arin-Dan*. I don't know when you will see me again, but you will. Don't worry about me. Your love shall lend wings to my feet, and they will never catch me."

Kay held out his hand. "Sam, take these. I don't know what they are, but they shall somehow hinder those who chase you. Take them."

Sam took the objects in his hand and looked at them. She smiled. "Oh, so adorable. Thank you for this Gift, Kay! I should have known; I should have seen this!"

In Kay's side vision, he caught a glimpse of several small figurines in Sam's hand. They seemed to be in the shape of blue seals.

Sam then moved her gown aside, exposing her collarbone. In Kay's amber Sight, he could see there was some sort of studded collar there—wait! He'd seen it before near the bathhouse, stitched into her neck. With her strong hands, she pawed at it, and ripped it bleeding from around her neck. She held the thing for a moment and regarded it with hatred. She then flung it with all her might a considerable distance away. "Now, I am free, Kay, for good or ill. Your love has freed me."

His Sight began to waver. "Go, Sam. Be safe and know that I love you."

She turned and removed Snugs from her bleeding neck. She looked at him one last time and mouthed the words in Anuie: "*I run for you.*"

Then she was gone.

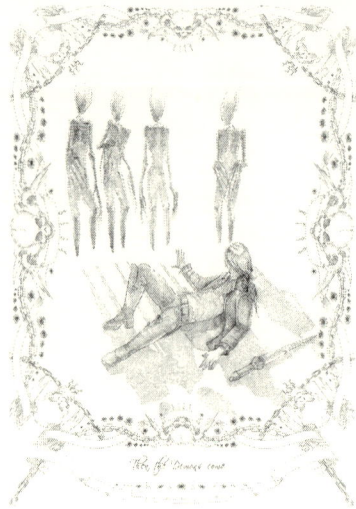

16—Return to Castle Durst

G*reat work, kid!"* the voice exclaimed as Kay returned to his room.

"What just happened?"

"You made her day; that's what just happened. So, one big mess down, one to go!"

He tried to look through the walls and into the castle, but he couldn't see through the stone of his room.

"Don't worry about your folks—they're fine now. What you need to be worrying about is that damn light atop Castle Durst. You need to get over there pronto and take care of it—for good this time."

Kay began feeling the effects of the Insanity Light coming from Castle Durst again. Things became a tad muddled.

"What? I'll get my father and we'll go …"

"No time. Out the window! Hurry!"

Obediently, he started going to the window.

"Wait… Out the window? What am I supposed to do?"

The voice appeared to get angry. *"Use your Gifts and be a Man, Kay! Go to Castle Durst and destroy that damn light! Do it!"*

Kay began to climb out the window. "Wait! How am I supposed to get down?"

With that, something head-butted Kay out of the window, making the decision for him.

He plummeted through the air toward the dark, night-washed ground far below. Sam had threatened several times to bodily throw him out a window to force his use of Gifts but had never done it.

Now, here it was and he didn't like it one little bit!

Falling, feeling the wind tickle his face and muss his hair, he panicked for a moment.

He thought about everybody in the Castle, on the ground, laid low, attacked by something coming from Castle Durst. Covered in bugs. The cold night air cleared his head a little, and he concentrated.

Better than dead, though, better than dead. He had made up with Sam, and she knew he loved her, and given her hope. Now she was running from ... whomever.

He began to Waft. He had about two thousand feet before he hit the waiting rocks below. He tried to imagine himself standing in the Grove with his cousins charging him, a nice sunny day, not a care in the world, Sarah and Phillip laughing and cavorting.

Sarah and Phillip lying in a death-like state in their rooms, previously gutted!

The biting wind flew past him as he plummeted. His hat was gone. Who knew where it was.

Relax.

He began feeling the air slowly spiraling around him, the beginning of a Waft—the random hand of the wind beginning to take shape and organize in a cylinder around his plummeting body.

Remember what Father said—the wind is not the Waft, but the by-product of it.

Waft! Just Waft!

"Kay!!" someone shrieked from above. Kay thought he saw a small, silvery head peeking out his window and two little round eyes fixed on him. "Waft, Kay!! You're going to hit the ground!!"

Thanks for that confidence-shattering update!

The air began moving faster. *Almost. Just Waft!*

He thought he saw the large stained glass windows of Maserfeld's Cathedral go whizzing by, lit up in gothic reds and blues. If that were the case, he didn't have long.

"Kay!!!"

A small tornado of wind formed around his body.

He hit the cold, rocky ground, but instead of a crushing, life-ending collision, he was only vaguely aware of the impact. It was a rather muffled, blunted hit, like landing in a pile of pillows. He felt himself moving through the air, Wafting, as a ghost. He came out of it several yards away with a skittering blast.

Getting his bearings, he began running.

Pain, sudden pain in his leg. He fell and slid to a stop, skinning his palms. His left ankle was broken from the fall. Must have hit the ground just before he Wafted. It could have been worse. A lot worse.

He limped into the covered park to the west of the castle—a great number of ripcars of various sizes and makes were parked there. At the front of the line was a modest little green one—the tortured one his mother favored using, though she was a terrible pilot, just like he was. Mother's green ripcar was dinged up from the many little accidents she'd had with it. She rarely used it anymore, favoring her perfected *Seeker,* which she could enlarge in size for quick and effortless transportation.

Next was the big silver one they had taken to Castle Durst for their bowling adventure. He thought about hopping into it, but the ignition pan wasn't there—Phillip always removed it, a habit the Duke had taught him.

Nearby was Hath's little souped up blue one. It was sleek and fast, and not quite legal—Lord Peter and Lord Milos of Probert himself had made several choice modifications to the thrust system. It had large tailpipes sticking out the back. It didn't create exhaust per se, and, therefore, didn't need tailpipes, but it had them anyway for show. The name "HATH" was painted in a sparkly, flowing script on the hood. Lady Hathaline loved this little ripcar.

The ignition pan was there, snapped into place. Hath never removed it—who would dare make off in her ripcar?

He thought of her lying dead in the castle. Surly, she wouldn't mind in this desperate situation.

He hopped in and started fiddling with the controls. Hath had all sorts of girly beads and trinkets hanging from the controls, and Kay wiped them away with a sweep of his hand and turned the pan, firing it up in a rumble

He didn't know what he was doing. In this regard, Kay was certainly not his father, who could fly anything. He wasn't even his little sister who could fly this ripcar with surprising skill. He'd seen her do it many times. She'd crushed Lord Phineas of Tyrol with it during the Falling in Love ball, creating quite a scandal in Tyrol and a huge increase in Hath's correspondence pile.

The car roared, stalled, lurched with a puff of ions and careened into the silver one. The big silver ripcar lurched over and smashed into the little green one—his mother's favorite, now partially destroyed.

He would apologize to the both of them later.

Somehow, he got the protesting blue ripcar out of the park and into the air, flying through several trees in the process.

Lurching, he fell onto his broken ankle and was livid and in pain. Pain.

The dark of night fell away into a pall of amber, and in that moment, he could see everything, for miles and miles. He could see Castle Durst like it was right there—he could see every detail of it. It was overwhelming. After a moment passed, everything faded back to night.

He hit the thrusters and hung on for dear life. Barely under control, the ripcar roared into the mountain passes heading west.

There was a mountain ahead, coming up fast out of the darkness: smooth, steep and cone-shaped—Mt. Durst from the looks of it—a slightly smaller twin of Mt. Vith to the east. He tried to go around it, but the ripcar kept on going straight. He moved the sticks but nothing happened; the cursed car kept plowing ahead toward the waiting mountain.

As the bulk of the mountain rapidly approached, he found himself oddly fascinated by the movement of Hath's beads on the dash.

Good Creation, his family was dying and he was going to fly his little sister's ripcar into Mt. Durst while gawking at her beads. He was probably the worst pilot ever, even worse than his mother. His father, should he live, would surely laugh, or possibly cry.

He remembered one afternoon his father showing Lady Hathaline something about having to use the foot pedals to bank when in-atmosphere. The sticks only were effective in orbit. And then he remembered Lady Hathaline stepping on the pedals and successfully turning the craft.

He glanced down and saw the pedals.

Mt. Durst was a hulking shadow in the dark getting closer every second. The bare trees growing on its side seemed to be reaching out for him.

His red-headed, gown-wearing, pasty-faced sister could bank the car.

He stepped on the pedal, and the ripcar banked so hard it almost dumped him out.

Recovering, he went around the mountain, righted the ripcar and set a direct course for Castle Durst.

The old, empty castle emerged ahead like a bleached white hand with patina-clogged fingernails. Wanting more speed, he risked using the thrusters and punched them; the car surged ahead, again almost dumping him out.

He aimed for the top of Rhoda Tower. He could see something there in the gallery at the top creating a bright focused light pointed at Castle Blanchefort, and it pointed in several other directions as well to the north, east and west. Several people milled about in the gallery. He would be there in seconds.

His thoughts momentarily wandered to Clatera and Mitz, his friends, now dead.

Wait! How does one stop this crazy contraption? He was speeding toward the high gallery of Rhoda Tower, and there was no way of stopping the ripcar ... none that he could see. He tested the various controllers and buttons in a frenzy, and none produced the desired effect of slowing the craft down. Moments before impact, he released the controls, leapt over the side and began to Waft, again testing fate.

As he fell, the speeding ripcar plunged into the tower face, taking off a good part of the eastward gallery. Bits of composite materials, stone, and flaming shards of metal came spiraling down, keeping pace with his fall. There was screaming, too—people clad in scant golden robes were falling amidst the debris.

Golden robes: Golden People. That seemed familiar to him.

Just as the Waft took hold, he thought he saw the falling gold-robed people change shape.

Changing shape; again, that was familiar.

One appeared to turn into a large bird of some sort, and another turned into an alien, starfish-like creature. That was impressive. Sam could change shape, but only into other types of humanoids. She couldn't make herself into a bird or a starfish like these Golden People had just done.

With a blast, Kay Wafted and appeared near the ruined, flaming edge of the gallery. Nursing his ankle, he lurched in.

Sitting in the middle of the lounge, where the extinct Dursts once entertained guests (he and his family included), was a tall, strange-looking device. It was shaped something like a Xandarrian oil lamp, having a tapering base expanding into a bulbous center section going to a thin, stalk-like top. It was composed of a smooth pearly, pinkish material with a harness of black circuitry strapped to it at various points. A strong yellowish light glowed at its top, sending several quiet but deadly shafts of light out in various directions—including one toward distant Castle Blanchefort.

It looked like it had previously; only now, it was alive and functioning.   Clatera and Mitz must have been placed here as Berserkacides to guard this device.

And twelve golden figures milled about it, their light gold robes waving in the breeze of Kay's Waft. They looked at Kay impassively. A moment later, a large bird and strange alien creature with starfish-like limbs appeared over the gallery and entered the lounge.

The bird, talons flashing, swooped at Kay and he dove aside, hitting his broken ankle.

Again, pain washed over him.   In amber he saw one of the golden females standing next to the device raise her arm and bathe Kay in a beam of reddish light.

He saw himself melting in the light, leaving only his clothes and his skeleton behind. The amber haze faded, and he saw the golden people standing there next to the device, the bird and starfish joining them and quickly changing shape back into golden, toga-clad people.

What had he seen—the future perhaps?

One of the golden females raised her arm, finger extended.

Kay pointed his CARG and loosed a blast of Silver tech.   The female produced a cone of red light from her finger and met Kay's blast in the middle, the red and silver swirling together for a moment. Two energies wiped each other out and faded with a crack.

Kay and the group of golden people stared at each other for a moment. They began chortling amongst themselves in an odd language. One of them produced a controller and pressed a few buttons.   A type of greenish gate opened behind them, and they were gone.

He approached the odd device. It was casting powerful beams of light in various directions. One beam was bathing Castle Blanchefort. Another was heading east, in the general direction of Bloodstein. Another pointed north toward the Holts of Shirster Point, and a vast beam, pointing southwest, seemed to be shining on the city of Mt. Holly.

This one odd machine was attacking several of the more prominent Vith strongholds all at once from this central location.

He hauled back and gave it a good whack with his CARG as he had previously. Nothing appeared to happen. He hit it again with similar results. His CARG was just bouncing off.

Creation!

"Blood-gutted Shocktyte!" he yelled as he stepped back, pointed his CARG, and let fly with another blast of Silver tech. His blast hit the device in a wave of silver fire.

Ah! It was somehow shielded, the mass of silver being reflected and diverted away. He could see it plain as day. He laid into it, and, after a few moments, the power of his blast began to take effect. The shield faltered and fizzled out.

He tried to blast it again, but, of course, no more Silver tech; the CARG sputtered, needing to recharge. He shambled up to it and gave it several hard cutting blows, the tubular shaft of the CARG this time biting deep into the device's pearly surface in angry furrows.

The lights at the top of the device sputtered and went out. The deadly beams were quieted.

Good, good!

Before Kay could catch his breath and chop the device into bits, another misty green gate opened. Three forms were dumped out roughly, and the gate closed.

They were naked, stark white with thick black hair that went down to the floor. They were tied up at the wrists and ankles with dark chains. They wore odd collars studded with long, diamond-shape crystals. They shivered.

Collars—just like Sam's, the one she tore out and was terrified of.

Monamas. They looked like Monamas.

He then ran to them. There were two men and a woman. Just like Sam, they were thin and ghostly pale, their black hair bursting and thick, their eyes black as midnight.

The woman appeared to be having trouble breathing. He knew what was wrong with her, the cold. Monamas couldn't take the cold, and here they were, stark naked in the open gallery. He took his coat off and draped it over her. He then began working to undo her ties. "I know you're cold. I'm going to release you; then, I'm going to get you warmth."

He grabbed the collars around their necks and made to pull them off. They didn't budge. They were stitched deep into their flesh, as Sam's was, and he couldn't pull it loose with all his strength.

It would have to be cut off.

As Kay worked, the Monamas didn't respond much. They sat there, heads lolled, mouths open and drooling.

Head Swarm. Is this what happens to a Monama when they go into Head Swarm?

He shook them trying to roust them from it.

Slowly, they started to stir. They looked dazed.

"Are you all right?" Kay asked, gently shaking them.

Gradually, they came into focus. They were terrified. "Not ... not safe ..." one of the men said, shivering. "It's not safe ..."

"It's all right," Kay said. "I'm not going to hurt you. I'm going to get you someplace warm, and I'm going to get these collars off you."

All three of them looked grief-stricken.

The woman struggled to say something. Kay leaned in to listen.

"... run ..." she said breathlessly. "Run, sir, please! Run for your life!"

The crystals embedded in the collars at their necks began glowing a rosy reddish color.

Their black Monama eyes suddenly lit up with a crimson glow. As Kay watched in horror, the glow compressed into a strange glyph, and the Monamas, like rabid animals, suddenly lurched in their chains, roaring and slavering. They raised their arms up toward the ceiling and, with a sudden sickening crunch of cartilage and bone, an extra set of arms, complete with delicate hands, fingers and claws, came shooting out under their armpits.

Berserkacides! They're Berserkacides!

He jumped back.

As the rabid Monamas bloodied themselves trying to get out of their chains, three misshapen people emerged from the back of the tower, a man and two women. The man was clad in armor that appeared to have been a gold color at one point, but was smeared with some sort of brown, stinking substance. The women were clad in fibrous reddish gowns or dresses that were heavily sewn with odd beads.

The man's armor was anatomically correct, down to the smallest and most modest of details; yet, his body was strange and malformed—as if his bones had been broken and deliberately mended in incorrect positions. The women appeared to be skinless, and their dresses were sticky against their bleeding bodies. As they stood there, blood and urine pooled beneath them. Their joints, too, were malformed.

Kay was horrified.

One of the women approached the roaring Monamas and held up a reddish prism, which seemed to enthrall them. The other approached the tall device in the center of the room and pressed a few buttons on its pinkish surface. The harness of black circuitry strapped to it began moving and twisting, re-wiring itself like a tangle of sinewy snakes. Then, the light at the top of the device began glowing again, bright as ever. The machine and its deadly light were back in action.

Kay made to finish the device off, and the armored man jumped forward and raised a hideous-looking weapon that was fashioned to resemble a male phallus.

Kay raised his CARG and held it out, one-handed as usual. He leaned forward and felt the angry protest of his broken ankle.

"This machine stands before my family's life, and by Creation, I'll see it in pieces!"

One of the women opened her terrible mouth and made a hideous noise—a sort of half screech, half moan.

Kay couldn't move. He couldn't move a muscle. A spell, she had cast some sort of arcane spell, and he was in its thrall.

"Release the Berserkacides and kill him," one of them said in a hollow voice.

Casually, the other woman slinked forward, swinging her hips in a seductive fashion. "Oh, but why waste this wonderful piece of meat? They'll spoil it. He's not going anywhere." She looked Kay up and down, and, with her blood-crusted hands, began touching him all over. She breathed graveyard breath into his ear and began kissing him, her hands going to forbidden places.

Kay's flesh recoiled at her touch, but there was nothing he could do. He couldn't move. He was be-spelled.

These beasts! These were what Sam, and Clatera and Mitz and all the Monamas were so terrified of.

The woman roughly pushed him down and climbed on top of

him, the others watching with perverted glee. She produced a small, blunt-looking knife and danced it over the surface of his clothes, slowly slicing them off.

Kay, under the woman, became aware of a growing sound coming from outside—a steady buzz or droning sound. The sound got louder and louder, penetrating his ears and settling into his brain.

He noticed a mass of small bluish objects filtering into the gallery, flying on shiny, reddish wings.

Bugs! The gallery was filling with huge, buzzing insects! They swarmed around and settled on the walls, covering them in a moving carpet. They then began buzzing in earnest, making a loud melancholy drone which saturated Kay's mind, pushing all else out.

And … he could move. The spell had been broken!

Quickly, he spun his CARG around and rammed it into the woman's midsection, the shaft of his weapon thudding to a stop at the base of her spine. He threw her off, and she landed a few feet away, dropping her knife and gushing blood.

Kay quickly stood and raised his CARG.

The mass of bugs lining the walls had very shiny wings, and coupled together as a whole, they made a coppery-looking reflective surface, like a mirror that slightly undulated with the movement of the wings. He could clearly see himself in it.

The woman Kay had stabbed was also looking at herself in the "mirror" at her mangled face, her skinned body and broken joints. She looked at her image as if seeing herself as a monster for the first time.

She slowly put her hands to her face and, in the din of buzzing, began a long, pitiful scream. She stood, gushing blood from her wound. She glanced back at Kay once—a look of genuine horror and shame etched in her ruined face.

She turned and ran, gibbering, to the broken rim of the gallery where she threw herself over the side without hesitation and was gone.

The armored man, averting his gaze, mumbled something drowned out in the buzzing, and then sprang to attack. The remaining woman drew a dirty-looking knife and moved to Kay's right.

The man swung his penis-shaped weapon in a cleaving stroke, and Kay raised the CARG one-handed to meet it. Their weapons clanged, and Kay lurched backwards, his ankle proving to be inconvenient. Another collision of weapons, and Kay tried to move to his left to rest his ankle. Bugs swirled around, bouncing off of each other as Kay and the monsters fought. The noise they created was becoming deafening.

Suddenly, the woman grabbed him from behind. Her skinned arm was slick with partially dried blood and stank of innards. He felt something sharp jab into his back.

Pain.

Everything turned to amber for a moment. For an instant, he could see this mutilated woman as a smiling, pretty girl wearing a fine gown, her hair set in a pleasing style. She sat with her family enjoying an outing by the sea.

Another image entered his head—the girl confined in a small, transparent container, full of a noxious brown substance. She screamed for help, for relief. None came apparently.

He saw her come out of the container a monster, lost in an evil dream.

It was heart-breaking. Kay pushed the images from his head.

She jabbed him again, and this time he flipped her over his head, and she landed with a slippery thud. Like a panther, she sprang to her feet. Without allowing himself time to think about it, Kay swung his CARG and took her head off.

A smiling, pretty girl with her whole life ahead of her, turned into a wrecked monster.

Who could do such a thing? He recalled the Golden People in their togas, and a remembered word popped into his head: *enemy.* They were the enemy, the masters of it all.

The man came at him, and they clashed weapons a few times.

Around and around they went: jab, slash, counter and thrust, their weapons ringing off one another. As they exerted themselves, the flying bugs began trying to land on Kay. With his free hand, he tried to shoo them away, but they were big and persistent.

The man tried to run Kay though. He just barely countered, his concentration being disrupted by the bugs. As they neared the broken railing of the gallery to the sheer drop beyond, the man tried to hook Kay's CARG out of his grasp. They spun around and, when the man's back was facing the edge, Kay extended the shaft of the CARG like a piston and forced him out into open space where he fell.

He laughed and tittered all the way down, his grotesque weapon falling with him.

He was gone. Kay turned his attention back to the machine.

The Golden People had returned, and they stood next to the machine as the bugs buzzed in a cloud. An oiled, golden female walked over to the raging, tied up Monamas and held up another red prism. She showed it to them. They slavered in renewed fury.

With a wave of her hand, their chains unlocked and the three of them, bounding on all fours, came at Kay in a lather.

A scene right out of Sarah's eager nightmares was coming true. Berserkacides, on the move, four-armed and lusting for blood—his blood, in this case.

They didn't run upright; rather they bounded on all fours, holding their newly grown extra set of arms over their heads in a grotesque fashion.

They were moving fast.

He pointed his CARG and tried to fire off a Silver tech blast.

It sputtered.

As they came at him, he couldn't see any good way out of this. The machine still functioned. His family still suffered beneath it.

He threw his CARG in a spiral, hitting the device right in the center—impaling it deeply. The device shuddered and began trembling as energy built up within. As the Berserkacides reached him, he allowed himself to fall backwards out over the edge of the smashed gallery, preferring the cool, lonely fall to a bloody death at their claws. He fell out into the night as the mortally stricken machine exploded in a ball of fire that devastated Rhoda Tower, caving it in and toppling the spire above. The Berserkacides were thrown out into space with the force of the explosion, one of them in pieces, another on fire.

I got it, he thought as the night air raged past him. *Mother, Father … I got it.*

He readied to Waft away and noticed a form falling nearby.

It was the female Monama, who, just minutes earlier, had shivered under his coat, had feared for his life and begged him to run. Now she reached out for him, straining to rend her claws into his flesh, her face puckered in bestial rage.

He looked at her, and, despite his situation, felt nothing but grief for this woman.

So much like Sam … and Mitz.

Forgoing the Waft, he reached out for her; his outstretched hand and her grasping, clutching claws almost but not quite touching.

And he fell and fell, the flailing Berserkacide nearby. He didn't try to Waft—there was no time. He'd let the fall have him.

The device and its light were gone, for good this time. He'd done his job.

* * * * *

He was swimming in darkness. He felt comfortable and warm. He moved his arms and felt soft bed clothes. His ankle felt like normal. Was he dead?

Something leaned over Kay and smiled. A silvery seal's head and round, bright eyes looked down on him. "You all right, Kay?" he asked.

He was pretty sure it was Carahil—Elemental Spirit and god, born right here at Castle Blanchefort by his Aunt Poe's hand.

"I think so. What happened tonight? Who were those people?"

Carahil gave him a nudge. "People who don't fight fair. People who use others to do their fighting for them."

"The Monamas. They became Berserkacides. Are they all right? Did you save them, too?"

Carahil paused. "You're never all right after you're made to become a Berserkacide—there's no going back. They're dead, Kay, and better off."

Kay thought of the woman, before and after her transformation. All he could think of was she, chained up, his coat draped over her shivering shoulders. A woman very much like Sam, possibly with somebody waiting for her back home, somebody who loved her, somebody who would never see her again. A tear came to his eye.

"Those poor people. They were so frightened. They tried to warn me. I wish they were home safe in their beds right now."

Carahil blinked. "I do, too. See, that's why I'm on your side, because you care." He looked hard at Kay.

Kay sighed. "How did I get here?"

"A little bird flew by and saved you," Carahil said. "Why didn't you Waft, Kay? Why did you let yourself fall?"

"The woman. I wanted to stay with her. I didn't want to let her go. I saw Sam in her face. Is she at peace, Carahil, the woman? Does her soul rest?"

Carahil backed away. "I guarantee it. Get some sleep; you did good tonight, Kay, and I'm proud of you. You've often wondered if you're actually a Vith Lord. I think tonight proves that. You saved your House, and you saved your love, too. I'll not let them do such a thing again; I swear it. Now I am at guard. I am summoned."

""Where's Sam? I need to help her!"

"She is in a place where you can't get to her now, Kay. She's all right, I promise. She's out there running for you, Kay, and for the possibility of what might one day be."

Carahil leaned down and gave Kay a nuzzle on the forehead. "Well, you know the drill by now. I'm going to take this from you, Kay, this whole day—it's for your own good. You'll go to sleep and not remember a thing about what happened tonight. You'll just have some vague memories of another bland day. It'll be like one of those days that you sleep through and can't remember except as a dream. Nobody here will remember this attack, except for two people. But, I have to say, sooner or later, we're going to have to come to grips with those whom you saw tonight. Sooner or later there will be a fight that must be fought, and it must be won. For the sake of the League, okay?"

And Kay slept, and the whole thing was forgotten.

17—The Wraith

Kay wanted little to do with Sarah for the next few days, partially blaming her for his reaction to Sam. Sam hadn't shown up, and she didn't join him in bed. This absence, discounting the mandatory summer lay-off, was by far longest he'd been without Sam in years.

Sarah and her mouth.

Phillip seemed to understand and gave Kay his space. Sarah, knowing that Kay was hurting, partially because of her, tried to occupy his time, make him forget, but it didn't work. He avoided her, and when their paths did happen to cross, he ignored her. As the days passed, Kay could tell Sarah was starting to feel quite guilty about what she'd said. She'd convicted Sam without good reason, and she saw how crushed Kay was.

She was sorry and didn't know what to say, which was odd for her.

Kay wasn't the only sad person in the castle—Lady Hathaline, normally unflappable, was beside herself. Her beloved ripcar appeared to have been stolen and flown into the ruins of Castle Durst by some miscreant whom she swore to hunt down and slay. Lord Davage promised he would get her another one—a faster one, and she brightened. A day later he and Countess Sygillis took her to Minz and bought her a fast, new red ripcar.

Kay drifted around the castle lost in a stupor.

He had a dim notion that he'd not seen the last of Sam—that she wasn't going to go out that easily. If she were going, she'd go swinging. She would not let all they'd created together go without a struggle. He kept that thought close to him.

Or maybe his words were so hurtful he knocked the love right out of her. That was a possibility as well.

In any event, if she didn't show up soon, he would go to her. He would go to Lake Monama and, welcome or not, visit her ancestral castle by the shores of the lake. There, he would beg her forgiveness.

* * * * *

Arin-Dan ...

Kay awoke in bed alone. He had a feeling that Sam had recently been there, sitting in a chair, gazing at him in the dark. Maybe it was a dream, but he didn't think so. Sam had been there with him earlier, but now she was gone.

Additionally, he had a feeling that she was around in the castle somewhere at that moment.

He grabbed a robe and headed out of his tower, determined to find her. The lofty hallways of the castle were dark and craggy with shadow. The noisy silence of night filled the air—alive with creaks and taps and other bower sounds that were drowned out in the daytime.

He made his way into the central area of the castle, and he heard a faint droning sound, like a continuous chanting, coming from somewhere nearby. He couldn't make out the words of the chant, but it sounded like Sam's voice.

The sound seemed to be everywhere. He moved around, trying to locate the source of the sound, and soon, heading west, he stood at the darkened entryway to Cathomere's Cathedral.

Sitting in a pew near the doorway was Sam. She was fully dressed in her black gown and elegant black shoes. She was sitting straight, her long arms extended in front of her, hands open, palms up.

Her delicate neck had bandages stuck all around it.

She appeared to be in a sort of trance. She was chanting, and her voice was hoarse from it. Tears leaked from her closed eyes.

She said, over and over again in Anuie: *"Now's the time. Now's the time. Now's the time. Now's the time."*

Elated, he ran to her. After a moment or two, she became aware of his presence. She slowly opened her eyes and looked at him, her face drawn and haggard.

"Now's the time, Kay," she said in Elder. Then she winked at him and disappeared, the sound of her chanting voice still echoing through the silent castle.

* * * * *

Two foggy days later, Sam returned to him again.

Kay lay asleep in his bed as usual waiting for Sam, hoping she would come. A partially read posting that Sarah had shoved under his door lay on his bed:

BERSERKACIDE SCOURGE UNCOVERED IN VITHLAND!
—MONSTERS FOUND IN MT. HOLLY, SHIRSTER POINT AND CASTLES DURST AND BLOODSTEIN!
—LOCAL MAGISTRATES BAFFLED. SISTERS INVESTIGATING.

He hadn't read the rest. It didn't interest him.

As he lay there staring at the high ceiling, he thought he caught a hint of movement beyond his window.

He sat up.

He saw something lit up and murky through his curtains. A mass of light came nearer and nearer.

A few moments later, something glowing came in through his window, moving like smoke.

It was Sam, wreathed in black cloud. She was floating on air, her body glowing with a sort of inner light, her black hair alive with serpentine movement. Her long arms waved about in a sort of dance macabre. Her nude body was coursing with yellow light and was partially obscured by seething black clouds that twisted around her. Kay noticed her mouth was missing—just a blank spot where her mouth should go. Moving through her body, as if through liquid, was her Snugs medallion.

She was wearing a long necklace made of white flowers. It, too, moved with a weightless fluidity.

He recognized the flower—small, daisy-like with a black button: White Emilia.

Glowing, clouded and necklace flowing, she settled over his bed.

Kay reached up to touch her, and his hand passed right through her chest.

"Sam?" he said quietly.

She stared down at him, her mouthless expression unreadable.

She stared at him for a long time.

Finally, *"I will first ask: do you love me?"* she said in Anuie in a grave-like voice though she had no mouth.

Kay responded. His voice came out in a whisper. "Yes, Sam—I'm sorry, I didn't mean what I said. I was hurt and angry, and I struck out at you. I'm sorry. Of course I still love you. I want you to come back home to me."

Then, *"You wish to court a daughter of Monama, then you will be put to Trial in accordance with the traditions of the House of Monama and the tribe of Astralon. You will be Tried, and you will be Judged! I tried to shield you. I tried to protect you and give you time to get a bit older. I BEGGED you to develop your Gifts—but now, it... it's too late! They come for me. There is no time! There is no time!"*

She pulled a long hair pin out of her black mane and showed it to him. It was centered with a black jewel. *"Do you see this?"* she asked. *"This is the NIGHTMARE, and Monama females have been using it for centuries. With it I can alter reality and create images from my deepest of fears. With this, I put you to Trial according to our customs. I cannot allow my feelings for you to color or temper my thoughts or my actions—I must test you to your limits. With the NIGHTMARE, I will place perils before you that, should you misstep, will bring about your death. Hence is the price of Monama and Astralon."*

She dropped down on him and hovered just inches from his face and put the NIGHTMARE back into her hair. She seized the flower necklace and presented it to him. *"The White Emilia is before you— the flower that offers either sweet riches or death. Are you ready to face Trial?"*

Kay made to say something and she interrupted. *"Before you answer—be it known and made perfectly clear that, should you fail in the Trials to come ... you, and I, will die. Are you ready?"*

"Yes."

"Then follow me."

Kay climbed out of bed and followed Sam as she drifted through the door and down the hall. He was wearing nothing but a pair of pajama bottoms, and wanted to grab a robe or a sheet or something to cover up with, but Sam wasn't waiting around.

She glided out of the castle and into the Grove, Kay following.

They went a long way into the tangle; Kay tried to ask questions as he stumbled along, but the ghostly, illuminated Sam nested in a thundercloud wasn't answering.

Finally, they reached a clearing. Kay looked around. It was the same clearing where Sam had previously run through the snow and yelled *"Olonol"* years ago.

In the clearing were three black, potato-shaped objects of indistinct smoky material floating above the ground. Sam stopped and turned to Kay, bobbing up and down slightly as she floated. The black nest of clouds swirled around her. Sitting nearby were two small figurines floating on pillars of cloud. The figurines look like tiny blue Carahils in a fun pose. Those seemed awfully familiar to him, and they were important for some reason.

She took off the necklace of White Emilia and held it out.

"You have one final chance, Kabyl, Lord of Blanchefort. If you choose to proceed now, if you accept this necklace, there is no turning back, and your life will be forfeit to me. I will ask you again, and for the last time; do I mean enough to you to risk your life? Does

a life and future with me mean that much to you? Do you wish to be put to Trial? Death awaits should you fail."

"Yes."

The clouds around Sam became excited and probing, wrapping around Kay. *"Then, let it begin."*

She placed the necklace around his neck. For a moment, it came to life and began squeezing his throat. Then, it relaxed and settled.

"I will introduce to you the Judges of the Trials. I have created these manifestations with the NIGHTMARE—they will have a life all their own, and they are here to assist you in progressing from one stage of the Trials to another. They will not help you other than to provide information with which you will need to proceed. They might even have to kill you should you fail. Do you understand?"

Kay didn't really know what was going on, but he nodded anyway.

Sam drifted over to the first mass and touched it. The dark material twisted around and elongated into the shape of a huge bronze man, about twenty feet tall, standing in a pewter chariot. He looked just like the statue of Lord Cathomere from Cathomere's Cathedral, only much larger and animated into life. Carved into his chest was a sturdy-looking, shield-shaped coat of arms (the House of Blanchefort coat-of-arms). The whole thing was very shiny. Harnessed to the front of his chariot were three naked women, tall, their eyes alight with orange fire. The women appeared to be constructed of dabbed mud or clay. They seethed in their harness and giggled as they looked at Kay.

Sam touched the next mass. A strange deer-like creature emerged from the dark. Its legs appeared gnarled and broken, its angry head hung on a broken neck. Its body twisted with unnatural flexibility. It gazed at Kay with its lolled head.

She moved to the last mass and touched it. Another form emerged from the dark—the strangest yet. It was a skeleton suspended in a flowing, golden protoplasmic mass.

Kay stood there staring at this horrific collection of creatures. Sam drifted behind him, and her voice changed back to normal, though Kay couldn't see her.

"Kay, oh my *Arin-Dan*. The Trial is upon us; we can wait no longer. It is now in motion and beyond my control. You must succeed in what is to come … for both our sakes. My love, you are going to be made to feel great pain in the upcoming days … and I am sorry. If

you are to survive, you must have your Gifts, and, to fully activate them, you must be made to suffer—I wish there was some other way. I watched you fight those Berserkacides alone and survive, and so I have hope. Know that I love you, and I do this in the hopes that the *Olonol* will one day stand here, and we will be free."

She put her arms around him. "I—I'm sorry for this ... I should have left you alone. Why couldn't I just stay away, and you wouldn't have to worry about what is coming ... I have brought all this upon you ..."

Kay gently pulled her around to his front, her face was flush with tears. "Because, if you had stayed away, I never would have met my true love, my *Cerri-Tela*. I'll face these trials, Sam. I promise I'll succeed."

"You promise?"

"I promise. I won't fail you, Sam."

She took his face in her hands. "Be true to these Trials, *Arin-Dan*, to this symbolic necklace of White Emilia, and we may be together as man and woman, no matter how bleak the future seems. I love you, Kay." She paused. "They're coming—they're coming for me!!" Her voice shook with panic.

There was a sizzling flash, and a cloudy green slit appeared in mid air. One of the blue Carahil figures took flight and began swimming or dancing in the midst of the green slit. The slit then vanished with a 'pop', along with the figurine.

The tall bronze man reached out and took Sam in his hands. Though still glowing, she appeared to be solid and whole as she sat in his hands. The coat of arms in his chest opened like two halves of a clam-shell revealing a hollow cavity within. Sam stepped in and looked at Kay one last time. She waved as the two halves of his chest closed with a solid-sounding thud, entombing Sam within. Gears engaged, locking tight.

Nearby, the green slit appeared again. The last Carahil figurine came to life and dispelled it.

The statue-man in the image of Lord Cathomere finally spoke in a brassy voice. "I am the Judge of your Gifts, the Vessel of your Love, and the Judge of your First Trial, Lord Blanchefort. Within me rests your love, safe from all who wish to harm her. There she will remain until the Trials are concluded. I am also tasked with enabling your Gifts, and, when that is done, I shall set you to your first Trial."

The three women unharnessed themselves from the chariot and surrounded Kay. They snickered and circled him. They pushed him and acted in a haughty and aggressive fashion. Kay tried to stand his ground. He noticed that all three of them looked just like muddy, rough statues of Sam.

"My 'horses' represent your three Gifts," the statue-man said. "When you can defeat them, you have progressed enough to continue on to the Trials."

One of the women grimaced in fury and suddenly punched him in the stomach, doubling him over and sending him wheezing to the ground.

The three stood naked over him and laughed.

One of them pulled him up.

"I am your Waft," she said, laughing. "You have long to go before you can best me. Frankly, I think your sister would be a tougher fight than you." She pushed him away.

A second woman lifted him and seemed loving and kind "I am your Cloak," she said, "You're as handsome as I thought you'd be."

The last woman tackled him and, seizing him by the hair, pushed his face into the hard, cold ground. She appeared enraged. She then flipped him over and, by the scruff of his neck, lifted him close to her furious face. "Look at me! I am your Sight, which you've ignored your entire life!! You will either master me, or you will die. I will kill you! I want to kill you!"

She stood up and, with strength unheard of, mashed Kay's face into the ground again with her foot.

"Stop it!" Cloak said.

The three of them returned to their harness and strapped themselves in. The one who called herself "Cloak" was concerned. "Are you all right, Kay?" she asked quietly.

The statue-man continued. "You are at Trial, Lord Blanchefort. There is no time limit to constrain you, but I advise haste. Your first task will be to go to the planet Xandarr. There you will train, and there you will develop your Gifts. Again, if you fail, you will die. We will speak again at the correct time."

With a few ground-shaking steps, he hopped back into his chariot and with a lash, took to the air, pulled by the snickering, naked women, all arms and legs, as the chariot climbed into the starry night.

The strange broken deer-creature and the mass of protoplasm lingered for a moment and then were gone as well.

What happened next was a blur of sound and confusion.

The green slit returned, and this time there were no Carahil figurines to ward it off. Two figures stepped out of the slit: a tall man in golden armor and a bent woman in a red beaded dress. "Sam!" the woman screamed. "You can't run from us, Sam! Where'd she go?"

The man and woman noticed Kay and, before he could react, attacked. In a wretched, ugly voice, the woman cast some sort of screeching spell.

The sound was terrible to listen to, and was somehow vaguely familiar, like he'd heard it before. He couldn't move, he could barely think—the sound filled his head and froze his muscles in place. He toppled over, helpless.

They approached Kay's fallen body.

In the distance, Kay thought he could hear buzzing, like a swarm of insects. Again, vaguely familiar, though he couldn't place it.

The man was tall, over six feet. He was clad in golden armor that was hammered to resemble a robust male musculature, complete, as Kay noted, with an angry phallus that was bolted to the base of his chest plate. The interlocking pieces of his armor were formed to look like fingers coming together at the knuckles. He had a strange heart-shaped helmet that covered his whole head except for his mouth.

The woman was tall and gangly, thin to the point of been utterly famished and decidedly bent in the torso, like a broken yard stick. She was wearing a strange sort of beaded red and black dress. She had long, curly red hair that was wound up over her head like a beehive, held in place with cords of what looked and smelled like clotted blood. She also had on a gold mask that covered her forehead, eyes and cheekbones, leaving her mouth and chin exposed. Her exposed skin appeared to be glistening with—blood maybe—and her flesh was deeply cut into, as if she had mutilated herself.

The two carried an odd smell with them—a burnt stench mixed heavily with dry blood. It was a terrible smell.

The woman slinked up to Kay and stared down at him. She stopped the screech that she was making, though the sound of it lingered in his head.

Her voice was thin and ugly. "Hi,ya, Kay," she said. "Remember me? No?"

The woman reached down and stood Kay's immobile body back up like a mannequin, showing a fair amount of strength for such a skinny person. "I been having sex with you for years. Don't remember?" She licked his face with a horrid tongue. "You and your girlfriend are in a lot of trouble. Sam removed her shockers—they never do that—they're too scared, but she did anyway. She loves you, don't she? Awwww... ain't that just sweet?"

She grabbed him by the face, squeezing his cheeks together.

Her hand, skinned and bloody, stank.

"She was supposed to kill you the other night—supposed to appear in your room and go Berserk on you, rip you limb from limb—wouldn't that have been a sorry story in some League rag? People should be saying 'Oh, look what happened to the now extinct House of Blanchefort, tsk, tsk,' but, here you are. We had it all planned out. She pulled her little shockers right off her neck, and you destroyed the Boss's light. The Bosses are real mad at you, and her, too."

She pushed his immobile face away with a jerk. She then produced some sort of small knife and quickly cut Kay out of his pajama bottoms with a savage ripping of cloth.

When she was done, she hauled back and seized him by his male parts with a slap.

Pain, unimaginable pain.

The clearing lit up in amber. He could see a cloud of movement beyond the clearing—like a fast approaching storm cloud. And, for a moment, for a tiny moment, he thought he saw the terrible woman standing before him as a smiling girl, soaring through the sky in a fast ripcar. He thought she looked like ...

The man in golden armor slapped her hand away. "Trying to make me jealous?" he said.

"Awww," she said. "I just wanted to have a little taste for old time's sake."

With Kay incapacitated, the two casually looked around the clearing. "Hmm," the man said. "We're going to get in a lot of trouble over this, and it's all that little bitch's fault. I have had it with her. She knows the penalty for pulling her shockers out. Her purpose has come and gone—and what a mess she made. Let's kill this idiot, eat him, and manually trigger her just for fun, shall we? We'll make an example out of her little ass."

"Ain't got no Shockers to trigger her with. Gonna' have to run her down," the woman said. She pulled the necklace of White Emilia away from his neck and held it. "Ah, young love."

The woman reared back and waved the necklace around. "That's right, Sam!" she yelled into the air. "We're going to kill your fella' here! We're going to take him apart and eat him! Then we're coming for you!"

The woman cozied up to the armored man. He bent down, and they kissed sloppily.

"I could do you right now, she said."

"Patience. I'm hungry."

A loud buzzing began to fill the grove. Kay saw black flying objects come swarming in.

The man picked Kay up by the neck with one hand and regarded him with disgust. "I've waited to kill this fool for years. Look at him. So soft and weak. I used to look up to him—admire him, can you believe that? This is too easy—what fun is this?" With his free hand, he swatted at large bugs that were starting to swarm around his head.

"What are these?" the man asked, bothered by them.

The woman sneered. "Who cares? Just bugs. Let me have him for a bit. I want him."

The man cuffed her across the face with a bone-cracking slap. "I said I'll kill him, and you can have fun with his dead body. Then, we'll eat hearty!"

"Awwww ..." the woman said. "I just want to have a little taste while he's alive. It tastes so much better when they're nice and fresh."

The man, troubled by the growing number of bugs in the clearing, threw Kay down to the ground. The woman, shooing bugs, began slobbering with excitement and produced the small, blunt-looking knife again.

"You may have him, love. Take him. Be quick about it."

"Can I mess him up?"

"Please do."

And, screeching, the woman fell on Kay and did terrible things to him as the armored man casually watched, the growing number of bugs beginning to perturb him.

As her knife, covered with blood, rose and fell, the clearing filled with giant bugs, their shiny wings reflecting in the moonlight.

Coppery light and buzzing.

Ren Garcia, author of the League of Elder series, graduated from Ohio State University with a degree in Literature. When he has free time he enjoys playing volleyball and ice hockey. He lives in Columbus, Ohio, with his wife and their four dogs.

VISIT THE LOCONEAL BLOG AT

www.loconeal.com

Breaking News
Forthcoming Releases
Links to Author Sites
Loconeal Events

Made in the USA
Charleston, SC
21 April 2011